Blue Rain
A *Los Angeles Times* Bestseller

"Mind-grabbing . . . fast-paced . . . Will make any reader believe 'what if' could happen."
Fort Worth Star-Telegram

"Freadhoff puts a different spin on the Vietnam POW story, and in Johnny Rose he has created a character who is comforting in his normality, a man whose plodding pace is more impressive than a superman."
Orlando Sentinel

"Freadhoff conjures up enough paranoia to chill readers, all the while offering an insider's take on how a good reporter goes about digging out the facts, no matter what the obstacles."
Publishers Weekly

"A satisfying mystery featuring a very human protagonist."
Booklist

"A dastardly plot . . . You can't get a much better glimpse of a reporter pushing his nose after news."
Poisoned Pen

Also by Chuck Freadhoff

Blue Rain

A
PERMANENT
TWILIGHT

CHUCK FREADHOFF

HarperTorch
An Imprint of HarperCollins*Publishers*

This is a work of fiction. Names, characters, places, and incidents are products of the author's imagination or are used fictitiously and are not to be construed as real. Any resemblance to actual events, locales, organizations, or persons, living or dead, is entirely coincidental.

HARPERTORCH
An Imprint of HarperCollins*Publishers*
10 East 53rd Street
New York, New York 10022-5299

First HarperTorch paperback printing: December 2001
First HarperCollins hardcover printing: September 2000

10 9 8 7 6 5 4 3 2 1

For
My Friend's Place

Acknowledgments

●━━━━━━━━━━━━●

*O*nce again my friend Jane Preuss played a pivotal role in helping me understand the characters in this book and I owe her a debt of gratitude. I also received immeasurable help and insight into the world of street kids from Brian Newhouse and Wade Trimmer of My Friend's Place. Doris Miller spent countless hours proofreading this book. She made a very tough job a lot easier and I want to thank her. Thanks go to Karolyn Connell for the excellent medical advice she gave me. I also want to thank Gretchen Easter of the California State Parole Board and Scott Carrier of the L.A. County Coroner's Office for their help and professional guidance. Most of all, I want to thank Steve LePore, the founder of My Friend's Place, for giving me the opportunity to meet and get to know these children in the first place.

Foreword

*T*here is no way to know how many street kids there are in America today. One recent estimate by the Better Homes Fund put the number at more than one million. That's more than at the height of the Great Depression. Each year many of these kids come to Hollywood, California. Some are drawn by the false hope of becoming a movie star or a rock singer. But many more come not because they have great ambition or big dreams but simply because Hollywood is "glamorous." They soon find that the streets of Hollywood can be just as cruel as the streets of any town, maybe even more so because the myth here is so strong.

As mean as the streets are, they are not without hope. Within a day of arriving in Hollywood, most of the kids learn about My Friend's Place, a drop-in center dedicated to helping them survive and eventually leave the streets. On a typical day My Friend's Place will see between seventy and one hundred kids.

For the past ten years my wife and I have volunteered at the center, serving meals on Hollywood Boulevard and talking with the kids in the dayroom. I drew heavily upon these experiences in writing *A Permanent Twilight*. Although none of the characters in the book are based directly on real people, many of them are composites of people I've met at the center. While none of the characters are real, the circumstances of their existence—diving in Dumpsters for their dinner and living in abandoned buildings and under bridges—are very real.

It's common to think of these kids as runaways. Most of them, though, are not runaways, they're throwaways. But it doesn't really matter what you call them. They're still kids, and I hope I've captured that in *A Permanent Twilight*.

One

●━━━━━━━━━━━━━━━●

Sara tore a match from the book and leaned toward the candle on the floor near her feet. She dipped the match toward the flame but heard a car on the street and froze. She looked up, wondering if she would see headlights play across the wall. But the plywood across the windows and doors sealed the house tight. Dallas had been right. They could burn candles. No one outside would see the light. No one would know they were there.

She lowered the match to the candle, little more than a wick in a puddle of melted wax, and held it to the flame. A second later it flared and she lit the second candle, this one tall and full, next to it. It was amazing how much light a single candle could give in a dark, empty room. It was enough to see the scrawls spray-painted on the dirty plaster walls, the tagging of kids who'd been in the house before them, before the owners boarded it up.

She looked at the girl lying on a thin pile of dirty blankets across the room, her backpack near her head. Behind the girl huge chunks of plaster had been torn from the wall, revealing the broken lath beneath. Random destruction, like the generations of graffiti sprayed on all the walls and the trash scattered throughout the house.

Even in the semidarkness, Sara could see the girl was pretty. At first you didn't notice it because of the colors, the blues and blacks she used to streak her hair, and the leather choker and the hardness in her eyes that warned you away. But they were family now, the three of them, and her eyes were gentle and she was pretty.

"Where is he, Gem? Why isn't he back?" Sara asked.

"I don't know. Don't worry."

But Sara was worried. "He said it would just take a little while to get the money. He should be here by now. What time is it anyway?"

But Sara didn't expect an answer, and the other girl laughed. "How the hell would I know? You know I don't have a watch."

"Maybe we should look for him. Go check the boulevard."

"He said to stay here. It's safe in here. No one knows where we are. He's coming back. He didn't leave us."

"Yeah."

Sara hugged her knees to her chest and rocked back and forth. She stopped for a moment and leaned her head against the wall.

"Hey, you okay? You feeling all right?" Gem asked. She sat up and looked at Sara, then stood and crossed the hardwood floor, leaving footprints in the plaster dust and dirt as she walked. She knelt next to Sara. "You feeling okay?"

"Yeah, Gem, I'm fine. I'm just worried."

"Don't be."

A creak and a slow groan of an old house settling came from the hall, and Sara tensed. "What was that?"

"Nothing, just the house. No one's here. Nobody's been here for months. It's empty."

Sara leaned against the wall. In the shadows she could make out the edge of the stairs and the outline of the newel post, but the hallway that led to the back of the house was dark. They sat quietly for almost thirty minutes, each with her own dreams. In the end the waiting became too much, and Sara got to her feet and picked up her backpack.

"I gotta go look for him."

"He told us to wait here."

"I'm going. You coming or staying?"

"Shit," Gem said. "I'm coming." She crossed the room and picked up her own pack, and with Sara holding the candle to light their way, they started toward the back of the house.

They climbed through a window and lifted the plywood from the weeds, hoisting it together onto the sill and leaning it to cover the glass. It wouldn't fool anyone up close, but from the street it would be hard to spot.

The night was warm, but after the closed-up house the air felt cool and refreshing for a few minutes. Sara and Gem walked north toward Hollywood Boulevard, constantly watching the other side of the street and scanning the people coming toward them, each silently asking herself the same question: Had he left them and run away?

At the boulevard they turned east and walked as far as Vine before crossing to the north side and going west toward La Brea. The boulevard was busy; the warm weather seemed to invite the tourists to leave their hotels and stroll along the famous street. They mingled with shopkeepers, street kids, and nearby residents who had left their small, hot apartments with no air-conditioning to seek a little relief in the night air.

Sara and Gem doubled back at La Brea and were near Cherokee when Sara suddenly felt weak and a wave of nausea swept over her. She slumped onto a bus bench, and beads of sweat popped onto her forehead. She waved her hand listlessly in front of her face, trying to stir the air and cool down. Gem settled next to her.

"You feeling all right?" Gem asked.

"It's just the heat."

"We should go back to the squat," Gem said. "He's probably already there, wondering where we are."

"Yeah, okay."

But as they stood they heard someone shouting at them. "Hey, Gem! Sara!" The voice came from down the boule-

vard, the stretch they'd just covered. The girls looked and
saw a boy coming fast toward them, weaving through the
crowd on a skateboard. He wore a dark T-shirt and baggy
jeans that barely stayed on his hips as he pushed hard along
the sidewalk. A multitude of small silver earrings outlined
his left ear, and his baseball cap was backward, the brim
pointing almost straight down. A moment later he skidded to
a stop, and the skateboard flew from under his foot and
crashed into the bench. He retrieved it and held it against his
hip.

"Hey, Sara, two guys are looking for you." He began tap-
ping the skateboard against his hip and looked over his
shoulder in the direction he'd come. His breath came in
large gulps. "I just saw 'em up the street."

"Who are they, Billy?"

"I don't know 'em. But they're asking about you."

"Shit. I knew this was going to go all wrong." She
grabbed her backpack from the bench and looked at Gem,
who touched her arm and tried to smile, but there was no re-
assurance in her eyes.

"Calm down. Maybe it's that asshole Griffin," she said
and looked at Billy. "Is one of them a short little fucker
wearing glasses?"

"No, these guys are big."

Gem turned quickly to Sara. "Come on, we better get
back to the squat."

Billy looked back down the street. "That's them," he said
and a second later had pushed off, the wheels of the skateboard grinding across the cement as he hurried away.

Gem looked and saw two men she'd never seen before
standing by a shopping cart overloaded with crushed aluminum cans and clothes. They were talking to the old man
who gripped the cart's handle, a regular on the boulevard.
They had passed him only minutes before. Now the old man
was turning and looking toward them.

"Run," Gem said, and they sprinted down the street,
clutching their backpacks as they ran.

They rounded the next corner, and Gem glanced over her shoulder. The two had started after them, dodging the tourists and locals who clogged the sidewalks. One of the men waved and shouted at her, but she couldn't make out the words.

"Shit, they saw us," she said. Fear gave them speed, and Gem's knowledge of the streets gave them an edge. They ran halfway down the block, then cut east across a parking lot, bending low, using the cars to shield them from view. They doubled back toward Hollywood Boulevard and then down one alley and another, going east before turning south. Finally, they reached the old house. They scrambled through the window, not worrying about the plywood, and walked slowly, cautiously, down the pitch-black hall, their rapid breathing echoing off the walls.

"Dallas?" Sara called quietly, but there was no response from the darkness ahead.

They reached the living room, and Gem lit the candle. They sank onto the floor and waited until their breathing was quiet.

"Did you know them?" Gem finally asked. Sara just shook her head, the motion sending elongated shadows across the wall behind her. Her breathing was normal now, but she could still feel her heart racing and the fear and tension in her muscles.

"What are we going to do, Gem?" she asked and could hear the anxiety in her own voice.

"We're going to wait here, like Dallas told us to. He'll come. I know he will. Come on, I still got some pot. Let's burn one. It'll make us feel better."

"Yeah, okay."

Gem bent forward and in the light from the candle deftly rolled the joint and twisted the ends. Holding it between her lips, she lowered her face to the candle, lit it, and inhaled deeply before passing it to Sara. A moment later the sweet smell of marijuana filled the living room, and the girls sat side by side passing the joint between them.

When they'd finished, Gem stood and shuffled across the room to the blankets and lay down.

"God, I'm tired," she said. "The running, the dope." She laughed suddenly. "You know, we're a lot faster than those two thought," she said. But Sara didn't respond, and Gem lay on the blankets. A few minutes later Sara could hear the rhythmic breathing of her friend's sleep. She bent and blew the candle out and lay in the darkness on the hard floor, her head resting on her backpack. For a second, anger and bitterness surged through her and she clenched her fists, but it was gone a second later, replaced by a deep sense of resignation and sadness.

It didn't matter what Gem said. He wasn't coming back. Sara felt tears well in her eyes and spill down her cheeks because there was nothing else to do now. She had been tough for so long, proved that she didn't need anyone else, that she could handle anything. But not anymore. Now she needed help and there was nowhere else to turn. She had to go home. She knew, without the slightest debate, that it had all gone wrong. She rolled onto her side to face the wall and drifted into a restless sleep.

When she awoke, she lay on her back and stared into the blackness in front of her, listening to Gem breathing. She didn't know how long she'd been asleep and ran her hand over the floor until she found the matches and lit the candle before lying back.

Rising slowly, she walked quietly down the dark hall to the rear of the house and climbed out through the window. Light was just breaking, the sky was a muted gray, the darkness beginning to give way when she reached a pay phone a block away. She realized then that she'd left Johnny's home number in her pack in the boarded-up house. She found the main number for his work in the phone book and dialed.

"LA Journal."

"Johnny Rose, please."

"I don't believe he's in yet, miss. Would you like his voice-mail?"

"Yes."

A moment later she heard his mechanical voice telling her to leave a message, then a beep. For a second she reconsidered, thinking she could tough it out and stay on the streets, but after a moment of silence she blundered on.

"Ah, hi, Uncle Johnny, it's Sara. I, ah . . . Listen, I need to see you, you know, if it's okay. I'll call you back. I gotta go. Bye."

She looked up the street and saw a bakery delivery van pass on the side street and suddenly realized how hungry she was. She hadn't eaten since noon the day before. She touched her stomach for a second and started back toward the house. Maybe Gem could go out and bring something back. She was good at it. She knew the streets almost better than anyone.

Two

Johnny Rose heard the fear in her voice and turned cold. His muscles stiffened, and he took a deep breath. His hand moved quickly to the replay button, and he listened to the message again as he sank into his chair and set his coffee mug on his desk.

"Ah, shit, Sara, where are you? What's wrong?" he whispered to the phone. He'd never heard her voice like that before. She'd always been tough, distant, acting as though she didn't need him or anyone. And now this call.

"Shit," he whispered again and played the message a third time, confirming the time she'd called—five-thirty. Almost four hours ago. It could be nothing or a lifetime. He stood quickly, almost knocking his chair over, and looked across the newsroom to where Stan Kuscyk, the metro editor, sat like a huge rumpled Buddha hunched over his keyboard, his fat fingers slowly pounding some hapless reporter's story into submission. Johnny grabbed his notebook and almost ran across the room.

"Stan, I gotta go for a while."

"What? Go where?" Kuscyk didn't look away from the screen.

"Hollywood. I don't know how long I'll be gone. With any luck I can be back before lunch."

"What the hell's going on in Hollywood, Rose?" Kuscyk stopped typing and turned to face him.

Johnny looked at the metro editor and for a moment almost told him, but the words didn't come and he simply shook his head. "It's personal," he said.

"Personal? Hey, I gotta get a newspaper out. That's business, and the last I knew you were still working here. Can't it wait?"

"No. I have to go now."

"Okay, okay. Listen, since you're going to be there anyway, you can cover something for me. Here." He turned away, bent down, fished a press release out of his trash can, and handed it to Johnny.

"Stan, I don't have time."

"Look, you can take the whole damned day over there, I don't care. But cover this and I get something out of it. It won't take half an hour. Besides, it's your old buddy Roberts. Figured maybe you'd like to see him."

Johnny looked away from Kuscyk and read the release. It was from the Hollywood Restoration Committee. The Reverend Richard Roberts and the actress Carol Holland were being named this year's honorary chairpersons at a ceremony on Hollywood Boulevard's Walk of Fame.

"Yeah, okay," Johnny said and began to walk away.

"Keep it short, Rose, and don't go too much on him winning the gold medal in the Olympics. That's old news. Besides, the guy's getting famous enough without our help."

Johnny waved but barely heard. He was almost out the door, the press release folded and stuffed in his coat pocket. Moments later he was hurrying across the parking lot toward his car, an aging 280Z. Maybe the press conference was a good idea. If anyone knew the street kids, Roberts did, and Kuscyk was right. Johnny and the reverend had been friends, at least as close as a reporter and subject can be. He tossed his jacket on the passenger seat and sped from the lot.

He slowed the car when he drew close. He cruised Sunset

Boulevard first, watching the sidewalks closely, looking for anyone who resembled Sara. But it was still early by Hollywood standards, and the hookers and street kids who lean into car windows weren't on the corners yet. The citizens were just starting to fill the streets. He fruitlessly cruised the north-south streets and alleys and finally, after an hour, left the Z at a meter and walked Hollywood Boulevard. There were too many hiding places, recessed doorways, Dumpsters, rooftops, and abandoned buildings to see them all from a passing car, he knew. Even on foot it could take weeks to search the area.

He passed empty storefronts, fast-food restaurants selling pizza by the slice, and tourist shops, their aisles stacked with Hollywood T-shirts and plastic souvenirs. The stores were starting to fill with tourists searching for mementos of their visit to a place that existed only in their minds: Hollywood, California, the glamour capital of the world.

To Johnny, Hollywood wasn't glamorous. He'd spent too many nights walking the streets and sitting on the bus benches with Sara. To him, the small stores run by immigrants from eastern Europe, Iran, and the Middle East selling stereos, cameras, and incense had an air of desperation, a sense that they were clinging to commercial life one month at a time. The mannequins in the lingerie shop windows displayed the attire of an adolescent boy's fantasy that made Johnny turn away. As he walked he glanced down a few times, looking at the stars and reading the names on the Walk of Fame. But the street itself seemed shabby, the sidewalk worn with decades of dirt and foot traffic, making the stars forlorn, like ornaments on a dried-out tree two weeks after the holidays.

Still the tourists came: the Japanese crowding around taking turns crouching next to a star, smiling up at their friends' cameras; the stout middle-class Germans with their sensible shoes and utilitarian clothing, the women clutching their handbags to their sides as they strolled the boulevard. The French, the Brits, the Mexicans, the Americans from Ohio,

Texas, and Florida here to see Disneyland, Universal Studios, and Hollywood, where it all started in sunshine and orange groves.

By midafternoon Johnny had walked or driven down almost every street and alley. He was exhausted from the worry, tension, and the physical demands of walking miles on the concrete in the heat. When he reached the Z again, he looked at his watch and realized the press conference would start in less than twenty minutes. It was only a few blocks away, but he decided to drive and quickly questioned his decision. Up ahead traffic was coagulating, the slow flow coming to a dead stop. "Come on, come on," he urged under his breath. He was already late, and the heat in the car rubbed his nerves. Then he heard the faint wail of a siren, and the anger slipped away. A slight nagging at the back of his head replaced it.

Don't be stupid, it's not Sara, he told himself. Still, he checked his mirrors and strained to see past the car in front of him, but it was impossible to know from where the noise came. Half a block ahead, Johnny saw an MTA bus pull from the curb in a puff of diesel and stop suddenly halfway into the intersection. As he watched, two patrol cars, their lights and sirens on, shot past the front of the bus, one on the bumper of the other, and headed toward the summer-dried Hollywood Hills on Johnny's left. He looked at his watch. The press conference would start in fifteen minutes. It wasn't much time, but it might be just enough.

"Come on, come on. Move it, move it," Johnny said. His right foot wavered on the accelerator while his left played with the clutch, anxious to let it slip and have the Z leap forward. The traffic broke free, and Johnny swerved to the middle lane, barely missing the bumper of the car in front of him. But a second later the light turned red and the cars stacked up again.

Johnny swore aloud, slammed his fist against the steering wheel, and turned to look again at the Hollywood Hills. It wasn't Sara, he told himself again. It's something else. But the nagging in the back of his head had grown from a whisper to an urgent demand. The moment the light turned green, Johnny pushed the Z forward, swerving across the oncoming traffic to a blare of horns. As he neared Franklin Avenue he slowed the Z and searched the side street, looking west and east and finally straight ahead, but there was no evidence of the patrol cars. No sign the police had sped past less than a minute before. He gambled and turned east and within minutes knew he'd guessed wrong.

Pulling to the curb, he stretched his legs straight and leaned his head back against the seat. He realized how hard he was gripping the steering wheel and forced his hands to relax. He'd never find them now, he knew. The cops could be anywhere in the hills. Besides, he told himself again, it wasn't about Sara. Checking for traffic, Johnny pulled back onto Franklin and turned south toward Hollywood Boulevard and the press conference.

Five minutes later he joined a crowd of pink-skinned tourists in Bermuda shorts and tank tops gathered in front of a small podium on the sidewalk. The president of the chamber of commerce was speaking, and the people shuffled restlessly. Johnny stood at the back of the crowd and within minutes of arriving had all he needed for a story. The piece would be no more than eight inches. That would make Kuscyk happy.

Johnny glanced at the speaker's podium and spotted Roberts, a tall, lean man in his mid-fifties, who had addressed the press conference a few minutes before. He wore a long-sleeved white shirt open at the neck, with no tie, and khaki slacks, and his dark hair was swept back over the tops of his ears. He was smiling as he looked at the crowd. When he saw Johnny he winked, glanced at the speaker, and rolled his eyes. Johnny smiled, nodded back, and wagged his finger between his chest and Roberts. "I need to talk to you," he mouthed, and the minister nodded that he understood.

The sound of another siren, this one far behind him, drifted down the boulevard, just another note in the urban background symphony that plays in every major city every day. But Johnny heard it and turned. Blocks away, he saw a red paramedic van from the LA Fire Department heading down the boulevard toward them. A few blocks away it slowed at an intersection and turned north toward the hills. At almost the same moment, the crowd behind came to life and he heard the click and flash of a dozen point-and-shoot cameras. He turned back just as Carol Holland, whom the tourists had come to see, stepped to the microphone. The television lights clicked on, and the cameras began rolling. Four o'clock on a slow news day; the event was almost guaranteed to get airplay.

Damn, if she was going to be on the news, he'd need a quote from her in the story. Johnny took his notebook from his pocket, flipped it open, and glanced back down the block before turning to the front again. Thrilled at the sight of a real celebrity, the tourists pressed forward, trying to steal a view of the movie star. She was a pretty woman: tall, with short, dark hair that framed her face and large brown eyes.

"Thank you very much for coming. We're here today because we all want the same thing, to continue restoring Hollywood to the glory and grandeur it once enjoyed." She spoke with a well-practiced sincerity about the deterioration of the buildings and the pressure on the small businesses. Blah, blah, blah, Johnny thought.

"I also want to speak to you about the homeless kids you see on the streets every day," Holland said and paused. Johnny turned and looked across the crowd to the actress. Her voice had changed, suddenly carrying an edge of anger and pain he hadn't heard before. It caught him off guard, and he lowered his notebook and studied Holland as she spoke. If she was acting, it was an Academy Award–winning performance.

He jotted a couple of lines and closed his notebook just as the press conference ended. The television reporters moved aside to do their quick stand-ups, and the crowd began to melt away. He saw Roberts coming toward him, smiling as he moved past the tourists and reporters. Suddenly an old man with a camera around his neck grabbed the minister's sleeve and began talking to him. Johnny couldn't hear the words, but a moment later Roberts had his arm draped across the man's shoulder while another tourist fiddled with a camera. Johnny turned and looked back down the street. A copper-brown Chevy Caprice with whip antenna, a detective's car, was crossing Hollywood Boulevard going north.

"Johnny. It's so good to see you." Roberts embraced him, then stepped back and held Johnny by the shoulders. "I'm glad you could come. Tell the truth, though. Not much of a story, is it? Not for someone like you."

"It's a legitimate story, Dick," Johnny said. He was forcing himself not to look back down the street, not to run for his car.

"I know, but I wasn't sure your editor would think so. Anyway, something you want to talk about?"

"I, ah, you know, ah, I know this sounds weird, but I've got to go check something, okay? Can I call you later?"

"Of course. Better yet, are you coming to the party?"

"What?"

"Carol Holland's hosting a reception at her house in about an hour. Why don't you come by. Here." Roberts stuffed an envelope into Johnny's pocket. "It's an invitation, has the address and a map too. Come by, we can talk there."

"I'll try," Johnny said. He started to turn but stopped and looked back at the minister. "Thanks, Dick."

It took less than four minutes to get to his car, and he headed north to Franklin Avenue. This time he went straight into the maze of two-lane roads that twisted like vines around the Hollywood Hills. As he sped into the hills, the nagging in the back of his head had become a gut-deep fear of what he would find ahead.

Three

———————●—————————————●———————

*J*ohnny sped around a corner and slammed on the brakes, skidding the Z to a halt. A young cop, tall with broad shoulders, stood in the middle of the road, holding up his hand.

"Whoa, slow down. Just hold it a second, bud," the cop said. Anger flashed through his eyes. Johnny was halfway out the door, looking past the cop to the lineup of police cruisers, detectives' cars, paramedics, and a coroner's wagon lining the road ahead.

"What's going on?" Johnny asked.

"A body was found on the hillside," the officer said. He half-turned and looked behind him.

"Car over the side?" Johnny asked.

"No," the cop said without looking back, and Johnny could feel his stomach muscles tighten. The cop said nothing more, and Johnny looked to the hillside where four men struggled to carry a body wrapped in a sheet and strapped to a board up to the road. The men were breathing heavily from the weight and the strain of the climb.

The body was too big, Johnny told himself. Sara was short, thin. They wouldn't struggle like that. But he knew it was a lie. He could tell nothing from that distance. When they reached the street, their clothes were covered with dust, their faces streaked with dirt and sweat. They carried the body to the coroner's wagon farther down the road and

15

loaded it in the back. Johnny recognized one of the four, a coroner's investigator he had known since childhood. The men loaded the body, and the investigator walked to the side of the van and leaned against it. The cop in the roadway looked back at Johnny.

"Okay, you can go on now."

He hurried, barely glancing down the hill as he went. He could see six people, most of them in uniform, still on the slope combing the hillside. He heard someone shout and saw a cop waving. "Hey, over here! I've got something," he yelled, and the others began picking their way cautiously across the steep hillside toward him.

Johnny stopped the Z next to the coroner's wagon, lowered the passenger window, and called to the investigator.

"Doc, what is it? What do you have?" His voice was demanding.

The investigator looked at him quizzically. "Just a dead kid, Johnny. Relax."

"Boy, girl? Who?"

"Some boy. What the hell's with you, Johnny?"

"Nothing. Give me a minute to park, okay?"

"Sure."

Johnny felt his shoulder muscles relax and his fingers loosen on the wheel. He took a deep breath, exhaled, and let the clutch out slowly, drove on, and parked.

As he walked back to the van, Johnny could hear the buzz of the Hollywood Freeway below and then the growing noise of a helicopter overhead. He glanced at the downtown skyline and the palm trees rising off the ridges of the hills between him and the city. Veiled in the late afternoon smog, the skyscrapers were little more than outlines.

Doc was watching the helicopters, holding a hand in the air to shade his eyes from the sun. His slacks were covered with dust, round spots of dirt marked the knees, and half-moons of sweat darkened his blue shirt under the arms. He glanced at Johnny and looked at the sky again.

"Looks like the television stations got the word. How'd you get here so fast?"

The noise of the helicopter grew louder as the chopper moved closer and hovered above the hillside. A moment later another helicopter appeared on the horizon.

"I was in Hollywood and saw the cars. So, what can you tell me, Doc?"

Doc's real name was Roy Whetmore. He'd earned the nickname while a medic in Vietnam and never lost it. He still wore his thick hair in a military cut with white sidewalls around his ears. He and Johnny had grown up on the same block, gone to the same elementary and high schools. They were always a trio—Johnny, his little brother, Jimmy, and Doc.

Doc lowered his hand and blinked for a moment before looking to the back of the van.

"It's a weird one. Unidentified white male, probably between eighteen and twenty. Body's been on the hillside for a while. Maybe since last night, maybe early this morning. Looks like he died someplace else and was dumped here."

"Murdered?"

"I don't know. There's nothing obvious. No gunshot or stab wounds. We'll have to wait for the autopsy."

"So what's weird?"

Doc looked back at the helicopters again, raising his hand to shade his eyes. He did not look at Johnny when he spoke. "Look, a dead body dumped on a Hollywood hillside and there are no visible signs. You gotta figure it's an OD. Someone had too much coke or smack. His friends panicked and dumped the body. That's the logical explanation, right?"

Johnny was taking notes but paying only partial attention. It was just another crime story, and he was happy because he'd been wrong. It wasn't Sara. An edge of guilt crowded into his consciousness. How could he be happy? Someone was dead. He focused his attention on Doc.

"Yeah, OD. That'd be my guess."

"Johnny, this kid doesn't belong in this neighborhood. The party crowd up here's not sharing their stash with this kid."

"How do you know that?"

"I think he was a street kid."

Johnny stopped taking notes in midword, his hand poised above his pad. He lowered his hands to his sides, stepped away from the van to the middle of the road, and looked at the city below. Hundreds, probably thousands of street kids pass through Hollywood every year. If the dead boy was a street kid, it didn't necessarily mean anything. Probably just another story.

"Why do you think he was living on the streets?"

"His hands are rough, nails broken and dirty. His teeth are a mess."

Johnny turned and walked back to the side of the van. "So what's he doing up here, Doc? It's a long hike from Hollywood Boulevard."

"How the hell should I know? You'll have to ask Detective Towers. That's him." Doc gestured to a plainclothes cop who was just coming up the hillside onto the road. In his right hand he carried a black plastic garbage bag that bulged at the bottom.

A third helicopter was overhead now, and Johnny looked up. He could barely make out the cameraman in the side door, the lens pointed toward the cops on the hillside. He watched the choppers for a moment, then looked at Detective Towers, who was squatting next to the bag in front of the copper-colored Caprice.

"Any idea what's in the bag?" Johnny asked.

"Probably the kid's clothes."

"Clothes?"

"He was naked."

Johnny watched as Towers unfastened a twist tie and peered into the bag. The cop stood up and walked back toward the Caprice. Johnny glanced at Doc again. "And no signs of foul play?"

"None that I saw."

"Thanks, Doc." Johnny started to walk away, but Doc reached out and touched his arm. Johnny looked back.

"There's something else."

"What?"

"The kid's been in water." Doc shoved away from the side of the van and walked to the back of the vehicle. Johnny turned and scanned the brown hillsides behind him. Where do you find water in the arid Hollywood Hills? The answer was obvious—any one of the hundreds or even thousands of swimming pools within a few minutes' drive. But what was a street kid doing in a swimming pool in this neighborhood?

"Did he drown?" Johnny asked.

Doc paused at the corner of the van and looked back. "Maybe. We'll have to wait for the autopsy, but I don't think so. I saw something on the body, but I don't want to say until I'm sure. I've got to wait until the cutters are done."

"Come on, Doc, don't give me this cloak and dagger. Give me something I can use."

"Ask Towers if he found any jewelry with the kid's clothes. Maybe that'll help you."

"What the hell does that mean?"

"I gotta go, Johnny. Good luck." He disappeared behind the van, and a moment later Johnny heard the doors slam shut.

The front door of the Caprice was open, and Towers stood behind it watching Johnny approach. He wore a dark gray houndstooth sports coat, an open-necked black polo shirt beneath it. His olive slacks were dusty, and the cuffs had caught weeds on the hill. He was about six feet with a thick black mustache and kind, dark eyes that looked at the world with a weary curiosity.

"My name's Johnny Rose. I'm a reporter with the *Journal.*"

"Detective Al Towers."

"Nice to meet you. So, what can you tell me about the body?"

Towers gave him a brief description, and Johnny took notes.

"Do you have an ID yet?" Johnny asked.

"Not yet. It's still a little early."

"Okay, what was in the bag?" Johnny asked, gesturing to the back of the Caprice.

"Clothes."

"The victim's?"

"Probably. We don't know for sure yet."

"So he wasn't dressed?"

"No."

"Nothing, no jewelry, watch, necklace, ID bracelet, nothing like that?"

"No."

"Find anything in with the clothes?"

Towers looked at him for a moment, as though weighing the question, wondering why he was asking it. "No, nothing."

"Who discovered the body?"

"Guy across the valley, trying out a new telescope."

He asked a few more routine questions, thanked Towers, and turned to look back up the road. The coroner's van was gone, and the police had already strewn the yellow crime-scene tape across an area of the hillside. He walked to the edge of the road and looked down the hill. The slope was steep and covered with scrub oak and weeds bleached the color of straw by the late summer sun. It was inaccessible but very visible. It was a terrible place to dump a body, Johnny thought, unless you wanted it seen or you panicked and literally dumped it at the first wide spot in the road.

He walked back to his car and glanced at the city below once again. Through the veil of smog he could make out the back of a huge neon sign atop one of the tallest buildings on Hollywood Boulevard. At night the sign's blue and yellow letters spelled out God's House and were visible from the freeway and the hills and the office towers in downtown LA. In the afternoon, though, the sign was dull and stark, lifeless neon tubing and a crisscross of support beams outlined against the haze and smog.

Johnny looked at it and remembered the invitation in his pocket. He pulled it out and scanned the map. Carol Holland's house wasn't a mile away. It was probably the closest phone, and it would give him a chance to talk to Roberts. Johnny fired the Z's engine and headed up the hill to the actress's house.

Later, when the small details would come together like random atoms colliding in an endless universe, Johnny Rose would think back and wonder how different everything would have been if he hadn't seen the neon sign.

Four

●━━━━━━━━━━━━━━━━━━━●

As he climbed farther into the hills, the houses became bigger, the lots larger, the prices escalating with the elevation. Just a few miles west mansions devoured half an acre each in Beverly Hills, or crowned hilltops, making first-time visitors to LA wonder if they were hospitals or hotels and doubt the sanity of their hosts when they insisted they were nothing more than single-family homes. But the houses near Carol Holland's were older and somewhat smaller than the faux Tudor mansions and Motel 6 castles favored by LA's new wealthy. Smaller, but still big even by Hollywood standards.

Her house was near the top of a hill at the end of a small cul-de-sac, which had been turned into a big patio for the party. A portable bar sat at the end of a neighbor's driveway next to a line of linen-draped tables covered with chafing dishes and plates of finger hors d'oeuvres. A small trio—bass, guitar, and singer—was tuning in front of a second driveway.

Johnny ignored them as he hurried across the lawn and into the house. The Spanish-tiled entry led to a crowded living room with a dark hardwood floor and a cathedral ceiling. The rear wall was floor-to-ceiling glass and gave a view of the valley below. He stood at the edge of the crowd and fruitlessly scanned the living room for a phone. He looked at his watch. The first deadline was coming fast. Kuscyk would be wondering where the hell he was. A moment later a waiter with a silver tray full of tiny quiches approached and held them out to Johnny.

"No, thanks, I've got to find a phone." The waiter shrugged. "Okay, then, which way's the kitchen?" Johnny asked.

The waiter gestured to the other side of the living room. "Down the hall," he said and walked on.

Johnny pushed through the crowd and worked his way down a corridor and into the kitchen. It was a cavernous room with a chopping-block cook island in the middle and copper-bottomed pots and pans hanging from a rack suspended from the ceiling above the cook island. Blond wood cabinets and black marble countertops whispered of handcraftsmanship and wealth. He turned sideways as a young woman with a tray of full wineglasses moved past.

"Phone, where's the phone?" he asked.

"I think I saw one at the end of the counter," she said and walked on, focusing on her tray full of drinks.

Johnny found the phone and called the metro desk. Kuscyk answered.

"Stan, it's Johnny."

"Jesus, where the hell are you? What's all that banging?"

"I'm in a kitchen. It's the only phone I could find."

"When the hell you going to get a cell phone like everyone else in LA, Rose?"

"When the *Journal* pays for it."

"We've been through this, Rose. Get one and bill us for the business calls. Someday you're going to need one and not have it."

"Look, Stan, I've been a reporter for more than twenty-five years and I haven't missed a story yet, have I? Besides those things give you brain cancer."

"Jesus, Rose, you're stubborn."

"Forget that, Stan. I got a story. You got someone to take dictation?"

"Yeah, it's about damned time you called. Thing was supposed to be over long time ago."

"No, Stan, it's not the press conference. I got something else. A body was found on a hillside in Hollywood. I came across it by accident." He realized he was shouting and looked back at the people in the kitchen. If they heard, they paid no attention.

"Man, woman, murdered, what?"

"Unidentified white male. The body was naked. Probably killed somewhere else and dumped."

"Another Hillside Strangler?"

"No, but, well . . . ," Johnny said, remembering Doc's cryptic remark. He'd seen something on the body.

"Well what?" Kuscyk asked.

"Right now there's nothing, but I can't believe it was natural causes. No one dies naked on a hillside in Hollywood. Just doesn't happen. I'll follow it up tomorrow."

"Okay. Give it to Jim Lawrence and forget about the press conference. We don't have the space and this is a hell of a lot better." The line went dead, and a moment later Lawrence was on the line.

Johnny turned to the wall, blocking out the noise of the caterer shouting at her employees as they loaded trays and headed back into the living room.

"I'm ready," Lawrence said, and Johnny began. He confined himself to what Towers had told him, leaving out the details Doc had provided. The story was short, and he was done a few minutes later. He checked his voice-mail at work and called his answering machine at home, hoping Sara had called again. But she hadn't. He hung up and retreated down the hall to the living room. He scanned the crowd for Roberts but didn't see him, so he went outside to a wide redwood deck to wait.

The deck stretched almost the entire length of the house, and Johnny moved to the far end. He leaned on the railing and looked down at the narrow yard terraced out of the hillside below. It was just wide enough for a swimming pool and Jacuzzi with a pool house at the end. A short brick wall, topped with ornamental wrought iron, edged the property just beyond the pool. A wooden stairway switchbacked the hillside to the pool area. He shifted his gaze to the hillside across the valley, and in the fading daylight he saw the outline of a police cruiser near where the boy's body had been found.

As he looked at the cruiser, he thought again about the body. Okay, figure the kid had been in a pool. So why was he naked? Skinny-dipping with the rich and famous? But the Hollywood elite don't hang out with street kids. Johnny shook his head, trying to push from his mind the image of the men struggling with the body up the hillside. He'd make a few phone calls tomorrow, maybe get some answers then. As he watched, the cruiser was swallowed by the night, and Johnny shifted his gaze to the skyscrapers downtown. He heard the first chorus of coyotes in the canyons beginning their evening, and it made him think again of Sara and her friends. For the first time in months, he wished he had a cigarette. He'd quit several years before, but at odd times he missed the comfort they seemed to provide.

"It's a spectacular view, isn't it?" Johnny turned and in the dim light saw Carol Holland standing near the railing a few feet away.

"Yes, it is. You have a very nice home, Miss Holland."

"Thank you." She walked to the railing and leaned, pressed her thighs against it, folded her arms across her chest, and looked at the city for a moment before turning to face Johnny. "You were at the press conference today."

"Yes, I was." He crossed the space between them. "I'm Johnny Rose. I'm a reporter for the *Journal*."

"Carol Holland." Her hand was small and delicate. She had worn a dress at the press conference but was now in slacks.

"So, did you do a nice write-up about this year's campaign?" she asked.

"Well, to tell you the truth, it got bumped."

"Photos?"

"I'm afraid not."

Her smile surprised him. "I was hoping it was a slow news day."

"What can I tell you?"

"Oh, it's okay, I understand. We've known from the beginning that this would be a long struggle, but we'll get there."

"I hope you do."

She smiled at him again, and Johnny realized she was older than he thought. He could see the small lines at the edge of her eyes that were invisible from a few feet.

"Oh, we will, Mr. Rose. Believe me, we will. Ask anybody. They'll tell you I'm a very determined woman." A smile that told Johnny she was mocking herself but deadly serious at the same time crossed her face.

She crossed the balcony to a sliding glass door and turned before going in.

"There's food and a bar out front, if you want anything."

"By the way, have you seen Dick, ah, I mean Reverend Roberts?" Johnny asked.

"No, not yet."

"Okay, thanks. But, before you go can I ask you something?"

She cocked her head. "What?"

"Why do you care what happens down there?" He gestured to the valley.

"Hollywood is my home. Doesn't everyone care about his home?" The answer came quickly and easily.

"No. They don't," he said. His voice sounded tired and angry even to his own ears.

Carol Holland stopped and looked at him. "Perhaps you underestimate people."

"I don't think so. Did you know the body of a young man was found on the other side of the canyon this afternoon?"

"No."

"They don't know yet how he died. But the point is, the

people at the party tonight, I'm sure they care about cleaning up Hollywood and homeless kids and all that, but they probably won't even read the story I wrote. And if they do, they'll forget about it in a day or two."

"You're being awfully cynical, aren't you, Mr. Rose?" She stepped back to the middle of the deck.

"No. Just realistic. He was probably a street kid. No one will care. But since we're talking about street kids, let me ask you another question."

"Is this an interview, Mr. Rose?"

"No. I'm just curious. When you were talking today, your whole demeanor changed when you mentioned street kids. Why was that?"

"I don't think I understand." She stiffened, and her eyes were suddenly veiled, her face a beautiful disguise. She stared at Johnny as though searching for a hidden message. A moment later, she crossed the deck to the railing and stared at the lights spread below like a suburban Milky Way trying to burn the blackness away. After a few moments of silence she looked directly at him.

"Did you know I graduated from Hollywood High?"

"No." Johnny shook his head and studied her. Her words rang with sincerity but seemed practiced, and it bothered him that he couldn't tell whether she was speaking from her heart or merely from an internal script.

"Well, I did, class of '77, and even back then I saw kids living on the streets. I made friends with a couple of them. I've seen these kids all my life. One year, five years, ten, it doesn't seem to matter. Nothing seems to change. The kids run away and come here expecting to become rock stars or actresses and they end up on the street. People do horrible things to them. I think someone has to do something to stop it." She was quiet for a moment and said, "You're very perceptive, Mr. Rose."

"Please, call me Johnny."

"Well, Johnny, as I said, someone has to do something. I care about these kids. Now and then I even hire one or two of them to do odd jobs around here. Maybe some gardening, or cleaning out the pool house. It's not much but it's something."

"So you actually know some of these kids?"

"Know them? I guess you could say that, why?"

"You ever run across a girl named Sara? She's short, with thin, brown hair."

"No, why?"

"Just wondering, that's all."

"You certainly ask a lot of questions."

"It's a habit."

She studied him for a moment, her brow furrowed, then smiled suddenly, a switch thrown. "Well, it's been a pleasure, Johnny. And as I said before, there's food and drinks out front. I hope you enjoy yourself."

She crossed the balcony and walked into the living room. Johnny watched her through the floor-to-ceiling windows as she moved next to a man in an elegant dark green suit who was just her height. He was portly and balding and, Johnny guessed, a good ten or fifteen years older than she. Putting her arm partially around his waist, she leaned her head against his. Without seeing his face, Johnny knew that the man was her husband, Melvin Plank, one of LA's wealthiest industrialists.

He was still watching them when a young man and woman came from the living room. They were laughing as they clung to each other, and Johnny wondered if they were drunk. When they each lit a cigar, Johnny left the balcony and walked back through the house to the street where he got a beer and stood at the end of the bar watching the people and looking for Roberts as he sipped it. He recognized a TV reporter and a couple of people he'd seen standing behind Carol Holland at the press conference but no one he knew.

He finished the beer quickly and tossed the empty bottle into a big plastic garbage can. When he looked up, he saw the minister half a block away walking down the street toward the party. Another man, much younger than Roberts, walked at his side. Johnny skirted the people, moved to the street, and waited for the minister. Roberts was still twenty yards away when he saw Johnny, smiled, and waved.

"Johnny, I didn't think I'd see you. Thanks for coming." They shook hands. He gestured to the man with him. "Have you met Buddy?"

"No, it's nice to meet you."

"Buddy's our outreach coordinator. Buddy, this is Johnny Rose. He's a reporter for the *Journal*. He covered the press conference today."

Buddy was about six feet and lean with short black hair. Johnny guessed Buddy was in his early thirties. He wore a long-sleeved gray shirt buttoned at the neck and blue jeans.

"Hi, nice to meet you, Mr. Rose." His hands were big and strong and his handshake firm. His eyes were dark and hard. He looked uncomfortable, out of place.

"Thanks," Johnny said and looked at Roberts again, but the minister was still looking at Buddy.

"He's a real inspiration for me," Roberts said. "Gave me the idea for my current series of sermons, 'Jesus Got Your Back.'"

"'Got your back'?" Johnny said.

"Tell him about it, Buddy."

Buddy smiled uncomfortably. "Well, I mean, it's just . . . I told Dick, man, you got my back. No one ever did that for me before, you know?"

"That's when I told him, no, it's not me, it's Jesus. And the idea just jumped into my head." He turned to Johnny again, smiling. After a moment, he went on. "Anyway, Johnny, you mentioned something at the press conference about wanting to talk. Is there something I can do?"

"I hope so. It's about this girl, a street kid I've been trying to help." Johnny stopped and looked back toward the people in front of the bar. It was harder than he'd thought it would be, even with Roberts, whom he'd known for years. Even after the phone call. He almost stopped but pressed on. "She's from Atlanta, ended up here. You know, it's the old story."

"What's her name, Johnny?"

"Sara Bradley."

Roberts looked at Buddy. "Do we know the child?" Buddy shook his head. "What about her friends? Do you know who she spends time with, Johnny?"

"I really only know one of them, a girl named Gem. She's talked about a boy named Dallas, but I've never met him."

Roberts looked at Buddy. "Do you know a Dallas?"

"No."

Buddy's answer, so quick and sure, bothered Johnny. How can you help the kids if you don't even know them? he wondered. And how could Buddy not know them? He was supposed to be the outreach coordinator, wasn't he?

Perhaps Roberts saw the question in Johnny's face or just felt the answer needed amplification. "There are a lot of kids out there, Johnny," he said. "Buddy's only been our outreach coordinator for a couple of months. Besides, they don't all come into the center. We'll ask about her, okay? We'll do what we can, make a special effort. And I'll say a prayer for her tonight. Never underestimate the power of prayer, Johnny."

"Thanks, but what I really need is some advice, maybe a suggestion about—"

But before Johnny could finish, a woman's strong voice came from behind him, and Roberts looked away.

"There you are, Dick. I've been looking all over for you. We've got some people who want to meet you." Johnny turned and followed Roberts's eyes.

A woman, perhaps five foot six in a dark maroon skirt that came to midcalf, a white blouse, and a silk scarf of gold, blue, and red on her neck was approaching. She stopped at the edge of the crowd.

"Susan Michael, our PR person. Duty calls," Roberts whispered. "Johnny, I'd like to talk to you more about the girl, but I can't now. I've got to meet some people here. Substantial donors." He sighed and shrugged his shoulders slightly, a "What can I do?" gesture. "You know how it is," he said with a smile.

"Sure, I know. Maybe later."

"Yes, of course. I'd like to help if I can. Come by the center. I'd love to show you the new facilities, especially the new youth center. We named it after Hank."

"Jefferson?"

"Yes. Our choir isn't quite the same since he retired. Living in South Central with his daughter now. But anyway, promise me you'll come by."

"I'll try."

"Great. I look forward to it."

Roberts and Buddy moved on, stopping only a few yards away as the minister talked to a small group of men and women in dark suits and evening dresses. A moment later he moved on, following Susan Michael toward the house, and Johnny thought again of Roberts's response to his plea for help. The minister had offered a prayer and a tour of his new building. Not what Johnny wanted, not what he needed. He looked at the crowd and thought of getting something more to eat before heading into the city again. His gaze moved to a small group at the edge of the cul-de-sac, a man in an expensive dark suit, an older woman who wore heavy makeup, and two young women in tight dresses. They had formed a semicircle in front of a short, thin man with a long, gray ponytail that hung to his waist. He wore faded blue jeans, a baseball cap, a T-shirt, Rockport loafers without socks, and a gold Rolex. LA, the city without a dress code.

Johnny looked at the hors d'oeuvres. A crowd had gathered in front of them, and he didn't feel like pushing his way through just for finger food. He looked up the empty street away from the party and back at the crowded cul-de-sac. It was a beautiful setting with beautiful people on a wonderful, warm, late summer evening, and Johnny felt as out of place as a wet dog at a wedding. He turned and walked up the street to his car.

Five

*H*e spent the next two hours searching the same streets and alleys he'd been on before. Finally, he idled the Z through an alley and saw two boys inside a Dumpster foraging for food. They stood straight up as he drove past, only their upper bodies visible. The harsh light of the security lamps gave their features a hard, stark edge. One wore a blue windbreaker despite the heat, and the second was bare chested, his right shoulder covered with tattoos, his hair cut almost to the scalp. As Johnny drove past, they stopped moving and stood motionless, staring at him, their faces filled with a look that managed to transmit distance and intimate rage simultaneously.

When he reached the street, he glanced in the mirror and saw the boys bent over the garbage once again. He headed for the freeway. It was time to go home.

By late afternoon they'd eaten the granola bars and fruit rollups and almost finished the small boxes of fruit punch that Gem got from the drop-in centers. It was still dark in the house but not as bad as at night. Gem sucked the last juice out of a box and threw it on the floor in the corner. She looked at Sara and tried to smile.

"Maybe it won't be so bad," she said. "You can try to work it out with your mom, you know. Me, I'm never going home. I hate my dad. I'd fucking get a gun and shoot the bastard first. I would."

Sara looked across the room at her and nodded. "I don't want to leave you, Gem. But I don't know what else to do." She stood up and looked at her friend. "I gotta go call Johnny."

"You should wait until it's dark," Gem said.

"No. I gotta go now. I'm afraid. I want to go soon."

"I'll come with you. Keep an eye out."

"Thanks."

A few minutes later, Sara stepped into the phone booth and pulled the door closed while Gem watched, looking one way then the other for the two who had chased them the night before. Sara dropped two quarters into the phone and dialed. She smiled when she heard him answer.

"This is Johnny Rose."

"Uncle Johnny, it's me, Sara."

"Oh, God, Sara. I'm glad you called. I've been worried about you. Are you okay?" She could hear the concern in his voice and it made her smile.

"I want to go home," she blurted out.

"Go home?"

"You said you'd send me." Suddenly she was afraid that he'd changed his mind, that he'd lied to her like all the other adults.

"Yes, of course I will."

"Can I go right away?"

"You mean today?"

"You said I could go anytime I wanted. You promised."

"Yes, of course, Sara. Of course you can go today."

"Good. I want to go right away."

"What is it, Sara? Are you okay?"

"Yeah, I'm fine. I just want to go home."

"Are you sure you're okay? You sound funny."

"Yes, I told you, I'm fine. So it's okay, I can go tonight?"

"Of course. I just need to book the flight, that's all. Look, why don't you call me back in fifteen minutes? I'll buy the ticket and have everything arranged by then, okay?"

"No, no, I can't call you back."

"Why?"

"I can't. I just can't, okay?"

"Yeah, that's fine. Listen, I'm going to put you on hold and order the ticket. Don't go away."

"Yeah." Sara looked through the Plexiglas at Gem, who was staring down the street, scanning the sidewalk, studying the pedestrians. Gem turned to her and made a rolling motion with her hand.

"Come on, what's taking so long?" Gem said.

"He's making the reservation." And Johnny was back on the line.

"Okay, Sara, we're all set. It's a red-eye, leaves at eleven and gets there about six in the morning. Sorry, it's the best I could do. Everything else seems to be booked."

"That's okay. Can you come get me now, right away?"

"Of course."

Suddenly Gem pounded on the booth. Watching the sidewalks, she'd almost missed them as they cruised past in a pickup on the opposite side of the street. "It's them," she hissed. "In the blue pickup."

At that moment the driver glanced at them. He saw Gem and smiled.

"Shit! Come on, Sara." She pounded on the booth's side again. Sara heard the screeching of tires as the pickup cut off a car in the middle lane and swerved across the oncoming traffic into a driveway.

"Uncle Johnny, I gotta go. I'm staying in an old house. I'll meet you on the corner." She looked up and saw the truck sticking halfway into the street, backing out. The oncoming cars blared their horns. The truck pulled back only a few feet, then accelerated forward, its right front wheel climbing the curb, then slamming onto the street, jolting the whole vehicle. She blurted out the cross streets to Johnny and ran.

"I'll be there in ninety minutes," Johnny said.

"This way," Gem said and grabbed Sara's sleeve. The

girls sprinted down a side street. They could hear the truck's horn and its engine revving as they ran.

"Down here, down here," Gem yelled and turned down an alley that divided the street-front buildings from the back-yards of the houses on the next block. Straight ahead an old beat-up pickup lumbered down the center of the alley toward them. Its sides had been extended upward with plywood and bulged outward under the weight of an oversized load of tree trimmings. The truck's hood was dinged and decades away from its last paint. Two men, their brown faces weathered and creased, sat in the cab. They watched impassively as the girls ran toward them. Gem turned sideways and slipped past the truck. A moment later, Sara followed.

Gem stopped suddenly and watched as Sara got past the truck. Sara's face was pale and she was breathing heavily. She couldn't run far, but in a minute the tree trimmers would be out of the alley.

"Here, get behind this Dumpster," Gem shouted and shoved Sara toward the garbage bin.

"They'll see us," Sara protested.

"No, I'm going. They'll see me. Everyone sees me." She smiled and ran her fingers through her hair, but Sara could see the fear in her eyes. "They'll follow me. They'll think we're together. I'll see you at the squat."

"But—" Sara tried to protest as Gem pushed her toward the Dumpster and ran. A moment later she heard a blast of horns and angry shouts. She peeked from her hiding place and saw the brake lights of the gardeners' truck. She ducked down behind the Dumpster just as the overloaded pickup began its crawl into the street. A few seconds later the blue pickup flew past, and, down the alley, she caught a quick glimpse of Gem's blonde hair as she scampered over a concrete-block fence into someone's backyard.

Johnny hung up and immediately picked the receiver up again. He dialed the number from memory. "Come on, Maggie, pick up. Pick up, I got great news," he whispered to himself. But he got the machine. He spoke quickly.

"Maggie, it's Johnny. I just talked to Sara. She's booked on the red-eye to Atlanta. Delta. It arrives about six from LAX. I'll call you later with the flight numbers and we'll talk."

He grabbed his corduroy sport coat from the back of his chair as he stood. But the phone rang before he could leave and he grabbed it.

"Sara?"

"No. No. This is Detective Towers, Hollywood substation. I got a couple of messages that you called. Sorry I didn't get back to you sooner. I've been out."

Johnny glanced at his watch and made the quick calculation that he could do the interview quickly and still have plenty of time to pick up Sara. He pulled his notebook out, holding the phone between his shoulder and ear.

"Yeah, I'm following up on the story from yesterday. Do you have an ID for that boy yet?" He pulled the top of the pen off with his teeth.

"Yeah. Kid's name was James Randall. He was nineteen."

"You have an address?"

"Nothing local. He was from Texas."

"What was he doing in LA?"

"We're not sure. Looks like he was a runaway." Johnny jotted the information down. Doc had been right.

"You have a cause of death?"

"No, not yet. It's still early."

"But you're treating it as a homicide?"

"Until we find out differently, we have to."

"Suspects?"

"No."

"Any idea what he was doing in the Hollywood Hills?"

"The body was moved, we don't know where he died."

"Isn't that an odd place to dump a body? I mean, it's not exactly out of sight."

"No, it's not. Maybe we'll know more when we figure out what killed him."

"Right. Thanks for calling me back, Detective Towers."

"You're welcome."

Johnny dropped the phone into its cradle and ran for the elevator.

He drove fast, got lucky with the lights, and made it to Hollywood with ten minutes to spare. As he passed the boarded-up house, he slowed the car to get a better look. Its roof sagged and the house numbers were missing, but it was at the intersection Sara had mentioned. Every door and window, except one in the back, was covered tight with plywood. A waist-high chain-link fence bordered the yard, a blend of dry weeds and dirt.

He looked up and down the sidewalk but didn't see Sara, so he drove on until he found a parking spot almost a block away. He climbed out and shoved the door closed. He began walking past a row of narrow, two-story stucco-sided apartment buildings. The sound of a baby crying drifted down from one. A radio in a window of another blared salsa music. Johnny turned and looked up at the window, thought about Sara, and smiled as he walked.

It was good that she was going home, finally leaving the streets. But still, he was uneasy and, to his surprise, a little sad. Sara had become an important part of his life the last few months. Without the two ever saying anything about it, Fridays had become the night they met. He'd buy her dinner and give her a small bottle of hand lotion or a toothbrush that he'd picked up for her, things that could make life on the streets slightly less miserable.

They never hugged, and they never spoke of the bond they had developed. In truth, much of their time together was spent in silence. But Johnny had started looking forward to their meetings, anticipating seeing her. It made him realize how shut off he'd become, how the lack of human affection had begun to close in around him. And he knew that she welcomed his unspoken affection.

Suddenly, a huge sucking sound and a roar like the sound of an oncoming train shattered the afternoon. A scream of pain and terror came almost simultaneously. Black smoke shot into the sky at the corner, and Johnny heard the unmistakable crackle of a hungry wood fire with plenty of fuel.

"Sara!" he screamed and sprinted for the house. The roar grew louder with each step until it was deafening. He could feel the heat and smell the smoke three buildings away.

He heard another scream and knew someone was trapped inside. He inhaled smoke as he ran and his lungs screamed. His legs weakened but he ran on adrenaline, sprinting down the sidewalk. At the front gate, he grabbed the fence to slow himself, then ran to the porch, taking the steps in two leaps. But as he reached the top, the thick smoke and intense heat forced him to turn his head away. Smoke poured past the plywood nailed over the front door. The heat saturated the air, searing his lungs with each breath.

"Sara!" He tried to scream, but his voice was barely a whisper in the heat and smoke. "Sara!"

He tore off his jacket, wrapped his hands, and turned back to the plywood, forcing his fingertips under the edge. But it wouldn't move, and he couldn't hold it. The fire and smoke were too much. He stumbled backward and almost fell down the stairs. The fabric of his shirt and pants was singed.

The sirens and the blaring of a fire-engine horn came from the distance, but Johnny knew the firemen would not arrive in time. There had to be a way in, a way to save the girl he knew was inside. He remembered the uncovered window in the rear and stumbled to the back of the house. The back door hung open, and flames engulfed the door frame. Smoke poured out of the nearby window and Johnny stopped. He heard the noise of the fire and the sirens growing louder, but the screams had stopped. He turned to run back to the front, desperate to find a way in, but after two steps he stopped and didn't move because he knew there was no hope.

He backed slowly away from the house, his mouth open, his throat dry. But as he went he saw something through the flames. From across the yard, beyond the smoke and fire, a girl stared back at him. He caught only a glimpse of her blonde hair streaked black and deep blue and the black leather choker around her neck. Her face and arms were smudged black, and she looked at him with a terror that seemed to transcend madness.

"Gem!" he managed, but his voice was only a weak croak. "Gem!" A cloud of black smoke billowed from the house, forcing him to turn away. He staggered a few steps back and looked again, but the girl was gone.

The fire engines were at the curb, and Johnny stumbled to the first pumper.

"There's someone inside. I heard screams from inside the house," he said.

Later, although he tried to remember the minutes that followed the firemen's arrival, he could find only bits of conversation and fleeting images. He'd hear himself saying, "It all happened so fast," and wonder how many times he'd listened with no real understanding as victims and witnesses said the same thing. In his years as a reporter he'd been to fires, fatal traffic accidents, and murder sites, but he had never been the first to arrive, never tried to save another's life and failed. It all happened so fast.

The first fire engines deployed, and the firefighters began pouring water on the house. A paramedic gave Johnny water, checked him for smoke inhalation, examined his hands, and led him across the street, where Johnny sat on the curb watching the fire. The ground floor was exploding in flames, and the paint on the siding was blistering and curling. Pops and creaks from small explosions hidden among the flames punctuated the roar of the fire. Overhead, debris rode the heat waves from the fire and drifted to nearby lawns.

A crowd gathered while the firefighters ran the heavy hoses to the pumpers and dragged them over the fence and through the bushes to the front lawn. A wave of nausea swept over him, and Johnny picked up his coat, stood unsteadily, and worked his way back through the crowd to lean against the side of a brick industrial building just beyond the sidewalk. His body was covered with a film of moisture, dirt, and soot, and he thought he might collapse. He lowered himself to the ground and stared blankly at the backs of the people surrounding him.

Eventually the people drifted away, and Johnny was alone to watch the coroner's van arrive. He saw them pull the gurney from the back and push it into the house. He rose slowly and crossed the street to stand amid the hoses and water washing across the sidewalk and down the gutter. A few minutes later a man came through the front door of the house and walked down the steps, moving cautiously, looking above and behind him as he went. He was in his late thirties or early forties and ruggedly handsome with a long nose and chiseled features and black hair combed straight back from his forehead. He wore the dark gray-blue slacks and shirt of a fireman but not the heavy firefighting equipment. When he reached the fence, Johnny stepped forward.

"Do you know her name?"

The fireman stopped and studied him. Johnny knew he looked dirty and tired, and the expression on the fireman's face spoke to the wildness he saw in Johnny's eyes.

"No, not yet," the fireman said.

"I think I know her."

The man stopped and stood straighter and looked at Johnny with new interest. "I didn't catch your name."

"Johnny Rose."

"Rose? You the one who tried to get in?" Johnny nodded. "I'm Inspector Garfield." His handshake was gentle. "Mr. Rose, what makes you think you know the victim?"

"I think it's my niece. Well, my cousin actually. I was like an uncle to her. I was supposed to meet her here. She's a street kid, been squatting in this house. Was the victim a girl?"

He hesitated for a second, then nodded. "Yes, I'm afraid so." His voice was soft and kind, and he looked back over his shoulder at the burned building for a second. Firemen continued to move in and out through the front door, their heavy coats smudged with soot. A stream of water, blackened from the fire, ran down the porch steps. The inspector seemed to study it for a moment and looked back at Johnny.

"Mr. Rose, you need to know there was no way you could have saved that girl. No way."

"That doesn't make much difference, does it?"

"No, I know it doesn't." They were quiet for a moment before Garfield said, "So she was your cousin, you said?"

"My second cousin. My cousin's daughter. I came to get her tonight to send her home. She's from Atlanta. I've even got the ticket." He touched his breast pocket and looked away for a moment. He turned back to Garfield. "If you want, I can try to identify the body."

"Thank you, but that's not going to be possible. I'm sorry, Mr. Rose, but the body was too badly burned for a visual identification. We'll probably need dental records for a positive ID."

"Okay."

"What was your cousin's name?"

"Sara Bradley."

"Can you help us with that? Help us get Sara's dental records? It's usually better if a family member makes the call."

Johnny lowered his eyes to the sidewalk and nodded slightly. Yes, he would make the call. Maggie should hear it from him, not a stranger. He looked at the black, dead building and then at Garfield. "Yes. I'll call tonight."

"Okay, thank you very much. I know this isn't a good time, but can you give me your cousin's name and the names and address and phone number of her parents?"

"I only know her mom's address. They're divorced. I don't know where her father is."

"Sure, I understand," Garfield said.

Johnny gave him Maggie's name, address, and number.

"Here's my card," Garfield said. "Please call me tomorrow. I won't contact the family unless I don't hear anything."

"Okay."

Johnny turned to leave but stopped when two men wheeled the gurney out the front door and started down the steps. A small mound, covered with a thick blue sheet, lay atop it. Johnny stared at the gurney numbly. Garfield stepped aside as they pushed it through the gate and went down the sidewalk.

Johnny watched the two men and their precious cargo until they reached the back of the wagon, then turned to see Garfield looking at him.

"Thank you again, Mr. Rose," he said.

Johnny heard the doors of the wagon slam and without deliberation asked Garfield, "It was arson, wasn't it?"

"Why do you ask?"

"I've covered a lot of fires."

"Covered?"

"I'm a reporter for the *Journal*."

"Are you writing a story about this?" His tone shifted from comforting and sympathetic to neutral, all business.

"No," Johnny shook his head. "I'm not writing anything. But I've got to call them. Tell 'em about the fire."

"Okay, but about all I can say right now is that the cause of the fire is undetermined."

"The place went up awful fast."

Garfield hesitated, then nodded. "Yes, it did. But a lot of things could cause that."

"Yeah, I know. Can I tell 'em that the origin looks suspicious?"

"Yeah, that'd probably be okay."

Johnny heard the engine of the coroner's wagon fire up, and he turned to see it pull away from the curb and watched it drive slowly down the street. He looked at Garfield again. Garfield returned the look, as though waiting for Johnny to say something. When he was silent, Garfield said, "Well, thank you, Mr. Rose. You did your best. No one could have saved her."

"Maybe not tonight, but . . . "

"What?"

"Ah ... nothing. Listen, there's something you should know. When Sara called me, she was scared. She wanted to leave right away."

"Scared of what?"

"I don't know. She didn't tell me but I could hear it in her voice. She's never talked about going home before and now ... " Johnny looked toward the house. "By the way, did you talk to any other street kids? Maybe a blonde girl with streaked hair, wears a choker?"

"No. No one like that. Why? Who is she?"

"Sara's friend. Her name's Gem. At least that's what they call her. I saw her here. Maybe she can help you."

"We'll look, but I haven't seen anyone like that," Garfield said again.

"Okay, thank you," Johnny said and walked away, feeling the crushing weight of hope turned to dust.

Six

Johnny circled the buildings near the burned-out house and walked the side streets but found no sign of Gem. It was close to the *Journal*'s final deadline when he gave up and went to a pay phone about a block away.

"You going to dictate?" the night metro editor asked when Johnny called.

Johnny squeezed his eyes shut and sagged against the side of the booth. He could smell the smoke clinging to his clothes and hear Sara's screams as though she were standing next to him. He tried to block it out, to turn away and tell the editor only what he saw, to adopt a neutral tone like on a scratchy radio report from the edge of the Arctic; you can make out the words, but there's no hint of emotion.

"Rose, you there? What the hell's going on?"

He opened his eyes and blinked against the harsh streetlight. Down the street he saw a homeless man sitting next to a mound of clothes and rags. The man smoked, moving the cigarette to his lips with a slow, steady determination. Johnny looked back at the phone.

"Yeah, I'm here, ah, I was just thinking about it, that's all."

"Hey, you know you're the king of dead bodies lately, aren't you?"

"What the hell's that mean?"

"Jesus, Johnny, relax. I'm just saying there was that naked guy on the hillside, now this. Just forget it, okay? You dictating?"

Johnny's head was swimming. "Yeah, okay. No, I mean I'm not dictating? No, I, ah. No, I can't."

"What do you mean you can't? You were there, right? Give me at least a couple of graphs on this. It's not worth more than that anyway."

"Not worth it? Jesus, a kid was killed," he said but then caught himself, sighed heavily, and said, "I can't . . . I just. Look, get someone else on it. I'm going home. I'll explain it tomorrow."

"You at least get an ID on the dead kid? You get that much?"

Johnny closed his eyes again. The phone felt moist and heavy in his hand, and he mumbled when he spoke. "No. No ID. She was burned too badly for positive identification."

"Yeah, okay, just give me what you got, then."

A car passed slowly on the road behind him, and Johnny could hear the instrumental beginning of Elton John's "Candle in the Wind" on the radio. It seemed to be coming from another universe. He closed his eyes and began telling the editor what had happened, giving him the time and location of the fire and a description of the house and mentioning Garfield.

"Okay, Rose, anything else?"

"Ah, you can say that witnesses reported that the fire spread rapidly. The whole house went up in seconds."

"Arson?"

"I don't know. Garfield said the cause is suspicious."

"Okay. Go home, get some rest. You sound tired."

"Yeah, I'm just tired," he said.

He walked, unaware of his surroundings or his movement, until suddenly he was at his car. He stood on the curb and looked at the Z for a moment as though surprised to see it, then moved to the driver's door and unlocked it. He'd just swung the door open when someone called his name, and he turned.

A boy was watching him from the rear of the car. He wore a black T-shirt that hung loosely on him, accentuating his thin frame, and blue jeans. Even in the semilight of the street lamp his skin was dark and roughened by the weather. A multitude of earrings ran along the edge of his ear. He carried a skateboard in his left hand and beat a constant rhythm on his hip.

"You're Rose, right?"

Johnny looked at him, trying to remember him. Had he been among the street kids with Sara? But Johnny had no memory of the boy.

"Do I know you?"

"Look, man, you gotta come over here for a minute. Okay?"

"Why?"

"Gem needs to talk to you."

His fatigue vanished. He stepped toward the boy, who moved away. "You know where Gem is?" The boy could hear the intensity in his voice and moved back again, stepping onto the curb.

"You gotta help her."

"Where is she?"

"Over there in the alley. Come on."

"I looked in the alley. I didn't see her."

The boy looked at him again, and his instant expression spoke volumes. Another adult who didn't believe him, another adult to keep at arm's length. "Well, fuck. You didn't look in the right place then, did you?"

"Does she know about the fire? Did she see how it started?" Johnny was at the end of the Z.

The boy dropped his skateboard and without taking his eyes from Johnny, kicked it upright next to his foot.

"Man, she was *inside* when it started." He stepped on the board and was halfway down the block by the time Johnny reached the sidewalk. Johnny ran after him. The boy stopped a block away, looked back at Johnny, rounded a corner, and disappeared in the alley behind a block-long brick building.

The alley was a tunnel of darkness, broken by lights in the middle and at the end of the building. The boy had stopped halfway down the alley and watched as Johnny walked toward him. The building's walls carried the tagging of street artists and gang members. A half dozen wooden pallets were haphazardly stacked near a Dumpster behind the boy. Johnny was less than a hundred feet from him when the boy looked at the Dumpster.

"Hey, Gem, he's here."

The outline of a head appeared above the edge of the trash bin, and then Gem was there.

"Okay, Gem, I got him, now I'm outta here," the boy said, stepped on his skateboard, and shoved away. A moment later he was halfway down the alley.

"Billy! Billy!" Gem shouted. But the boy rounded the corner and disappeared without looking back. She stared down the alley, her back to Johnny for a few moments, then turned and looked at him.

The expression of loss that filled her was so absolute that Johnny started to run to her, but the expression was gone in a second and he stopped. "Gem, are you okay?"

Gem walked toward him until she was standing under the light mounted high on the building. "Yeah, I'm all right."

But she wasn't all right, and Johnny could see it. This wasn't the same girl he'd met so often with Sara. He'd known from the time Sara introduced her, from her first words, that Gem was smarter, maybe better educated, than the other street kids. But she was tougher too. A kid who learned early that Santa was a myth and accepted without question that the house always wins. She barely spoke to him the first month, but he knew she was watching him, studying him. After almost a month, she'd come to accept the fact he wasn't an exploiter, that he wouldn't harm Sara, that he cared for her. And eventually he'd come to understand something of Gem too. Gem protected Sara on the streets, like a big sister forced into adulthood too early. Slowly they reached an unspoken understanding. Sara was family for each of them. They would help her and protect her.

And now they stood facing each other in the alley, the death of their separate but shared families hanging in the air between them. Johnny stepped toward Gem, thinking to hug her, tell her it was okay. But her eyes warned him away, her defenses on red alert.

"Are you sure you're okay?"

"Yeah."

Johnny looked at her for a moment and saw that her blonde hair was speckled with black and that ash had darkened her face. Streaks cut through the soot on her cheeks, and he wondered if she'd been crying.

"What happened at that house?"

"It caught on fire."

"You were inside when it started?"

"Yeah, but I couldn't get to her."

"No one's blaming you, Gem."

"Fuck that. She's dead, isn't she? I was there and I couldn't save her."

"I was there too. We both lost her."

"Yeah, well." She turned away suddenly and sniffed. Johnny knew she was crying, and when she looked back at him, she'd rubbed the tears from her eyes and her face was smeared.

"Gem, tell me what happened." Johnny's voice was softer as he tried to pull the information from her.

"I was in the back when it started. I heard Sara screaming. I couldn't get to the living room. I had to get out. There was nothing I could do. Nothing!"

"But was it arson?" She didn't answer. "Gem, if it was arson, you've got to talk to the police or the fire inspector. Somebody. You have to help them find the one who started the fire."

"No, the cops will arrest me. They'll put me back in the system. I won't go back."

"They won't arrest you."

"Yes, they will. I got a warrant out."

She lowered her eyes to the asphalt at her feet, and Johnny waited a moment. When he spoke again, his voice was barely above a whisper. "Please. We both loved Sara. She was family for both of us. Look, help me. I won't take you to the police, I promise."

"Maybe you can help me instead," she said, her eyes still on the ground.

"What?"

Suddenly she brought her head up, cocked it to one side, and looked at Johnny coyly. She was a different person. She smiled a sweet, little-girl smile, but it had a distinctly lurid edge that made Johnny uneasy. "I was thinking maybe I could do something for you and then maybe you'd help me out. This doesn't have to be about the fire."

"Don't do this."

"You were going to send her to Atlanta. I was thinking maybe you could just let me go instead." Days hence he would remember the look on her face and the closed-off expression in her eyes and understand its origin. But at that moment he understood almost nothing. Unconsciously he touched his breast pocket, feeling the ticket there.

"I can't give you her ticket."

"Maybe you could lend me some money then? My folks are rich. They'll pay you back." She smiled, but when he shook his head no, Johnny saw anger and desperation flash through her eyes.

"The hell with you then. I don't need your money. I'm leaving anyway."

"What happened in that house? Why are you so anxious to get out of LA?"

She turned and walked away. But she had gone less than ten yards when a police cruiser drove slowly past the end of the alley on the street she was facing. She was walking back to him even before it disappeared down the street. She stopped short and looked back at him. "Come on, Mr. Rose, you've got to help me. Please. Is that what you want to hear? Okay, please, please."

"Is Atlanta where you're from? Is that your home? Is that why you want to go there?"

"No. I'm from here."

"Okay, I'll take you home if you want to go." The words came with no thought, no planning, but the moment he said them, Johnny knew it was the right thing to do.

Her shoulders sagged, and she looked at him with an expression of desperation, like a cornered animal. "Don't take me there. Please. I hate it there."

"I'll take you home," Johnny repeated. He was playing a dangerous game. He needed more time with her, time to learn why someone had killed Sara. If he left her in the alley, she could disappear into another squat or hitchhike out of LA, and if he gave her the airline ticket, he'd never see her again.

"I'll help you. I promise I will. First, just let me give you a ride home so I know you're safe tonight. We'll go one day at a time, okay?"

"No! I'm not going home ever." She stared at him, and he could see the absolute determination in her eyes. He was about to speak when a car swung into the alley, its headlights bathing them in harsh light. Johnny held his hand up, shading his eyes, and looked. Through the darkness he could make out the light bar on top of the vehicle and moments later understood it was the police cruiser they'd seen moments before.

"Ah, shit," Gem swore.

Johnny could hear the gravel crunching under its tires as the patrol car rolled slowly toward them. Gem moved to Johnny's side and touched his arm as the cruiser slowed to a stop next to them.

A black man in his mid-thirties was behind the wheel. The second cop was thin, blond, and looked very young.

"Good evening," the black cop said.

"Hello."

"What's going on here?"

"Nothing," Gem said. "My uncle here was just taking me home. I don't live far from here."

"Your uncle?"

"Yeah. His car's just over there," Gem gestured toward the end of the alley.

"That right, mister?" The cop looked at Johnny.

"That's right, I'm taking her to her place right now."

The cop looked from Johnny to Gem. "You sure you're okay?"

"Yes. I'm fine."

"Okay." He slipped the car into gear, and it moved on down the alley.

Gem watched the cruiser silently for a moment again and looked at Johnny. "How the hell you gonna help me with something like that, huh?"

"I don't know. But I always tried to help Sara. You were her friend so you know it's true, don't you?" She said nothing. "Don't you?" he insisted.

She looked back down the street, and Johnny followed her eyes. The cruiser paused at the end of the alley, its brake lights on. "No police?" she asked.

"No, I won't make you go to the police."

"All right. I'll let you take me home," she said and walked past him up the alley toward the burned-out house and away from the police cruiser.

Johnny followed until they neared the end of the alley and stepped next to her. The top of her head barely reached his chest. He glanced down as they walked. She was lost in her own thoughts, paying no attention to him, and Johnny realized how small and vulnerable she looked when the anger slipped back below the surface.

They walked silently to the car, and he held the door for her. She stopped and looked at him for a moment, her eyes searching his face for meaning in the unexpected gesture. For a second he saw the vulnerability of a child in her eyes.

It was a look he'd seen only once or twice with Sara.

"What?" she demanded, and the expression was gone.

"Nothing," he said.

"I got it," she said and pushed his hand off the top of the door.

She stared straight ahead as he got in the car a moment later. He caught her reflection in the windshield. Her face was blank, her eyes hollow and lifeless; the look of a prisoner who's lost her last appeal to the governor.

Johnny started the car. "Which way?" he asked.

"Not far. Go west on Santa Monica, I'll tell you where to turn."

They rode in silence for a few blocks. She curled against the door, her head down, and despite the heat of the evening, she shivered.

"Would you like a blanket? I have one in the back," he asked.

"No," she said, but he paid no attention and steered the car to the curb. He circled to the back of the car, popped the hatchback, and grabbed an old cotton blanket. Leaning in the driver's door, his weight on his knee on the seat, he draped the blanket across her. She didn't protest, and a moment later she pulled it to her chin and laid her head against the window, as though she were sleeping.

After a few more blocks, Johnny turned to her. "Just tell me how it started," he said. "Just tell me that much."

His words seemed to wake her, although he was certain she hadn't been asleep. She looked at him for a moment but said nothing.

"Please," Johnny said. "Just tell me. You don't have to go to the police. Just tell me. Maybe I can do something myself."

Gem pulled the blanket down from her chin and looked at him for a second, turned to the windshield, and spoke. "There was a window in the back. We pulled the plywood off. That's how you get in. We only opened it day before yesterday. We weren't planning on staying. We were going to go up to San Francisco and live in a nice hotel and order room service."

"Okay, you were in the back," Johnny said, turning the conversation back to the fire. "Then what happened?"

"Sara was already there. I came in later. When I got in, I smelled gasoline and I heard Sara yelling."

"What was she saying?"

"Something like, 'Hey, what are you doing here? You can't do that.' Then she said something like 'what the fuck,' and there was all this yelling back and forth and then all this smoke and fire. I heard her screaming and I started to go to the hall but there was all this smoke and fire. I couldn't get out of the room so I just got back out the window. That's when I saw you."

Gem turned away and looked out the side window at the car in the next lane. Johnny watched the road for a moment, aware that his own car now smelled like smoke and ashes. He turned back to the girl and tried again.

"Why'd this guy want to burn that house down?"

"I don't know." He glanced at her and knew she was lying.

"Look, Gem, you gotta tell me the truth, okay? You can't lie to me on this." He could feel the intensity seeping into his voice again. She stared out the window and said nothing.

They rode silently for a few minutes, and she waved at the windshield. "Take the next left and go down a few blocks."

He turned the corner and silently questioned the directions the girl was giving him. The bungalows and working-class immigrant neighborhood would be behind them in a few minutes. They were headed toward upscale real estate and some very pricey homes. Why was she directing him there? But he pushed the thought from his mind. He didn't want to fight with her about that. He needed her to be calm. He glanced at her. "Tell me something." She looked at him. Her jaw was set, her lips pressed tight. "What's your real name?"

"It doesn't matter, does it?"

"Oh, I don't know. I'd just like to know. That's all."

"Just call me Gem. Everybody does. Turn left at the corner."

Johnny made the turn and wondered again what the hell they were doing in Hancock Park, one of the wealthiest areas in Los Angeles.

"Is this where you live? Hancock Park?" She looked out the window and said nothing. Suddenly she said, "Stop here at the corner."

Johnny pulled to the curb. "You sure you live here? This is your neighborhood?"

It took Johnny a moment to understand the look in her eyes. It was disappointment and hurt. But at what?

"Wait a second." He spoke softly, trying to erase the pain he'd seen in her eyes a moment before. "Will you be here tomorrow? Is this where I'll find you?"

"I'll be around."

"Okay, just one more thing."

"What?"

"Who lived in the house with you and Sara? Was anyone else inside?"

"No. It was just the three of us. Me, Sara, and Dallas. But he left, ran away."

"Who's Dallas?"

"That's Sara's boyfriend."

"That his real name? Dallas?"

"No, we just called him that because he's from there."

And the penny dropped. Through the fatigue and mind-numbing sadness of losing Sara, Johnny understood. He leaned across the car and grabbed Gem's arm.

"He's from Texas?"

"Yeah, Dallas."

"What was his real name? Was it James?"

"Jesus, man." She jerked her arm away. "Yeah, Jimmy, but we called him Dallas. So?"

"The police found the body of a boy named James Randall yesterday afternoon in the Hollywood Hills."

"Ah, shit," she whispered and jerked sideways in the car and shoved the door open. Johnny caught a glimpse of her eyes and saw the raw fear in them. It was the same look he'd seen through the smoke and flames at the back of the house. She struggled to climb out of the bucket seat, but Johnny lunged toward her, catching her sleeve again.

"Wait! What is it?"

"No! No! Let go of me." She jerked free, flailing her arms at him, stumbled from the car, got to her feet, and ran, a dead sprint down the sidewalk.

"Gem!" Johnny shouted, but it was useless. She ran along a tall, thick hedge and suddenly disappeared up a driveway that cut through it.

Johnny moved as quickly as he could, but Gem was already gone by the time he got to the driveway, the first break in the hedge that extended to the corner. The drive was a long, narrow ribbon of used brick and cement, and he stared up it toward a huge, two-story house but stopped well shy of it. The house was dark, and there was no sign of movement within. He listened but didn't hear a door close, and he slowly scanned the wide yard. He saw a huge sycamore in the far corner, but nothing moved. He walked slowly back to the car, got in, and looked at the blanket on the empty passenger seat. The exhaustion he'd held at bay suddenly over-whelmed him, and he leaned his head against the steering wheel for a moment, then glanced at his watch. It was just pushing midnight, about seven hours since he first heard her screams.

It felt like days.

Seven

●━━━━━━━━━━━━━━━━━●

*J*ohnny could see the phone on the kitchen counter, waiting for him like a plague carrier. He tossed his jacket on the couch, grabbed the remote control, and turned on the television. He ignored the phone. At first he told himself he was doing Maggie a favor by letting her sleep. There was no point in waking her in the middle of the night. When he left the couch to get a beer, he didn't even look at the phone. But in his heart Johnny knew he wasn't doing Maggie a favor. He was stalling, trying to find the courage within himself and the words to tell her.

He opened the refrigerator and reached for a beer but hesitated, grabbed a quart of milk instead, pulled a paper towel off the roll on the counter, went to the front door, and stepped outside. He crossed the narrow strip of grass to the thick oleander hedge that separated his building from the one next door, squatted, and peered into the blackness where the bottom branches grew thick. Nothing moved. In the dim light from the apartment, he could see the small saucer he'd left there. After pulling it out, he waved it in the air, wiped off the dirt with the paper towel, filled the saucer with milk, and put it down on the grass just beyond the edge of the dirt. He waited, but when the cat didn't come, he walked back to the front door and watched from there, taking care not to block the light from the apartment. Soon a black-and-gray

56

cat poked its head from under the bushes and looked around warily, studied Johnny for a moment, and then moved cautiously to the saucer and lapped the milk, glancing up occasionally to watch him for a moment before returning to the milk.

He had spotted the stray about a week before. Guessing its age was tough. It was years past a kitten but still not old. It wasn't big, but its gnarled right ear and scars above the eye told Johnny it was a fighter. The first time he put the milk out the cat ignored it, disdaining the offer. But after several days, the animal had started to take the milk, to trust it would be there. Now it waited for Johnny but still wouldn't come out until he had walked away. When it was done, the cat looked at Johnny for a moment, the superiority and disdain still obvious in its eyes. It turned abruptly and sauntered to the bush and disappeared among the low branches. Johnny smiled at the retreating animal and went back inside.

He watched television until three the next morning, when he knew he couldn't avoid it any longer. Going into the kitchen, he picked the phone out of its holder on the counter. It would be six in Atlanta, and he knew she would be up, getting ready to go to the airport.

He sat at his kitchen table looking into his unlit apartment, wondering what he would say, what words he could use, when she answered. He glanced at the clock on the microwave, the numbers glowing green in the dark kitchen. It was three-fifteen. He dialed from memory and listened to the phone ring. The sound was crystal clear, as though the phone were ringing across the street, not thousands of miles away, and it made him dread the conversation even more.

"Hello." Her voice was strong and upbeat.

"Maggie, it's Johnny."

"Hi."

"Yeah, I, ah . . ."

"Good grief, what time is it there, anyway?"

"About three."

"You always were a night owl."

"I waited until I knew you'd be up."

"Why? Has something happened?" Fear seeped into her voice like a burgundy stain on a fine new white carpet.

"There was a fire. This abandoned house where Sara was living, it caught fire. She was inside."

"Oh, my God. Is she all right?"

He stared into the darkness and felt saturated with the helplessness of being three time zones away from someone you love who needs you to touch and hold her and in some tiny way salve the pain that will never go away. He didn't know how to say it, what words to use, and so he said nothing, and the silence built as loudly as the onset of a hurricane.

"Did she get out? I mean, is she hurt, is she . . . Goddamn it, Johnny, say something."

"She was killed in the fire, Maggie. She died almost instantly," Johnny said.

"No! No!" He heard her scream and then the sudden burst of tears. She was sobbing into the phone, and Johnny blundered on.

"It happened just as I got there to pick her up," he said, knowing how stupid that sounded. For a fleeting second he thought of telling her it was arson. But there seemed little point.

"I knew when she ran away, I just knew I'd never see her again, and then I got that postcard and she called me and, oh, God, Johnny . . . " Her words were thick, and Johnny sat and just listened for a few moments.

"Maggie, I'm so sorry. I just . . . " His voice trailed off, and he listened to her sobs, feeling helpless and wishing he hadn't called, although he knew there was no choice.

"She was a wonderful child, Maggie. I got to know her. She was a good kid," he said. But his words didn't lessen Maggie's pain, and for a while Johnny just listened to her cry. After a while she choked back the tears and Johnny stumbled forward, helping her concentrate and make arrangements for dental records and for Maggie to contact a funeral director there and give permission to release the body. And then, when there was nothing left to say, no comfort possible, he said good-bye with a promise to call again soon. He gently put the receiver back in its holder.

Despite the exhaustion, Johnny knew he wouldn't sleep, and he sat at the table and thought of the first time he'd seen Sara on the streets. She'd run away from Atlanta two years before. Maggie called Johnny when she got a postcard from Sara postmarked Hollywood. She asked him to find Sara, talk to her, make sure she was okay. Johnny didn't ask why she ran away, and Maggie never told him. Now, as he sat at the table, he wondered if he'd been wrong. Should he have pressed, done more? Would she be alive if he hadn't stayed on the sidelines? But there was no way to answer the question, and finally he climbed the stairs to his bedroom and got in bed. The curtains were open, and the streetlight glinted off the silver frame of a picture atop his dresser.

In the photo, he and Jimmy stood on opposite sides of Maggie, the cousin who had lived down the street when they were growing up and was like a little sister to them. The photo was decades old, taken when all three still smiled easily, before the years had introduced them to failed marriages and war. Before the pain of death and lost loved ones had permanently entered their lives. Johnny got off the bed and picked up the picture and studied it for a moment before gently putting it back.

He lay in bed for almost an hour before finally sleeping. But he was restless, and after only a few hours he awoke and got up, feeling his age in his knees and hips. He showered and dressed and headed downstairs.

He made coffee, and while it brewed he called Doc Whetmore. But his friend wasn't in yet, and Johnny had to leave a message on his machine. "Doc, it's Johnny. Call me. It's pretty important."

He got the *Los Angeles Times* from the front porch and skimmed the front and the Metro sections for a story on the fire. But the *Times* didn't have the piece, and finally he folded it up again and put it aside without reading anything while he drank his coffee and ate an English muffin. Half an hour after he'd left the message for Doc, Johnny picked up the phone and called the *Journal*. He dialed in Kuscyk's extension and got an answering machine.

"Stan, I'm going to Hollywood this morning. Following up that arson fire from last night. I should be in by noon." He grabbed his keys off the table and was halfway across the living room when the phone rang.

"Hey, Johnny, it's Doc. I just got your message."

"Hi, thanks for calling.

"What's so urgent?"

"There was a fire last night in Hollywood. A girl was killed."

"Yeah, I heard about it. A street kid, right?"

"Yes. Doc, do you remember Maggie?"

"Your cousin? Of course. We still trade Christmas cards."

"The girl was her daughter Sara."

"Oh, God, I'm so sorry. I had no idea. I mean, it's not my case. I . . . ah . . . is there anything I can do?"

"Maybe. Do you know anything more about that boy, the one on the hillside, James Randall?"

"Randall? Why? What does he have to do with it?"

"I'm not sure, but I think they're connected."

"You're not serious?"

"Yes, I am. Look, right now all I know is that he was staying in the same house as Sara. And they were killed one day apart. It's not much, but it's enough. You know how he died?"

"Yeah, we got the results yesterday."

"Did he drown?"

"No. You're not going to believe this. He was electrocuted."

"Jesus, electrocuted?"

"Yeah. You remember at the scene I told you I had an idea about what killed him?"

"Of course."

"He had a burn mark on the inside of the fingers of his right hand. I think he was holding on to some kind of metal when he got it."

"That's how you knew? The burn mark?"

"That and the water. I told you he'd been in the water. But there was something else too. There was a burn mark on his neck and one on his chest, like he was wearing a medallion."

"A Saint Christopher, something like that?"

"Well, sort of. But this one was different. The burn was pretty faint. I had a hard time making it out at first."

"What was it?"

"I don't know exactly. It was a *P* with an *X* over it."

"What the hell's that?"

"I don't know. I've never seen it before. Maybe it was some kind of gang thing or something. By the way, did Towers tell you if he found any jewelry in the kid's clothes?"

"He said he didn't. Which raises an interesting question."

"Where's the necklace?"

"Right. Tell me, you think the kid was murdered?"

"I don't know. It could be accidental, but who knows?"

"Right. Listen, can you do me a favor? Can you check on Sara's case? Maybe just see if there's anything unusual?"

"I'll see what I can find out. Hey, how's Maggie handling it?"

"I just called her a few hours ago. I think she's still in shock."

"Yeah, I'll bet. I'll get back to you as soon as I can."

"Thanks."

Johnny set the phone back in its cradle and looked at it for a moment, bouncing the keys in his hand, then walked out and locked the door behind him.

He drove first to the burned-out building, wanting to see it in daylight. The yellow crime-scene tape that the police had strung across the front of the house danced in the breeze. Johnny pushed the gate aside and walked up the short sidewalk to the house. His heartbeat accelerated as he came close to the porch. He could hear the roar of the fire again and feel the heat. The lawn was littered with fragments of burned wood and shingles and scorched paper. Near a bush Johnny saw a gray blanket, soaked and splattered with mud. Had it been Sara's?

At the bottom of the steps, he hesitated. The plywood that had been nailed across the front door was gone, leaving only a blackened hole, like the entrance to a mine. After a moment he began to climb the steps, his eyes on the door. His heart was beating faster, his breathing accelerated. The acid after-odor of water and fire, of loss and destruction, filled his nostrils. He stopped on the second step, knowing he'd find nothing inside but more pain. Turning back, he began walking the perimeter of the house.

He found the window that hadn't been covered with plywood and stood on his toes to look into a small room that might have been a back bedroom. He continued until he'd circled the house. Back in front, he moved through the gate and glanced again at the house. Just then a new black Lincoln Continental stopped at the curb. A short, thin man in an expensive dark blue suit, white shirt and a conservative tie, and wire-rimmed glasses got out and looked at Johnny across the hood.

"Hello. Tell me, do you live around here?" he asked. His voice was friendly. Johnny guessed his age at close to sixty. His eyes were alert and full of energy.

"No."

"Well, maybe you can help me anyway. I'm looking for someone who can tell me something about this building and maybe about the fire."

"I don't know anything about the building."

"I couldn't help but notice you walking around it, though. Looked like you were looking for something. Maybe someone?"

Johnny looked at the dapper little man for a moment, studying him openly, before speaking. "Who are you?"

"Oh, pardon me. I'm Clay Griffin." He took a gold-plated business-card holder from his coat pocket, extracted a card, rounded the front of the car to the sidewalk, and held it out. Johnny studied the card. It had the man's name and phone number but nothing else.

"I didn't catch your name," Griffin said.

"Johnny Rose."

"You're the reporter, right?"

"Yes, ah, how did you know?"

"Your byline. You know, maybe you can help me after all. I have a client who is very anxious to learn more about this fire."

"Oh?" Where was this going? Who was this guy?

"The story mentioned witnesses."

"I was a witness. I got here just as it went up," Johnny said.

"Did you see anyone else here?"

"Your client own the building?"

"No."

"Look, Mr."—Johnny glanced at the card and then at the man standing by the Lincoln's fender—"Griffin, why don't you tell me what this is about? What are you looking for? Then I'll know if I can really help you."

"I'm trying to locate a young girl who lived in this house."

"What girl? You mean Sara, the girl who was killed?"

"No, the other child."

Johnny looked at the man, trying to see into him, making a quick judgment. "I'm not sure who you mean."

"A young blonde girl. She goes by the street name Gem."

"Why do you want to find her?"

"Like I said, it's a personal matter with my client."

"Well, I'm sorry, I can't help you, Mr. Griffin."

"Okay. But if you see her or have any information about her, please call me. My client is very motivated to find her."

"What's that mean exactly? Motivated?" But Griffin simply smiled.

"Who's your client?" Johnny asked.

"I'm afraid that's confidential."

"You an investigator, an attorney, or what?"

"That's not really important. I'm acting more as a friend right now."

"Why's your client want to find her?"

"That's a private matter, Mr. Rose."

"Well, I can't help you."

Griffin opened the door on the driver's side. "Thank you for your time, Mr. Rose. If you change your mind or if circumstances change, you have my number."

"Right."

Griffin got into the car, and a moment later it slid silently away from the curb. Johnny watched it go, looking at the rear bumper, but it was a new car and there was no license plate.

He read the business card again, stuck it in his pocket, and went to his car. Inside the Z he sat for a moment and thought again of Griffin's words. *"If circumstances change, you have my number."* What the hell did that mean?

He spent the next hour driving through Hollywood, the window rolled down and his elbow protruding into the sun. He scanned the crowded sidewalks and glanced into the storefronts, pulling into a parking space and climbing out every time he saw a street kid, anyone he even vaguely recognized from the times he'd been with Sara. But his questions about Sara and Gem were met with blank looks and hostile stares. "I'll be around," Gem had said. But Johnny knew she wouldn't be near Hancock Park, and he could find no one who would admit seeing her in Hollywood.

Finally, he parked on Ivar and walked to the boulevard. Towering above the street was the huge neon sign for God's House. He glanced at the sign and walked on toward the church. When he reached the revolving door leading to the church lobby, he stopped abruptly, stepped back into the middle of the sidewalk, and looked around, trying to reconcile what he saw with his personal memories of Richard Roberts.

When Johnny had first written about the Reverend Roberts, his church was a storefront with folding metal chairs, worn hymnals, and a simple pulpit. His wife played the upright piano, and Hank Jefferson, an aging Hollywood studio musician, led the choir. An open front door and several large fans were the only cooling system, and the cleaning crew was Roberts with a broom. In those days, Roberts spent every night walking the streets of Hollywood, telling the winos, the runaways, and the homeless that a life of happiness and reward awaited them if they would accept God's love. Occasionally, he would hit the rubber-chicken circuit, leveraging his Olympic glory into after-dinner honorariums that he plowed back into his mission.

Johnny spent a week with Roberts, as much as twelve hours a day, and even walked the streets with him. One night Johnny watched Roberts squat on his haunches next to a wino, his running shoes only inches from the pool of vomit at the man's side. The minister looked into the man's face, burned the deep red of a beet from exposure and alcohol, put his hand on the man's shoulder, and spoke to him by name, telling him that God loved him. Later he talked to a young woman, no more than sixteen, trying to convince her not to sell her body on Sunset Boulevard.

"Look, I'm not asking you to make a decision about the rest of your life right now. Just stay off the street for one night. Don't prostitute yourself tonight, okay? Come by God's House tomorrow. We can help you." But the girl's reaction was muted and noncommittal, and Roberts left her with the words "God will always love you."

Later that night Johnny sat on a folding chair in the church, exhausted from the day, and watched as Roberts straightened the rows of chairs, put hymnals on each, and swept the dirty linoleum floor, preparing for the next morning's service. He talked as he worked, saying that someday he wanted to open a live-in shelter for street kids and have a church that could minister to the community's secular needs, not just save their souls. His words were upbeat and full of energy and held no hint of weariness despite the long day.

"We should be helping the immigrants get through the bu-reaucracy. We should be visiting the shut-ins and helping the elderly get to the doctor. We should be running a halfway house for prisoners who accept the Lord and want to give back to society, make amends. God's work isn't just about going to church and singing hymns. It's about people." He stopped sweeping and looked up from the floor, his gaze fix-ing on Johnny. "You know, God wants you to succeed. He wants people to be successful and happy. Personally, I have never doubted why God put me on this earth. He wants me to accomplish something great. I know he does."

Now, standing outside the church's new headquarters, Johnny thought how close Roberts was to fulfilling the dream. Johnny had to crane his neck to see the top of the tall brick building that held the neon sign. It wasn't just the building, though. Roberts was earning a national reputation for his work. A few months back he'd been in *Time* maga-zine, prominent in an article titled "America's 12 Moral Leaders." *60 Minutes* had done a piece a year ago, and dona-tions now came from across the country.

Johnny pushed through the revolving door into the lobby and stopped for a moment to admire the marble and brass and beamed ceilings. He looked around the lobby, seeing the large silver and brass cross mounted on the wall.

"Mr. Rose, hello." Johnny heard the voice and turned to see Buddy and Carol Holland standing on the other side of the lobby. Buddy waved and smiled. He wore blue jeans and a long-sleeved white shirt open at the collar. Carol Holland wore gray wool tights, a white T-shirt that hung to midcalf, a baseball cap, and sunglasses. She looked as though she'd just come from the gym. They started across the lobby to him.

"Hi, Buddy. Ms. Holland."

"It's a pleasure to see you again." She smiled broadly at him and took off her sunglasses and held them dangling at her side.

"Thank you." He looked at Buddy. "I'm looking for Dick. Is he here?"

"No. He's attending a prayer breakfast in Pasadena. Is there anything I can do?"

"Maybe. At the party the other night I mentioned a girl, Sara Bradley. Were you able to find out anything about her?"

"I'm sorry, Mr. Rose. I checked our records and asked the counselors but . . ." He shrugged. "If she came in, it was probably just once or twice. She wasn't in any of our programs."

Johnny exhaled, feeling his hopes slip. "Okay. Well, thanks anyway for trying."

"Wait a minute, Mr. Rose," Buddy said. "Sara Bradley. Isn't she the one who was killed in the fire last night?"

"Yes."

"You doing a story for your newspaper about her?"

"No." A silence settled over them. Buddy and Carol Holland looked at Johnny, the expectation obvious in their eyes. "She was my cousin. I've been trying to help her out. That's why I'm interested."

"The girl, the one who was killed, she was your cousin?" Carol Holland asked.

"Yes."

"Oh, Mr. Rose, I'm very sorry. I just heard about it this morning. It was a real tragedy. I'm so sorry."

"Yes, thank you for your concern," he said and looked to Buddy again. "Listen, while I'm here maybe you can tell me about another boy, a kid named James Randall? Does that ring a bell?"

"No. I, ah, no. I don't know him either. Why?"

Johnny looked back to Carol Holland. "He's the boy who was found on the hillside the other day. I told you about him at your party, remember?"

"Yes, of course. It was very sad. I know how hard life can be for these children. That's why I'm helping with the Hollywood Restoration Committee. We're having a meeting here in just a few minutes. I'd love to have you join us, find out a little more about what we're doing. Do you have a little time?"

"Thank you, but no, I've got to be going." He shifted his gaze to Buddy again. "Thanks for your help."

Johnny walked back across the lobby to the revolving door but stopped two feet in front of it, turned, and looked back at Carol Holland and Buddy. "Hey, Buddy," he called. "Tell Dick I stopped by. Ask him to call me, okay?"

"Sure."

Johnny watched them for a moment longer. He started toward the revolving door but had to wait as a group of tourists in shorts and T-shirts, with cameras around their necks, led by a young woman in a white blouse and gray jacket, flooded into the lobby. The woman was telling the story of God's House.

"After Reverend Roberts won the gold medal in the hurdles in the Olympics, he dedicated himself to helping the less fortunate . . ."

As the last of the tourists came through the door, Johnny moved around the crowd. He was almost at the door when a young woman with thin dishwater blonde hair to her shoulders and the scarred lip of a poorly repaired cleft palate left the tourists and approached him. She wore the same white blouse and gray blazer as the woman leading the tour.

"Excuse me, would you like to join our tour?"

"No, thanks. I was just leaving," he said and pushed through the revolving door to the sidewalk.

Johnny paused on the sidewalk, listening to the noise of the cars on Hollywood Boulevard and feeling the trapped heat radiating off the sidewalk, street, and the nearby buildings. He could smell diesel fumes as a bus pulled from a nearby stop, sending a plume of purple and black smoke into the air. He turned away from the revolving door and walked toward his car, his pace unhurried, and as he walked he thought of Sara dying in the fire and Dallas, dead and dumped naked on a hillside. The City of Angels had swallowed two children, and it seemed that no one even noticed. Maybe, Johnny thought, he could do something about that.

A large banner hanging in the lobby said: WELCOME TO HOLLYWOOD STATION, BIENVENIDOS A LAS ESTATICION DE HOLLYWOOD. Johnny glanced at it as he reached the information counter.

"Can I help you?" The cop behind the counter was young, with dark hair in a crew cut, broad shoulders, and strong upper arms that showed long hours in the weight room. But his face was soft, as though he hadn't quite lost all his baby fat. His name tag said Rodriguez.

"I hope so. My name's Johnny Rose. I'd like to see Detective Towers."

"Okay, Mr. Rose, have a seat and I'll let him know you're here." He motioned to a bench against a wall near the front door.

A moment after he sat down, a young Hispanic couple with two children in a stroller and a third in the woman's arms entered the station. It took a moment for them to get the double-wide stroller through the door, and they approached the counter slowly, cautiously, moving with the aura of supplication so common to the poor living in a country whose language is not their own. Johnny tried to listen but couldn't follow the Spanish. The woman stood a step behind her husband, hoisting the baby from one shoulder to the other. Rodriguez nodded as he listened, then leaned forward and spoke in a low voice. He did not look toward Johnny again, and after twenty minutes Johnny wondered if Rodriguez had forgotten him.

He stood and stretched, debating whether to remind the cop, but at that moment Towers stepped into the lobby from an inner office and motioned him over.

"What can I do for you, Mr. Rose?"

"It's about the boy on the hillside. Look, it's kind of complicated." Johnny looked past Towers's shoulder toward the door he'd come through.

"We have an interview room in the back. We can talk there, if you want."

"Good. I think that would be better."

Towers led him through the detective bureau, a room where the desks, pushed together in groups of four, were piled high with papers and in and out boxes were stacked full. The interview room opened off the detective bureau like a closet. It was small, barely big enough for two chairs and a round table. The walls and ceiling were covered with gray acoustic tile that showed the insults and scars of thousands of bored and angry people who had passed through the room.

Johnny entered first and squeezed into the corner between the table and the wall. Towers sat with his back to the door and took a small notebook and pen from his coat pocket, put them on the table, and leaned back.

"You said you have some information on the Randall boy?"

Johnny glanced at Towers's notebook and looked at the detective.

"He was living in that house that was torched last night. The girl that was killed in that fire, Sara Bradley, was my cousin, Detective."

"I'm sorry for your loss. You have my sympathy." He said it slowly, probably wondering where this was leading, but prepared to let this reporter talk for a minute or two.

"I think they're connected."

"Oh, why's that?"

"Sara called me yesterday. She was scared, I mean, really scared, which was a complete change for her. She always acted really tough."

"Scared of what, of who?"

"I don't know, I never got a chance to ask."

Towers flipped open his notebook and jotted something down. "Well, it's possible they're linked in some way, but, well, frankly, just living in the same house . . . I mean, it could be coincidence. The boy was way up on the hillside, the house was down here, and they sure didn't die the same way."

Johnny thought of Gem fleeing from the car when she heard that Dallas was dead. She knew something of the murders, he was positive. But he'd promised no cops and now regretted his quick action the night before.

Towers tapped his pen against his notebook for a moment longer. "Let me ask you a couple of questions. They're tough, but I need to ask them, okay?"

"Sure."

"Your cousin into drugs? You think it's possible she and this Randall ripped someone off?"

"No. I don't think so. I really don't."

"Steal something that someone wants back? Money, property of some kind? Maybe a gun or something like that?"

"I don't think she was a thief or a druggie."

"But you don't know for sure?"

"Listen, Detective Towers, I knew this girl. She wasn't like that." But even as he said it, Johnny knew he was speaking from gut instinct, without proof. He saw her once a week for an hour or two. How well did he really know her?

"You know, Mr. Rose, a lot of times we don't know these kids as well as we think," Towers said as if he'd read Johnny's thoughts. "I see it all the time. We get a kid in here who's a stoned crazy. But you listen to his parents tell it and the kid's a choirboy. Never been in trouble before, loves his family, looks after his little sister, and, by the way, why are we harassing him all the time?"

"It's not like that."

"I'm not saying it is. But just the same, we don't always know these kids as well as we think."

"Look, everything you say may be true, but so what? It doesn't change the fact she was murdered."

Towers nodded. "You're right, of course. But that's assuming it was murder. Look, I'm going to talk to the detective investigating the arson, tell him what you told me. It gives us another angle, another way to look at things. I'll ask juvenile too. See if they've heard anything. I don't want you to think your coming in wasn't helpful. But frankly, I don't want you to get your hopes up either." Towers leaned forward and reached for his notebook. The interview was over.

"That's it?"

"You've given us something that could be important, but like I said, I can't promise anything. You've been a reporter for a long time, right?"

"Yeah."

"Then you know these things can take time."

"Sure, of course. Thanks for seeing me," Johnny said. They shook hands, and a couple of minutes later he walked from the police station. As he crossed the street to his car, he asked himself again how well he really knew Sara. Well enough, he decided. Well enough.

Eight

———————●————————————●———————

*J*ohnny was ten feet past the newsroom door when he heard Kuscyk bellow.

"Rose!" Johnny looked to the far end of the newsroom. Kuscyk never turned when he called someone. He simply yelled. Johnny had no idea how Kuscyk knew he'd just come in.

The metro editor was about sixty and wore his black-and-gray hair in a crew cut. He'd always worn it that way, skipping the long-hair days of the sixties and seventies. His tie was loose, and the sleeves of his white shirt were rolled at the cuffs and smudged with ink.

Johnny sat on the corner of a desk across the narrow aisle from him. The metro editor swiveled in his chair, leaned back, and laced his fingers behind his head.

"Tell me about that fire. What the hell's so special about it?"

"The girl who was killed was my cousin."

Kuscyk opened his mouth to speak but stopped, swallowed, and said, "Damn, Rose, I'm sorry. I didn't know."

"I didn't tell anyone."

"You want to take some time off, a day or two?"

"No." His answer was cold and flat and tinged with anger.

"Yeah?" Kuscyk cocked his head, waiting for Johnny to go on.

"This isn't just a fire. There's more to it. I think it's tied to that body they found up on the hillside."

"The one you covered?"

"Yes. After the fire I talked to a girl, a friend of my cousin. She was in the house when the fire started. She told me the dead boy lived there with them."

The editor's eyes held Johnny in a steady gaze. "Tell me the rest," he said, and Johnny went through the story, keeping it brief.

When he finished, Kuscyk lowered his hands and rested them on his stomach. "Rose, you have any idea why I offered you a job after you quit the *Chronicle*?"

Before joining the *Journal*, Johnny had been a columnist and reporter at the rival *Chronicle*. It had been a great job. He was free to write what he wanted and pursue only those stories that interested him. Total freedom, the dream of every reporter. But the paper had been sold, and he'd had a bitter falling out with the paper's ambitious and soulless new owner and had quit. Things went poorly after that. Johnny had tried freelancing but was a terrible businessman and often failed to collect from the publications that ran his stories. When Kuscyk called from the smaller, less prestigious *Journal*, Johnny was two months behind on his rent and had less than two hundred dollars in his checking account. He'd taken the job without hesitation.

"Why you hired me?"

"Yeah."

"I figured you were shorthanded."

"We're always shorthanded. No, the reason I called you is you've got one of the best instincts for stories I've seen. That's why I'm sitting here listening to this. Anyone else, I'd have told them how sorry I was about the girl and then gone back to work. So you want to tell me where this is leading?"

"I want some time to check it out."

"Time? Shit, you already took half of today without asking me. All I got was a message you'd be in late."

"This could be an important story, Stan."

"Every story's important."

"Not like this one."

"Listen to me, Rose. Right now you've got a fatal fire in Hollywood that killed a street kid and you've got another body on a hillside. The dead boy's not even officially a homicide, and the fire's not officially an arson, right?"

"The boy was murdered, and the fire was set. I know it, Stan."

"You're probably right. But listen to me, Rose. Harsh as this may sound, that's not of a lot of interest to our readers."

"Two kids were murdered, for Christ sake. Isn't that enough?"

"No, not right now it isn't. You got two kids dead but you can't prove they're connected. You can't even prove they were murdered."

Johnny leaned forward, cutting the distance between him and the editor. "And if they were, and we break the story? No one else has this story, Stan. Not the *Times*, not the wires, not broadcast. No one's made the connection. Just me."

Kuscyk grunted. "Maybe that's because there's no connection to make."

"Damn it, Stan, I'm right about this. I know. I was there. In both places, remember?"

Kuscyk looked at him for a long time. "You're sure they're connected? Your judgment isn't clouded because the dead girl's your cousin?"

"They were murdered, Stan. And they're connected. The only questions are by who, and why."

"Where do you stand on that zoning story?"

"It's half written."

"Finish it by tonight and take a day, two at the most. You find something and we'll talk. Otherwise you do the legwork on your own time."

"Thanks, Stan."

"Just bring me something besides a hunch. Something I can use. Get someone to tell you these are connected. Someone who'll talk on the record. Otherwise we don't have squat. And keep in mind you're a reporter, not a cop. Don't do anything stupid."

"Don't worry, Stan."

"Yeah, I've heard that from you before, Rose. It always makes me nervous."

"Yeah, yeah," Johnny said.

Before turning on his computer, though, Johnny called the arson investigator. But Garfield wasn't in and he left a brief message.

"Inspector Garfield, it's Johnny Rose, Sara Bradley's cousin. Please give me a call. I have a few questions about the fire." He left his home and work numbers, hung up, and turned to the computer.

It was almost eight by the time Johnny finished the zoning story Kuscyk wanted and sent it to the editor's file in the system. He left the paper and drove to West LA, ate dinner at Eduardo's, a Mexican take-out place on Westwood Boulevard, and then drove a couple of blocks north to Rhino Records. He spent almost an hour wandering through the store with nothing in mind, picking out CDs, reading the song titles and credits. Just killing time, keeping his mind from focusing on Sara and Dallas and shoving aside the nagging worry about Gem. Where was she? Was she in danger too? He finally settled on a Slim Harpo CD, paid, and left.

He tossed the new CD on the passenger seat, stuck a cassette in the deck, and headed home. It was dark when he pulled into the carport, and Johnny noticed that the overhead fluorescent light was out. His headlight sparkled on something like broken glass on the cement, but he didn't connect the two. The Z's tires crunched the glass, and Johnny swore softly, simultaneously thinking that the light must have exploded and how odd that was.

When he got out, he craned his neck to see the broken light suspended from the bare beams of the carport. He heard a scrape like leather on concrete behind him and started to turn, but a fist caught him behind the ear. Johnny staggered forward, and his hand smashed against the fender, sending the CD he carried flying across the carport. His head was ringing, and he slithered down the side of the car to his hands and knees. He started to push up, but the man hit him again, his fist landing hard on the side of Johnny's face. His head jerked sideways, and Johnny collapsed completely onto the concrete. He lay on the cement for a moment, struggling to understand what had happened. The smell of oil and transmission fluid filled his nostrils, and he finally summoned the strength to get off the cement. Wavering unsteadily just inches off the carport floor, he turned his head and could see the bulk of the man, but his face was invisible in the darkness. The man kicked suddenly, bringing his weight forward and driving his toe under Johnny's rib cage.

The breath exploded from Johnny's lungs, and he collapsed forward, fighting for air like a man tied to an anchor and watching the bottom of a boat recede above him. Johnny tried to turn and see the man, but he knelt quickly, and with nothing more than the palm of his hand on Johnny's cheek, he drove him back to the ground. Johnny lay on the cement, fighting to breathe. He heard a ping as the car's engine cooled. The man shifted, pushing Johnny's head harder into the pavement.

"Where are they, Rose?"

"What? Where's what?" His words were high-pitched squeaks.

"Where are they?"

"I don't know what you're talking about."

"You telling me the girl didn't give 'em to you? Well, fuck you, Rose. I think she did."

"What girl? I don't know—"

The man grabbed Johnny's hair and lifted his head off the concrete and flicked it back down. His jaw hit the cement with a thud, and for a second Johnny thought he would lose consciousness. He tasted blood in his mouth where his teeth had broken the skin. He was too weak to spit.

"Don't fuck with me, Rose."

"I don't know what you're talking about."

The man grabbed Johnny's hair again and pulled his head back.

"Hey, a car." It was another voice. A man was standing at the rear of the carport.

Johnny heard it then, the music from the car's stereo preceding it like the fife and drums of an invading army. The man leaned down next to his ear, and Johnny could feel his breath warm on his neck.

"Give it up, Rose. The boy's dead and the girl's already a crispy critter. We'll get the other one too. You got no way to win here. Just give 'em to me, that's all."

Johnny could hear Sara's screams suddenly loud in his mind. Anger jolted through him and he struggled to push himself off the cement, but the man shoved his face into the pavement again with ease.

"Fuck you," Johnny managed.

"Hey, man, come on." The voice from the edge of the carport was urgent, demanding.

The man leaned down and whispered into Johnny's ear. "I'll be back, asshole."

The man stood and walked toward the alley and was gone. Moments later, the approaching car rolled past and down the alley, and Johnny closed his eyes and wavered on the edge of consciousness. He wasn't sure how long he was in the carport, but it seemed as if hours had passed before he finally struggled into his apartment and called the police.

When they arrived he could tell them little. The sergeant, a man in his late thirties with short brown hair and bulging biceps, sat on a chair near the couch and took notes while his partner, a short, heavy black woman, walked out to the carport. She returned a few moments later and shook her head.

"Are these yours?" she asked, holding out Johnny's car keys and the CD.

"Yes," Johnny said and reached up for them.

"You didn't see the man at all?" asked the sergeant.

"No, it was dark."

"Looks like they busted out the light," the female cop said.

The sergeant looked from his partner to Johnny. "Okay, once again, this guy didn't take anything, not your wallet, your watch, nothing?"

"No. Like I told you, he said he wanted something a girl had given me."

"What girl?"

"He meant my cousin. She was a street kid in Hollywood."

"Was?"

"She was killed in an arson fire in an empty house over there a couple of days ago."

"Oh, right. I read about that. What did she give you?"

"Nothing. That's just it. She never gave me anything. I don't know what he wanted."

"Is it possible this guy had you mixed up with someone else, then?"

"No, he knew my name. He had the right guy."

"How'd he know where you live?"

"I don't know. I'm not trying to hide."

"But you have no idea what it is he thinks you have?"

"None."

"This cousin of yours, was she mixed up in drugs or prostitution or anything like that?"

Johnny looked at the cop, holding his eyes for a moment, then shook his head. The movement hurt. "No. I'm sure she wasn't."

The sergeant stood and closed his notebook. "To be real honest with you, Mr. Rose, I don't know how much luck we're going to have with this. You didn't get a look at the guy and you can't seem to provide us with a clear motive. We'll check the robbery angle, of course. But beyond that, I don't know what I can tell you."

"Wait. The guy said something else. He said they'd get the other one too. I think he meant a girl named Gem. She lived in the same squat as my cousin."

"What's this Gem's real name, do you know?"

"No."

"And you have no idea what these kids have that your attacker wants, right?"

"No, no idea."

"Okay. Look, about all I can do is pass this information on to the detectives in Hollywood. Maybe they can put something together."

"But—" Johnny started to tell him to call Towers but he stopped. His head throbbed, and all he wanted to do was be done with it. He'd call Towers himself. "Well, thanks for taking the report."

"It's what we're here for. Look, I'll ask a patrol car to swing by a couple of times during the night just to make sure everything looks okay."

"Thanks, but I figure the guy's probably gone by now."

"You're probably right. But you know, I have one last question, if you don't mind."

"No, go ahead."

"How'd they connect you with the dead girl?"

"What?"

"They think the girl gave you something. How'd they make the connection?"

Johnny looked at the sergeant for a moment, then slowly shook his head. "I don't have any idea. Maybe they saw her with me."

"Well, if you think of anything else, give us a call, okay?"

"Yeah."

Later as he lay awake, staring at the ceiling, he heard the man's words again: *"You telling me the girl didn't give 'em to you?"* Johnny tried to remember every conversation, every visit with Sara, everything she'd said. But he could find no clues in his memory. Had she talked about him to the other kids? To adults? What did they think he had? He was still struggling with the questions when he fell asleep. About three in the morning he awoke and felt the pain in his head and jaw. He swung his legs to the side of the bed and slowly sat up and reminded himself of the old newspaper saying:

"You're not doing your job if someone's not angry." After a few minutes he stumbled to the bathroom, took three more aspirin, went back to bed, and wondered who was angry and why.

Nine

•────────────•

Johnny moved slowly the next day. He took more aspirin and stood in the shower a long time, washing his face gently to erase the last elements of oil from the carport floor. After dressing, he went downstairs. He got the newspaper from the front porch, feeling the stiffness in his back and knees as he bent to pick it up. When he stood, he looked at the oleander bush. The saucer was empty, but there was no sign of the cat.

"Hey, Archie," he called, but the cat didn't show, and Johnny retreated to the apartment and made coffee. He was on his second cup when Maggie called.

"Hi, Johnny."

"Hi, Maggie, how are you?" He knew the question sounded stupid, but he also knew it was a genuine expression of concern and not a throwaway line. Her answer didn't surprise him.

"I'm not doing very well."

"I'm sorry, Maggie, I wish—"

But she interrupted him. "I tried to call you at work. They said you weren't in yet."

"Yeah, I'm going out on a story from here." For a moment he considered telling her of the attack but decided against it. There was no point.

"I called a funeral home. I drive by it all the time, I mean it's just a mile or so away, you know. They were the only ones I knew. They'll take care of everything." She sighed, and there was a long pause before she continued. When she spoke, her words came quickly, as though she were rushing to get through the business. "I asked our dentist to send the X rays overnight so they can release the body and we can . . . They should have gotten them yesterday, maybe today." She started crying, and Johnny gripped the phone hard and squeezed his eyes shut against the pain in his head and the ache in his heart.

"Maggie, is there anything I can do?"

"Can you come?"

"There, to Atlanta?"

"Yes."

"Of course I'll come. But what about Jeff?"

"I called him yesterday and told him. He said he couldn't get away. Something about, oh, I don't know. I didn't understand. He can't get away. God, right now I don't think I understand anything." Her voice trembled, and Johnny knew she was struggling to maintain her composure and not cry again.

"Yes, I'll come, Maggie."

"We're going to have a memorial service the day after tomorrow." Her voice was calm again, in control.

"I'll get there as soon as I can. I need to make a reservation, that's all. I still have . . ." But he didn't finish the sentence, didn't mention the airline ticket to Atlanta that he still held, and Maggie went on.

"Let me know when you're coming. I'll pick you up."

"I can take a cab, Maggie."

"No, I'll pick you up. I want to."

"Okay. I'll call as soon as I have my reservations."

"Good. Thanks, Johnny. I'll see you soon."

"Wait, Maggie! Before you go, I wanted to ask you something."

"What?"

"Did Sara ever talk about her friends, maybe a boy named Dallas or a girl called Gem?"

"No, why?"

"Ah, I met Gem. She was living in the house with Sara. I thought I'd talk to her before I come to Atlanta but I have no idea where to find her now."

"She never talked much about her friends. There was a place she'd go to sometimes. She mentioned it once. God, what was it called? Wait, I got it. My Home. It's a drop-in center of some kind."

"Sure, she mentioned that to me too. Maybe I'll go by, see if I can find Gem."

"But you'll come to Atlanta?"

"Yes, of course. Don't worry. I'll be there tomorrow."

"See you then."

They said good-bye, and Johnny was at the door when his phone rang again. He swore under his breath and hurried across the living room to grab the phone before it rolled to the answering machine.

"Hello."

"What the hell happened last night?" It was Kuscyk. As always, he went straight to the point.

"How'd you find out?"

"I used to be a reporter, remember?" He paused a second. "An old friend, he's a cop, heard about it and called me."

"There's not much to tell. A couple of guys jumped me. They wanted something they thought Sara had given me. Something I didn't have."

"Any idea what they were after?"

"None."

"Okay. So how are you? You holding up okay? You came through it all right?"

"Yeah, Stan, I'm fine."

"Any way to connect this to the kid on the hillside?"

"Not officially, but the guy who jumped me said something about the boy. He had to mean the kid on the hillside. He also said they'd get the other one. He means Gem. I know he does. Who else can it be?"

"Hunches and leaps of faith. That's all you got right now. Get something concrete."

"I'm on my way to Hollywood now."

"Good. But remember, Rose, I told you, be careful and keep me in the loop."

"Sure, Stan, don't worry," he said and hung up. Three minutes later he was backing the Z out of the carport.

The aspirin held most of the pain to a minimum, but Johnny still felt a small throbbing at the back of his skull, and when he walked toward My Home, it was with a slow, measured pace. He'd just turned down the side street from Hollywood Boulevard when a group of teenagers came out of the center trailing helium-filled balloons tethered to thin white strings. They gathered on the sidewalk in front of the center, and the balloons hovered over their heads, bumping each other, pulling at the restraints. A woman who looked to be in her late thirties or early forties was the last person out. She, too, trailed a balloon behind her. Johnny stopped and watched as the kids formed a half circle in front of her. He looked from one to the next, searching for Gem or the boy called Billy, but they were not among the crowd.

From the kids' faces Johnny knew they were listening intently to the woman, but the distance and city noise drowned out her words. He started toward the group, but suddenly the balloons shot into the sky like a startled covey of multicolored quail. Johnny stopped and watched as the balloons drifted apart and quickly became small bright dots scattered across the gray-blue sky.

The kids watched the progress of the balloons for a few moments, then one by one lowered their eyes and drifted away themselves. A few minutes later the woman was alone on the sidewalk, staring into the sky. She lowered her gaze, glanced at Johnny, and turned toward the center.

"Excuse me," Johnny said. She stopped and looked at him. She was short and wore a white blouse unbuttoned at the collar, navy blue slacks, and white jogging shoes. She had thick black hair, her skin was a deep brown, and her dark eyes were red and rimmed with tears.

"My name's Johnny Rose."

Ignoring Johnny for a moment, she glanced at the sky, then lowered her head, looked at the sidewalk, and wiped her eyes. When she finally looked at him again, the pain he'd glimpsed a moment before had been hidden behind a thin veneer of polite professionalism. "How can I help you, Mr. Rose?"

"Do you work at the center?"

"Yes. I'm the director." The skin under her eyes was dark and slightly swollen, giving her the look of someone for whom sleep was a distant memory.

"Can you tell me what I just saw here?" Johnny asked.

"The balloon release?"

"Yes."

She inhaled deeply, as though she could draw energy from the city's polluted air, and exhaled. "When we lose a child we do a balloon release a few days later. The kids write messages and put them in the balloons or tie them on the end of a string. I say a few words in the center or out here on the street and we let the balloons go. It's a way of saying good-bye."

"Like a memorial service."

"Yes. For most of our kids it's the only memorial service they'll attend."

Johnny looked at the sky and thought of how quickly the balloons had drifted away, how quickly everything had changed.

"Was this for Dallas or Sara?"

She raised her eyebrows, stood straighter, and studied him more openly. "Yes. Dallas. Did you know him?"

"No, but he's part of the reason I'm here. Look, is there someplace we can talk?"

"Are you with the police?"

"No."

"Dallas's family?"

"No, not directly. You know, I'd really prefer not to do this outside."

She looked at him silently for several moments. Her eyes seemed to concentrate on the swelling and red skin where his face had been ground into the cement. She finally nodded.

"Okay, Mr. Rose. We can go to my office."

"Thank you."

She pushed open the door. "My office is upstairs," she said without turning around. She crossed the room and began to climb the stairs. Johnny followed but stopped on the first step and looked back. It was easy for him to see Sara here, preferring to be with these kids instead of outside with the tourists, shop owners, cops, and crazies.

About twenty kids in shorts, jeans, T-shirts, and sweatshirts wandered through the room or sat in white, formed plastic chairs at square tables topped with brown Formica, eating, talking, and playing board games. Near one table, a six-foot black man wearing rouge, bright orange lipstick, and a tight white dress that needed washing laughed loudly at a joke. Johnny heard a buzz and looked across the room to where two boys were taking burritos out of a microwave oven. A cork bulletin board hung on the wall above the microwave. A neatly lettered sign at the top read: MESSAGES. He saw it all in a glance, his eyes sweeping the center, reading the signs without being aware he was doing it. He looked up the stairs and saw her waiting, watching him.

"It's up here," she called.

"Right." He followed her up the steps, and by the time he reached the second floor she was already in her office. Johnny tapped lightly on the door frame and looked in. She was seated behind a brown metal desk, studying the screen of a laptop.

"Please come in." She motioned across the desk to a chair. He glanced around her office as he approached. It was sparse and clean but surprisingly comfortable. The walls were a soft apricot, and a framed poster of Monet's lilies hung near the desk. Behind her an unpainted pine bookcase was filled with paperbacks and pictures of street kids in clear plastic cube frames. A cork bulletin board with more snapshots of her hugging the kids and mugging for the camera with them hung on the wall over her right shoulder.

"I'm sorry I didn't introduce myself out front. I was a little distracted. My name's Katherine St. Croix." She half-stood, extending her hand across the desk. Her handshake was strong.

"It's nice to meet you."

"Thank you. So, Mr. Rose, how can I help you?"

"I'm looking for a girl who goes by the name Gem. I'm hoping you can help me find her."

"I'm sorry, Mr. Rose, but we have a rule here. We don't help adults find kids. So, I'm not going to be able to help you, I'm afraid." She smiled as she said it, keeping their conversation cordial, friendly.

But Johnny could tell there was no room for compromise, and he felt a rush of unfocused anger. Not necessarily at the woman across the desk but anger at Sara's death, at the murder, at Gem for refusing to help, and even at the kids downstairs for being alive when Sara was dead. He knew it was stupid, but he didn't care.

"Why not?" he demanded.

Her hands rested on the desk on opposite sides of the computer. Anger flashed through her dark eyes in reaction to his words. But she bit her lower lip for a second, and when she spoke her words were controlled, even. This was her house, her rules, and she was perfectly comfortable making all the calls.

"We're trying to help the kids and that's our policy, Mr. Rose."

"This is really important, Ms. St. Croix."

"So is our policy," she said, and her eyes sent him a silent message: Say what you want, I won't change my mind.

But Johnny wouldn't give up. He pushed harder, his anger driving him. "I'm not asking you to break the law, Ms. St.

Croix. I'm just looking for a little help here, that's all."

She leaned back in her chair and folded her arms across her chest. "Tell me something, Mr. Rose. Why is this so important to you? If you're not the police, and you're not family, why do you want to find her?"

He turned away from the woman and looked at the Monet poster, taking a moment to breathe slowly, to calm himself. When he looked back, she was still staring at him, waiting for an answer. He leaned back in his chair, letting the silence grow, and she continued to stare at him until she finally spoke.

"Mr. Rose, was there something else you wanted to ask me or something else I can do for you? Because if not, we have a lot of kids downstairs and I do have a lot of work to do."

But Johnny didn't get up. He lowered his gaze to the floor, trying to set his own anger aside and focus on getting the information he needed. He'd started it off all wrong and now wasn't sure how to retreat and start over. He exhaled deeply, looked up, and simply said, "Ms. St. Croix, I apologize." He felt himself relax as he said it. "I didn't mean to sound so demanding. Let me start again."

"If you want, but I honestly don't think there's much I can do for you."

"Maybe not. But . . . well, Sara Bradley, the girl who was killed in that house fire the other night, was my cousin. She shared that house with Dallas and Gem. I need to talk to Gem about the fire. That's why I want to find her."

"Oh, Mr. Rose, I'm so sorry. We were all deeply saddened by Sara's death. She was a nice girl. Very bright. We enjoyed having her in the center. Her death was a terrible tragedy."

The muscles in Katherine St. Croix's face relaxed and her features softened. Johnny realized he was really seeing her for the first time. She was a pretty woman. Not drop-dead gorgeous, but pretty in the way that grows on you and shows on a woman who is comfortable with who she is.

"How well did you know Sara?" Johnny asked.

"Not well. She came in often, but she didn't usually stay very long."

"Was she in trouble?"

The question seemed to surprise her. "I don't know. But even if I did know, I couldn't tell you. We don't discuss our clients' private lives, even with their families. That may sound harsh, even cruel, but we have to do it that way."

Johnny looked at her for a moment, then stood slowly and paced to the door, turned, and looked at the woman across the room.

"Ms. St. Croix, that fire wasn't an accident."

"Yes, the newspaper said the cause was suspicious. That usually means arson, doesn't it?"

"That's not what I mean. I think someone wanted to kill Sara. It wasn't random."

"You're not serious?" Her brow furrowed, and she squinted at him, taken aback by his words.

"I am completely serious. Ms. St. Croix, Sara called me that day. She wanted to go home, to leave LA as soon as possible. She was scared to death of something." He crossed the room quickly, pulled the chair back, and sat down again. He leaned forward, resting his palms on the edge of the desk. "Do you have any idea what was she afraid of? Why she'd want to leave the streets in such a hurry?"

Katherine slowly shook her head. "I don't know. Life on the streets is very dangerous. You must know that. She could have been afraid of a dozen different things."

"How about Dallas?"

"What about him?"

"He shared the house with Sara and Gem and he was killed, too, the day before she was. I don't believe that was a coincidence. These deaths are connected."

"Oh, Mr. Rose, I know Sara's death was very hard for you personally. Believe me, I know what it's like to lose someone. But think about what you're saying. Ask yourself why in the world someone would want to kill these children?

Why? What possible motive could someone have?" She stopped, waiting for him to answer.

"I don't know, but I think Gem does. That's why I want to find her."

"Why would Gem know anything?"

Johnny breathed deeply and laid his hands on his kneecaps. He let his gaze wander to the floor for a moment, then suddenly looked up at Katherine St. Croix. She was asking good questions, questions for which he had no answers.

"I was at the fire. I tried to save Sara, but I couldn't get her out of the building. Afterward, after it was over, I saw Gem. Some kid named Billy took me to her. She was hiding in an alley. When I got there she told me she'd been in the house when the fire started. I think she knows who started it and why."

"Mr. Rose, I'm sorry, I really am, but my answer is the same. Our policy is that we don't help adults look for our clients under any circumstances. And that means *any* circumstances. You have to understand, if these kids can't trust us, if they think we're helping people hunt for them even once, they'll never trust us again. If that happens, we might as well close our doors. Trust is all we have. If Gem comes in, I'll tell her to call you. I'll gladly do that. But I'm afraid that's the best I can do."

"Ms. St. Croix, I know you mean well, but your policy could get Gem hurt. Someone's already hunting for her."

"What? Who?"

"A man named Clay Griffin. I was over at the burned-out house yesterday. He was there looking for her."

"Who's Clay Griffin?"

"I don't know."

"Well, it doesn't matter. I can't, I just can't change our policy."

Johnny lowered his head. He only raised it again after he'd started speaking. "Last night two men beat me up. I'd just gotten home and they jumped me in the carport of my apartment. They wanted something they thought Sara had given me. I don't know what it was, but they were very serious. I think they're looking for Gem too. They said something like 'We'll get the other one too.' They had to mean Gem. I don't want to see her hurt."

Katherine leaned forward, her arms on either side of her computer. She wore a simple watch with a black plastic wristband and no rings. She stared at him, holding his eyes. Her words were no longer defiant. She simply seemed tired when she spoke. "Mr. Rose, I don't know where Gem is. I honestly don't know. I haven't seen her in days. She could be anywhere."

"How often does she usually come in?"

Small lines formed on her forehead as she considered the question. "She and Sara and Dallas were here a lot. Not every day, but quite a bit. I haven't seen her for at least three days, maybe four, but, Mr. Rose, you really can't make too much out of that. These kids don't keep a schedule. She's likely to come in again today and be here every day for a week, then we wouldn't see her for a month."

Johnny closed his eyes and rubbed them with the finger and thumb of his right hand for a moment, then looked at Katherine again.

"When I talked to her, she claimed she was going to San Francisco. Said she was going to live in a nice hotel and order room service. Is that possible? Do you think she went up there?"

Katherine sighed and nodded.

"Mr. Rose, many of these children live in two worlds at the same time. They have a wonderful fantasy life. They pretend their parents are rich or that they're movie stars with huge mansions and three or four babies and everything is wonderful. And then there's reality. That means diving in Dumpsters or panhandling for their dinner and sleeping on rooftops and in doorways or maybe selling themselves or posing for pictures. I can take you to a 'movie studio'"—she made small quote marks in the air with her fingers—"right down the street from here. They tell the kids they're going to be movie stars and they end up doing hard-core pornography. The girls especially. They use a lot of makeup and make them look pretty and exploit them. And you know what they do with the photos? They post them on the porno sites on the Internet. I could show you some of our kids right here," she said, waving at her laptop, "if I could stomach looking at it. So they become stars but they're not. I guess that's a long way of answering your question. Is Gem going to San Francisco? Maybe. Is she going to live in a hotel? Maybe a night or two in a fleabag. Is what she told you true? No. Is it a lie? No, not exactly. These kids live in a permanent twilight, Mr. Rose."

Johnny stood up slowly. "I have to find her. Are you sure you won't help me?"

"You can leave a note on the message board downstairs. If she comes in, I'll make sure she gets it."

"That's it?"

"I can't do any more. Besides, I'm sure she'll be in today or tomorrow. It's not like her to just stay away. Come on, I'll show you the message board."

She led him down the stairs, and Johnny stopped on the last step and looked at her. "This looks like a very nice place. It's very clean. I know why Sara liked coming here," he said.

"Thank you. It's part of the message we're trying to send the kids. We keep the place nice because they deserve a nice place. They won't leave the streets until they believe they deserve better, until they understand they don't have to lean in car windows and sell themselves for enough money to get a room for the night. By the way, that's the message board over there."

"Thanks, that's probably a good idea."

"You can get some paper at the desk," she said and pointed to the receptionist near the front door. Johnny got a piece of notebook paper and wrote a simple note: *Gem, call me collect. Anytime day or night. It's very important. Johnny Rose.* He added his home and work numbers, folded the note and put "For Gem" on the outside, crossed back to the board, and pinned it up.

Katherine was standing near the front desk when Johnny walked to the door. He stopped and held out his hand.

"Thank you, Ms. St. Croix."

"I'm sorry we can't do more. I'll ask some of the kids, make sure they spread the word. If they see her, they'll tell her to come in and pick up the note."

"Thanks."

"Good luck. I hope you find her and that she's well."

Johnny was half a block away when he looked back at My Home. It was unobtrusive, just another storefront. A small sign on the outside wall above the door said MY HOME. There were no other signs or markings. You could walk past it a dozen times and never know it was there. As he watched, one of the boys he'd seen in the center, his long dirty hair sticking from under his baseball cap, stepped through the door to the sidewalk. He swung his backpack onto his shoulder and walked away. Johnny looked again at the small sign above the door. The kids obviously knew where the center was. That was probably enough.

Kuscyk had his briefcase on his desk and was tossing papers into it when Johnny crossed the newsroom. The metro editor looked up when Johnny was only a few feet away.

"You look like shit."

Johnny touched the side of his face. "Nice to see you too."

"You okay? I checked with my friend in the department. They haven't got anything new on the assault."

"They're not going to find these guys, Stan. We both know that."

"You're probably right. So how'd it go in Tinseltown?"

"Okay, I guess. On my way back here, I went by the Hollywood substation to see Towers and tell him about the assault. He wasn't there so I left him a message."

"Okay, good. So what else you got?"

"Come on, Stan. Progress is always slow in the beginning. You know that."

"In other words, you got dick," Kuscyk said and closed his briefcase with a snap.

"It's not exactly that bad. You ever hear of a guy named Clay Griffin?"

Kuscyk turned and leaned back. His chair almost disappeared beneath his huge frame, and Johnny thought that someday it would simply collapse under him.

"No. Who the hell is he?"

"I don't know. When I went back to the burned-out house yesterday, he was there. He's looking for Gem too."

"Why?"

"I don't know. Told me he represented a client who's *motivated* to find her."

"He tied into the two that attacked you last night?"

"I don't know."

"Well, it sounds like you're stirring up some interest. Maybe there is a story here after all. Take a couple more days. See what you can find."

"Ah, that's something I wanted to talk to you about. Is your offer of bereavement time still open?" The question was obvious on Kuscyk's face, and Johnny went on. "Maggie, Sara's mom, called. She wants me to come to the memorial service. Sara's dad isn't going to make it. I think it's important I go."

Kuscyk shoved himself to his feet and pulled his briefcase from the desktop.

"Get on this story as soon as you get back. And ask a few questions while you're down there. Find out a little more about the girl. You never know what'll help. And leave me that Griffin guy's name. I'll see what I can find out for you while you're gone. I still have a few friends in the right places."

"Thanks, Stan."

Johnny watched Kuscyk walk across the newsroom and

disappear through the door, then went to his desk. He called Towers again but he still wasn't in, and this time he didn't leave a message. Turning to his keyboard, he signed onto his computer and began searching the paper's files and other databases for Clay Griffin. Two hours later, he'd found nothing. He sent Kuscyk a quick note on his search, including the name and phone number on Griffin's card, and shut the computer down.

Johnny glanced at the blank computer terminal as he stood up. He was anxious to follow the story, but Maggie needed him. He was going to Atlanta.

Ten

●━━━━━━━━━━━━━━━━━━━━━━━━━━━●

Maggie lived in a single-story house with an old aluminum awning over a picture window in the living room. The blue paint was peeling, and when they turned up the driveway, Johnny could see that the eaves were full and the shingles worn.

He had caught an early morning flight, but it was late afternoon by the time Maggie drove down the gravel drive that ran straight back along the edge of the yard and parked in the open carport attached to the house. She took his carry-on bag from the backseat and turned toward the house.

"I'll put you in the girls' room," she said and pushed through the door into the kitchen.

"What about Annie?" he asked as he followed her into the house.

"She'll sleep with me for a few days." She set his overnight bag down and looked at him. A weak smile pushed the edges of her mouth. "Annie's only twelve. Sleeping with her mother's not so terrible."

"Maggie, I can get a motel room. You don't have to do this."

"I want to. Just your being here will help. It'll be good for Annie too. She doesn't have a lot of family left. Sara was her only sister. I mean, first Jeff left and now this."

"Okay."

She smiled at him, and Johnny was struck by how small and frail she looked. She'd always been thin but strong and determined. Maggie's mom had called her stubborn and willful. Theirs had not been a loving nor kind relationship, and for long stretches of years, especially after her marriage to Jeff, they'd barely spoken. But now, looking at her hollow cheeks and her dark, puffy eyes, Johnny saw only the adult version of the little girl who knew in her heart that fierceness and bravado will carry you only so far.

She seemed to understand his thoughts because she turned away and said, "The bedroom's this way," and disappeared through the living room. But Johnny didn't follow immediately. He put down his suit bag and studied the house. Through the window he could see the last few days' newspapers in the front yard, yellowing in the sun. In the kitchen fruit flies buzzed around spotted bananas in a bowl on the counter, and a stick of butter was melting on a small saucer, forming a puddle along its edges.

Johnny picked up his bag again and saw a calendar hanging on the wall near the door. Maggie had written Sara's flight number in large letters and underlined it three times. He looked away, grabbed his bag, and followed Maggie through the sparsely furnished living room. A maple and plaid couch was pushed against the wall under the picture window, and two chairs faced it across a coffee table. An end table and floor lamp were the only other furnishings. A pile of mail, unopened sympathy cards and bills, spilled across the top of the coffee table. A layer of dust covered the hardwood floor and gathered in the corners.

Maggie was pushing back the curtains when he walked into the bedroom.

"Drop your stuff and I'll make us some coffee, okay?"

"Sure."

Two single beds filled the middle of the room. One was crowded with a petting zoo of stuffed animals, but the other was unadorned, made up with military efficiency, the worn green spread pulled tight at the edges. Maggie had put his carry-on piece on the empty bed, and Johnny swung his suit bag next to it. He sank slowly to the edge of the other bed and looked around, trying to envision Sara in the room, to see her as a little girl before she ran away. He plucked a white rabbit from the zoo, turned it in his hands, and looked at a poster of a young heartthrob taped to the wall above the dresser. Johnny didn't recognize the boy, and the tape had turned yellow with time and appeared brittle. He could find no feeling for Sara in the room, no hint that she'd ever lived there. It could be any child's room in any city or suburb.

The sound of a whistling teakettle brought his thoughts back to the bedroom. He took his suit and shirts from his bag, hung them in the closet, and went to the kitchen. Maggie stood at the counter, spooning coffee from a jar into two mugs.

"I'm sorry, all I have is instant. I haven't been to the store. Things have been a little crazy around here." She gestured to a clear glass pot on the counter, a thick residue of coffee turning to sludge in the bottom. "Been a little lax on my chores."

"Instant's fine," Johnny said.

She carried the teakettle from the stove, filled the mugs, turned, and leaned against the counter.

"The coroner's office called late yesterday. I mean, I knew they would but . . . I don't know, I guess somehow I was hoping. Anyway, the dental records proved . . ." She lifted her shoulders, a weary gesture. "The match was positive."

"Maggie, I'm so sorry."

She wiped a tear from her cheek, then waved his words away. "No, don't say it. Besides, I've been meaning to tell you . . . well, to thank you for looking after Sara."

"Oh, Maggie, don't. I didn't do a very good job, did I? I keep thinking that if I'd done something different. If I'd maybe just tried a little harder to get her off the streets earlier, she might be here."

"Well, if she hadn't run away, she'd still be alive, too, wouldn't she? And if Jeff had been there for her . . . If that prick had . . ." She shook her head and turned away with a weak wave of her hand. "Oh, the hell with it," she said, her back turned to him. She opened a cupboard above the counter and took down a fifth of Jim Beam and held it up.

"You too?"

"No, thanks."

She studied the bottle for a moment, then put it back on the shelf. "Yeah, I guess you're right. I keep thinking it'll kill the pain but it doesn't. Nothing does."

She crossed to the table and handed Johnny the mug and slid into a chair. She sighed deeply and closed her eyes for a moment. When she opened them, tears had gathered in the corners and her voice quivered when she spoke. "This whole thing was my fault. I know that. It's not anyone else's." She lowered her gaze to the table.

"That's not true. You didn't kill her. Someone else did."

"But she ran away from me. She ran away from my house." She sniffed loudly. "She was my baby, Johnny. She was fifteen and I let her go." She took two deep breaths and looked up at Johnny for a moment, but she was unable to hold his eyes and looked down again. "I as much as forced her out." She pulled a white paper napkin from a wooden container stuffed with them and wiped her nose. "I loved her, I really did. But . . ." Her lip trembled, and when she raised the cup to her mouth her hand shook slightly and she had to use both hands to steady the mug.

"Every mother and daughter fight. That's normal."

"Not like us. I was really hard on her. It's just that she looked, I mean, every time I looked at her I saw Jeff. I was still furious with him and she was just like him, smart and stubborn and just so damned sure she was right. I was really mean to her. We fought all the time, horrible, bad fights. I'm . . ." She put the cup down again and wiped her eyes with the napkin. "Jesus, Johnny, I hit her. More than once. What kind of mother hits her own kid? I never meant to hurt her, I just . . ."

Johnny sipped his coffee because he had nothing else to

do. "She knew you loved her. I'm convinced she knew that."

"Fat lot of good it did her."

"She was coming home, and someone killed her. Someone set that fire on purpose. You're not responsible for that."

But if she'd heard him, she gave no indication. Her hands clutched the mug and she sat stiffly, as though fearing that if she relaxed even the smallest muscle, she would collapse.

"I've never told anyone this. No one." She was quiet for a moment, and when she spoke again it was to the table, not to him. "The night before she ran away we had a terrible fight. I said some very hurtful things to her. Jeff was more than two months behind in child support, and I just had a big car-repair bill. I'd called him to tell him to send the money and he told me he'd met someone else and they were talking about getting married and money was tight and he couldn't send us anything for a while, that I'd just have to make do. Make do. I'm shopping thrift stores and flea markets to keep these girls in clothes and driving across town to save ten cents on a gallon of milk and that cheap bastard tells me I'll have to make do." She breathed deeply for a moment and glanced at Johnny but looked to her mug again and went on. "Then Sara did something that really pissed me off. I'd bought her this cute dress at a yard sale and she didn't like it. She said she was tired of being poor and wearing other people's hand-me-downs. I started in on her and told her Jeff was an asshole and if he'd act like a man and take care of his family I wouldn't have to shop in thrift stores. She just got mad and fought back. That kid was a fighter, Johnny. Just like her dad. She said she wished she lived with him instead of me, because even if he didn't have much money, he was always fun and never yelled at her like I was always doing. Of course not, that son of a bitch never did any discipline around here. God, no, that might interfere with his good-guy image."

Maggie raised her eyes and stared at him, and he could see the tension in her face, her muscles taut, her lips stretched tight, the anger fed by guilt just below the surface.

"I was just so mad, I just . . . I held the dress up in front of her. It was just a simple cotton dress, there wasn't anything to it, and I ripped it apart and threw it in her face and then . . . and then I slapped her, I hit her hard right across the face and told her that she could go anytime she wanted, that I wasn't keeping her here. That if she thought her piece-of-shit father was so goddamned great, she ought to go live with him for a while and see what an SOB he really was. In fact, I'd love to see her go. Give me one less mouth to feed. But when she found out what a jerk he was she'd better not come to me begging for help. If she went, that was it. She wouldn't be coming home. The next day when I got home from work she was gone. No note, nothing. Just the dress in a pile on the kitchen table. She went to Jeff's but didn't stay. She ran away from him, too, but she didn't come home and I knew why. It was because of what I said, what I did. She was so prideful and stubborn. Damn her, Johnny. Why'd she have to be so stubborn?" Her hands gripped the mug so tightly Johnny was afraid she'd break it. "She lived on the streets rather than come home. She was so damned stubborn. She was doing it to punish me. Or maybe . . . or maybe it was just better for her on the streets than here."

The tears broke through then, and Maggie began to cry. Sobs ran through her body like electric shocks. "Oh, God, I killed my little girl. I killed her."

He moved around the table quickly and stood at her side, and she wrapped her arms around his waist and he pulled her head into his stomach and gently stroked the back of her head and mumbled the words, "It's going to be okay, sweetheart. It's going to be okay," and he knew the lie even as he was telling it.

That night they ate at a restaurant, the three of them in a booth, Maggie in the middle. Johnny looked past her at Annie, who sat close to her mom and eyed him warily, making a silent judgment. She was short like her mother but had inherited her father's round face and curly hair. He smiled and tried to start a conversation, asking what her favorite subject was and what did she like about school. But she said little, and Maggie nagged her to sit up straight, and when she spilled ketchup on her blouse, Maggie dipped a napkin in the water glass and tried to rub it out.

"Damn it, I told you to be careful. Now this stain is going to set. You've probably ruined it."

"Mom," Annie protested but said nothing more, her eyes filled with humiliation and defeat.

Ninety minutes after they left home, they were back. The moment they were in the house, Annie ran to her mother's bedroom and turned on the television.

"Turn it down," Maggie yelled, and the volume fell away. She moved to the kitchen and took the Jim Beam bottle from the cupboard.

"You want a drink?"

"No, thanks."

She grunted and put the bottle back. "Yeah, you're probably right. I've been drinking a little too much lately." She took ice cubes from the freezer, dropped them in a glass, and filled it from the tap.

"Maggie, I need to talk to you about something. About Sara," Johnny said as she ran the water.

"Sure, but not tonight, okay? I'm not up to it." She turned off the water and looked at him. "Can we do it some other time, maybe tomorrow?"

"Of course."

"I'm going to go wade through that stack of mail. I've been putting off reading the cards. Just couldn't handle it before."

"Sure, I understand." She stopped at the edge of the living room and looked back at Johnny sitting at the kitchen table. "I'm glad you're here," she said.

"I'm glad I came. Look, I'm going to take a walk. Why don't you let the cards go for a while and join me? The exercise will be good for you."

She shook her head. "No, thanks. I've got to read those

cards before the service. Then I'm going to bed. I'll probably be asleep by the time you get back."

"Okay, I'll see you in the morning."

"The service is at eleven." Johnny nodded, and Maggie walked into the living room. He could hear the opener slitting the envelopes and, a few moments later, her soft weeping.

The night air was thick and humid, and moments after he left the house his body was covered with a fine sheen of perspiration. He could hear crickets and several times had to slap mosquitoes from his arms and wave them away from his ears. He walked in a loop through the neighborhood and an hour later was nearing the house again when a bolt of lightning cracked across the sky and the first few fat drops fell, filling the air with the smell of warm, wet asphalt and rain-puckered dirt. He jogged to the house and stepped under the carport roof just as the space between the raindrops disappeared and the sky was full of rain and lightning, followed by thunder so loud it rattled the windows. From the edge of the carport, he watched the lightning and listened to the thunder, feeling the cool breeze and sudden drop in temperature. A few minutes later, he turned when he heard the back door open and saw Annie standing a few feet away dressed in pajamas, a robe, and slippers.

"What're you doing?" she asked.

He smiled and said, "Watching the rain. We don't get thunderstorms in Los Angeles, at least not like these." He looked back into the night to watch the rain for a moment more before going to Annie's side. "Come on, we'd better go in. If we stay out here we'll just get wet." He put his hand gently on her shoulder to guide her into the house.

Annie walked to the living room and snuggled into a corner of the couch, clutching the stuffed rabbit he'd held earlier. He moved to one of the chairs facing the sofa, and Annie stared at him as he sat down, as though waiting for him to say something. She looked younger than twelve, and

Johnny sensed that grief had stripped years from her and that she was retreating to preadolescence for comfort.

"Your mom asleep already?" he asked, and she nodded. A silence filled the living room, and Johnny glanced out the front window at the rain, unsure what to say to the young girl sitting across from him. Across the street, a neighbor switched off the porch light, and the front window seemed slightly darker.

"Do you miss your sister?" he finally asked, and she nodded but didn't say anything. "We all miss her," Johnny said.

"My mom says you tried to help her."

"Yes, I did, Annie. I liked Sara a lot. She was a good kid. She really was."

"Was Sara in trouble?"

"Trouble? Why do you ask that? Did your mom say something?"

Annie shook her head and looked down at the rabbit in her lap and tugged lightly at its ear.

"Why did you think she might be in trouble?" He leaned forward slowly and smiled at Annie, trying to sound casual. But he could feel tension building in his stomach, the muscles tightening as he waited for the answer.

"She said." Her voice was that of a small child.

"You mean Sara?" Annie nodded, her eyes still on her rabbit. "You talked to her, to Sara?"

"No. She sent me a birthday card with a note in it." She looked up at him.

"What did the note say?"

Annie shrugged. "I don't remember."

"Do you still have the card?" She nodded again. "Could I see it?"

She slid off the couch, holding her rabbit, and walked down the hallway to her room. She returned a few moments later and handed him the card. He glanced at the drawing of a young girl in a swing on the front and opened it. Sara's handwriting was neat.

Dear Annie,

Happy Birthday. Sorry I can't be there to say it in person. Maybe next year. I'm thinking of coming home. Tell Mom I've got big news for you two but she's got to promise not to get mad at me. Annie, I love you. See you soon, I hope.

Love, Sara

"Do you know what the big news was?" She shook her head. "Does your mom?" Another head shake.

"Did Maggie tell you what happened? To Sara, I mean."

"Sara was killed in a fire."

"That's right." He hesitated a moment and tried to smile at Annie. "How are you doing, Annie? Are you okay?"

"I'm okay."

"Are you sure? It can be tough losing a brother or sister."

Her chin quivered and tears welled in her eyes. "I miss her. I miss Sara. I just wish she could come home," she said.

Johnny crossed the short distance to the couch and sat next to Annie. He put his arm around her small shoulders, and she leaned against him and cried silently.

"It's okay to cry. We all miss her," Johnny said. "We all miss her."

"Mom's mad at me all the time."

Johnny pulled her a little closer and leaned down to kiss the top of her head.

"No, she's not, Annie. She's upset because Sara died. It's not fair but sometimes we yell at the people we love when we're upset. Your mom loves you very much. You know that, don't you?"

"I guess."

Annie curled her legs under her, wriggled against Johnny's side seeking comfort, and a moment later fell asleep. Johnny carried her into Maggie's bedroom and slipped her under the covers next to her mother. Maggie was asleep on her side of the bed and never moved. Annie stirred a moment as he pulled the covers over her and tucked the rabbit to her chin, but she was sound asleep again seconds later.

He stood in the doorway for a moment and watched them sleep, then went back to the living room and reread the birthday card. *"I'm thinking of coming home."* She made it sound like a casual decision, just something she might or might not do. But on the phone, Sara hadn't been casual. She'd been desperate and afraid. Then he read it all again and wondered why Sara had feared her mother would be angry. *"Tell Mom I've got big news for you two but she's got to promise not to get mad at me."*

He put the card down, drummed his fingers on his knee, picked up the card, and read it again. The note seemed an odd blend of joy and fear. He closed the card and held it for a moment as he looked out the window at the rain. A bolt of lightning cut the sky, and for an instant Johnny could see well enough to read the house number on the home across the street. But a second later the light was gone and the world outside was dark again. He put the card on the coffee table and walked through the dark house to his bedroom.

The memorial service was held in a small, narrow church with white wood siding. Inside the front door, a large photo of Sara, a blowup of her high school yearbook photo taken three years before, stood on a tripod. Flowers in vases on pedestals stood on both sides of the photo.

The small church was only partially full. Johnny sat in the front row with Maggie and Annie and stared straight ahead when the minister emerged from a door behind the pulpit. He was an older man in a dark suit and said he'd known Sara from the church's youth group and that she was a kind and gentle soul. He could offer no explanation for why the Lord had called Sara to him at such a young age, but it was not ours to question God's will. As the minister spoke, Johnny thought again of the flames in the house and Sara's screams.

He lowered his head during the prayer and stared at the hardwood floor beneath his feet. He tried to believe that God hadn't wanted him to get into the house, that he'd arrived moments too late because God wanted it that way. But he saw himself stumbling backward off the porch amid the heat and smoke and didn't believe that God had meant him to come that close and fail. Sara's death wasn't God's will. Sara's death wasn't a random act. It was a murder.

The minister finished, and a soprano soloist at the rear of the church began "Amazing Grace." Maggie reached over and gripped Johnny's hand, and he stole a glance and saw the sparkle of tears on her cheeks as she listened to the music. When the service concluded, Johnny stood and looked again at the crowd, expecting to see Jeff, sure that Sara's father would have come in at the last minute. Positive that he wouldn't miss his own daughter's funeral.

But Jeff was not at the church, nor in the parking lot where Maggie's friends approached and hugged her and spoke softly of their sorrow at Sara's death. Later, when the people from the church and friends from work and elsewhere stopped at Maggie's house and ate the cold cuts and coffee cakes and cookies and drank the iced tea and coffee, Johnny received the guests and helped, shifting his mind into a neutral hospitality and wondering the whole time why Jeff hadn't come.

A few friends stayed and washed and dried the dishes and put them away, returning them to the wrong cupboards and to the wrong shelves. It was late afternoon when Maggie waved from the front window as the last of the visitors pulled from the driveway.

"I'm changing. I'm sick of this black dress. I don't ever want to see it again," she said to her reflection in the window. Johnny walked to Annie's room to change, but the little girl was playing with her Barbie dolls on her bed. She looked up when Johnny stepped to the door.

"Why didn't my dad come?" she asked.

Johnny sat beside her on the bed and put his arm around

her shoulder. Unlike the night before, though, she didn't move close to him but sat stiffly upright. "I don't know," Johnny said. "I'm sure he wanted to. But sometimes we can't do what we want, Annie."

"That's what Mom said too."

"I know, it's hard. But it will get better. I know it will. All the people are gone. Do you want to come to the living room now?"

"No."

"Okay."

Johnny pulled his tie and coat off and threw them on the bed. He pulled his shirttails out as he walked down the short hall to the living room. Maggie followed him a few moments later. She wore cutoff jeans and a loose T-shirt and no shoes or socks. She stood at the kitchen counter, dropped cubes in glasses and poured them half full of iced tea, then took the Beam bottle from the cupboard, held it aloft, and looked at Johnny. He nodded.

She handed Johnny his and walked on to the living room, where she pulled a cushion off the couch to lean against and sat on the floor, her legs stretched straight under the coffee table. Johnny followed and sat on the couch just long enough to take off his shoes. He pulled a second cushion down and sat at her side just beyond the end of the table.

"You know, I'm sick of being an adult. I'm sick of holding up and not showing how much it hurts. I'm goddamned sick of it."

"Yes, I know."

She held her glass up, and Johnny touched hers with his. "Here's to my daughter Sara. She was a fine human being." She took a long drink, set the glass down.

"She was, Maggie. She was a fine girl," Johnny said. He held his drink loosely in his fingers, swinging it slightly back and forth in front of him. The sound of crickets and of a car accelerating on the street drifted through the window, but nothing else disturbed the quiet in the living room. Maggie took another gulp of her tea and bourbon, and Johnny reached over and set his glass on the coffee table.

"You know, I'm still amazed Jeff didn't come. She was his daughter."

"Who knows? Maybe he really didn't have the money. It's expensive, booking at the last minute. Hell, what am I telling you for? You know how much it cost."

"What?"

Maggie looked at him for a moment, her head cocked to the side. "You don't know, do you? But how would you?"

"Know what?"

"Jeff moved to LA three or four years ago. Greener pastures, land of opportunity. That's why Sara was in LA in the first place. Because of Jeff. Shit, you'd think he'd at least have the decency to feel guilty enough about that to come to the funeral."

"I had no idea he was in LA."

"Well, in Torrance really. South of LA someplace."

"I thought she ran away to Hollywood to be discovered or something crazy like that."

"She probably did. She just didn't have as far to go, that's all."

"Yeah, I guess. What's Jeff doing in LA?"

"I don't know. He went out there to sell real estate when the market was booming. I don't know what he's doing now. You know Jeff, always looking for a better opportunity."

"He's a good salesman."

"Yeah, churn 'em and burn 'em."

"That's not quite fair, Maggie."

She looked at Johnny for a long time, and he saw the bitterness in her eyes, the anger at the failed marriage, the burden of being a single mother, her daughter's death, and Jeff's absence from the funeral. But as she stared at him the weight of the hatred apparently became too much because her eyes softened and the hard set of her jaw slackened.

"Maybe you're right. Maybe. You know, I heard an expression once that sums Jeff up: 'the curse of easy charm.' Boy, that's him."

"Yeah, he's very charming."

"I know. God, don't I know. But it made everything too easy for him. At least it was always easy in the beginning. He could get in someplace and make a sale to anyone. But he couldn't sustain it. He'd lose interest, get bored. Maybe that's what happened with us. He thought he could just charm me and the girls and not have to do the hard work of being a husband and father." She paused for a moment, her eyes focused on an uncertain distance in front of her. She turned to Johnny, and he saw the strength in her face. "Only I wouldn't let him get away with it."

Her eyes softened and a wistful smile played at the corners of her mouth. "The funny thing is, he really did love the girls. He really wanted to be a good father, but just didn't have a clue how to do it."

They were quiet again. A breeze kicked the horizontal blinds up in the window behind the couch and dropped them against the sill with a soft *thump, thump*. Maggie picked up her glass and took another long drink and put the glass back, the ice cubes clinking as they sought their place. She glanced back at the blinds.

"That's the problem. I hate air-conditioning, but if you leave the windows open all you get is bam, bam, bam all night. That or the humidity." She turned sideways to face him. "You said before you wanted to ask me something. Something about Sara."

"Yeah. Look, I know this isn't a good time, but I've got to ask. Okay?"

"Sure."

"Was Sara in any kind of trouble? Did she have any enemies?"

"What do you mean, enemies? What are you talking about?" He was quiet for a moment and could hear the blinds behind him. "Johnny, what's this all about?" She was staring at him, demanding the truth.

"I don't know for sure. But I think there's a possibility that Sara was murdered. That someone set the fire to kill her."

She picked up her glass of iced tea and bourbon, saw that it was empty, and slowly set it back on the coffee table. "Jesus Christ," she muttered. "Murdered. That's crazy. Why the hell would someone want to kill her?"

"I don't know. But when she called me, she was scared. I could hear it. Then after the fire, I met Gem, this girl who lived in the house with Sara. She was scared too."

"What are you saying? That Sara was a criminal? Is that what you mean?" An edge of anger crept into her voice, and her eyes narrowed. She looked at Johnny as though he were a stranger she'd never seen before.

"No, Maggie, that's not what I mean. Look, there were three of them living in that house. Sara, Gem, and a kid named Dallas. Maggie, Dallas was killed two nights before Sara died. His body was dumped in the Hollywood Hills."

"Oh, Jesus. What the hell is this?" She leaned back slightly, putting a few inches more distance between her and Johnny.

"I don't know. Look, I know this isn't easy. But I need your help." She shifted uncomfortably on the floor and folded her arms across her chest. When she looked at Johnny again, her neck was red and the color was creeping toward her face. She nodded.

"Yeah, okay," she said.

"Annie showed me the birthday card she got. Do you have any idea what her big news was or why she was worried you'd be mad at her?"

"No."

"Did she ever mention Gem or this boy named Dallas?"

"No. All she ever said was she had some friends and they all looked after each other."

"Maggie, there's something else I gotta tell you."

"What now?"

"A couple of nights ago, two guys jumped me in the carport at my place. They think Sara gave me something and they want it."

"Want what?"

"1 don't know. She never gave me anything. But these guys didn't believe me when I told them I didn't have it."

Her eyes had widened, and fear had edged out the anger he'd seen moments before. "Jesus, what the hell's going on?"

"I don't know. I really don't know."

"The police. What are the police doing about this?"

"They're doing the best they can. I've been talking to a Detective Towers in Hollywood. He's a straight shooter, Maggie. He's doing all he can."

They were quiet for a moment. "She wasn't a criminal. She wasn't. I don't care what anyone says. She was stubborn and angry, but she wasn't a criminal. My little girl wasn't a criminal."

"I know that, Maggie. I know that."

She stood and held up her empty glass. "I'm going to have another one. You ready?"

"Damn, I'm half drunk already."

"Yeah, me too. Now I'm going to finish the job. You going to join me?"

Johnny held up his glass, and Maggie took it and wandered off toward the kitchen. "What the hell, I'll sleep on the plane."

Eleven

●━━━━━━━━━━━━━●

*H*e was back in LA by early evening the next day. He stopped at a convenience store for a quart of milk and a packaged sandwich. The shadows were stretching longer into the east, and the lights outside his neighbors' apartments were already on as he moved up the narrow walkway that ran alongside the building from the carport to the sidewalk out front.

He stopped at his front door and glanced toward the bushes, wondering if Archie was still there or had lost faith. But he could see nothing in the darkness. Turning, he unlocked the door and swung his suit bag into the apartment. Instantly, he knew something was wrong. He started to reach for the light switch but saw movement from the corner of his eye. As he turned, a man rushed across the living room toward him. Johnny dropped his groceries and suit bag as he turned to face the man.

"Hey, what the hell," he shouted and tried to brace himself. But the man was coming too quickly and caught Johnny off balance. He ducked and drove his shoulder into Johnny, hitting him just below the rib cage. Johnny was hurled backward into the door frame, his wind exploding from his lungs, his head smashed against the wood. He slumped to the floor as the man sprinted out the door.

Johnny rolled onto his hands and knees, staggered to his

feet, and stumbled outside. He looked toward the street and back to the carport, but the man was gone. Clutching his stomach, he moved doubled over to the door, reached inside, and turned on the light to see the wreckage in his apartment. Every book, every CD was on the floor. The cushions on the couch were scattered, the television and stereo moved, the kitchen cabinets opened, the drawers dumped. The sliding glass door at the rear of the apartment was ajar, and the vertical blinds moved gently in the breeze.

"Jesus," Johnny said under his breath. He walked carefully across the living room, picked the phone out of its stand on the kitchen counter, and dialed 911.

The same two who had responded when Johnny was attacked before arrived about twenty minutes later. Johnny stood in the living room looking at the clutter as the sergeant ascended the stairs and his partner checked the sliding door in the back.

"Looks like the lock was forced," she told the sergeant when he came back downstairs.

"Okay, thanks," the cop said. He jotted something in a small notebook and looked up at Johnny. "You think this is related to the other night?"

"It must be. Why else would someone tear my place apart?"

The sergeant's eyes swept the living room and settled on Johnny again. "And you still have no idea what they're after?"

"Not a clue."

The sergeant looked at him for a moment, and Johnny knew the cop thought he was lying. "Okay. Well, I think I'd better call out a detective from the burglary squad."

"Yeah, I think that would be a good idea."

Johnny walked to the door, picked the milk up off the floor, and went to the bushes, where he squatted down and reached into the darkness and ran his fingers along the dirt until he found the saucer. Looking over his shoulder, he could see the sergeant in the middle of the living room, surrounded by the burglar's chaos, talking into his radio. Johnny wiped the saucer on the grass and filled it with milk.

"Hey, Archie, you old fighter. You want some milk?" His voice was low, barely above a whisper, the tone of a man at prayer. After a few moments, Johnny stood and walked back to his apartment and switched on the porch light. He could see the saucer, but five minutes later the cat still hadn't come, and Johnny went into the apartment to wait.

The cop stepped to the door as Johnny approached. "I'm sorry, Mr. Rose, but none of the detectives is available. We'll have the technicians come out and check for prints and, if you want, a detective can probably come out tomorrow."

Johnny surveyed the disaster in his apartment and shook his head. "No, that's okay. I'm sure they didn't find what they were looking for anyway."

"You're sure you don't want someone to come by tomorrow?"

"Yes."

"Okay. I still have the report from the other night. I'll pass that along."

"Great."

It was two hours before the last technician left, and Johnny spent another three hours cleaning the fingerprint powder off the counters and cabinets and glass and straightening the disarray. Finally, he knelt by the stacks of books and CDs he'd assembled on the floor and picked a CD off the top of the pile. He looked at the stacks and knew it would take at least another hour to get them in alphabetical order and back on the shelves. He put the CD back, stood, and went to the front door, opened it, and looked out.

In the dim light, he could just make out the saucer's surface. The milk was gone. He turned off the porch light and went upstairs.

In the morning, he called the *Journal* while his coffee brewed. He left a message on Kuscyk's machine saying he was back in LA and would be heading to Hollywood. He poured his coffee and had just added milk to it when the phone rang. He put the carton into the refrigerator and shoved the door closed with his hip as he grabbed the phone.

"Hello."

"Hi, Johnny, it's Doc. How'd it go in Atlanta? How's Maggie holding up?"

"As well as can be expected, I guess. She's tough, but this is probably the hardest thing she's ever been through."

"I can imagine."

He set the mug down and ran his finger around the edge. He looked at the living room and saw the stacks of books and CDs and felt a sudden surge of anger at his home being violated.

"I checked on Sara's case."

"Good, thanks. Did you find anything?"

"No, not really. I mean, there's nothing connecting her death to that boy, if that's what you mean."

"Okay. It was a long shot anyway."

"She died almost instantly. She had a pretty high level of THC in her blood. Looks like she'd been smoking some strong stuff. Either that or smoking a lot of it. And, ah . . ." Doc stopped, and an awkward silence filled the line.

"What?"

"It would be tough to prove this in court, but it looks like the gasoline, or whatever it was, was poured on her."

As the shock of Doc's words sank in, images of Sara flooded his mind. He saw her the first time he'd bought her dinner, the time they'd sat for nearly two hours on a bus bench talking. He shook his head.

"Jesus," he mumbled. "So, she was murdered?"

"Oh, hell, I don't know. Maybe it just splashed on her. I don't know, I really don't."

"But that's not what you think happened, is it?"

"No," Doc said weakly. "It's not. I think someone wanted to make sure she didn't come out of the building. Maybe I shouldn't have even told you this, but I thought you should know."

"Yeah, thanks, Doc. Thanks for telling me." Johnny opened his eyes. "Thanks for calling."

After he hung up, Johnny sat at the table, staring across the living room and through the open front window to the row of oleanders outside. But none of it registered. He felt a cold emptiness inside that he didn't want to consider or explore.

A gentle breeze came through the window, and Johnny could hear the whine of an electric leaf blower somewhere in the neighborhood. He picked up the phone to call Maggie but didn't dial immediately. Did he really have to tell her? What good would it do? Sara was dead, why deliver more pain? He looked away from the telephone then back again, hesitated a moment, and dialed. Maggie should know the truth, Johnny told himself. As harsh as it was, in the end the truth would be less painful than one more lie.

He heard the phone ring four times and felt the tension in his shoulders ease when the answering machine picked up.

"Hi, Maggie, it's Johnny. I'm just checking in, letting you know I got home okay. There are a couple of things I wanted to talk to you about but I'll try later. Say 'hi' to Annie for me, okay? Tell her I love her. Bye."

He sipped his coffee and dialed the Hollywood police station. The man who answered the phone told him to wait, and a moment later Towers was on the phone.

"This is Towers."

"Hi, it's Johnny Rose."

"Oh, hi, Mr. Rose. Sorry I missed you when you called before. I heard about you being attacked. You okay now?"

"Yeah, I'm fine. But last night someone burglarized my house. Tore it apart. Whoever did it thinks Sara gave me something, but I don't have a clue what it is." Johnny's words met with silence, and after a moment he went on. "I thought you should know. I thought it might help."

"Well, I don't know how it ties in, but thanks for calling."

"Yeah."

"Listen, after you were in here the other day, I had a

friend in juvenile look for any records on James Randall, your niece, or any kid using the street name Gem. I'm sorry, but we didn't come up with anything."

"So, what are you telling me, Detective?"

"Mr. Rose, I want you to know we're taking this seriously. We're looking at all the angles. I'll talk to the officers who made the report at your place last night. It's just that sometimes these things take a while, that's all. But I appreciate your calling."

"I thought you should know."

"Thank you."

Johnny stared at the phone after he disconnected it. Towers's sincerity was obvious. The guy wanted to find Dallas's killer and probably understood the connection to the fire. But how many cases did the detective have? How much effort could he really put into it? Johnny stuck the phone back in its holder, flicked off the coffee machine, and headed for the door. The cops might have the tools to find Sara's killer, but he had the determination.

Katherine St. Croix was behind the front desk at My Home and looked up when Johnny walked into the center.

"Hello. What brings you by My Home, Mr. Rose?" She smiled, a polite business greeting.

"I'm still looking for Gem. Have you seen her? Has she been in?"

"No, and your note's still on the board."

Johnny turned and looked across the room to the board. Even from the distance he could see the note pinned to it.

"How about that boy, Billy? Maybe he knows where she is."

"I'm afraid I haven't seen him either."

"Did she have any other close friends, anyone I could talk to?"

"Not that I know of. I only ever saw the three of them together."

"No one else, no other guys with her or Sara?"

"No."

"Okay." Johnny turned and glanced around the room, then looked back at her. "Listen, would it be all right if I just talked to some of the kids? I'd like to ask 'em to pass the word to Gem or Billy if they see 'em."

She hesitated a moment, obviously weighing her decision. "All right, but with two stipulations. You can tell them you're looking for Billy and Gem but you have to tell them who you are and you can't give them your home phone number or address. If any of the kids wants to reach you, they tell me and I'll make the call."

"Why can't I have them call me?"

"We don't allow our staff or volunteers to give out addresses or phone numbers. All contact has to be through the center. It protects everybody and, frankly, the kids may trust you a little more this way."

"I already put my phone numbers on the note for Gem."

"That's okay, I think she'll understand. Good luck." She sat down, and Johnny approached a table where a black woman who looked a few years past thirty sat alone. Her eyebrows had been plucked away and replaced by pencil. Her hands were large and the skin rough and scaly. But her red lipstick was precisely placed, and she was overdressed in clothes that didn't quite match or fit her.

"Hi, my name's Johnny Rose. You mind if I sit down?"

"Suit yourself."

"What's your name?"

"Beverly."

Johnny took it slowly at first, asking her questions about herself, getting her to talk. She was reluctant in the beginning, but eventually talked to him about her hopes of joining the Job Corps and learning a skill.

"They're going to send me to Idaho. I'm supposed to fly up there in a week or so. I've never been on an airplane."

"What will you learn to do?"

"I don't know yet. I'm still getting it set up, you know?"

"Yeah, I know what you mean. You've got to take your time and make the right decision."

They talked more, and he told her about being Sara's cousin and looking for Gem. But in the end she said she hadn't seen either Gem or Billy in the last few days.

"But you know them?"

"I know Gem pretty good. We used to hang out together when she first got to Hollywood. That was a couple of years ago."

"And you haven't seen her?"

Beverly studied his face, and Johnny sensed she was deciding what to tell him. She shook her head and said no.

"If you do see her, ask her to call me. I left a note for her on the board, okay?"

"Sure," she said and looked away.

He stopped next at a table where a boy and a girl sat eating quietly. Small empty Styrofoam cups were on the table in front of them, a red halo of fruit punch at the bottom of each cup. They wore identical red T-shirts, and the boy wore shorts that hung below his knees and a baseball cap pulled backward on his head. The girl was plump, with wavy blonde hair that hung to her shoulders. A spray of pimples crept along her forehead at the hairline.

"You mind if I sit down?" Johnny asked.

"Sure, go ahead," the boy said.

Johnny pulled out a chair. "My name's Johnny. What's your name?"

"Bear," the boy said. Johnny looked at the girl.

"Melanie."

"So where are you guys from?" Johnny asked.

"I came from New Orleans," Bear said. "She's from Riverside."

"How'd you get here?" he asked the girl.

"I worked a job and saved up enough to take the bus." Her voice was high and light, and Johnny wondered if anyone knew where she was or cared.

He looked at Bear. "How about you?"

"Trains."

"You're train hopping?"

"Yeah, me and that kid over there." He motioned to a boy in a torn sweatshirt and jeans black with street grime. His hair, thick with grease, was formed in a multispiked Mohawk. He sat at a table playing checkers with Kate St. Croix. He was tall and lanky and towered over Kate. As Johnny watched, he saw Kate lean close and touch the boy's arm. The boy smiled, reached out, and moved one of the checkers. As he did, Kate threw up her hands and laughed, and her smile lit up her face, a look of genuine delight the most accomplished actress couldn't manufacture. Johnny looked away, suddenly feeling like a voyeur intruding on her privacy.

"Why are you taking trains?"

"You pretty much have to. It's hard hitchhiking from New Orleans to here. Nobody will pick you up. I knew one guy hitchhiked, took him three weeks to get here."

"Isn't it dangerous?"

"You gotta be careful, that's all. As long as you don't try to hop a moving train, you'll be okay."

"I'll try to remember that. You know, maybe you can help me out. Did either of you know a girl named Sara? She's the one who was killed in the fire the other night."

"Nah. We heard about the fire, but we didn't know her," the boy said.

"How about a girl named Gem. Do you know her?" They both shook their heads. "How about Billy? Ever heard of him?"

"No. Why you asking about them?"

"Oh, I gotta talk to Gem about something." He shook their hands, and Johnny moved two tables over.

"Can I sit down?" Johnny asked one of the two girls at the table.

The girl, her hair a tangle of blonde and red streaks, looked at him for a moment, her eyes distant and mistrustful.

He waited until she nodded, her head barely moving.

"My name's Johnny Rose."

Neither girl said anything, and Johnny leaned back in the molded plastic chair and waited a moment.

"What's your name?" he asked the girl with the strawberry hair.

"Blaze." She looked at the tabletop as she spoke, her answer a one-syllable acknowledgment of the question that invited no further discussion. Johnny noticed her fingers, dirty, with the nails bitten and ragged. He turned to the second girl, a slender young woman in cutoff jeans and a spaghetti-strap top that ended above her midriff. She cradled a black duffel bag in her lap.

"What's your name?"

"Alexandra."

"So, Alexandra, what's in the bag?"

"Food." She smiled, and Johnny was surprised to see she wore braces. "Here, look," she said and unzipped the bag and held it open for Johnny's inspection. It was full of granola bars, bags of chips, fruit rolls, and cookies.

"I'm the food mama," she said.

"I can see that," Johnny said. "Where do you get it all?"

"At the shelters. I'm the one who doesn't ever get kicked out, so I'm in charge of getting all the food for everybody."

"Who's everybody?"

"Our family. Just a group of us."

"A group, huh? That include a girl named Gem or a boy named Billy?"

"The ones that used to hang with Sara?"

"Did you know Sara?"

"I've seen her around."

"Was she part of your family?"

"Nah."

Johnny looked at Blaze. "I was Sara's cousin and I'm trying to get in touch with Billy or Gem."

"I don't know 'em." She looked away.

"How about you, Alexandra?"

"If you're looking for Billy, try the bridge squat. I hear he was staying there for a while."

"Shut up!" Blaze snarled, and Alexandra dropped her eyes to the bag in her lap.

"Well, thanks," Johnny said and moved on. He tried a few more tables, taking the time to talk to the kids about their lives, where they were from and how they got to Hollywood. Finally, though, he gave up and crossed to the front desk where Kate sat. She watched him approach.

"How'd it go?"

Johnny didn't answer at first. He looked back at the day-room and watched as a tall, gangly boy who wore an empty scabbard on his belt laughed loudly, his voice full of adolescent energy and swagger. Just as quickly the boy dropped his gaze to the table and color crept into his face as he realized that the other kids were staring at him. Johnny saw the backpacks and skateboards, and the kids talking softly and eating burritos and cookies. Many of the teenagers were clean and neatly dressed, and Johnny thought that at first glance it could be a classroom in almost any high school in America. Except he'd sat at the tables with them and heard the anger, suspicion, and pain in their voices and seen an isolation and desperation in their eyes that went far beyond concern over a Friday night football game or a poor yearbook photo.

"I'm afraid I didn't find out much. One of the kids said Billy was staying at something called the bridge squat. What's that?" Her expression darkened, and Johnny held up his hands. "Whoa, I didn't ask where to look for him. I just said I wanted to get in touch and the girl mentioned it."

"Okay, I understand. Sometimes I'm more cautious than I need to be. But some of these kids just don't understand how dangerous it can be."

"What about the bridge squat, Ms. St. Croix?"

"Some of the kids used to stay under the bridge where Hollywood Boulevard crosses the freeway. On the west side. The city closed it up when they started throwing garbage down on the freeway and urinating on passing cars."

"Could he have gotten back in?"

"Maybe. It's been locked up for a long time but . . ." She shrugged. "Maybe."

"I think I'd better take a look. Maybe he can help me find Gem."

"Mr. Rose, don't go in there. If that squat's open it could be dangerous."

"I don't have a choice. I've got to look everywhere I can."

"Don't do this. I'm not kidding when I say those places can be dangerous."

"I'll be careful. Thanks for your help." He turned to leave.

"Wait!" He looked back at her. "If I can't talk you out of going, at least take this." She pulled open a drawer in the desk, searched through it for a moment, and took out a flashlight, flicked it once to make sure it worked, and held it out to him. "It'll be dark in there."

"Thank you," he said. He took the flashlight and started toward the door but stopped and looked back at her.

"Thanks for helping me, Ms. St. Croix," he said.

"You're welcome, and please, call me Kate."

"Okay, I will, and I'm Johnny. I'll bring this back when I'm done."

"There's no hurry." She hesitated for a moment and went on. "I watched you, Johnny. You do very well with the kids." For the first time she smiled at him, a relaxed and open smile full of warmth, as though he were a friend.

"Well, I've had a lot of experience asking people questions."

"I think it's more than that."

"A lot of them remind me of Sara. I mean, like you said, they're just kids."

"Yes, they are, but you'd be surprised how many people refuse to see that."

"Yeah, I'll bet. People used to look at me and Sara when we'd be sitting on a bench sometimes and I knew what they were thinking. Sara knew, too, and to tell the you the truth, sometimes it made me want to punch them out. Anyway"—

he held up the flashlight—"thanks for this. I gotta go."

"Good luck."

Johnny was just pushing the door open when she called him. "Johnny, wait a minute." He turned. "There's something I wanted to show you." She pointed across the room. It took him a moment to see that she was pointing at a bulletin board on the floor, leaning against the wall. It was nearly hidden by the tables and chairs. Johnny walked past three tables until he had a better view. It was full of pictures of street kids, each held in place with pushpins, and across the top were the words "Who We Are."

Johnny squatted down in front of it, and Kate walked up behind him.

"This was in one of the offices upstairs. I brought it down today, I just haven't gotten around to hanging it yet." She knelt on the carpet next to him. "There's a picture of Sara and one with Gem too. If you'd like, please take them." She pointed to a photo near the left-hand corner.

Johnny saw the photo and slowly took it off the board to study it. Sara and Gem were standing on the boulevard, laughing and mugging for the camera.

"Who took this?"

"I'm not sure, maybe Beverly."

Johnny looked from the picture to Kate. "You mean the kids took these?"

"Yes. A local artist, Alex Taylor from Pasadena, did an art and photography project with the kids about a month ago. He gave several kids in his workshop a throwaway camera and told them to take pictures of the world the way they saw it. Some others he had do drawings, then they put several montages together. This was one of them. Moving, isn't it?"

"Sara never mentioned it."

"I don't know how interested she was. Dallas actually did pretty well in it." She sighed and shook her head.

"What?"

"Alex said Dallas was the only kid he ever saw who liked

working in the darkroom more than taking pictures. He only shot one roll but spent hours in the darkroom. I teased him that he was doing it because he liked the chemicals."

"What'd he say?"

"He blushed. He was like so many of these kids. Smart and dumb at the same time. Not too different from most teenagers, I guess."

"Yeah, I know what you mean."

"That's a picture of him, there." She pointed to a photo on the right side of the board. Johnny saw a tall, strong boy in a sweatshirt with the sleeves cut off, his short hair bleached a straw white, a mustache growing in brown. In the photo Dallas was leaning against a brick-and-wrought-iron fence. A small Jacuzzi was in the foreground, and behind and below him Hollywood gave way to the LA sprawl.

"He told me it was a self-portrait," she said. "Here's another one of Sara." She pointed to a photo in the opposite corner of the bulletin board. Johnny heard a girl giggle behind him and a boy brushed past, jostling him with his backpack, but Johnny didn't turn; his eyes were on the picture.

"Dallas take this one?"

"No, I think Bev took that one too. Like I said, Dallas only took one roll that I know of."

"May I take them?"

"Sure, you can keep them."

He pulled the second picture from the board, stood, and waited while Kate rose from the floor. He studied the picture of Dallas and tapped it slowly with his finger. "Did he tell you where he took this?"

"No. Why?"

"I think I've been there."

"Are you sure?"

"No, not completely but it looks like Carol Holland's backyard. Dallas or Sara ever mention her?"

"No, not to me at least."

"Maybe I should go up there and ask her about it?"

"You mean to her house?"

Johnny smiled. "Sure. You know, it's amazing what people will tell you if you just ask."

Johnny thanked Kate again for the flashlight and photos and left the center. A few minutes later he reached the Z, stepped off the curb, and walked to the driver's door, where he paused and pulled the picture of Dallas from his coat pocket. He studied it again, staring at the background, the brick fence and the view of the city below. But the details were blurry and it was hard to be sure. How many brick-and-wrought-iron fences were there in the hills overlooking LA? In truth, Johnny knew, there could be hundreds, even thousands. It was far from a unique style. He stuck the picture back in his pocket, tossed his jacket on the passenger seat, and was about to get in when he heard Gem's voice.

"I saw your car."

Johnny glanced up, studying the people on the sidewalk, searching for her, but saw no one he recognized. His eyes drifted up the sidewalk and down again over the tourists and past the storefronts and finally to a long, recessed doorway leading to a boarded-up shop. The wind had collected paper and dirt in the front of the narrow passage, and in the far corner he saw a dark figure. She moved then, her blonde hair catching just enough light to be visible. Gem stepped closer to the sidewalk but hung back in the doorway. Johnny could see her face, a veneer of toughness that almost but couldn't quite hide the fear in her eyes. Her face was dirty, her hair oily and stringy, and he wasn't sure if she'd bathed since the fire.

"Gem," Johnny said as he closed the door on the Z slowly, deliberately. "Are you okay?" She said something, but a car passing behind him drowned out her words. He moved quickly to the sidewalk and stopped in front of the entrance. "I'm sorry, I didn't hear you," he said.

"I said I'm fine." She moved forward slightly, and he could see her better now.

"Good. I'm glad. I've been worried about you."

"Oh, yeah?"

"Yeah. I just came from My Home. They said you haven't been in for a few days."

"I'm looking for Billy. Maybe he can help me get out of LA." She stressed the word "he" but paused for a moment, looking from the darkness into the sunlight of the street, and locked on Johnny's eyes. "Unless you've changed your mind." Her words came as a direct challenge, and she lifted her chin at him.

"I'm not going to help you run." She was quiet, and Johnny went on. "You didn't stay home."

"This is my home." She gestured toward the street, moved back into the darkness of the recessed doorway, and slid down until she was on the cement, her back against the wall.

Johnny waited as a short, paunchy man in a frayed white shirt with a wide striped tie, his thin dark hair slicked back, walked past. The man glanced at Johnny but never looked into the doorway. Johnny walked to the edge of the entranceway.

"Gem, I'm worried about you and I want to help, but I can't if you run."

Without looking at him, she dragged her backpack to her feet and dug through it until she found a pack of cigarettes. She lit one and inhaled deeply, looked straight ahead, and blew the smoke out, her wrist resting on her knee, the cigarette held between two fingers dangling inches away. She looked at him and smiled, but there was no joy in her face. Sadness, resignation, and loss filled her eyes.

"I know you want to help. You know how I know?"

"How?"

"The way you look at me."

"What?"

"It's not like everyone else. It's like with Sara."

"I don't understand."

"All those times you were with Sara, you didn't look at me like they do." She waved toward the sidewalk, smoke trailing off the cigarette. "Like I was an animal or wasn't even there. Or the other ones who, like, see me for the first time and say you're really pretty and what they really mean . . . Oh, well, what the hell . .." She paused and took another drag on the cigarette before going on. "So, yeah, you're a good person but you haven't got a clue."

"Then tell me. Tell me what this is all about. Tell me why someone wanted to kill Sara and I'll do everything I can to help you."

"Help me get out of LA, because I can't stay here and I'm not talking to the cops."

Johnny moved into the doorway and squatted across from her, his back pressed against the wall, trying to get closer, hoping he could convince her. His shoes were less than two feet from her.

"Gem, listen to me. You could be in danger. Some men beat me up a few days ago. They burglarized my apartment last night. They want something I don't have. Something they think Sara gave me. What if they're looking for you? What if they think you have it? I'm worried about you."

The end of her cigarette glowed brightly for a second as Gem inhaled. When she looked at him again, she smiled but looked sad. When she spoke, her voice had the timbre and tone of a woman decades older than the child sitting only a few feet away.

"You're sweet, you know. You really are," she said, and Johnny felt like an underclassman being turned down for a date by the prom queen.

"This is serious, you've got to listen to me. I met a man named Griffin at the burned-out house. He asked about you, Gem. Not Sara or Dallas. About you. You have to listen to me. These men are looking for you."

"Griffin's a piece of shit."

"Who is he, Gem? Why's he looking for you?" But she looked away from him and stared silently at the wall opposite her and took another drag on the cigarette. Johnny could hear the traffic on the street and glanced at the boulevard and saw an old Yellow Cab drift by. He looked at her again.

"What's Griffin want? What are these guys looking for? What did you do? What was Sara doing? Was it drugs, guns? What?"

"She never did anything wrong."

His patience was wearing thin, and his anger at the young street girl and her evasiveness and refusal to help was growing. "Look," he snapped, "I just got back from Atlanta. I read a letter that Sara sent her sister while I was there. She said she was coming home but her mom would be pissed. So I know she did something wrong. What was it? Was she hooking? Was that it? Damn it, Gem, tell me."

"Jesus, I can't believe you asked that," she said and turned away from him. She flicked the cigarette to the end of the doorway. It bounced off the wall, and sparks cascaded onto the cement. She stared at him, and her eyes had hardened. "She didn't do a damned thing." She stood in a fluid, easy movement, swept her pack to her shoulder, and stepped over his feet to the edge of the doorway. Johnny struggled to stand straight, pushing himself up, his palms flat on the dirty cement, but his knees ached, and he was slow and awkward. A second later Gem spoke to him, and her words hit like a brick slammed into his chest.

"She wasn't in trouble, man. She was pregnant."

"Pregnant? Jesus." He froze for a moment and sank down the wall to the cement. "Who?" Johnny managed.

"Who do you think?"

Images of Sara filled his mind. She was just a kid, a skinny little girl with thin dark hair who acted tough but wasn't, not really. God, she didn't look older than twelve. Pregnant? No. It just couldn't be. She'd have told him, wouldn't she? He stared at the wall across from him, oblivious to the noise on the street and the people passing on the sidewalk only a few feet away. He was lost in his own thoughts for seconds, not long. But long enough. When he turned back toward the sidewalk, the entrance was empty. Gem had slipped silently and easily away. Johnny scrambled to his feet and hobbled out of the doorway as quickly as he could. But by the time he got to the sidewalk, she was gone.

"Shit," he swore aloud. He scanned the sidewalk again in a futile effort. "Gem!" he shouted in one direction, then turned and called in the other. "Gem!" he yelled. The pedestrians ignored him, and traffic flowed past without missing a beat. "Oh, Christ," he whispered. "You don't understand. They'll kill you." But as he pulled the door to the Z open, he realized that maybe she did understand after all.

Twelve

———————•———————

*T*he cul-de-sac was empty, all evidence of the party gone. He parked in front of the house, and as he got out of the car, Carol Holland's garage door jerked up a few inches, hesitated, then slowly rose the rest of the way. Johnny walked to the bottom of the driveway and waited, facing the house, as a white Mercedes 300E backed out, Carol Holland behind the wheel. She saw him, stopped, and lowered the window, leaving the engine idling.

"Well, Mr. Rose, this is a surprise."

"I wanted to ask you a question. About something you told me the other night."

"The other night?"

"At the party here. When we were out on the deck."

"Oh, yes, of course. What is it?" She seemed slightly bewildered.

"You said you used to hire street kids to do chores around here."

"Yes, I did. Just odd jobs." The confusion he'd seen in her eyes a moment before slipped away, and her smile intensified. "You know, I want to help them, if I can."

"You ever hire that boy whose body was found over there on the hillside? He used the street name Dallas."

"So that was his name, Dallas?" she asked.

"His real name was James Randall." He thought of Gem's

———

133

answer, "Who do you think?" Had she meant Dallas? He focused again on Carol Holland and reached into his pocket. "Here, let me show you a picture of him." Johnny pulled the photo out and held it in front of her. "Do you recognize him?"

She glanced at the picture and shook her head. "Sometimes the kids come up here and I barely see them. Why?"

"But that's your backyard, isn't it?"

The actress shrugged. "Who can tell? It's kind of out of focus."

"So you're telling me you don't know this boy, is that right?" Johnny felt an odd intensity, a blend of anger and frustration, and knew he was still reacting to the news of Sara's pregnancy. He forced himself to focus on Carol Holland, struggling to push Sara from his thoughts.

"You came all the way up here to ask me if I know this boy? I don't see the point."

"Just look again. Take a close look. You might recognize him." He pushed the photo a little closer. Her eyes slid over it and back to Johnny. Her smile intensified. Maybe he was supposed to be flattered because she was a beautiful movie star making him the sole object of her attention. But her calm, reassured smile simply angered him. "Look at the fence real closely. This is your backyard, isn't it?"

She was still smiling at him, but an edge of anger had begun to pinch the corners of her eyes. "Is this what passes for serious journalism today, checking on who hires day laborers?"

"I'm only interested in the day laborers who get murdered and dumped on hillsides."

"You're being awfully melodramatic, don't you think?"

"Did Dallas work for you, Miss Holland?"

"I told you, I don't know. Why are you interested in the street kids I hire, Mr. Rose? What? You want to know if I pay their Social Security taxes? Well, I don't. I pay 'em cash. Okay? So now I'll never be able to run for president. Is that what this is all about?"

"I'm interested in how Dallas's death and the fire that killed my cousin are tied together."

The smile was gone now, and she looked at him with a blank face that hid all emotion.

"Mr. Rose, I try to help these kids. I want to help them, I really do. And this is what I get, a reporter throwing wild accusations at me? If you'll excuse me, I have an appointment."

She stepped on the accelerator, and the Mercedes lunged back, then stalled. She restarted it. When the engine caught, she turned to look behind her as she backed up. The car slid into the street and jerked to a stop, and she drove away without looking back.

He started back to his car but noticed an elderly man, perhaps seventy-five, standing in the gutter across the street, clutching a rake and watching him. When Johnny looked at him, the man smiled, shook his head, and chuckled. He was almost bald, with age spots on his head. He wore chocolate colored polyester pants that were too big in the waist and a few inches too short, a faded blue polo shirt over a white T-shirt, and worn cotton gardening gloves.

Johnny crossed the street as the man slowly raked a small pile of leaves together in the gutter. "Hi. My name's Johnny Rose. I'm a reporter for the *Journal*. You know Carol Holland?"

"Name's Henry. Nice to meet you. Sure, I know Miss Holland. Been neighbors ever since she moved in. I saw the way she was acting. You must have really got her mad. She doesn't get like that very much."

"I'll have to take your word for that." Johnny looked back up the street where the Mercedes had disappeared.

Henry laughed. "Well, son, I won't say a word against her, if that's what you're after. She's a great neighbor. Besides, us Hoosiers stick together, you know." He chuckled.

"Pardon me?"

"Hoosiers. From Indiana."

"I thought she grew up here, in Hollywood."

Henry shrugged. "Don't know. Told me she grew up in Indianapolis. I'm from Fort Wayne myself. Moved out here right after the war. Went into real estate." When he realized that Johnny wasn't listening, he began sweeping the leaves again.

"Sorry, Henry, I was thinking of something else. But she told you she was from Indianapolis?"

"That's right."

"Okay. Thank you for your time, sir."

"Sorry I couldn't help. But like I said, she's really a nice lady."

"Yes, I'm sure she is," Johnny said.

Ten minutes later, Johnny walked up the wide cement steps from Sunset Boulevard into Hollywood High School. The hallway was clean, the tile floor waxed and polished. Red stars with names of congressmen, writers, musicians, and other famous graduates were painted on the walls, and Johnny read them as he walked.

He found the office, stepped to the chest-high counter, and watched as a small, wiry Asian woman who appeared frail and old slowly slid from behind her desk and began to shuffle across the office to the counter. As he waited, Johnny turned and looked around the office.

His eyes were caught by photos of famous actors and actresses hung above a row of teachers' mailboxes on the wall opposite the counter. He saw a *Time* magazine cover of Mickey Rooney and a *Life* magazine cover of Lana Turner, a series of *TV Guide* covers with James Garner and Stefanie Powers and others. He studied every photo and magazine cover on the wall, and when he turned back the woman had reached the counter. She was smiling.

"Yes, they all went to Hollywood High," she said without waiting for him to ask.

"I guess a lot of famous people went here."

"Yes, we've had quite a few."

"But you don't have a picture of Carol Holland?"

"Why would we? She didn't go to Hollywood High." The

timbre of her voice told Johnny not to misjudge her. She could easily be seventy, but she wasn't frail and miles away from senile.

"You're sure? I thought she graduated in the class of '77."

The woman shook her head. "I've been working in this office since 1967. I don't know all the kids, but I know a lot of them. I go to the school plays and know the ones who go into the movie business. I still hear from one or two now and then."

"But you don't know Carol Holland?"

"No."

"Maybe she changed her name when she went into show business."

"That could be. Stefanie Powers used the last name Paul when she was here, but I'd still know Carol Holland, and I know she didn't go here."

Johnny glanced at the pictures, leaned on the counter again, and looked at the woman. "Thanks for your help."

"That's all you wanted?"

"It's all I need," he said and walked out of the office, through the hall, and back down the stairs to Sunset Boulevard.

He sat in the car, oblivious to the cauldron of motion on the street around him, and thought about Carol Holland. She'd skillfully sidestepped his questions about Dallas. She hadn't admitted that he'd worked for her, but she hadn't denied it either. So why dance around a subject like that and lie about something as simple and stupid as going to Hollywood High? It made no sense, and he could imagine no answer. Finally, he pulled from the curb and headed toward Hollywood Boulevard.

The freeway was below ground level where it passes under Hollywood Boulevard, and Johnny stood at the edge of the bridge spanning the highway. Two cars turned down the on-ramp and picked up speed as they went. Johnny watched them for a moment and turned back to the bridge.

He noticed the noise then. The sounds of the vehicles

speeding by on the eight lanes below funneled up to the bridge in a roar. Each car and truck contributed its own whine of grinding gears, growling engines, and screaming tires. It all came together like an orchestra of discordant instruments in the hands of angry musicians.

A short cement wall ran along both sides of the on-ramp. On the freeway side the wall separated the ramp from a weed- and ivy-covered hillside that dropped quickly to the highway's edge. Under the bridge but high above the freeway, street kids had in times past made a home. Concrete panels now enclosed the space under the bridge. Johnny climbed over the wall and almost slipped. He caught his balance and moved slowly down the slope along the edge of the bridge. A metal service door, set in the panel closest to the edge, hung open. A pile of rusted chains someone had cut lay at the foot of the door. Johnny saw a small roll of toilet paper wedged in a crack between two of the panels. The smell of feces and urine drifting from under the bridge was overpowering. He swallowed hard, exhaled deeply, and stepped inside. Pointing the flashlight in front of him, he flicked it on.

"Stay away, I've got a knife." The voice echoed in the closed-in space and was instantly lost amid the roar of the traffic. "I'll kill you. I swear it."

Johnny turned the light toward the voice, high on the slope, just below the bridge. The beam fell on a boy in filthy clothes with greasy, spiked hair. He squatted on his haunches, holding a pocketknife in front of him. His backpack and a dirty, worn sleeping bag lay on the ground just to his right.

"Get away," the boy said. Johnny could hear the fear in his voice and wondered if the boy would charge down the slope.

"I saw you talking to Kate at My Home, didn't I?" Johnny said. He flicked off the flashlight. In the sudden darkness he lost sight of the boy. "I was in there earlier, you two were playing checkers." His eyes were adjusting now, and he could just make out the form of the boy.

"What do you want?" the boy demanded, but Johnny no longer heard the fear in his voice.

"My name's Johnny Rose. Sara Bradley, the girl who was killed in the fire, was my cousin."

"So?"

"I'm trying to find Sara's friend, Gem. She might be in trouble. I know Gem's friends with Billy and I heard Billy squatted here sometimes."

"He ain't here."

The sound of a siren came from overhead as an ambulance or police car raced across the bridge. Johnny was still until the sound faded.

"What's your name?" he asked when he was sure the boy could hear him again.

"Spider."

"Well, Spider, I'm going to turn on the flashlight again, okay?"

"Do whatever you want, but Billy isn't here."

Johnny still had not moved, but he shined the light around the dirt-and-cement cavern. Someone had dragged an old roll of carpet into the space, and it lay near the highest part of the slope. Newspapers, Styrofoam cups, aluminum soda cans, and broken bottles were scattered across the dirt. He played the flashlight across the backs of the concrete panels tagged with bright swirls of color and messages: "Toy Loves Bear" and "Punkers Forever" and a sloppily formed marijuana leaf.

He turned the light off again and looked at the boy.

"Is this where Billy usually squats?"

"Sometimes, yeah."

"What about Gem?"

"She's Billy's friend. I don't know anything about her, man."

"But you're Billy's friend, right?"

"Yeah. We travel together sometimes."

"Hopping trains?"

"Yeah, so?"

"Nothing, just wondering. Tell me, Spider, you have any idea where I can find Billy or Gem now?"

"No." The answer was quick and firm, and Johnny knew he was lying.

"Yeah, sure," Johnny said. He flicked on the flashlight and scanned the area again before turning it off and looking up toward Spider. "Thanks for your help," he said.

He walked back through the door, scrambled up the slope to the edge of the on-ramp, and stood breathing the hot, smog-filled air that suddenly seemed fresh and cool.

He'd left the Z half a block away, and as he approached it, he saw a billboard high above the boulevard. It bore a picture of a reclining woman wearing a very small bikini, peering over heart-shaped sunglasses at the street below. Her enormous breasts revealed a mile of cleavage before the bikini restored the barest hint of modesty. Above the picture was one name: "Angelyne." She was LA's most famous wanna-be, a woman whose billboards and signs had appeared around Hollywood for more than two decades, yet she never seemed to appear in movies or on television. A woman famous for wanting to be famous.

Johnny turned from the soft-focused photo of Angelyne, looked back at the freeway, and realized that the billboard and the bridge had captured Hollywood like bookends; three blocks from the city's magical sunshine allure to its most brutal reality.

It was near closing time when Johnny arrived at My Home. Kate was talking to the receptionist but looked up when he walked in. Johnny smiled.

"I saw Gem," he said. "She was waiting for me near my car when I left here."

"Is she okay?"

"She was, but I'm worried about her. I don't think she understands the danger."

"These kids know all about that."

"Maybe. Look, there's something I need to ask you."

"What?"

"Gem told me that Sara was pregnant." He waited, but she said nothing. "Do you think Dallas was the father?"

"I don't know. Maybe, probably. I mean, they were together all the time. If she was pregnant, then he was probably the father. Gem wouldn't tell you?"

"No."

"Did she talk to you about the fire?"

"No. I tried to get her to go to the police. But she wouldn't."

"I'm not surprised. Most of these kids are afraid of the cops. They get hassled by them all the time."

"She said they have a warrant out for her arrest."

"A lot of them do. That's another reason they don't want to have anything to do with the cops."

"So she's not lying about the warrant?"

"Probably not. We had one kid in here six months ago. He'd come here from St. Louis, where he'd shot his stepfather and almost killed him. The police picked him up for jaywalking, ran a check, and found an attempted murder warrant out for him."

"Okay, well . . ." He could think of nothing else to say. "Well, look, ah." He held up the flashlight up. "I just came by to give this back to you."

"Did it do any good?"

"I'm not really sure. Someone opened up that place under the bridge again. Cut the chains to get in. I went in. Spider was there." Her eyes widened in question. "It was okay. He seemed scared when I first came in, but I told him I'd seen him playing checkers with you."

"He's a good kid, he really is. He's just got a lot of problems, like so many of these kids. Did he help?"

"No. Billy's been squatting there, but Spider said he didn't know anything about Gem. Or if he did, he wasn't saying anything. Well, anyway, thanks for this." He handed her the flashlight.

"You're welcome." She smiled, but Johnny caught something in her eyes, a flicker of concern.

"You're worried, too, aren't you?"

"With these kids you always worry."

"You didn't answer my question."

"I don't know how to answer it." She waited a moment. "Don't take this personally, but sometimes the only way to survive is to put a little distance between you and what's happening to them. You know, not everything makes sense all the time."

"I know, but . . ." He stopped and dismissed the thought with a quick wave.

"We're still open for another half hour or so, Gem still might come in."

"I hope so. Anyway I just wanted to give you back your flashlight. Thanks again."

"You're welcome."

A silence filled the space between them. Johnny looked around the empty center, and his eyes came to rest on her again. "Hey, Kate, would you like to have dinner with me?"

"What?" From the shocked look in her eyes, Johnny wondered if he'd offended her.

"I just asked if you'd like to have dinner with me."

"You mean now? Tonight?"

"Yes. Unless you're married or something like that."

"No, nothing like that. It's just that, well . . . I don't think that would be a good idea. I don't even know you." Her answer was polite, but firm.

To his own surprise, Johnny laughed. "That's the whole point."

"Thank you, but . . ." She shook her head no.

"Look, the last few days have been hard for both of us. Let's forget about it for a while. It's just dinner. Let someone else cook. Take a break. What do you say?"

She looked at him for a moment before smiling, holding his eyes. "Okay, sure. Why not?"

"You want to eat somewhere around here?"

"No. When I'm off work, I get away from Hollywood."

"Where do you live?"

"Culver City."

"Good. I'm in Santa Monica. Do you know the Sidewalk Café on the boardwalk in Venice?"

"Sure, it's right next to that small bookstore."

"That's the place. I'll meet you there in, say, an hour and a half?"

"Better make it two."

"Okay, see you then."

Thirteen

●─────────────────────────●

Johnny got to Venice Beach early and walked toward the ocean, crossing a wide grassy area and moving to the edge of the cement bike path that on Sundays is crowded with a blend of bikers and in-line skaters, some of whom struggled against gravity like dogs on ice and others who whipped past at speeds that were way past the redline and bordered on the foolhardy. But early in the evening of a weekday, only a few solitary, lazy bikers and leisurely skaters moved past. A young couple skated toward him, their hands clutched together for balance as they wobbled forward, and they spoke in hushed, emotion-filled voices. The setting sun lit their faces, and as they slid past, Johnny noticed acne on the boy's chin and forehead and guessed the couple was sixteen, perhaps even eighteen, but no older. He felt a sudden jolt of loss and thought of Sara and wondered what she had thought when she learned she was pregnant. It should have been a joyous time, a cause for celebration. He doubted it was.

Why hadn't she told him? Had she been afraid of what he'd say? Scared he'd send her back to Maggie? But she'd planned to go anyway, hadn't she? Johnny watched the young couple skate past again and realized with renewed sorrow that he'd probably never understand what Sara thought or felt.

He was still thinking of Sara as he crossed back to the

144

boardwalk and stood waiting near the restaurant. A few moments later he saw Kate walking toward him, her eyes scanning the people ahead of her. When she saw him, waved, and smiled, Johnny's thoughts of Sara melted away.

"Hi. I hope I haven't kept you waiting," she said.

"No, I just got here a minute ago."

"Good."

"Ah, Kate, I was wondering . . . "

"No. I left a little early, but Gem hadn't come in. If that's what you were going to ask."

"Yes. Thanks. I really hadn't planned on asking. I didn't want this to be about work. We're supposed to leave it in Hollywood tonight. So, let's go eat."

"Great, I'm starving."

She followed him to the edge of the restaurant's awning-covered patio where they waited until a barrel-chested maître d' wearing a checked sport shirt approached. He handed them menus and pointed to a table next to the short brick wall that separated the patio from the Venice boardwalk.

"You can sit there, if you want," he said and turned away.

Kate followed Johnny as he led them through the tables, and she smiled when he pulled out her chair, an unexpected gesture.

"Thank you," she said.

For a fleeting second he considered attempting a joke, but instead he simply said, "You're welcome."

He sat down and looked past her shoulder down the boardwalk. Most of the street performers, the musicians and comedians, the jugglers and unicyclists, were packing up or running through their last performances of the day. The portrait artists had taken their easels down, and a lazy, early evening calm seemed to hover. He shifted his gaze, studying Kate as she read the menu.

She wore an unbuttoned denim shirt over a white top, and, Johnny noticed, she had taken the time to put on small pearl earrings and fresh lipstick. It was her only makeup.

Johnny shifted his gaze to the menu and a moment later was aware of someone standing to his left, just beyond the short wall. He turned and was looking at a barefoot man with a long, unkempt gray beard and unwashed, disheveled hair. The man wore tattered jeans and a T-shirt and held a small dog to his chest. Guessing his age seemed impossible.

"Hey, man, you got about eighteen cents? I'm trying to get about eighteen cents today, okay?"

Johnny heard the waiter to his right before he saw him. "There's nothing for you here. You'll have to move on." The waiter, a young man in faded jeans and a polo shirt, moved next to their table. His words had been firm but not harsh, and he repeated them. "You'll have to move on. There's nothing for you here."

"Can I get a bone for my dog?"

The young man said nothing but continued to return the stare of the man with the dog. They remained that way for a moment; then the man shuffled away and the waiter smiled at Johnny and Kate. Another bum moved along. It must happen a hundred times a day here.

"I'm Jim. I'm your waiter. Can I get you something to drink?"

Johnny ordered a beer, Kate iced tea, and they fell into silence again as they watched the people parade past: those who were down and out and those from out of town, the muscle beach weight lifters in spandex and the shapely girls in next to nothing. It was a measure of Venice Beach, Johnny thought, that the only two who really stood out were a man and woman dressed for the office. He wore a dark blue suit and she, heels and hose. They walked along the sidewalk like black bugs trapped in a kaleidoscope.

"You know, I haven't been to Venice Beach in, well, I don't know. I guess it's been at least five years, maybe longer. Can you believe that?" Kate said.

"Really? You ought to get down here more often. Never a dull moment. Back there"—Johnny pointed north—"where the skating path bends and the Venice part of the boardwalk begins, there used to be a homemade sign. It said something like 'Venice Beach the Eternal Circus.' That about captures it. This place would make P. T. Barnum jealous."

She laughed lightly, and Johnny realized that she had changed. It was a subtle, almost imperceptible shift. She was different here on the edge of the ocean miles away from Hollywood. Her lips looked fuller, her eyes less narrow, the shadows under them not as dark.

"You know, it's good to see you away from your office."

"Really? Why's that?"

Johnny sensed her stiffen, and a caution seemed to rise in her eyes.

"Oh, I don't know. You just look more relaxed."

Before she could respond, the waiter returned, served their drinks, took their orders, and left. They sat quietly for a moment and Johnny said nothing, letting her decide to pick up the conversation or change the subject.

"Maybe you're right. Sometimes distance helps." She was quiet for a second, letting her gaze fall to the tabletop. "You never really get used to losing kids," she said and looked up at him. The edges of her mouth softened, and for a second he thought she would cry, but she simply looked at him.

"How'd you get started at My Home?"

Kate lowered her eyes to her iced tea and twirled the straw with her finger. "Oh, it was an accident, really. I was a social worker, and a friend told me about My Home. Arranged an interview and, well, you know." She shrugged.

"Must have been a good friend. Seems to have put you in the right place." His tone was light, making it sound like a compliment.

But her expression changed, and she looked at him as if searching for a hidden meaning in his words before smiling, a thin smile that held no joy. She turned and looked toward the ocean. "It really is a beautiful night. I forget how nice it is being so close to the ocean."

Johnny waited a moment, wondering if she would say more. But she continued to look at the ocean, seemingly lost in thought.

"Yes, it really is nice, especially this time of the day. When we were kids, my dad would bring us to Santa Monica sometimes and I'd think, 'Someday I'm going to live here.' Maybe that's why I'm still buying lottery tickets. If I win, I'm getting a place on the beach. I even promised my kid brother I'd put a room on for him."

She turned slowly back to look at him, and a playful smile appeared in her eyes. "And you get to move into his spare bedroom if he wins, right? That would be fair, wouldn't it?"

"Oh, well, you know, Jimmy doesn't play the lottery." He tried to say it with a casual nonchalance, but Johnny could never mention Jimmy without emotion in his voice. Even now, years later, his voice grew thick just talking about him. He picked up his beer, avoiding her eyes for a moment.

"Why?"

"Why what?"

"Why doesn't he play the lottery? I get the feeling there's more going on here than what you just said."

Johnny took a long drink from his beer, set the glass down, and watched the foam slip down the inside and spread across the amber surface. Kate didn't interrupt the silence but waited for him. When he spoke, he kept his gaze on the glass.

"Jimmy's in the long-term psychiatric care facility at the VA."

"The one on Wilshire?"

"Yeah. He's been there for a long time, pretty much since he came back from 'Nam."

He looked at her, knowing her expression would tell him whether to continue. Her eyes held an unspoken invitation to trust, but he wasn't sure he wanted to cover that old, painful ground with someone he'd just met. He exhaled and looked at the tabletop, concentrating on the small red-and-white squares on the oilcloth covering.

He started slowly and then spoke more rapidly, telling her

of Jimmy's inability to fight the ghosts of Vietnam or forgive himself for the horrors he'd committed while there. He talked of his brother's struggle with drugs and alcohol and his attempted suicides and finally his self-commitment to the hospital.

The waiter appeared just as he finished and set their plates on the table. Johnny poured ketchup on his fries, ate two, and took a bite from his burger. He chewed slowly, thinking about how Kate had gotten him to tell her things he rarely told anyone. No wonder she was good with the kids. She was easy to trust.

The sounds of a young boy shouting, his voice full of energy, drifted from the boardwalk into the restaurant. Johnny looked up as two boys flew past on their skateboards, yelling at each other as they went. One was short and thin, with an enormous earring, his baseball cap on backward. Johnny thought immediately of Billy.

"I know I promised I wouldn't bring this up, but well . . ." He looked at her expectantly, awaiting permission, and she smiled.

"Go ahead."

"Do you think Sara was doing something illegal? Maybe something she and Dallas and Gem were doing together? Something that would piss someone off enough to want to kill them?"

She studied him for a moment, perhaps wondering whether he was joking. She dabbed the edge of her mouth with her napkin, then set it on the table.

"Johnny, I know Sara's death upset you. I can't imagine what it was like trying to get into that house to save her. But to answer your question, no. Those are good kids. They're not criminals. You need to make peace with this. I mean, I don't quite know how to say this but you, well . . ."

"You think I'm overreacting, seeing things that aren't there?"

She was quiet for a moment, and when she did speak, it was obvious that she was picking her words carefully. "It's very hard on all of us when we lose a child. But death is a very real part of life on the street. You have to understand that first. But, more important, ask yourself this: Why bother? I mean, what could possibly be so important that someone would kill them? Johnny, they were street kids. The fact is, most of them have a very short life. Someone once asked me if our kids are runaways and I told him no. They're not runaways, they're throwaways. More of them are going to die before they turn thirty than you want to know about. So why kill them?"

Johnny started to speak but stopped and sat quietly for a moment. "I don't know. But I also don't know why someone beat me up and demanded I give them something I don't have."

"It's a long way from a mugging to murder, don't you think?"

"You know what, I promised not to bring work up and here we are talking about it again. I guess I get a little obsessive sometimes. I don't normally take a woman to dinner and then tell her all my latest conspiracy theories. I guess I'm a little off my game."

She smiled, and the tension between them seemed to break. "Hey, enough of this. No more work stuff, I promise. And this time I mean it. You ever been in the bookstore here?" Johnny waved at Small World Books and the Mystery Annex attached to the café. "It's small but a pretty neat little place."

"No, I've never been."

"Well, you're in for a treat."

They didn't mention Dallas or Sara again, talking instead about growing up in Orange County and the San Fernando Valley.

"Both of my parents were born in California. Can you believe that? Everyone I knew growing up was from someplace else," Kate said.

"Sounds like us. We moved out here from the Midwest when I was only five." He shook his head and rolled his eyes. "To me, family reunions meant a four-day car trip across the country to be kissed by a bunch of powdered-up old women in flowered dresses who I didn't remember ever seeing before."

The waiter cleared their table and brought them coffee. They spent half an hour in the bookstore, then strolled along the boardwalk. Johnny offered Kate his arm, and they walked in that odd fashion that can be a precursor to intimacy or simply an indication of courtesy, until they reached the end of the boardwalk and retraced their steps.

As they talked, Johnny felt an odd mix of nervous energy and total calm. He felt comfortable, as though he'd known Kate for decades but was anxious to please like a teen on a first date. As they approached the restaurant, Kate said, "Venice is a lot like Hollywood, except you don't get the sensation of sleaze you get there. It's hard to describe."

"Maybe it's because Venice never claimed to be anything but what it is. Hollywood is Tinseltown, the Walk of Fame, Venice is the eternal circus."

"I guess."

"Hey, I've got an idea. You can get Carol Holland and the Reverend Roberts to clean up Venice after they conquer the evils of Hollywood."

"Yeah, maybe."

Johnny stopped and turned to face her. He wanted to reach out and touch her arm but left his hands at his side. "What, you don't think much of the Hollywood Restoration Committee?"

Kate gave a half shrug and said, "It's not that. I hope they succeed. It's just that some people equate cleaning up Hollywood with getting rid of all the street kids. I don't know where they think they'll go, but renovating some buildings doesn't mean the kids are going to be any better off. They'll still run away and end up here. Hollywood is always going to be a magnet for kids from all over the country. They're always coming out here to be rock stars and movie stars."

They began walking again, this time side by side, Kate not on his arm.

"How well do you know Carol Holland?"

"I don't really know her at all. I met her for the first time a few weeks ago. We had an open-mike night at the center. Some of the kids sang, or read poetry, one even played a violin. I have no idea where he got it. Anyway, Dick brought her by to watch. I guess he thought it would be fun for the kids to have a movie star watch their performance."

"And?"

"They were impressed, but to tell you the truth, I don't think many of them knew who she was, even after Dick told them."

"She seem pretty straight arrow to you?"

"Yeah, I guess. Why all the questions?"

"I went to her house today and asked her about Dallas. Even showed her the picture. She didn't deny knowing him but she didn't confirm it either. She just danced around it. The funny thing is, I think she lied to me about where she went to high school."

"High school? Where did that come from?"

"She told me she went to Hollywood High, but they don't have any record of her."

"You checked on where she went to high school?" Her tone was halfway between amused and shocked.

"Kate, she's lying about something."

Kate stopped. They were at the end of the open-air stalls that line the boardwalk and give Venice Beach the feel of a swap meet. One vendor was packing his racks of mirrored and colored sunglasses into an old white van. The smell of incense hung in the air. Kate turned the corner and began walking up the street that dead-ended into the boardwalk. They had taken only a few steps when she stopped again.

"Johnny, stop and think about what you're doing here. You're going into squats, checking out a movie star's high school records, I mean, in my experience finding a movie star who lies about her background isn't, well—"

"You think I'm way off base."

"I just don't get the sense that there's a connection to all this."

"You weren't at the fire."

"No, I wasn't. But sometimes distance is a help, not a hurdle. So think about what I said, okay? Anyway, I parked up here. I should probably be getting home. I've got an early meeting in the morning. I had a great time, I really did."

"Me too. It was a lot of fun. I don't get down here very often, but it seemed like a good time to come."

They walked up the block in silence until Kate stopped and pulled keys from her purse and opened the door to a Honda Civic that was at least ten years old and needed washing.

"If you're in Hollywood again, drop by the center. We enjoy having visitors."

Kate pulled the door of her car open and turned to face Johnny.

"Thank you again."

"You're welcome."

"I had a good time."

"Yeah, me too. Say, ah, you know, maybe, I mean, I'd like to see you again, but I don't have your home number. Would it be okay?"

Kate smiled, took a business card from her purse, and wrote her number on the back. "Of course. I'll look forward to it. Thanks again. Bye."

Johnny stood on the curb as she backed out, thinking of what she'd said. He was going into squats, asking about a movie star's high school attendance records. Maybe it was all crazy, except she hadn't been at the fire and she hadn't been attacked, nor had her home been burglarized. He didn't need to understand it all to know he was right.

He'd just started to wave when her brake lights lit and the car stopped. He could hear the buzz of a cell phone and saw Kate lift one to her ear. A moment later she shoved the door open, stepped out quickly, and looked at Johnny. He could see fear in her eyes.

"Gem was in the center," she blurted out.

"Is she going to call me?" But Johnny had heard something in her voice and knew this wasn't good news.

"That was Jan, one of our counselors. She said Gem and Billy came into the center after I left, just minutes before we closed. I think they're running. They had their backpacks and asked for food. They took a bunch of granola bars and a few other things, just about all they could carry. Billy already had a bunch of stuff. He said he'd been to a couple of centers."

"Ah, shit."

"I think they're going to hop a train. That's how Billy travels, and he told Gem two or three times to take a couple of quarts of bottled water."

"Bottled water?"

"If you're in one of the exposed cars, the wind dehydrates you really quickly. The train hoppers always try to carry lots of water."

"Where will they go? Downtown? Union Station?"

"I don't know. I don't know much about train hopping. I just know that's how Billy and some of the other kids get around."

"I gotta go." He stepped from the curb and started past the car.

"Johnny, wait a second."

"What?"

"I, ah . . ." She hesitated. "I'm beginning to think you're right about the violence. I think those kids are in danger. Jan said they both seemed really scared. Johnny, I think you should call the police."

"And tell them what? That a scared street kid is leaving LA? No, I don't have time. I've got to find Gem. I'll call you soon."

"Johnny, wait!" she called, but he was already running down the alley toward the lot where he'd left his car.

Fourteen

•━━━━━━━━━━━━━━━━•

He stopped once for three minutes at a convenience store to buy a flashlight and was in Hollywood not long after dark. He parked in a red zone half a block from the bridge squat and ran up the sidewalk toward it. At the on-ramp, he had to stop as three cars turned down it in front of him. He was in too big a hurry getting over the short wall, and he fell on the other side and slid a few feet. He swore under his breath, picked up the flashlight, and moved cautiously down the slope to the squat.

The door still hung open and he stepped in. This time the smell of feces was cut by the odor of marijuana and incense. A candle flickered in a puddle of wax a few feet inside the door, giving the place an eerie half-light, like a cave. Johnny saw two kids lying on sleeping bags atop the carpet he'd seen earlier in the day. He could distinguish neither their age nor gender. He flicked the flashlight on and shined it on the two. One rolled and looked at him, holding up a hand to shade his eyes from the light. He didn't recognize either one.

"Hey, what the fuck . . ."

"Who are you? What do you want? Get out of here."

The voices came from different places under the bridge, and Johnny swept the light across the area. He saw Spider and three kids he'd talked to earlier in My Home near the top

155

of the slope. He pointed the beam to the ground near his feet but didn't turn it off.

"It's Johnny Rose. I talked to you at My Home. I need your help."

None of the kids said a word, and the space was filled with the noise of the freeway underneath them. A heavy truck rumbled across the bridge just feet above their heads, and the vibrations felt like the precursor to an earthquake. When the noise died, Johnny tried again.

"Gem's in trouble. I'm trying to help her. I need to know where she went."

"She left, man. That's all we know." Johnny recognized Spider's voice. He turned the beam on Spider and saw Bear, the boy from the center, sitting next to him.

"Spider, I know they're going to hop a train, just tell me where to look. That's all."

They were silent, and Johnny turned off the light and walked slowly up the slope toward them, stepping carefully among the trash. His eyes were adjusting to the darkness now, and the candle threw a huge shadow ahead of him onto the wall and the kids. He could see the pinpoint of red light where a stick of incense burned near Spider. Johnny stopped just a few feet down the slope from them and lowered himself to his haunches.

"Spider, I think the same person that killed Sara and Dallas wants to hurt Gem and maybe Billy. I don't know who or why but I've got to find them. I've got to at least talk to Gem."

"I don't know Gem, she's Billy's friend," Spider said. Johnny looked at him for a moment but knew he'd get nothing more from the boy. He turned to Bear.

"Okay, just tell me this. Where do you go to hop a train here in LA? Would you go downtown, near Union Station?"

"No." Bear said. "The freight yards. On Washington, near East LA. By the freeway bridge there's a place where all the tracks run next to each other. That's where you go."

"Thanks." He stood up and walked slowly to the door,

keeping the flashlight off, listening to the noise of the traffic but hearing only the silence of the street kids behind him.

The LA freight yards, an expanse of asphalt and tracks eating up more acreage than most stadium parking lots, was ablaze with lights, a snake bed of motion. Trains rolled up and back, and tractor-trailer rigs loaded with containers moved through the yard.

From the edge of it, Johnny could see the 710 freeway arching over on a high bridge, headlights forming a white-lined blur. He punched the Z and headed into the yard, swerving past cargo haulers and pickups as he drove toward the bridge, adjusting his course as he went, snaking across the blacktop, aiming always for dead center of the bridge. Moments later, he stopped next to a massive cement support column at the outer edge of the bridge, climbed from the car, and stood with the door open looking over the roof, scanning the area. A breeze blew from the west, and the smell of oil and diesel permeated the air. He could hear the hum of traffic on the bridge high above him. As he realized the size of the area under the bridge, his hopes sank. He could spend a long time searching the shadows and darkness beneath it and still miss them.

"Gem, Gem. It's Johnny Rose. I need to talk to you," he called, but it was useless. His voice was buried under the noise of traffic, diesel engines, tractor-trailer rigs, and rolling stock.

He slapped the Z's top in frustration and looked back toward the yard where boxcars, tankers, and flatbeds sat in parallel lines like dominoes on a board, creating another warren of hiding places. Gem and Billy could be anywhere. Maybe they'd already hopped a train and were halfway to Phoenix or Sacramento.

"Shit," he swore. He got in the car and followed the blacktop under the bridge heading east. On his left, five sets of tracks ran parallel under the bridge, heading east out of the yard. To his right, the blacktop was interspersed with tracks, and finally, at the far side of the freight yard, the freeway bridge descended and met the earth again just beyond the edge of the yard. A final lone set of tracks bent out of the yard and ran behind the backyards of tract houses that bordered the railroad property.

His impatience and frustration were mounting, and he stopped midway under the bridge, got out, walked to the edge of the blacktop, and looked at the multitude of tracks. The first two pairs of rails were empty, but on the third a train rolled slowly eastward. Stepping carefully over the rails, Johnny moved to the center of the second set of track, just a few feet from the rolling stock, and looked up and back. Down the track a line of cars awaited a locomotive. A man wearing an orange hard hat walked beside the cars, a series of flatbeds double-stacked with containers, inspecting each as he went.

"Hey, hey," Johnny shouted and trotted toward him. The man turned and watched Johnny approach. When Johnny got close, he took two quick breaths and said, "Have you seen a couple of kids? Train hoppers?"

"Train hoppin's against the law. I never tell anyone where to hop a train." The man turned away quickly and looked at the train rolling past them, pretending to study the cars.

"Look, I'm not a cop. I'm not with the railroad. Nobody's gonna get you in trouble." As the worker watched, the train slowed and stopped, but he continued to stare at it. "Okay, look, someone told me the kids hop the trains over there." Johnny waved toward the bridge. "Is that right? You must know that. Is that where I should look?"

"What's so special about those two, anyway? Everybody looking for 'em like they wuz Bonnie and Clyde or something."

"Everybody? What do you mean, everybody?" Johnny stepped next to the man.

The worker turned and looked at Johnny, only inches away. He was as tall as Johnny, black and strong with rough hands and a pockmarked face with the white stubble of a poorly shaved beard. But from this short distance, his eyes were gentle, and he seemed to find something in Johnny's face because his gruff manner disappeared.

"Two other guys were here looking for 'em. 'Bout half an hour ago," he said, his voice soft, almost apologetic.

"What did you tell 'em?"

The train on the parallel tracks started again suddenly, its movement so smooth and silent, Johnny almost didn't notice it. The worker looked toward the bridge.

"I told 'em the hobos sometimes go out east and catch a train after it leaves the yard. But I don't think they believed me. Look over there, I think that's them."

Johnny could see the dark outlines of two men walking slowly near the far side of the bridge, playing the beams of flashlights along the ground like they were searching for lost coins.

"Shit," Johnny swore. "Did you see the kids?"

"Back under the bridge," the man said quickly, then turned and walked away, his pace picking up as he moved.

Johnny looked back along the tracks. The noise of a tractor-trailer rig braking suddenly and the bleat of its air horn sounded under the bridge. Johnny saw two people burst through the truck's headlights inches from its grill and run toward the moving train. Their backpacks bounced, giving them an odd gait, slowing them. Johnny saw Gem's bright blonde hair. Billy was a few steps ahead of her.

Johnny looked at the far side of the bridge. The men with flashlights had seen them too. One of them yelled, and Johnny caught a wisp of the sound but couldn't distinguish the words. Gem and Billy had a head start, and the men had to wait to get around the truck. But the men, unburdened by backpacks, were much faster.

Johnny sprinted toward Gem and Billy, hoping to get to them before the flashlights. His heart was pounding and his feet unsure on the rough granite gravel. He could hear the huge steel wheels grinding on the tracks two feet away as the train rolled next to him. He was moving faster than the train, and he quickly passed a flatbed and an oil tanker, but Johnny was a distance runner, not a sprinter, and his lungs screamed quickly and his legs ached as he ran at the train's side.

He looked at the two men angling from his right. They had closed the gap, but if he could just keep up the pace, he was sure he'd reach Billy and Gem first. He looked ahead. Billy and Gem were beside the train now, running with it as it gained speed. He passed two more cars, coming closer to Billy and Gem.

He could hear the men now closing in from his right. They were yelling, "Stop! Hey you, stop!" They, too, were quickly gaining on the two street kids.

Billy and Gem were running next to an open boxcar, shrugging their backpacks off as they went. Billy tossed his in and trotted alongside. Gem was just a few feet behind. She caught up to him a second later, and the boy threw her backpack into the boxcar. He grabbed an iron handhold and pulled himself up in a quick, practiced, sure move. He hung off the train, his left foot on the bottom rung of the steps to the car.

"Come on, Gem. You can do it!" Billy yelled, his voice high and full of fear, excitement, and promised escape.

Johnny saw the next few seconds as though they were in slow motion. The train was rolling, not terribly fast but picking up speed. Gem stumbled and Billy reached for her and his foot slipped from the rung. A second later his right leg was under the train. The iron wheels snipped it off with cold indifference, and the train rolled on. Billy's agony rang through the train yard. Gem screamed hysterically.

Johnny reached them seconds later. Gem was at Billy's side. Her breath came in huge gulps, and Johnny had to fight the impulse to vomit. The train was moving quickly now, creating its own noise and wind, the steel wheels grinding, the cars starting to rock slightly. Johnny grabbed Billy and pulled him away from the track, bumping him across the rough granite gravel, leaving a trail of blood. Billy screamed as the stub of his leg bounced off the gravel. Gem scrambled after them. The leg was severed just below the knee. Billy was quickly slipping into shock, and his screams diminished.

Johnny jerked his belt out and tied a tourniquet on the leg, although the weight of the train had smashed the leg so completely it almost sealed the skin, like dough pressed along the edge of a pie plate. The men with flashlights hesitated and stood in the shadows watching as two rail workers, who had heard the screams, jogged down the tracks from the yard.

"Help! Help! A kid's been hurt. His leg's cut off," Johnny screamed to be heard across the distance. One of the rail workers stopped and pulled a walkie-talkie from his belt and began talking. The other kept coming, his hard hat bouncing as he ran. A moment later both rail workers were there.

"Holy shit," the first one said and turned away. The second grabbed his walkie-talkie again and started speaking rapidly, stumbling over his own words as he spoke.

From his knees at Billy's side, Johnny looked up at the two who had chased Billy. They were back under the bridge, almost hidden by the shadows, walking slowly away.

"Those men, you've got to stop them. They were chasing the kids. They're responsible," Johnny said. The rail workers exchanged a glance but did nothing. He looked at Billy, who lay on his back in the gravel staring at the underside of the bridge high in the night. Johnny stood and for a second thought of chasing them but glanced at Gem, who sat hugging her knees on the gravel, rocking and staring at the wheels of the passing train. He followed her gaze and saw the end of Billy's leg lying between the tracks, the cloth cut evenly and bloodied at the end, Billy's shoe still tied tightly to the foot. He moved to her and lowered himself to the gravel next to her, putting his arm around her shoulder.

"It's okay, Gem. He's going to be all right. The paramedics are on their way. It's going to be okay. It's going to be okay." They lapsed into a silence strong enough to shut out the industrial sounds of freeways and freight trains, and Johnny pulled her close and she leaned against him.

Within minutes a crowd had gathered. Johnny stood and walked to the edge of the small crowd that had formed around Billy. The tough, hardened rail workers looked at the small boy with the severed leg, and Johnny saw them divert their eyes to the ground and mumble platitudes about how it was a shame, and how dangerous hopping trains was and how they wished someone would tell these kids. They said these and other things because it was the only defense they could mount against such instant and predictable tragedy. One of the men had a first-aid kit and was trying to help Billy.

Johnny walked back to Gem and once again lowered himself to the ground next to her. The police and paramedics arrived almost simultaneously. The two cops, one a short, thin Asian and the other a Hispanic with large shoulders and a round face, moved everyone back from the scene.

The Hispanic cop approached Johnny and Gem and stopped a few feet away.

"I'm Officer Castro. I understand you saw what happened here. Can you give us a statement, Mr. . . . ah?"

"Rose. Johnny Rose." He looked at Gem and nodded. "They were trying to hop a train. The boy got up on the lower rung and slipped."

"The two of them, the boy and the girl?" He nodded at Gem.

"Yeah."

"One of the men I just talked to said you saw someone chasing them?"

"Yes, two men with flashlights. They were over there, under the bridge."

"Hmmm. Mr. Rose, would you mind talking to my partner over there while I talk to the girl."

"I'd like to stay with her."

"I'd like to talk to her alone. Would you mind giving your statement to Officer Yamada? Thank you." Castro's request was polite but firm and not really a request at all.

As Johnny stood, the paramedics were loading Billy into the back of the van. He walked to its side.

"Is he going to make it?" Johnny asked.

The paramedic, a young woman with a thick blonde braid down the middle of her back, looked at him with kind blue eyes. "I hope so," she said as she shoved the door closed. As the back door swung closed, Johnny got a glimpse of the lower part of Billy's leg, which had been loaded into the van. The shoe was still on the foot.

When Johnny turned, Yamada was waiting. "So, can you give me a brief rundown on what happened here? Let's start with your name."

Johnny turned and looked behind him and saw Castro squatted on his haunches talking with Gem. He looked back at Yamada and quickly told him the story, but the cop had questions. Twice he asked why Johnny was there. Was he sure the kids weren't running from him? Could he describe the two men with flashlights? Who were they? Where had they come from? When Yamada was finally done, Johnny turned and saw Castro standing alone beside the tracks. Gem was gone. He ran to the cop's side.

"Where's the girl? Where's the girl?" He could feel the panic swell inside him.

Castro looked behind him and shrugged. "Sara? She left, I guess."

Johnny scanned the rails, peering into the darkness, and turned and looked into the yard, trying to see details in the shadows among cars and the freight haulers, but as hard as he tried he could see no signs of her. Suddenly, it hit him.

"What did you call her?"

"She told me her name was Sara, ah,"—he looked at his notes—"Sara Bradley, from Atlanta. Why?"

Johnny looked at the cop for a moment, then shrugged. "I only knew her by her street name, Gem."

"Oh."

"But you didn't see her leave?" Johnny asked.

"No, sorry."

He walked to the car, despair settling across his soul like coal dust.

It was not far from sunrise when Johnny finished with the cops and the railroad inspectors and finally drove slowly out of the yard. In the distance he could just make out the tops of the skyscrapers in downtown LA, some of the offices still lit as the cleaning crews finished their work.

As he headed home on the Santa Monica Freeway, he thought of the empty apartment waiting for him and knew he'd never sleep but would sit in the dark, seeing Billy slip under the train and worrying about Gem. Near Overland Avenue he moved to the right lane, took the exit, found a pay phone at a gas station, and called Kate. The phone rang four times before she answered.

"Hello." She sounded alert, but sleep was evident in her voice.

"I'm sorry, I didn't know who else to call."

"Johnny?"

"Yeah. Look, I, ah . . . I." He looked away from the phone toward the gas pumps and back again. "Billy's been hurt. It's pretty bad. I don't know where Gem is. She's disappeared. I need . . ."

"Johnny, do you want to come over?"

"Yes."

"Where are you?"

"Overland and the Santa Monica Freeway."

She gave him directions, and fifteen minutes later he parked on the street and walked up the driveway past a tract house to a small cottage in the rear on a large lot. Kate watched him come and pushed open the screen door and stepped onto the small covered porch. In the yellow hue from the porch light, Johnny could see the worry in her eyes. He stepped onto the porch, and she reached up and hugged him in a comforting way. He stood bent over her, his arms around her, pulling her close, feeling the warmth of her body.

"Come in, I've made some herbal tea," she said, holding the door for him. "Sit over there." She pointed to a long sofa with a low back against the wall of the living room. He took the room in quickly, seeing the small television on the stand with wheels, a boom box on top of it. A framed Edward Hopper poster hung on the wall behind the couch. A small round table with a short, fat red candle in the middle stood next to a foam chair that looked as if it folded into a futon bed. It rested a few feet from the sofa. A doorway led to a bedroom off the living room, and Johnny could see the edge of a four-poster bed, a blue-and-white spread hanging down inches from the floor.

He lowered himself onto the couch, lay his head back against the cushion, stared at the ceiling, and listened to Kate getting the mugs from the cupboard and pouring the tea.

"Here." Kate stood over him a moment later, holding out a mug, steam rising from it. Johnny shifted slightly, took the mug, and sipped the tea as Kate pulled the futon chair across the hardwood until it was next to the couch.

"What happened?"

"They were trying to get on a moving train. Billy was." He stopped for a moment and took another sip of tea, seeing the accident again and hearing Billy's scream. "Billy was . . ." Johnny could hear his voice start to crack, and he cleared his throat. "Billy reached back for Gem and slipped. His right leg went under the train. It was amputated just below the knee."

"Oh, my God." Her hand fluttered to her mouth. Johnny looked away and sucked air deep into his lungs. "Is he . . . ?"

"They don't know. He was in shock. They're taking him to County USC."

"I'll go down today."

"Yeah." They were quiet, and Johnny sipped his tea again and looked at her. She wore sweatpants and a T-shirt, and her hair was disheveled and spiky. Worry pulled at the corners of her eyes. "Kate, someone was already there, in the freight yard. Two men. They chased Billy and Gem to that train. They took off as soon as Billy fell."

"Who?"

"I don't know."

"What do they want?" He said nothing. "How did they know they'd be there?"

The weight of all the deaths and pain and the questions he was powerless to answer piled on him, and suddenly it was more than he could shoulder.

"I don't understand any of it." He took a deep breath, but it didn't seem to help. "Jesus, what's happening? I got there too late for Sara and too late for Billy," he said and leaned his head back.

"Look, why don't you just lie down for a few minutes? Just get a little rest."

"I can't, I should go."

"No, you shouldn't. Look, it's six. Sleep till seven. That's just an hour. I'll wake you, I promise."

"Gem, I mean Kate, I should . . ." But Kate stood and looked down at him until he nodded his agreement and stretched out. A few seconds later he was asleep.

At ten after seven, she shook his shoulder gently and Johnny woke with a start. He sat up and stared ahead, disoriented, his eyes blurry. He rubbed his face with his hands and slowly shook his head from side to side.

"You take milk or sugar?" Kate held out a mug of coffee.

"Ah, normally I take milk but right now black is just fine," he said and took a long swallow. "Thank you, it's great."

"You're welcome," she said. "Johnny, I'm going to the hospital this morning, on my way to work. Why don't I call you and let you know how Billy is?"

"Thanks, I'd appreciate that."

"Okay, I'm going to head out. Stay as long as you want. There's more coffee in the kitchen. Just pull the door closed when you leave, okay?"

"Sure." She turned to leave, but Johnny leaned forward and grabbed her hand.

"Ah, Kate, thank you for this morning."

"I'm glad you came."

"Me too."

She smiled, turned, and walked out the door.

He moved slowly and drank another cup of coffee, staring out the window above the kitchen sink, then rinsed the cup and turned it upside down on the drain board.

Johnny was on his way out the door when he stopped and retreated to the telephone. He didn't expect a message but still hoped she'd called. He dialed the *Journal* first, and the message on his voice-mail startled him.

"Rose, I just left a message at your house," Kuscyk growled. "If you pick this up, get your ass in gear and get down here. Do it now! You can explain it to me when you get here and it better be good."

Johnny listened, hoping there was more, but the message ended abruptly. He put the phone down slowly, looked at it for a moment, then went to the bathroom, rinsed his face, and ran his fingers through his hair. He looked in the mirror but barely recognized the face he saw there. The man who looked back at him was older, with dark circles under his eyes and worry etched deep in his forehead. For a moment he thought of going straight to the office but knew he had to go home, shower, and get fresh clothes. He could still hear the urgency in Kuscyk's voice, but he'd just have to wait.

Fifteen

————————•————•————————

Kuscyk jerked his thumb upward toward the ceiling. "Come on, we're going upstairs. Knight's got some lawyers up there. His secretary called and told me to bring you up there the moment you got in."

The metro editor stood and moved past Johnny down the aisle toward the hallway and elevator. "No sense keeping Knight waiting."

Lawrence Knight was the *Journal*'s publisher. The paper was part of the Delaware Group, a chain of papers in mid-size cities and towns across the United States. The *Journal* was the group's only major market holding. At each paper, the publisher was given wide latitude to run things as he wanted. As long as the paper made a healthy profit, no one at corporate headquarters cared what went between the ads.

In the elevator, Kuscyk stared at the door and spoke without looking at Johnny. "Okay, Rose, who are these lawyers and what do they want?"

"They're probably from the railroad."

Kuscyk punched the emergency stop button and turned to face him. Johnny could hear an alarm bell in the distance.

"The railroad? What the hell's this?"

"A kid was maimed in the freight yard last night. His leg was severed below the knee."

"So?"

168

"I was there."

"Ah, shit, Rose. Tell me."

"He was being chased, and he started to get up on this moving train and he slipped."

"No, Rose. Stop. Tell me from the beginning. But do it fast, Knight's waiting."

"Sorry, I'm just really tired." Johnny told him about searching the yard for Billy and Gem and seeing the men chasing them.

"But you had nothing to do with those kids trying to get on the train? Nothing to do with them being in the yard? You were just there to interview them, right?"

"Yeah, that's right."

"Okay, one last question. You went there to interview this girl, this Gem?"

"Yeah."

"So, it's related to the arson story?"

"Yes, but I don't know how."

"Okay, we won't get into that. You went there because you had to talk to the girl for a story and had heard she was leaving and might be in trouble. No, on second thought, don't say anything about her being in trouble. You just wanted to interview her and you didn't have time to go through Union Pacific's PR department. That's it, right?"

"Yeah, I guess."

"Okay, okay. Let's just keep it at that," he said, feeling confident they had their story ready for the lawyers. Anything beyond that, the paper's own attorney would handle. He pulled the emergency stop button out, and the elevator continued for a few moments and slid to a stop. Kuscyk was first out the door.

The conference room was in a corner with windows on two walls, recessed ceiling lights, and a large oval table of polished walnut. Knight was halfway down the table, the two lawyers at the far end, their backs to a window ablaze in the morning sun. Johnny had to squint to see them. But he could make out their dark suits, white shirts, and striped ties.

One was about sixty, perhaps a few years older, and the other not much past thirty. A closed briefcase rested flat on the table in front of each. Kuscyk moved to the middle of the table near Knight, and Johnny slipped into the seat closest to the door.

"Thank you for joining us, gentlemen," Knight said. "This is Charles Carruthers and Michael Patrick." He waved nonchalantly at the two lawyers. "They're with Chatham, Carruthers, Sondheim, and Feist."

The young attorney, Michael Patrick, stood, leaned over the table, and held out a business card to Kuscyk, who rose halfway from his chair and stretched past Knight to take it. The lawyer turned toward the end of the table, but when Johnny made no effort to get up, he sat down again.

"They represent Carol Holland," Knight said.

"Who?" Kuscyk barked.

"Carol Holland, the actress," Knight said. Kuscyk looked at Johnny, his eyes asking "What the hell's this?" Johnny's shoulders raised, a half shrug.

"Johnny," Knight continued, "Mr. Carruthers told me that you showed up at Carol Holland's house yesterday and tried to interview her without telling her you were coming. Is that true?"

Johnny struggled to remember, to sort the brief conversation from the flood tide of yesterday's events. They were all watching him, waiting for him to speak.

"Yes, I went up there." He stopped for a moment and sat a little straighter. "She tell you about the murdered boy who was found near her house? She tell you he used to work for her?"

"Mr. Rose," Patrick said. "We're not here to talk about something that happened in Ms. Holland's neighborhood. We're here to talk about you."

"Me? I'm not the one who hired a day laborer who got murdered and dumped on a hillside not far from my house."

"Mr. Rose, we're not here to talk about that."

"So why are you here?"

"Let me start by saying we are staunch defenders of freedom of speech and we believe a free press is essential to the well-being of our democracy, and having said that, I'll tell you why we're here. We've come to insist personally that you stop harassing Miss Holland."

Johnny laughed. It was an involuntary reflex born of exhaustion and a sense of disbelief at what he was hearing. "You're kidding, right?" Neither lawyer spoke. "That wasn't harassment. I didn't accuse her of anything. I asked her if she knew the dead boy. I showed her a picture of the boy and asked her if it was taken in her backyard. That's not harassment. If I want to harass her, she'll know it."

"Mr. Rose, it may be true that one of the youths she occasionally hires died under unfortunate circumstances. But for you to try and somehow connect her to that unfortunate incident is far beyond the bounds of good journalism."

"What's she hiding, Mr. Patrick? I mean, why are you really here?"

"Mr. Rose, we realize Carol Holland is a public figure, and that gives you a certain license. But you should know she has a publicist who handles all media requests for interviews. In the future, if you want to talk to her, you'll go through her publicist."

Johnny looked from Patrick to Kuscyk, who shook his head slowly side to side, telling Johnny to let it go.

"Johnny," Knight said and waited until the reporter looked at him. "I've told Mr. Carruthers that the *Journal* won't abandon any stories that we think are legitimate and that is not negotiable. But I've also assured him you'll be happy to forward any future requests for interviews with Miss Holland through the studio. I think that's a fair solution. I personally don't believe in ambush interviews."

"Ambush? I didn't ambush her, I just went—"

"Can I ask a question?" Kuscyk interrupted. "What the hell's the lady afraid of? I just wandered into this, so I'm a little behind the game here, but helping some street kid isn't a federal offense, even if the kid ends up dead. What? She think *Hard Copy*'s going to make it their lead story tonight? Why don't you answer his question. What's this really about?"

Patrick started to speak, but Carruthers laid his hand gently on the young man's arm and he stopped in midword.

"What is this really about?" Carruthers asked. "Miss Holland has dedicated herself to the Hollywood Restoration Committee. She is the spokesperson for it. She believes in its mission. Now she's afraid that she will become the focus of the media, not the committee and its work. Frankly, she wants to help the street kids in Hollywood and she thinks you're getting in the way."

Kuscyk coughed and shook his head slowly from side to side, like a parent disappointed in his children. "You know, I think that's a load of crap. What's the lady really worried about? You tell us that and maybe we have a chance of making some kind of fair, honest judgment here."

Johnny smiled to himself, but he didn't look at Kuscyk; he was watching Knight, trying to judge his reaction. But the publisher sat silently and showed no emotion.

"I resent what you're implying, but at least you're direct. I'll give you that. Let me be equally direct," Carruthers said as he shifted his gaze from Kuscyk to Johnny. "If you attempt to interview Miss Holland again without going through her publicist, we'll seek a restraining order. I doubt we'll have any trouble obtaining one. In fact, I've already had one drawn up. We can file it at any time.

"Miss Holland's efforts to help the homeless may not be important to *Hard Copy,* but being stalked by a reporter for a supposedly legitimate newspaper would be. I'm sure you can see my point."

Carruthers stood; Patrick was on his feet a half beat behind. Carruthers turned to Knight and nodded. "Mr. Knight, I appreciate your seeing us on such short notice. I believe our position is clear."

"Yes, you've made yourself very clear," Knight said. He

stood, and the three men shook hands. "I'll be glad to escort you to the elevator," Knight said.

"That won't be necessary. We can show ourselves out," Carruthers said.

As they walked past the table, the young lawyer stopped at Johnny's side, looked at him for a moment as though he were a cockroach scurrying across the linoleum, then laid a business card in front of him.

"It's Carol's publicist's card. If you have any questions, you'll know who to call. It's his direct line."

Johnny pushed the card with the end of his finger until it was facing him and looked at the lawyer but said nothing. The two left the room, and as the door closed, Johnny looked back to Knight. Even from the end of the table Johnny could see a vein pulsating in his temple. He was watching the door the men had just gone through.

"Fucking lawyers," he said. He was quiet for a moment, then shifted his gaze to Kuscyk. "You want to know what that's about? This is about Melvin Plank. Chatham, Carruthers, Sondheim, and Feist represent Plank and all his businesses. So my guess is"—he looked at Johnny—"you pissed her off somehow and she went running to him and he sent his lawyers to deliver the message. It doesn't really matter. They're smart enough not to make a direct threat, but it's pretty obvious. If we keep bothering her, we'll lose all the ads for his grocery stores and other businesses, including his real estate. That's not a small amount of revenue."

Knight looked at Kuscyk. "I don't know what the story is you're working, but we'll do just what I told them. Johnny can keep going on it, but don't go near that actress without talking to her flack first. Keep this thing under control."

"This is bullshit," Johnny said.

Knight's eyes flared, but his voice was calm. "Maybe. I don't like some lawyer dictating our business any more than you do. But I won't have you questioning my judgment. Is that clear?"

"Yeah," he said.

"Good. I also don't want anyone pissing off one of my biggest advertisers for no purpose. Is that clear too?" He waited a moment, then turned to face Johnny. He said it again, drawing the question out. "Is . . . that . . . clear?"

"Yeah. I got it." Johnny stood.

"It's clear," Kuscyk added. "I'll keep an eye on it."

Knight was still standing near the end of the table when Johnny and the metro editor walked from the room. They didn't speak until they were in the elevator.

"Damn, Johnny, sometimes I wonder about you. What the hell's the point in pissing off Knight?"

"Look, Stan, it's been a long twenty-four hours. I'm not in the mood."

"Well, you'd better get in the mood." They rode in silence for a moment. Kuscyk exhaled, puffing out his cheeks as he blew the air out. "Okay, you think Holland's really concerned about the Hollywood Restoration Committee, or is there more to this?"

"There's more to it."

"Is it tied to that boy who was dumped on the hillside or the fire?"

"I don't know, but she's hiding something."

The elevator stopped, and Kuscyk stepped out, turned, and looked at Johnny. "Find out what the hell's going on," he said.

"I will."

"Good. Oh, by the way. I said I'd try to get a line on that Clay Griffin character."

"You find anything?"

Kuscyk smiled. "You know, it was kind of fun digging again. Made me feel like I was doing something worthwhile for a change. Anyway, he's a CPA by training but does personal finance and business management for the high-net-worth crowd. Everything from making your investments to helping you buy a pedigreed dog. Keeps a pretty low profile."

"So what the hell's he care about a street kid?"

"How would I know? You're the reporter, you find out. You can do it in your spare time, when you're not sifting through Carol Holland's garbage."

Kuscyk was chuckling when he walked away.

At his desk, Johnny started to sign on to his computer but stopped. He had hours, maybe days of legwork ahead of him, but there was something he needed to do before he started. He reached for the phone, hesitated a moment, then picked it up and dialed. Maggie answered almost immediately.

"Hi, Maggie, how are you?"

"Hi. I guess I'm doing okay. I'm keeping myself busy with chores and errands. I'm thinking of going back to work tomorrow, maybe the next day. I gotta have something to do. I can't just stay here. I think about it too much. Like today. I was walking through the grocery store looking at the cereal and I saw one Sara liked as a kid, and it hit me again. She's never coming home." Her voice thickened, but she didn't cry. He could hear her suck in a deep breath. "I'll get through this. I have to for Annie's sake. She needs me now. I mean, it's just the two of us."

"I know you will. You're a strong lady, Maggie."

"I don't feel particularly strong right now."

"Yeah," he said, but his mind was elsewhere, thinking of what Gem had told him. He didn't want to tell her, not now. But there would never be a good time.

"Ah, Maggie, there's something I need to tell you. It's about Sara."

"Oh, Christ, what now?"

"You remember I talked about a friend of Sara's? A girl named Gem?"

"Yeah, so?"

"I saw her, talked to her about Sara. I asked her about the card she sent Annie."

"What did she say?" Johnny could hear the apprehension in her voice.

"Maggie, Sara was pregnant."

"Oh, Jesus." The phone was quiet for a second, and then she spoke. "Is there no end to this?"

Suddenly she abandoned all attempts at control, making no effort to speak or disappear in the invisibility distance provided. Her sobs filled the line, and Johnny felt tears in his own eyes as he listened to her pain, as clear and sharp as the summer sun in the desert.

"I think it's what . . ." He had to stop and swallow hard to clear his throat before going on. "I think it's what she meant about why she was afraid you'd be mad at her."

"I can't take any more. God, I can't." He could hear her crying quietly, and her breathing became ragged. Slowly her crying ebbed, and after a few minutes she spoke again. "This is the hardest thing I've ever done. I wouldn't wish this pain on anyone."

"I know," he said, although in truth he had no idea of the desolation losing a child can visit on a person.

"Look, I gotta go. Okay? Call me soon," she said abruptly.

"Okay, we'll talk in a day or two. Bye, Maggie. Tell Annie I love her. You, too, you know that."

"Of course. Oh, Johnny, wait!"

"What?"

"Can you do one thing for me?"

"Of course."

"Tell Jeff, will you? Tell him about her being pregnant. He should know, but I don't think I could stand talking to him right now."

"Sure. I'll take care of it."

He jotted the numbers in his notebook, hung up, and stared at the blank screen in front of him. Suddenly the job seemed almost too big, almost hopeless.

Sixteen

●────────────────●

*J*ournalists are often drawn to the profession by a sense of glamour, an idea that people will read their bylines and remember their words. In truth, more people probably will read their names in the phone book than in the paper, and the pressure of deadlines will flatten their prose, often leaving it as compelling as a grocery list. But for many young reporters, the biggest surprise is how demanding reporting—getting the information and getting it right—can be, and few develop a real appetite for the digging, the endless interviews, the questions, and the rejections that are the foundation of every good story. But the best reporters understand that the more you know before you ask your first question, the greater the odds of success.

Johnny's first move was to look for Tracy Biggs, the *Journal*'s movie critic. His digging had started.

He found her outside on the edge of the sidewalk, smoking. Her right elbow rested in the palm of her left hand as the cigarette she held loitered near her mouth. She stared with a bored indifference at the side street that bordered the *Journal*'s offices. About fifty-five and with wide, full hips and stout legs, she dyed her hair jet black and wore bright red lipstick and gold hoop earrings. She watched Johnny approach but was silent until he spoke.

"Hey, Tracy, you got a minute?"

"I don't know. I'm working real hard on getting lung cancer here. But I guess I can spare a minute or two. Why?" Her voice was raspy, showing the effects years of smoking can have on vocal cords.

"I need some information about an actress, Carol Holland."

Tracy took a long drag, turned her head up and away from Johnny, and blew the smoke out. "Why? You thinking of changing beats? Maybe rub elbows with the rich and famous." She looked at him and smiled. "Might do you some good. You should get out more often anyway. Maybe get your ashes hauled once in a while."

"Do you know her?"

"Of course." She flicked an ash from the end of her cigarette. "Not much to tell. She had an okay run. Actually has some idea how to act, which is no guarantee of success but doesn't usually hurt too much either. Why?" She dropped her hand, holding the cigarette out from her side.

"I'm working on a story. She may be involved in some way, I'm not really sure."

"Oh, yeah, you covered that save-Hollywood press conference she held a few days ago, didn't you?"

"Yes."

"I was afraid Kuscyk was going to stick me with it."

"I got it and now I'm following up. So what else can you tell me about her?"

"Not much. She's got a movie coming out in a few months. Thanksgiving release, I think. Her husband produced it."

"Melvin Plank?"

"The same."

"I didn't know he was in the movie business."

Tracy laughed and dropped the cigarette onto the pavement and stepped on the glowing butt, grinding it into the cement with the toe of her shoe. "He's not. He just put up the money."

"That makes him a producer?"

"Sweetheart, in this town if you put up enough money you can be anything you want. Look." She started back along the sidewalk toward the door and hooked Johnny's arm in hers as she passed him. They walked together toward the door. "Plank and Holland got married maybe six or eight years ago. She's done a couple of made-for-TV movies since then, but that's about it. Couldn't get much else."

"If she's good, why couldn't she get more work?"

Tracy stopped and looked at Johnny without releasing his arm. "You're joking, right? She's too old. In Hollywood, if you're over thirty, you're too old. And believe me, if Carol Holland couldn't get a part, nobody could. That is one determined broad."

"So she gets Plank to put up the money when no one else will and she gets to be a star again. Is that it?"

"Exactly. She gets a movie and he gets a write-off on his taxes. Everybody wins. Isn't capitalism grand?" She laughed and went on. "Of course, a few of the more cynical people I know think that's what the whole marriage was about in the first place. He gets the trophy wife, she gets to be a star again. Successful marriages have been built on less."

"What's the movie about?"

"She plays an alcoholic woman trying to hang on to her teenage daughter. Family drama. Tearjerker. Early buzz is that she gives a hell of a performance. Could revive her career."

They had reached the door, and Tracy didn't wait for Johnny to open it. She pushed through, stopped a few feet inside, and looked at Johnny. "That help?"

"Yes. But there's one more thing. You have any idea where she went to high school?"

"High school? Man, you're really into this, aren't you?"

"Do you know?"

"No. Why do you care?"

"Just checking. Thanks for your help."

"Hey, there's a file on her in the system. Maybe you can

find it there. Let me know if you want anything more."

"Great, I'll check it out."

A pink "While You Were Out" slip was taped to Johnny's computer when he got back to his desk: *Reverend Richard Roberts called. Please call him.*

Roberts himself answered on the first ring. "This is Reverend Roberts, how may I help you?"

"Hi, Dick, it's Johnny. I just got your message."

"Thanks for calling. I've got someone coming in here in a minute, so I'll get right to it. Can you drop by? There's something I need to talk to you about. It's pretty important."

"Sure. When?"

"I've got to be at the halfway house until a little after four. So, say about five?"

"That's fine. What's this about, Dick?"

"I'd rather not say on the phone. We'll talk when you get here, okay?"

"Sure."

Johnny replaced the receiver slowly, wondering what could be important enough to prompt Roberts's call. He looked away from the phone, flipped open his notebook, signed on to his computer, and found the *Journal*'s scant files on Carol Holland. It took less than fifteen minutes to read the puff pieces, the flattering profiles, and the captions of the pictures that had run on the society pages. And he learned nothing. He read them a second time, shut down the computer, and stared at the blank screen. Maybe, he told himself, he was going at it wrong. Maybe, like all good stories, he should start at the beginning, start with the fire. Start with Sara.

He opened his notebook, found the numbers Maggie had given him, and called the work number of her ex-husband, Jeff. When the receptionist answered, he said, "Can you give me your address please?"

Jeff might not know anything, but it wouldn't hurt to talk to him. Besides, he'd promised Maggie that he'd talk to her ex.

* * *

Traffic was moving on the Golden State Freeway, and Johnny made it to Orange County before three o'clock. He had to check the address the receptionist had given him against the Auto Club map, but he found the industrial park easily. He found the company, Computer Direct, at the end of a series of long, low buildings with prefab cement walls and flat roofs. Johnny left his car in the long, narrow visitors' lot at the side of the building and went in.

The waiting area was smaller than some walk-in closets. A sign on an inside door said "Employees Only." A small, frosted-glass window to the right of the door was open a crack. He slid the glass back and looked at the small office beyond. A young woman seated at a desk looked up from a magazine. She was in her mid-twenties with dishwater blonde hair and too much eye makeup.

"Excuse me, I'm looking for Jeff Claymore."

"He expecting you?" She seemed bored.

"No, not really."

"Well, we don't allow visitors in back."

"Can you just call him and tell him I'm here. My name's Rose, Johnny Rose."

"I'm sorry, our salesmen don't meet the public. You'll have to call him, or send him an e-mail." She looked down at the magazine again.

"Look, I'm not a customer. This is a family matter. Okay? So can you just call him."

The woman looked at Johnny for a moment, sighed and picked up the phone, and dialed. "Jeff, there's a man named Johnny Rose here to see you. Says it's personal. Yeah, sure." She hung up and looked at Johnny. "He'll be out in a minute."

Still, it was another five minutes before the lock on the internal door buzzed and Jeff walked into the small waiting area.

He was five feet nine with his shoes on and carried ten or fifteen pounds too much in his upper body. His suit pants were stretched tight across his middle, and he wore a white shirt frayed at the neck from too many washings. The top button was undone, and his tie was loose. His hair, thick and curly, was turning to gray and spilled over his ears. He looked at Johnny and smiled, his blue eyes twinkling, giving him a gleeful, almost mischievous look.

"Hey, Johnny, God, it's good to see you. It's been a long time."

"Good to see you, too, Jeff."

"What brings you down behind the Orange Curtain?"

"Sara."

The smile faded, and Jeff nodded at the front door. "Yeah. I guess I'm not surprised. Let's take a walk, okay? I've just got a few minutes. A couple of customers are supposed to be calling me back."

They pushed through the door, and Jeff led the way to the street. He chatted as they walked, telling Johnny about his job. "We sell computer systems here. PCs, desktop publishing, small office-management systems, things like that. I can beat just about any price in the market. So, you know, if you need something for your home or whatever, let me know. I'll get you a great price. I could probably set something up for your newspaper. You're still in the news business, aren't you?"

Johnny didn't respond, and when they reached the street, a wide, empty boulevard that ran past a long row of identical buildings, Jeff continued. "Oh, well, anyway, it's all commission work, so I'm doing pretty well."

"I didn't come down here to talk about computers, Jeff."

"Yeah, I guess not."

"I went to Atlanta," Johnny said, letting the short statement deliver the volume of things he had to say.

They walked a little farther in silence, Johnny waiting for Jeff to respond, letting the silence force him to speak. "I wanted to go, Johnny. But you know how it is, sometimes it's just tough."

"She was your daughter, Jeff, and Annie kept asking

about you. So, no, I guess I don't know how it is. Why don't you tell me?"

Jeff stopped, folded his arms across his chest, and turned to face Johnny. The easy smile was gone, and his eyes didn't dance as they had a few moments before. He looked past Johnny's shoulder down the street to the Computer Direct building.

"Okay, I'll tell you, since you asked. There's no fucking business here. Our profit margins are paper thin and half the time the big discount houses can beat our price, anyway. I'm not making a dime. I'm in here ten hours a day pounding away on the phones, and at the end of the day I'm lucky to be making five bucks an hour. I'm maxed out on my credit cards."

"So find another job. You were always good at that."

Jeff looked at the street and scraped the blacktop with the edge of his shoe as though trying to wipe out a chalk line. "It's not that easy. I've burned a few bridges down here and word gets around. I just gotta wait it out, that's all. Lay low a little while. People forget, you know."

"I guess."

"Look, Johnny, I wanted to come to the funeral, but I didn't have the money. I honest to God didn't have it." A bitter anger lay just below the surface of his words, and Johnny sensed he was sincere.

"So, this is about money, that's it?"

"No, it's not, not completely anyway." He turned and continued down the street.

"Did you know I remarried?"

"Maggie mentioned it."

"Her name's Julie. She's a wonderful woman. She's stuck by me through some pretty hard times, and that hasn't been easy. She has a boy, Evan, from another marriage, and we have a little girl of our own named Kelly."

"Congratulations."

"Thanks." They strolled past the small, finely trimmed lawns and tiny green hills that filled the narrow space between the buildings and the street like an English country estate in miniature. "You probably think I'm a royal asshole, don't you?"

"No, Jeff, I don't think that. I didn't come down here to lay a guilt trip on you. I just came down here to get some information about Sara."

"What kind of information?"

"For starters, tell me why she left."

"Why she ran away?"

"Yeah."

"Yeah, okay." They walked a little farther before Jeff started speaking. "Sara got here a little over two years ago. Almost three now. She just showed up. There was a knock on the door and there she was. Julie and I were living together in this one-bedroom apartment and we had Evan with us too. It was really tight. I was still selling real estate then, working nights and weekends, but the market was absolutely in the toilet. Anyway, I didn't get to spend much time with her. Julie was working, and Sara was just sort of on her own. Then we found out Julie was pregnant, and Sara didn't handle it well. There was a lot of tension. Julie never said anything, but I could tell she didn't like having her here. I don't know, Johnny. I mean, I wanted to take Sara in, to have her live with us, but there just wasn't a place.

"Then she stopped going to school. When we found out about that, we tried to talk to her about it, to set up some kind of ground rules. We even drew up a contract and we all signed it. But that only lasted a few days. She ran away. The cops found her hitchhiking outside of Fresno on Interstate Five. She was going to San Francisco. They brought her home. We talked and I tried to tell her how dangerous it was, but a few days later she ran away again. I took off from work, ended up spending a whole week driving up and down that damned interstate, stopping at every truck stop and in every shithole town asking everybody I could find about her. You know what it costs to take a week off? Do you? Well,

I'll tell you, I couldn't afford it, but I did it. I put up flyers, talked to the cops. I did everything I could, Johnny, everything. Finally I figured she'd just gone back to Atlanta."

"Did you call Maggie and ask?"

Jeff looked at Johnny, his eyes filled with equal portions of anger and regret. "Of course I did. But Sara wasn't there so what the hell difference did it make? How was I supposed to know she'd end up in Hollywood? I couldn't be everywhere, could I?"

"No, I guess not."

"I did everything I could. Everything. I loved Sara. I don't care what Maggie says. I loved her."

"Did Sara ever call you and ask for help?"

"Help, are you kidding? No way. She was tough, resilient, resourceful, like her old man. Throw anything at us, we'll handle it. We're alike in that way. We can handle whatever comes along."

"Apparently not quite everything."

Jeff exhaled deeply and walked to the curb and sat down, his feet in the gutter, his pant legs hiked above his socks, revealing the white skin on his shins. He lowered his head like a man defeated. Johnny sat next to him. When Jeff looked up, Johnny saw the glistening of tears along the edges of his eyes.

"I kept telling myself she'd be okay, that she was a survivor like me." He grunted and half-smiled as he wiped the tears from his eyes. "She was like me, Johnny, she really was. I love Annie and Kelly, but both of them are like their mothers. Sara was just like me. I was so proud of who she was. I hated the fact she ran away, but, hell, I was sixteen when I told my old man to shove it up his ass and moved out, and I turned out fine. I thought she'd be okay. I really did. I mean, I had no idea this could happen." With the back of his hand, he brushed tears off his cheeks.

"Did you know she was pregnant?"

"Pregnant? God, no. Pregnant? Wow, you mean I was going to be a grandfather. Jesus." He smiled broadly for a moment, then lowered his head again and slowly shook it from side to side. "This is really fucked up."

"Jeff, I gotta ask you something."

"What?" The color had drained from his face, and he looked years older than just moments before.

"Did Sara ever mention a woman named Carol Holland?"

"The actress?"

"Never talked about working up at her house?"

"No, why?"

"Was Sara in any kind of trouble that you know of? Did anyone want to hurt her?"

"Hurt her? What are you talking about?"

"She have any enemies?"

"Johnny, what the hell are you talking about? What the fuck's this about?"

"Was she doing anything illegal? Was she dealing or anything like that?"

"What the hell are you saying? My girl wasn't a criminal. Don't fuck with me. She was a good kid. Don't try telling me any different."

"That fire was started on purpose. I think maybe someone was trying to kill her."

"Murder?"

"It's possible."

Jeff staggered to his feet and looked at Johnny, a storm raging in his bloodshot eyes. "Who? I'll kill the son of a bitch. I'll do it myself."

"I don't know. I'm not even sure it was murder."

"Bullshit, you wouldn't be here if you weren't sure." He licked his lips rapidly, leaving a spot of spittle in the corner of his mouth. He leaned forward, inches from Johnny's face. "I want to know who the fuck it was. Who killed my girl. You find out, Johnny, you tell me."

Jeff was almost screaming, and Johnny's heart rate kicked into high. He struggled not to react, to remind himself that he'd just given Jeff some very tough news. He waited until

Jeff stood up straight. When Johnny spoke, his voice was under control. "Jeff, I don't—"

"Bullshit, you're a reporter. You know how to find things out."

Johnny shook his head slowly from side to side. His hands clenched into fists. "I'm just trying to figure out what happened."

"You find the son of a bitch who killed her and you tell me, understand?" He jabbed the air with his finger. "You got that?"

"Jeff, calm down. I didn't come down here—"

"You got that?" He jabbed Johnny's shoulder.

Johnny brushed his hand away and Jeff stepped back. "Yeah, Jeff, I got it."

"Good." He stood up straight and squared his shoulders. "I gotta get back to work," he said and walked away without saying good-bye. Johnny sat on the curb and watched him go, his arms and legs pumping rapidly like an uncoordinated race walker heading for the finish line. He would have been a comic figure except for the aura of tightly wound menace that radiated from him like an atomic glow.

Johnny stood and walked back to his car in the lot next to Computer Direct and looked at the building again. He understood Jeff's grief and anger, but that didn't make his behavior easier to take. It didn't surprise him, either. Everything in Jeff's life had always been about Jeff.

Seventeen

———————•———————

*I*t was late afternoon, and Johnny was crawling up the 101 freeway toward the Hollywood Boulevard off-ramp. A school bus, its exhaust a yard from the driver's window, had him pinned in on the left, and the car behind him gave no quarter.

The drive from Orange County had been brutal. The heat seemed magnified by the smog and haze, which reduced the downtown skyline to an indistinct outline in the distance. Sweat trickled from his armpits down his sides, and twice Johnny almost fell asleep in the stop-and-grind traffic creeping northward.

His neck and shoulder muscles were coiled tight, and a pain was just starting to build behind his left eye when Johnny took the off-ramp. As he drove up it, he glanced across the freeway to the cement panels that blocked the view of the space under the bridge. He wondered if any of the kids were in there now, listening to the unending roar of traffic and trying to stay cool.

He turned onto the boulevard and a few minutes later pulled into a long, narrow driveway that ran along the side of the Hank Jefferson Center, a new two-story brick-and-glass building that extended to the edge of the sidewalk. In the small lot at the rear of the center, Johnny parked next to a white Dodge van, the words "God's House Chariot" painted in neat blue-and-yellow block letters on its side. He climbed out of the Z and stretched, arching his back, putting his hands on the car roof, leaning forward and stretching his legs, a classic runner's stretch. Standing up straight again, he closed his eyes, rubbed his neck, then massaged his eyelids with his thumb and finger.

When he opened his eyes he saw Buddy standing on the porch, his arms folded across his chest, watching him. Buddy wore khaki pants and a white long-sleeved shirt, open at the collar, the cuffs folded back once.

"Hello, Mr. Rose. Can I help you?" His face was blank, but his eyes showed an unfocused anger that Johnny couldn't quite read, like a polite but well-disciplined clerk still furious at the customer who just left.

"Dick called and asked me to drop by."

"He's inside. But don't keep him too long, okay? *People* magazine is coming by tomorrow to do a story on him and he's got a lot to do. He's got to get ready."

"He called me, Buddy. It's his show." Johnny crossed the lawn and stepped onto the porch, and Buddy turned and moved past Johnny to the edge of the porch. As he turned, the late afternoon sun glinted off a small medallion on his neck. Unconsciously, Johnny glanced at it and stopped abruptly.

"Hey," Johnny said, and Buddy looked back at him. "That's an interesting necklace." Johnny gestured to the crossed letters, *P* and *X*. "I just caught a glimpse of it. What is it? I don't think I've ever seen one like it. Can I see it?"

Buddy looked at him, trying to read the question, wondering if there was a hidden message. After a moment he nodded. "Sure. It's a Chi-Rho, the first two letters in the Greek word for Jesus." He pulled the medal away from his neck and held it up for Johnny to see.

"Where'd you get it?"

"I got it here, the day I was baptized. Why?"

"Oh, I was just wondering. A lot of kids have them?"

"A few." He tucked the necklace under his shirt. "Why are you so interested in the medallion?"

"You remember the boy whose body was dumped up in the hills a few days ago?"

Buddy's eyes narrowed, but he held Johnny's gaze. "Yeah. So?"

"I think he was wearing a medallion just like that when he was killed." Johnny waited, but Buddy said nothing. "But when I asked, you said you didn't know him."

Buddy squared his shoulders and seemed to stand a little taller. His jaw muscles tensed. "Of course I knew him. But you asked me about a boy named James Randall. I didn't know him by that name. I only knew his street name."

"Dallas?"

"That's right."

"So, did he get a medallion here too? Was Dallas baptized here?"

"I don't know where he got it, but I'll tell you something, Mr. Rose. This"—he pulled the medallion from under his shirt—"is more than just a symbol of baptism to me. It reminds me to keep cool, you know. Something we all need to remember now and again."

"That's why you're wearing it?"

"Helps me remember where I came from. We all want to keep that in mind."

"Really? Where'd you come from, Buddy?"

Buddy stared at him for a moment. "You know, Mr. Rose, I'm a little busy right now. Like I said, don't keep the reverend too long." Johnny didn't respond, and Buddy walked to the middle of the parking lot and turned back to Johnny. "You can go right in. You don't have to ring the bell. He'd never hear you anyway. His study's down the hall. Just knock."

Johnny watched Buddy until he was halfway down the driveway before going into the house. He stepped into a small entrance with hardwood floors and closed his eyes, trying to force his muscles to relax, to will away the pain behind his eyes. It was cooler inside the house but only by a few degrees, and after a moment's relief he felt the uncomfortable warmth of late summer closing in again. A hallway led from the entrance to the back of the house. On the second door, a simple, brown plastic sign said REVEREND R. ROBERTS. Johnny tapped lightly.

"Yeah, come on in." Roberts swiveled from his word processor as Johnny pushed the door open and leaned in. "Johnny, hi. Please come in. Let me just finish this up. Won't be a minute. Grab a seat." He waved to the chair across the desk from him and turned again to the computer on his desk.

Johnny took in the room slowly. Not large to begin with, it had a cramped but not uncomfortable feel. Bookshelves began on both sides of the door and bent around to fill the walls. Behind Roberts's desk, a vertical blind hung at an odd angle in a small window. A room air conditioner consumed the bottom of the window, but wasn't on. Through the slats in the blinds, Johnny got a view of a narrow side yard. A picture of Roberts in his clerical robes, with Buddy and Hank Jefferson smiling at his side, hung just behind Roberts's head. Next to it, two parallel rows of photos, framed in simple black metal, filled the wall. Each showed a different youth choir standing on risers, and in every one Hank Jefferson stood at the end of the first row, smiling proudly at the camera.

Johnny took his notebook from his hip pocket, put it on the edge of the desk, and sat just as Roberts finished typing.

"There." He punched a button and the screen went blank. He turned to face Johnny. "You know what it's like when you're on a roll. You hate to stop."

"Yes."

"Anyway, welcome." He leaned back and held his arms up and out in a wide gesture and looked around the room. "Tell the truth. It's not what you expected, is it?" he asked with a big smile, as though joking.

"I wasn't sure what to expect."

"Well, it catches a lot of people by surprise. They think that because God's House is successful, I should live in a nice home, maybe drive a fancy car, have a plush office. But, well, I don't know. It's not that important to me. After Barbara died I found myself spending more and more time at the center anyway. It was still over on Franklin then. When we bought this property, the house was already here so I told them to leave it up and I moved in. It's all I need. I've got a big office with a secretary at the other building. But I prefer it here. Besides"—he smiled—"I've got lots of company."

"Company?"

"The center." He gestured to the door. "A lot of staffers drop by before or after their shifts. A couple of 'em are college students, and they'll sleep over if they're working late and have early classes the next day. I don't have a lot of privacy. But I like it that way. It's like having an extended family now."

"That's good," said Johnny. "You know, Dick, I never got to tell you how sorry I was to hear about Barbara's death. I thought she was a terrific lady."

"Thank you, Johnny. During that whole time, when she was so sick, it was . . . it was awful. I wouldn't wish it on my worst enemy. The only thing that saved me was my work." He half-turned in his seat and glanced at the photo of him and Hank Jefferson with Buddy. "Sometimes we manage to save a few souls, like Buddy. He was the first person to complete the program at the halfway house. That was taken on the day he was baptized, the same day he finished the program. I asked Hank to come back and play that day."

"Yeah, you mentioned Hank had retired."

"He did. He's living with his daughter in South Central now. But he was here when Buddy first joined us. He was as proud as the rest of us."

They were quiet for a moment, and Roberts's thoughts seemed to drift and his eyes slipped out of focus. A moment later he was back.

"This may sound funny, Johnny, but despite Barbara's cancer and all, I think the Lord has blessed me. But"—he leaned forward and clasped his hands together on the desktop—"I didn't ask you to come here to listen to me preach."

"No."

"Johnny, I know this may sound strange, and frankly, if we hadn't known each other for so long, I'd never ask it."

"Ask what?" He could feel the tension building in his neck and shoulders again. The room seemed small and the air stale. Why the hell didn't Roberts turn on the air conditioner?

"The boy whose body was found on the hillside." He stopped speaking and looked at Johnny. Johnny said nothing, letting Roberts play it out. But his early warning signals were already buzzing. Where was this going?

"I know that you asked Carol about him and, well, I just . . . well, I know how this stuff can get blown all out of proportion."

"What stuff, Dick?"

Roberts leaned back in his chair and folded his arms across his chest. "How well do you know Carol Holland?"

"Not at all. We met at her party."

"Exactly. You don't really know her at all. But I know her pretty well, and, frankly, I think I'm a pretty good judge of character."

"Good, then you can tell me what she's hiding." The words came without thought.

"Oh, Johnny." He sighed deeply. "She's not hiding anything. That's why I asked you to come by."

"Come on, Dick. Her husband's lawyers were at the paper this morning threatening me with a restraining order. What's she afraid of?"

"Look." Roberts leaned forward again and clasped his hands on the desk. "Carol's a very private person. She's had some bad experiences with the press. She's terrified you'll blow this all out of proportion. I told her that was ridiculous, that you were a responsible journalist. But she wouldn't listen."

Johnny wanted to believe Roberts, to trust his friend and chalk it up to a minor misunderstanding. It would be the easiest thing in the world. The pain behind his eyes began to escalate, and he shut them for a moment. He wanted nothing more than to just go home, take some aspirin, and cool off. He squeezed his eyes tighter, but it didn't matter. He knew he couldn't let it go. Roberts was wrong. Only one thing had bothered Carol Holland when Johnny confronted her. She wasn't worried about Dallas or Sara or the other kids. She'd been worried because she hadn't been in control. This wasn't about bad publicity. This was about control.

Johnny opened his eyes and nodded at Roberts. "She ask you to talk to me?"

"No."

"So why did you call?"

"I'm asking you as a personal favor just to let the police handle this. We've worked too hard at the Restoration Committee, come too far to lose it all just because a boy died near Carol's house."

"He didn't die there, Dick. He was murdered and dumped there."

"Johnny, listen to yourself. What happened? You used to be, well, able to keep an open mind. That's how I always thought of you. Now I'm beginning to think you've become obsessed with this."

Johnny stood slowly and leaned forward on the desk, his arms stiff. "You know what, Dick? Last night I saw a boy maimed. Sucked under a train he was trying to hop. He fell and it cut off the lower part of his leg. He's going to be a cripple for the rest of his life. That's assuming he lives. You ever see a kid cut in pieces like that, Dick? You ever see something like that?"

"Johnny, I've seen some awful things, but I think I've kept my balance."

"Yeah, maybe so. But let me tell you the worst part. Someone was chasing him. The boy was running for his life and he ended up under the train. Two kids have already died. Someone murdered Dallas and dumped his body up there by Carol Holland's house. Someone set the fire that killed my cousin, Dick. Now this boy may die. So yes, maybe I am obsessed."

"You can't really believe that Carol's involved in all this."

Johnny pushed back from Roberts's desk and walked across the small room. He rolled his shoulders, trying to corral the anger running through his body, relieve the pain in his eyes. His mind was racing, jumping from Sara, to the train tracks, to Jeff's explosive anger, to seeing the medallion on Buddy's neck.

"Tell me something, Dick."

"What?"

"How did Buddy come to be here, at the center?"

"What?" The question, unconnected to the conversation and without preamble, seemed to shock Roberts.

"How'd he get here?"

"I already told you, through the halfway house."

Compassion and fury mingled in Roberts's eyes as he looked at Johnny. When he spoke, though, his voice was controlled, even. "Johnny, I understand how you must feel after seeing that boy hurt. But you're rambling. Maybe this is too much death and hardship to handle in such a short time. It would be hard for anyone to process. Perhaps you should consider taking some time off. A vacation. I'm afraid you're losing touch, acting irrationally."

"Where did Carol Holland go to high school?"

"Johnny, calm down. This is not like you."

"Where'd she go to high school? Just tell me that."

"What difference does that make?"

"What's she hiding?"

Roberts slowly shook his head, then stood. "Johnny, I'm going to ask you to leave now. Please get some rest, put some distance between you and these unfortunate incidents. Maybe even consider getting some counseling to help you with your grief."

"Why'd she lie to me about going to Hollywood High?"

"Johnny, please." The minister gestured to the door.

Johnny stared at Roberts for a moment, holding the minister's eyes. Roberts didn't waver, and finally Johnny walked to the door.

"I'm not going away, Dick."

"I'll remember you in my prayers tonight. It's all I can do until you decide to help yourself. Remember, you're not alone."

Johnny looked at Roberts, and for a second his focus shifted to the picture of the minister, Buddy, and Hank Jefferson behind him.

"Don't worry, Dick, I'll help myself, and I have a damned good idea where to start."

Eighteen

●━━━━━━━●

*H*ank Jefferson was still listed with the musicians' union, and it took the *Journal*'s resource librarian less than five minutes to get an address. Johnny thanked her and hung up the pay phone on the side of the 7-Eleven building. He started back to his car but stopped when he saw a boy standing next to a bus bench. The boy was bare chested but wore a long black leather coat. He smiled across the parking lot at Johnny, cocked his head, and raised his eyebrows, a nonverbal invitation.

Johnny shook his head no, hesitated as he watched the boy turn away, then retreated to the phone, pulled it off the hook, and dialed Kate. When her machine answered he spoke quickly. "Kate, it's Johnny. Have you heard anything about Gem? Anything at all? I'll call later to check in."

A moment later he was in the Z. He paused at the street's edge, then hit the gas and shot across the oncoming traffic and swung south.

Hank Jefferson lived on a street of small houses, neatly trimmed lawns, tall palms at the curb, and bars on the windows. When Johnny parked in front of the house, he checked the address again. He hadn't called ahead, and he knew he was taking a chance Jefferson wouldn't be home. But over the years, he'd learned it was a lot harder to turn someone away from your door than to simply hang up the phone. He had no reason to think Jefferson would turn him away, but he also saw no reason not to increase the odds.

As he got out of the car, he glanced down the street and saw a mix of late-model American cars, small imports, and pickups in the driveways and at the curb. A van turned into the drive next door, and a black man in khaki slacks and a short-sleeved white shirt and wide tie climbed out. He nodded at Johnny, taking a mental picture, getting a good look at his face, then leaned back into the van to get a briefcase.

A white man wasn't necessarily unusual in the neighborhood. But Los Angeles is a city fractured along ethnic lines like a mirror, shattered but still in the frame. You can see the reflection and get a glimpse of the whole here and there, but it's just not possible to hold it at a distance and get a clear picture of the entire mosaic. Johnny knew when he parked the car that he'd driven from one piece of the city to another, and he looked at his watch before walking up the sidewalk, because in LA it's never simply a question of neighborhood. It's also a question of the clock; an intricate interplay of race, place, and time of day, and most people instinctively know the rules of where to be when. Now, in the almost-evening, Johnny knew he stood out and his presence was probably already widely noted. The curtains moved in the window of the house across the street, and he imagined he could hear the comment, "What's that fool white man doing here at this time of day?"

He didn't cut across the lawn but went up the worn and cracked cement walk and climbed the steps to the wide porch and knocked on the screen door. A small girl, barefoot, in a yellow dress, came to the door. She looked through the mesh at him but didn't speak.

"Hi, I'm looking for Mr. Jefferson. Is he home?"

The girl spun and disappeared in a swirl of yellow, suddenly lost in the darkened interior. A moment later Hank Jefferson came to the door.

His ebony face was deeply creased, and he wore large, thick glasses in a simple black frame. But even through the lenses Johnny could see the sparkle and a hint of recognition in his brown eyes.

"Yes?"

"Mr. Jefferson, I don't know if you remember me. My name's Johnny Rose."

"Yes, of course, you're that newspaper man who wrote about Mr. Roberts."

"Yes. It's good to see you again."

Jefferson pushed open the screen and stretched out his hand. His fingers were strong and his grip firm.

"Please come in, Mr. Rose." Johnny stepped into the house, and Jefferson said, "Don't mind my granddaughter, she's a little shy. Let's go to the living room, we can talk in there. Can I offer you anything to drink, coffee or a soda?"

"No, thank you."

Jefferson led him into a comfortable room with hardwood floors and a large entertainment center against the side wall. An upright piano partially blocked the front window. "Please," Jefferson said, motioning to a terra-cotta-colored leather couch along the wall opposite the entertainment center.

Johnny lowered himself to the edge of the sofa.

"This is a very nice home, Mr. Jefferson."

"Thank you," Jefferson said as he moved to the piano bench and sat facing Johnny, his back to the piano.

"Tell me, Mr. Jefferson, how long have you been retired from God's House?"

"Oh, it's almost two years now. My daughter kept after me to come live with her, and God's House needed someone with a little more energy. So, I'm here with Charlene and my two granddaughters. That was Chantell you saw." He waited for Johnny, saying nothing more.

"I apologize for dropping by unexpectedly but I'm working on a story and I thought you might be able to help."

"You doing another story on the reverend?"

"No, actually I'm trying to get some information for another story."

Jefferson turned his back to Johnny, and his fingers skipped across a few keys; a musician doodling. "What kind of a story?"

"A couple of street kids were killed recently. One of them was a boy who used the street name Dallas. I was wondering if you knew him at God's House."

Jefferson shook his head. "Dallas? No, I'm afraid not. But like I said, I retired almost two years ago."

"Right. It was kind of a long shot but I thought I'd ask."

"What makes you think he came to God's House? There are a lot of agencies out there."

"The boy was wearing one of those medallions, a crossed *P* and *X.*"

Jefferson smiled. "The Chi-Rho. Yes, we give them to the kids when they accept Jesus as their savior. If that boy had one on, he definitely got it at God's House. You know, you should be talking to Dick."

"I already have. But it's good to get as much information as possible. I'm sure you understand."

"Yes." Jefferson said. He looked at Johnny for a moment, then turned to the piano again and played a few more quick notes, apparently lost in thought. He turned back and raised his eyes and seemed to be staring at a spot six inches in front of his face. When he focused on Johnny again, his gaze was sharp and clear.

"Did you really come all the way down here to ask about that boy, Mr. Rose?"

Johnny looked toward the big TV in the entertainment center, then back to Jefferson, who was watching him. His eyes were kindly but they demanded the truth.

"That's only part of it. I also need to learn a little more about Buddy."

"Is he in trouble?"

"Why do you ask?"

"Sometimes leaving the old ways behind isn't very easy, that's all."

"Will you tell me about the old ways? Tell me how he came to God's House?"

"Like I said, you really should ask Dick or Buddy himself, not me."

"I have and they won't tell me. Mr. Jefferson, I want to be fair. I don't want to misjudge him. If I understand him, understand his background, I can make a better judgment," Johnny said.

Jefferson nodded slowly. "Yes, it would be easy to misjudge him. He was in prison. Did you know that?"

"I knew he came through the halfway house, so I guess I knew he was an ex-con, yes."

Jefferson looked at him, and his eyes clouded. The sparkle Johnny had seen there a few minutes before disappeared, replaced by an expression of trouble and worry. After a few moments, he asked Johnny a question that seemed to come from nowhere.

"Tell me, Mr. Rose, do you think of Dick as an ambitious man?"

Johnny didn't respond at first. He sat, trying to both judge the reason behind the question and give an honest answer.

"Ah, ambitious. That's an interesting word." Johnny was quiet for a moment, thinking some more about it. "Yes, he's ambitious, but, well, I don't know, it's kind of hard to describe. I think he wants to accomplish great things, but not for himself."

"Yes," Jefferson nodded. "Yes, I think that too. Sometimes I think ambition is good. It helps us accomplish things we never thought possible. Other times it blinds us."

"Did it blind Reverend Roberts about Buddy?"

Jefferson looked at Johnny. His smile was kindly, but weary. "The reverend wants God's House to be more than just a church. I'm sure you know that. That's why he set up the youth center and established the halfway house for ex-cons and parolees."

"That's how he met Buddy? At the halfway house?"

"No, the reverend knew Buddy even before he went to prison the last time. Buddy used to be in a gang called the Hollywood Jackals. They were selling drugs, robbing, doing whatever they wanted."

Jefferson turned back to the piano and ran his fingers over the keys again, lost in his memories for a moment. He spoke to the instrument.

"After a while, though, the police arrested them and Buddy was sent to prison. That's where he found Jesus, in prison. It was a jailhouse conversion. The prison chaplain was a friend of Dick's and invited him to visit and he saw Buddy again there. Dick remembered him, and they started talking and then they exchanged letters. Dick sort of took him on as a pet project. Buddy had been up for parole a couple of times but never got it. The last time he came up, Dick stepped forward for him. He persuaded the board to let him come to the halfway house. He even said he'd help Buddy find a job and make sure he attended services and stayed out of trouble."

"That's how he became the outreach coordinator?"

"No, not at first. When Buddy first got to the halfway house, Dick found him a job as night janitor in a Christian elementary school." Jefferson sighed deeply and looked at Johnny. "But it didn't work out."

"What happened?"

"This all happened after I left, so I can only tell you what I heard. The principal came back to the school late one night and caught Buddy smoking a marijuana cigarette in one of the classrooms. He fired him and reported him to his parole officer."

"They didn't send him back to prison?"

"No. Dick stood up for him. He told them that Buddy had just slipped the one time and asked that they give him a second chance. He even said the church would hire him."

"That's when he became the outreach coordinator?"

"Yes. It would have been very hard for Buddy. He's already been to prison twice. If he goes back again, it'll be for a long, long time."

"You've got my back," Johnny said, his voice low, his eyes on the floor.

"Yes, that's what Buddy used to say. 'Dick's got my back.'"

"He's been through a lot."

"Yes, but I think he's come through it okay," Jefferson said.

"Mr. Jefferson, I need to ask you a tough question, okay?"

Jefferson turned to the piano and lowered the lid to cover the keys before looking back at Johnny. His eyes held a resignation, a sense that he knew the question before it was asked.

"Do you think Buddy's jailhouse conversion was sincere? Did he truly accept Jesus?"

"I would never question another man's faith, Mr. Rose. But to answer your question, I'm not quite sure. But I do believe his dedication to God's House and to the reverend is sincere."

The room was still, and through the window Johnny saw a UPS van hurry down the street.

"Thank you, Mr. Jefferson, for your time and candid answers."

Jefferson smiled at him. "You still haven't answered my question, Mr. Rose. Is Buddy in trouble?"

"I don't know."

"But still, you're here."

"Yes."

"Maybe I shouldn't have spoken so freely with you, not if you're going to write a story that's going to hurt the church."

"I would never write a story that wasn't accurate or balanced. You have my promise that I won't write a word about Buddy that isn't true."

Jefferson looked at Johnny for a full minute, holding his eyes before finally nodding. "You know, Mr. Rose, a lot of people have written about Reverend Roberts. They make a big deal out of his winning that gold medal, then doing the Lord's work. They make him sound like a saint or something. Your story was different. You wrote about the man. You were honest that time, so I guess I should trust you this time too."

Johnny stood. "Thank you. I should probably be going."

Jefferson fell in beside him, and they walked to the door. He pushed the screen open and smiled at Johnny. "You know, whatever it is, I hope you're wrong about Buddy."

"I hope you're right. Thank you for your time."

Johnny stepped onto the porch and turned back. "Oh, just one more question. Do you know Carol Holland?"

Johnny hadn't expected an answer that was anything more than a casual dismissal, but he asked the question from habit. A good reporter is always asking the obvious as well as the obscure questions.

"I saw her on television the other night. I know she's trying to help the reverend with the kids," Jefferson said and let the screen door close between them.

"Yes. How long has she known Reverend Roberts, do you know?" The screen blocked Johnny's vision, but it was light enough to see Jefferson step back from the door, farther into the shadows. His face was now completely dark, but his voice had changed.

"Oh, you'd have to ask the reverend about that."

It seemed an odd answer. Why not just say he didn't know? Johnny started to push it, but didn't. Instead he simply said, "Ah, thank you again for your time, Mr. Jefferson." He stepped off the porch and walked down the sidewalk to the car. He waved back at the darkened front door and wondered if Hank Jefferson even saw him.

Johnny slowed the Z at the edge of the *Journal*'s parking lot and waved at the elderly man in the small plywood guard shack. Sam smiled and touched the brim of his stiff, perfectly shaped baseball cap. Johnny could tell the noise of the car had awakened him. Johnny guessed he was seventy, maybe even older, and he always wondered if Sam was working out of boredom or if he really needed the money.

He found a parking space and glanced back at the guard shack as he got out. The side door hung open, and he could see Sam sitting comfortably in the corner, his head already on his chest. Another guard, a young man Johnny knew was just marking time until he could get into the police academy, cruised slowly past the guard shack in a golf cart and began to circle the lot, checking each vehicle for its *Journal* parking sticker. Johnny had always thought the precautions and the security were a pain, but now, after the attack and the burglary, he found them reassuring.

Johnny's original plan was to stop just long enough to check his messages and his e-mail. He didn't even bother sitting down when he dialed his voice-mail and listened to the first, a reminder from the accounting department that he hadn't signed a recent expense report. But he tensed when he heard the voice on the second message.

"Hi, it's Clay Griffin. I was wondering if you had any news about the girl. We all want what's best for her, Mr. Rose, believe me. Please give me a call, I'd like to talk."

Johnny wrote down the number and dialed immediately. "Shit," Johnny swore when a message machine answered.

"Mr. Griffin, this is Johnny Rose. I just got your message. You know, I'd find it a lot easier to believe how concerned you are if I knew who your clients are and why they want to find her. I'll be at the *Journal* for another hour if you want to call me."

He tried Kate next but got her machine again. He checked his e-mail and tried reading the paper to kill the hour. He wanted to give Griffin plenty of time. Finally, he tossed the paper into the trash and left, stopping at the edge of the newsroom just long enough to glance back to the phone and look at his watch. He'd been in the office almost two hours. It really wasn't that long.

But it was long enough.

The *Journal*'s parking lot was almost empty. The cars and pickup trucks of the pressmen and overnight editorial staffers who had arrived after the day shift were clustered in bunches near the building. Johnny's car had been surrounded by vehicles when he parked but now was alone in the middle of the blacktop. As he stepped onto the blacktop, he heard the whine of an electric motor and turned as the young guard pulled his golf cart to a stop a few yards away.

"Hey, Mr. Rose, want a lift?"

"No. Thanks anyway, Frank. I think I can walk it from here."

"Suit yourself. Have a good night," he said and steered the cart away. A moment later he disappeared around the end of the building.

At the car, Johnny pulled the door open and heard the first shot. The Z's side mirror exploded. Shards of glass, plastic, and metal flew through the air. Johnny felt a sharp pain in his left arm and doubled over. He heard another shot, like a whip cracking, and suddenly, through the pain and surprise, he understood. Someone was shooting at him, trying to kill him.

Instantly the pain in his arm was gone, forgotten, and he flattened himself on the macadam of the parking lot. His heart roared in his ears, his pulse raced, and his breathing was shallow and rapid. Johnny heard another shot, and the Z's headlight shattered at almost the same instant. He heard the glass falling on the asphalt. He inched forward, his belly pressed tight to the ground, until he could just peer past the front tire. There, just beyond the guard shack at the edge of the street, a man he didn't recognize stood next to a dark sedan, resting a rifle on its roof, aiming at him. Another crack and the barrel seemed to lift slightly and Johnny heard the bullet whiz past his head. It hadn't missed by more than a few inches.

"Ah, shit," Johnny swore and slithered backward like a snake, the rough asphalt pulling at his clothes and digging at his skin, rubbing his palms and knees raw. A second later another bullet hit the pavement with a thud, and almost instantaneously another struck the Z's open door.

At the rear of the car, Johnny lay flat on his stomach, fighting the urge to leap up and run for the *Journal*'s back door. Abruptly, the shooting stopped and a deafening silence filled the night. In the distance, Johnny could hear a helicopter flying across the city. Moments later the roar of an engine and the squeal of tires broke the quiet. He lay on the ground until silence filled the parking lot again. When he stood a few moments later he could smell the burning rubber and he saw Sam coming from the front of the building toward him. His gait was slow, but he was moving as quickly as possible.

"Mr. Johnny, Mr. Johnny, are you okay? I was inside, in the bathroom. I heard, I heard the shooting."

"Police?"

"I called."

"Good."

He walked back to the driver's door and looked at the side mirror, which dangled from the side of the car. A chunk of the mirror lay on the ground, and when he reached for it, a sharp pain shot through his left arm again. He looked down and saw a piece of the mirror protruding just below the elbow. Blood soaked his jacket, and he could see smears on the ground where he'd crawled, the pain in his arm masked by adrenaline and fear. He turned toward Sam.

"When the cops get here, tell 'em I'm in the newsroom," he said and started back across the lot toward the *Journal*'s back door, glancing at the street as he walked.

Nineteen

●━━━━━━━●

*T*he story would run on the *Journal*'s front page, not leading the edition but still there, just below the fold. It wasn't
every day that someone tried to kill a reporter, although the
police weren't certain it was an attempted assassination.

"Look, all I'm saying is that it's possible someone may be
just trying to send you a message. I mean, a drive-by with an
automatic weapon, or up close and personal with a Saturday
night special, yeah, no question someone wants you dead.
But long range like that, I don't know. I mean, it's just not
very accurate," the detective said to Johnny.

Johnny looked at the cop, a man near sixty, tall, with a
protruding stomach, a full head of white hair, and blossoms
on his cheeks that showed years of alcohol, and held up his
arm. The paramedics had cleaned the wound and bandaged
it even before the detectives arrived. Now, though, the blood
had begun to soak through. The cop glanced at it, unim-
pressed.

"If the first shot hadn't hit the mirror, I'd be dead. I'd say
that was pretty damned accurate. This isn't a warning."

"Could it be tied to a story you wrote?"

"No. I already told you this is not just someone pissed off
over a story. It's about street kids."

"Right, it's all tied to that dead boy on the hillside and the
arson in Hollywood that killed that girl."

"Yes, that's right. Look, call Detective Towers in Hollywood. He'll tell you. I've talked to him before."

"I will. But in the meantime, I'm here, so you'll have to talk to me. So one more time, you don't know anything about the fire or who started it or who killed the dead boy? You don't know anything special about these cases?"

"No." Johnny could feel the adrenaline ebbing away, exhaustion taking control of his body, sapping his will to argue. His left arm throbbed.

"Well, you can see how that might make it a little tougher for us to link them all together, can't you?"

"Jesus," Johnny mumbled and sighed loudly. The cop, whose name was Bennett, looked at him, his jovial demeanor gone. "Mr. Rose, I assure you we'll look at all the possibilities. Like I said, I'll check with Detective Towers about that boy on the hillside. And I'll get ahold of the two patrol officers who came to your house the night you were attacked. I'll even check with the railroad. I'm not dismissing this. We're treating it as an attempted murder. Look, I'm doing my job and frankly, I'm damned good at it." Bennett let the words sink in for a moment, and when Johnny said nothing, he continued. "We're checking the street for casings and we're looking for witnesses. But the fact is, I don't have a lot to go on here. A sniper attack like that, it's just . . . it's just odd, that's all."

"Yeah, okay," Johnny said.

"Listen, I've got to make a call. Is there a phone I can use and have a little privacy?"

Johnny stood and looked around the newsroom and pointed. "Over there, in the corner. That desk's empty. Dial nine to get out."

"Thanks."

He watched Bennett walk away. Once the cop picked up the phone, Johnny called Kuscyk at home and went over it with him. Finally, he ran through it all one more time for the young reporter assigned to write the piece. The reporter's name was Ben, and if Johnny remembered right, he'd just finished journalism school a few months before after abandoning a career as a stockbroker. Ben brushed a wayward lock of hair from his forehead a half dozen times while asking his first few cautious and disorganized questions. Finally, Johnny pointed to a chair in the empty cubicle across from him and said, "Sit down and just take notes, okay?"

Johnny led him through it, practically dictating the story, going slowly and not giving the kid much of a chance to ask questions. When he finished, Johnny leaned back in his chair, exhaled deeply, and gazed at the ceiling for a second before looking at the reporter again. Ben was about twenty-eight, tall and thin, and looked at Johnny with a mix of excitement and admiration, as though this interview were the best story he would ever be assigned in his career. Johnny remembered when he, too, had wanted nothing more than to write important, above-the-fold stories that carried his byline. It seemed light-years ago.

"What else do you need?" Johnny asked.

"Ah, nothing, I guess. Not unless you know why someone took those shots at you? Are you working on an important investigative piece or something like that? Or maybe it's a jealous husband?"

Ben meant it as a joke, but the look in Johnny's eyes told the reporter that he'd found little humor in it.

"I'm working on a couple of things, but there's no direct evidence they're connected," Johnny said. For a second he thought of telling Ben about the fire and Sara's death and the body on the hillside. But all he had were suspicions. There was no hook, nothing to use to connect these events to the shooting. "So, no. Without a connection, you can't mention it."

"What? Why not? You can just say what you're doing and we'll let the readers make up their own minds." The kid was smiling, sure he had a winning argument.

"And if there's no connection? If someone got the wrong person? If the whole thing is just mistaken identity? It'll just raise more questions than I have answers for. Just say I don't know who took the shots, or why. That's the truth."

"Yeah, okay," the kid said and stood and glanced down the aisle. Bennett was coming toward them. Ben moved aside, giving the cop room. He stepped in front of Johnny's desk.

"Mr. Rose, I'd like to ask you a couple more questions." The reporter looked at the cop, then back at Johnny.

"You need anything else?" Johnny asked Ben.

"Well, we'll need a picture of you."

"Get the one they shot for my press pass."

"Okay." Ben started to say something else but stopped and stood. "Be careful, Johnny. I don't want to write your obit next."

"Yeah," Johnny said. "I wouldn't particularly like that either."

"So you want to read this when I'm done?"

Johnny looked at him and slowly shook his head, an almost imperceptible side-to-side motion. "No, Ben," he said, barely above a whisper. "I'm the subject of the story. You never show the subject the article you've written about them. No point in pissing 'em off early, right?"

Johnny looked at the detective and gestured to the chair Ben had just left. "You want to sit?" he asked, but Bennett shook his head. He looked down at Johnny, his face a blank.

"You didn't tell me about the burglary."

"You mean at my place?"

"Where else?"

"Yeah, I guess I forgot about it. With the shooting and everything, it was pretty easy to forget."

"You just forgot about it?"

Johnny looked at the cop, trying to figure where this was going. "What's this about?"

"You sure your cousin didn't give you anything? Maybe something to hold on to for a while? Maybe something not strictly legal?"

"Jesus, not this again. No. She wasn't into drugs. She wasn't a thief. She wasn't a bad kid."

Bennett glanced behind him, backed into the cubicle across the aisle from Johnny, and lowered himself onto the desk.

"You know I have half a mind to believe you. But look at it from our point of view. Someone searches your house, beats you up and demands you return their property, and then tries to shoot you for a reason you don't understand. Now, that's not behavior usually associated with legal activities, is it?"

"Look," Johnny said and stood. He was almost too tired to care and way beyond being polite. He looked at the cop across the narrow aisle. "Find out about that fire, find out about Dallas. Find out who's killing these kids. That's what this is about. Just do your damned job, Detective. I'm not involved in this."

"Not involved?"

"I'm just trying to find out what's happening here, that's all."

Bennett stood up from the desk. He was less than two feet from Johnny but was slightly shorter and had to look up. His voice was low and controlled when he spoke. "Mr. Rose, that's all we're trying to do too." He walked away, his shoulder brushing Johnny's chest as he went.

Johnny watched him go and sat again. He stretched out his legs, slid down in the chair, and leaned his head back. In the distance he could hear Ben's voice as the young reporter told someone about the attack.

"A sniper, can you believe it?" His voice was charged with energy, and the words were eager.

Johnny stood and looked over the cubicle divider. Ben was standing in a small knot of writers and copy editors, telling the story he'd be writing in a few minutes, pleased with his own relationship to an attempted murder. As he watched the young reporters gathered around Ben, Johnny suddenly realized he was probably the oldest reporter in the room. He saw an assistant metro editor who was only a few years from retirement and knew the sports editor, who had just walked past, was pushing sixty. But all the others, the reporters and copy editors, were young. What the hell had happened to the years, he wondered? He rolled his shoulders and started to raise his arms above his head, but a sharp pain shot through his left arm and he stopped.

Shards from the shattered mirror had made two small holes in his notebook, and Johnny touched them with the fingers of his right hand, feeling the small tear in the cardboard. Just as he dropped the notebook back into his pocket, the phone rang. He just looked at it for a second and then picked it up, hoping it would be Kate.

"Johnny Rose."

"You're a lucky man. Next time, we'll be closer." A man's voice, one Johnny didn't recognize. But the man raised no fear, only anger in Johnny. In his mind he could see the man leaning across the roof, taking slow aim, and he wanted to reach through the phone and strangle the man on the other end.

"Who is this?" Johnny demanded as he looked around the newsroom searching for Bennett, but the cop was gone.

"Leave her alone, Rose. Just stay away and you won't have to look over your shoulder anymore."

"I'm not staying away. I'll find out who you are."

"Then you're a stupid man. Just stay away from her. We won't miss next time."

The line went dead. Johnny realized he was squeezing the phone, his arm muscles constricted, and he wanted to slam it on the desk. Instead he put it back gently and slumped into his chair, waited a moment, and called the police. But Bennett wasn't there and he had to leave a message.

When he left the *Journal,* he crossed the lot quickly, forcing himself not to glance toward the street. When he reached the car, he took a moment to examine the damage. He'd have to get the left front headlight replaced before long and the side mirror was a total loss, but the car was driveable. Leaving the door open, he got in and fired it up. The engine caught and ran smoothly. He climbed out again and walked to the rear of the car, where he opened the hatch and searched until he found the tire iron under a blanket and pile of bungee cords. He picked the iron up, feeling the cool steel in his hand. He tossed it on the passenger seat and looked at it again when he got in. It wasn't much, but it would have to do until he found something better.

He circled the block where his apartment building was and parked two streets away before approaching through the alley, swinging the tire iron at his side. He stopped at the edge of the carport and turned in a slow circle, scanning the area before crossing to the narrow walkway between the back of the small fenced patios of his building and the concrete block wall of the apartment complex next door.

As he moved up the narrow walkway, past the gas meters, his shoulder almost ran into the wooden fence to his left. As he neared his patio, he saw a shadow flicker across the grass near the front of the building. He slowed his pace and tightened his grip on the tire iron. The elongated figure, formed by someone standing in front of the landscape spotlights, wavered, then moved away from the building. Johnny stopped completely and watched the shadow for a moment. "Fuck 'em," he mumbled and started walking quickly down the path. His pace quickened as he moved past the last gas meter, and he was running when he rounded the corner. He raised the tire iron, cocking it near his right ear. But the small space of lawn at the end of the building was empty, and he ran onto the sidewalk when he saw a man walking away down the street. Johnny recognized him instantly.

"Jeff. What the hell are you doing?" he called.

Maggie's ex-husband stopped and looked over his shoulder and waved.

"Hey, Johnny, there you are. I just tried your place and didn't get an answer." Jeff turned and came up the sidewalk toward him. "I was in the neighborhood, figured I'd come by."

He stopped a few feet away and smiled, the charm coming

easily. Jeff saw the tire iron then, and his face clouded.

"What's with the tire iron? And what the hell happened to your arm?"

"It's a long story. It's nothing. You know, I've never known you to stop by. What are you doing here?"

Jeff wore a sport coat, shirt, and tie. He stuck his hands in the back pockets of his dress pants, half-turned, and glanced back down the street. When he looked at Johnny again, the easy smile was gone.

"Like I told you, I was in the neighborhood."

"Look, it hasn't been a particularly good day. So why don't you tell me why you're here."

"I was up here looking for a job. I heard this place in West LA was hiring."

"Yeah and . . . ?"

"Look, can we go inside?"

Johnny looked at him for a moment, weighing his decision. "All right."

They walked silently to his apartment. Inside, Johnny motioned to the chairs at the dining room table. He dropped the tire iron near the front door and followed Jeff across the apartment. Jeff pulled a chair out and sat down while Johnny took two beers from the back of the refrigerator, twisted off the tops, and set one on the table in front of Jeff.

"Glass?"

"No, thanks."

"You said you're here looking for a job?"

"Yes, but I don't think I have much of a chance. Not really my area. Medical supplies. What the hell do I know about medical supplies?"

"Sorry to hear that."

Jeff put the bottle in his mouth and took a long swallow, drinking half the beer. He set it on the table and looked at it for a moment before raising his eyes to Johnny.

"I wanted to apologize for the way I acted when you came to visit me. I was way out of line."

"It was hard news to get."

"You can say that again." He smiled at Johnny, but when the other man didn't respond, Jeff looked away, focusing on the top of his beer bottle. "Maggie called me the other night. Gave me a real load of shit about Sara's death. Said it was my fault. She blames me. Can you believe that shit?"

"Yes, I know. She told me." Jeff had started to pick up his beer but put it down again. He looked at Johnny and grunted, a disgusted explosion of air, and shook his head from side to side. "We talk. She's having a hard time, Jeff. Cut her a little slack, okay?"

"Oh, yeah, I forgot. You two were always close. I don't know what I figured coming here. That you'd understand? That you'd see my point of view on this? Jesus, I should have known better."

Jeff picked up the beer, finished the bottle, stood up, and carried it into the small kitchen. He set it on the counter and, without waiting for an invitation, opened the refrigerator, took out another, and twisted off the cap.

"You were always in the background, you know that?" he said, walking back to the table. He sat down heavily, almost falling into the chair, hitting it with a thud, as though he were trying to break it. "With her it was always 'Johnny.' She seemed to look at you like some kind of cross between a big brother and fucking rock star. Shit, she never said anything, but I always knew I was being compared to you. God, no one could live up to that."

"Why did you come here, Jeff?"

Jeff took a long swallow and put the bottle down. The insides of the bottle foamed, and there was less than an inch of beer left in the bottom.

"Tell me who killed Sara."

"Oh, for Christ sake, Jeff, I don't have any idea."

"That's bullshit."

"I wish it was but it isn't. I don't know anything."

"Johnny, I don't give a shit what Maggie told you about me. The fact is I love my daughters and I loved Sara."

"I know you did."

"Do you? I don't think so. You and Maggie. You both think this whole thing is my fault. If I hadn't driven her out, she'd be alive today. Yeah, well, how about Maggie? She wasn't exactly the perfect mother now, was she? Was she? She tell you about how she used to scream at Sara? She tell you that she used to hit Sara? Did she? No, nobody wants to talk about that. Nobody wants to talk about the fact that Sara ran away from Atlanta. Hell, no, it's just easier to blame Jeff, the father who wasn't there."

"What's this about, Jeff? What are you doing here? Why did you come?"

"I told you. I want to know who killed her."

"And I told you, I don't know."

"This is all just so much bullshit. Maggie calls me up and screams at me how I killed my own kid, my wife thinks I'm losing it, I can't catch a break on the job, and you just sit there and look at me like I'm some bug crawled out from under the carpet."

"Jeff, I can only tell you what I told Maggie. You're not responsible. The man who started that fire is responsible."

"And who is that?"

"Jesus, give it a rest. I told you, I don't know."

"Forget it, okay? Just forget it. I'll take care of this myself." He shoved the chair back, almost knocking it over as he stood. "Thanks for the beer. I can show myself out." He walked across the living room and banged out the front door, not bothering to close it.

Johnny sat at the table, staring out the open door for almost a minute.

"God, what an asshole," he mumbled. He tried to tell himself that Jeff's actions were just his way of mourning. Someday he'd calm down and understand and maybe even apologize. But at that moment, Johnny knew he didn't care if he ever saw or heard from Jeff again.

The living room door was still open, and after a moment Johnny stood, took the beer bottle Jeff had left on the table, threw it in the garbage, and walked to the front door. He only had to wait a moment before seeing Archie. The cat crept out to the small clearing where the empty saucer was and looked at Johnny on the porch. He waited but didn't meow. He'd come halfway; now it was up to Johnny.

Leaving the door open, Johnny went to the refrigerator. He found a loaf of white bread in the back of the bottom shelf, took out a slice, and picked up the quart of milk. Outside, the cat stepped a few feet away while Johnny tore the bread into small chunks and dropped them into the dish and poured the milk over them.

As Johnny walked away, the cat moved to the saucer and watched Johnny cautiously for a moment before beginning to eat the bread and milk. It was hard to tell in the dim light, but it looked like the cat had another scratch on his face. Another fight.

"Okay, Archie, tomorrow I'll get you something even better. Looks like you could use something to build up your strength. I know how it feels," Johnny said. The cat froze at the sound of Johnny's voice. Hunched over the saucer, it turned its head and watched Johnny. But Archie wasn't going to run, Johnny could see that. The cat was ready to fight if it needed to. After a moment, it turned its attention back to the food.

Johnny closed the door, leaned back against it, looked into the dark, empty apartment, and saw the phone on the kitchen counter. For a fleeting second he thought of calling her again but instead climbed the stairs to the bedroom. He picked up the picture of him and his brother and Maggie and studied it, looking at the young faces smiling at him. When he put it down and finally fell in bed, he lay awake for a moment and felt as alone as a lion spirited out of Africa to the "natural habitat" of a zoo. He might not ever fully comprehend how he got there, but he'd know intuitively that he would never go home again.

Twenty

•━━━━━━━━━━•

*T*he first call came a little after five the next morning. Johnny rolled over and picked the phone off the nightstand, and for a moment the echo of a transoceanic call and the British accent threw him off.

"Hello, is this John Rose?"

"Yeah, who's this?" He blinked, trying to fight off the sleep.

"Good morning. It's Clyde Haverman, from News One, Sydney's number one radio station. Sorry to bother you so early but it's already late here, you know."

"What?"

"Just read the story about the shooting. Must have been terrifying and all. Wondered if you'd be willing to do a few minutes with us. Just a quick chat."

"Chat?"

"Right. We'll record it and play it in the morning, drive time."

"This really isn't a good idea. Thanks for calling, but I'm not looking for publicity."

"But as a reporter, I was sure you'd understand. It's quite a story. Not one we hear every day."

"Yeah, I understand. Thanks for calling."

He hung up and lay on his back, staring at the ceiling. "Shit," he swore under his breath. The AP had obviously picked up the *Journal*'s story. It was probably already in papers around the world. He should have seen it coming. It was, after all, a great story. The attempted assassination of an American newspaper reporter. It screamed to lead the six o'clock news or get good play someplace in the paper.

The next call came half an hour later and then another a few minutes after that and then another. He didn't answer any of them. He didn't want people prying into his life, putting him on television, moving him off the sidelines to center stage. All he wanted was the truth. How the hell would being on *Hard Copy* and *Eyewitness News* help?

About six he gave up trying to sleep and showered, taking care to wash the wound in his left arm gently. He rewrapped it following the instructions the paramedics had given him, got dressed, and went downstairs. He stopped just long enough to listen to the messages the reporters had left. The first one convinced him he'd been right to ignore them.

"So, Johnny, what are you working on this time? Must be one hell of a story to get someone pissed off enough to try and kill you. Hey, this is Terry Fox, long time no see. I'm still at KJTV. Give me a call back, I'd love to talk to you, get some more on this. Any possibility you could make it into the studio today? We could do a full interview. We're thinking of dubbing the story 'Reporter and the Rifleman.' Got a nice ring to it, don't you think? You'll be famous. Listen, we'll even spring for the makeup. Sorry I missed you. I'll leave a message at the Journal, *just in case you're on your way in."*

The message clicked to an end, and a moment later the next one started. Johnny flipped open his notebook and wrote the names and phone numbers as he listened to the messages. Some were aggressive and insistent. Others took a softer approach, saying they'd just like a quick minute or two and maybe get a comment. As he listened to the last message, Johnny knew he was at ground zero in a budding media circus. He told himself that with any luck the whole thing would die down in a day or two. But as he headed to the front door, the phone began ringing again.

He ate breakfast at an all-night coffee shop, drove to the *Journal,* and parked near the building. As he walked across the lot toward the door, he saw two Hispanic pressmen speaking rapidly in Spanish near the back of an old Mazda pickup. One nudged the other as Johnny approached, and they averted their eyes in silence when he walked by.

The early crew was already in, a few reporters, editors, and a clerk. As he walked by the receptionist, a dough-faced woman with short, bleached hair, she smiled and said, "I'm glad you're okay."

"Thanks, Lisa," he mumbled. By the time he reached his desk, two young reporters were waiting and a third was working her way toward him.

"Hey, man, what happened last night?" one asked.

He looked at the two as he sat down. "Someone took a few shots at me."

"Yeah, I read the story. Was someone really trying to kill you?"

"Sure seemed like it at the time."

"Why?"

Johnny looked past them. "I'm not really sure. Listen, guys, I'd like to talk, but I've got to chat with Kuscyk."

They turned and saw the metro editor walking quickly toward them.

"Yeah, sure."

Kuscyk didn't slow down as he passed Johnny's desk.

"In the conference room," he said and walked on, leading the way, rolling from side to side as he went. Kuscyk closed the door, pulled out a chair, and dropped into it. Just after eight, and his tie was already loose and his cuffs rolled up. He looked at Johnny with a softness in his eyes that Johnny hadn't seen before.

"You okay, Rose?"

"Yeah. Like I told you last night, I got lucky. The first bullet hit my mirror."

"Good, good. Okay, so tell me."

"It's pretty much all in the story. Someone standing out on

the street opened up on me. Then, after Bennett left I got a call. Some guy telling me to stay away."

"Who was it?"

"Shit, Stan, I don't know. If I knew that I'd tell the police."

"Okay, so someone shoots at you and then calls in a warning just to make sure you got the message to stay away."

"Yup."

"But stay away from what?" Before Johnny could answer, an assistant metro editor knocked tentatively on the door. Kuscyk didn't even look, he simply yelled. "Go away!" He gestured to Johnny. "So?"

"The girl. He said, 'Stay away from her.' He had to mean Sara's friend Gem. I don't know who else it could be."

Kuscyk nodded and looked through the glass to the newsroom for a second, then turned back to Johnny. "I got a call from Knight a few minutes ago. He told me the paper's offering a ten-thousand-dollar reward for information that leads to an arrest. He's going to hold a press conference at nine. He wants you to be there."

"Me? Come on, Stan, I don't want to do that. This is a circus. Reporters aren't supposed to make the news, they're supposed to report it. If I stand up there, I'll look like a fool. I'll become known as the rifleman reporter."

Kuscyk smiled mischievously. "Hey, that's got a nice ring to it."

"Jesus, Stan."

"Okay, I get the point. But you'll be at the press conference. You don't have a choice."

"Stan, showing up at a press conference, being on the six o'clock news, isn't going to help me find out who killed Sara or why."

"Maybe not, but it might help circulation for a day or two. And I don't have to remind you that you're the guy that pissed off the paper's biggest advertiser and that Knight supported you."

"So now I'm supposed to be grateful?"

"No. You're supposed to be at the press conference. It starts at nine. And put on your tie and jacket."

"Do I have any choice at all in this?"

"No."

Johnny stared at the tabletop for a moment. "Okay then, I'm going to ask for help. I'm going to appeal to the public. Maybe someone saw something or knows something."

"Okay, that's not a bad idea," Kuscyk said, but he was tentative and watching Johnny closely. "You're just talking about getting help with this shooting, right?"

"No." Johnny raised his eyes to the metro editor and leaned into the table. "I'm going to talk about the whole thing, the fire, the body on the hillside. Everything. Maybe I'll even tell 'em about Carol Holland's lawyers threatening me with a restraining order. Then I'll tell 'em about the phone call."

"You said that guy was talking about Gem, not Carol Holland."

Johnny leaned back and threw his hands up. "I don't know who he was talking about."

Kuscyk looked at Johnny and let the silence build. "You're not going to do that, Rose. The last thing Knight said to me was you don't mention Carol Holland or the restraining order at the press conference. If it looks like we're trying to connect her with the shooting, even remotely, they'll sue us for slander."

"So? They can't win."

"Maybe not. But that's not why you're going to leave her out of it, and you know it."

"Oh? So why won't I mention her? Might shake her up pretty good."

"Because it's unprofessional. It's smear and innuendo. That's not who you are. It's not how you operate."

"It isn't? Someone killed those kids. Murdered them. You weren't there. You don't know."

"But I know you."

"So what the hell am I going to say?"

"Not much."

"This is bullshit," Johnny said and shoved the chair back from the table and walked out of the conference room into the newsroom. His phone was ringing, and Johnny sat in his chair and just watched it, feeling the frustration and anger bottled inside. The call rolled into his voice-mail, but a moment later the phone rang again. This time he answered it with a half shout.

"Yeah?"

"Mr. Rose?"

He recognized the voice, and the anger he'd felt a moment before began to disappear. "Yes."

"This is Clay Griffin. I'm sorry I missed you last night."

"Yeah."

"Well, I think you made an excellent point. If you have some time later this morning, say about eleven, my clients would like to meet you."

Johnny saw Kuscyk stand at his desk and point to his wrist. It was time for the press conference. "Good. I think that's a great idea. Give me the address and I'll be there."

He wrote the number in his notebook and read it back to Griffin.

"That's right. It's in Hancock Park. Do you know where that is?"

Johnny read the street name again. "Yeah, in fact, I think I know the house."

"You do?"

"I've been there."

"Oh." He seemed momentarily confused. "Well, good. We'll see you at eleven then."

"Rose, let's go," Kuscyk yelled.

"Yeah, see you then," Johnny said and followed Kuscyk to the *Journal*'s front door.

The press conference was held on the sidewalk in front of the paper. The independent news stations showed up, and two of the network affiliates sent reporters, as did the news radio stations, two newspapers, and the AP. Johnny stood behind Knight and listened as the publisher explained the *Journal*'s reward and offered to take questions. A television reporter was the first.

"Johnny, is this connected to a story you're working on?"

Johnny glanced at Kuscyk, who looked directly at him, holding his eyes for an instant.

"I have no proof that it's connected to anything I'm working on." He stepped back from the microphone, and Knight stepped up again hoping to gain control of the conference himself. But the next reporter's question was also aimed at Johnny.

"Mr. Rose, I did a quick scan of the *Journal* for the last few weeks." It was the AP reporter, a middle-aged woman who looked anorexic and wore a skirt that was too short. "You've only had one byline. It was on a story you wrote on an arson fire over in Hollywood. A girl was killed. Is it possible that's connected to this shooting incident?"

Johnny paused a moment to glance at Knight, whose eyes were small and dark. Johnny moved to the microphone.

"I have no proof that this is tied to any specific story I'm working on. But I am working on a couple of things and I have to get back to them now. So if you'll excuse me." He turned and walked back through the front door into the *Journal*.

He could hear the reporters shouting questions as he walked through the door and feel Knight's eyes boring into his back, but he didn't look back and he didn't stop in the newsroom. As he passed his desk, he grabbed his notebook and walked straight to the elevator in the rear of the building and left.

He arrived in Hancock Park thirty minutes early and drove through the streets looking at the big houses with wide porches, ornate white columns, and small colorful signs warning "Armed Response" stuck in the flower beds. He tried to imagine Gem growing up in this neighborhood of gardeners and pool men, maids and Spanish-speaking nannies.

At two minutes to eleven, he parked at the curb outside the tall, impenetrable hedge that obscured any view of the house. He'd recognized the house instantly. He'd been there only a few nights before. It was the house Gem had run to when she fled his car. No wonder he'd lost her. She knew every hiding place on the grounds. He crossed the small strip of grass between the sidewalk and the street. It was soggy from too much water, and he had to scrape his feet to get rid of the mud as he walked up the long, used-brick driveway. Halfway to the house, he saw an elaborate tree house built amid the branches of the big sycamore near the far edge of the property and wondered if she'd hid there. He doubted she'd gone into the big Tudor-style house. Gem hadn't gone home again, he was sure.

A moment after he pressed the doorbell, Griffin opened the door.

"Mr. Rose, you're right on time. Thank you for coming."

"You're welcome."

Griffin led Johnny through a formal living room with a thick oriental carpet and a curved couch with large white pillows, down a hall to a sunken family room in the back of the house. The room's rear wall was all windows and looked onto an expansive lawn, swimming pool, and tennis courts.

"I'll let them know you've arrived. Make yourself comfortable," Griffin said. He gestured to the sunken family room and walked away, leaving Johnny alone at the top of the steps.

Through the windows, Johnny could see a man, perhaps fifty, lean and fit, in white shorts and shirt playing tennis with a much younger man, who had him on the run. A moment later, the older man hit the ball hard, slamming it in apparent frustration. It sailed far wide of the court, and the young man stopped and walked patiently around the net. Although he couldn't hear, Johnny could tell from the gestures that the younger man was coaching, showing the proper stroke. The older man turned abruptly, walked back to the baseline, and glared at his coach.

Johnny turned to look at the rest of the room and in an instant forgot the tennis game in the backyard. His eyes were riveted by the pictures that covered the wide mantel of a large flagstone fireplace to his right. He walked down the steps, crossed the room, and stopped inches from the mantel and looked at the pictures, picking up each framed and matted photo of Gem and studying it carefully before moving to the next one. As he went, his stomach tightened, his breathing came more quickly, and he felt slightly nauseated, as though he were looking at an outrageous yet totally legal form of child pornography. None of the photos were candids. There were no shots of mom or dad steadying the bicycle while their little girl learned to ride. No girl in a soccer uniform awkwardly clutching the ball, no photos of pony rides or snapshots of a group of kids with silly hats and balloons at a birthday party. In each photograph Gem was a little statuette, a child in beautiful gowns and makeup, smiling at the camera. The smile was the worst. It made him want to close his eyes and look away. In the early pictures her smile was strained, a work of endurance and practice. But as she grew older it was more relaxed and assured as her lips formed a seductiveness inappropriate for her age. But as the pictures progressed, her eyes became more and more empty. In one picture she wore patent-leather shoes and stockings and her hair was perfect. In another a tutu, dancing slippers, and tights, and in another cowboy boots and a frilly cowgirl dress. Always in costume, always dressed expensively, her lips shone red with lipstick and her fingernails glowed with polish.

Johnny turned away and looked up just as Griffin walked to the top of the steps.

"Johnny Rose," he said but didn't finish because the man Johnny had seen on the tennis court walked past him and came quickly down into the room. He approached Johnny and held out his hand. He still wore the white shorts and shirt from the court and had a towel draped across his neck.

"I'm Ted Rottman and this is my wife, Joellen." He half-turned and gestured behind him to a woman, who had followed him but stopped on the top step.

Rottman was tall, a good six feet, with dark hair touched white at the temples and a tan that had come from hours on the court. Johnny shook his hand, turned, and nodded to Joellen Rottman, who smiled a distant, reserved smile. She wore a simple blue denim dress with a collar and, Johnny noticed, stockings and pumps. She came down the steps into the room but walked away from Johnny and her husband to the windows and looked out at the backyard, her back to them. Joellen turned again only when her husband began speaking.

"I saw you admiring the photos of Jeanette. She's a lovely young girl, isn't she? Takes after her mother, don't you think?"

Johnny looked at Joellen Rottman and back at her husband. Only then did he realize that Rottman was looking at the fireplace, not his wife. Johnny followed his eyes to a portrait of a very young and very beautiful Joellen in a long, slinky white gown, smiling at the painter, hung high above the mantel. As he studied it, Johnny saw an early hint of the reserved expression he'd seen in the photos on the mantel moments before.

"Yes, I see the resemblance," Johnny said, not sure how he'd missed the portrait when he first walked in. It was meant to dominate the room but seemed shunted to the shadows by the photos of Gem.

"Please, have a seat." Rottman gestured to the sofa. Johnny sat on the edge of it, his hands resting between his knees, and Rottman lowered himself into a wing-backed chair. Joellen stood by the windows, watching them.

"Mr. Rose, I'm due at the hospital shortly, so let me be brief," Rottman said.

"You're a doctor?"

"A thoracic surgeon. Now, as I was saying, our daughter, you probably know her by that awful name she uses now, what is it? Gem. That's it. Anyway, she first ran away about four years ago. I won't bore you with the reasons, and frankly I'm still not sure either Joellen or I understand them. But, suffice it to say that since then our lives have been a living hell. You have no idea what she's done to us."

"Mr. Rottman I don't—"

"Wait!" Rottman held up his hand; obviously a man used to talking, not listening. "Let me finish. We finally heard about two months ago that she was back in LA. In Hollywood, to be specific. A friend of my wife's saw her on Hollywood Boulevard and called her. I asked Mr. Griffin to try to find her. Clay and I have been friends since college. He handles all my personal business. An investigator who works for him was able to track her to that house that burned down. When we heard about the fire, we were worried sick that she was the girl who'd been killed. You can only imagine how relieved we were it wasn't her."

"Yes, I know how awful it is to lose someone," Johnny said, keeping his voice controlled, even. In his mind's eye he could see the gurney being pushed from the house toward the coroner's van. "But look, Mr. Rottman, since you're obviously very busy, why don't you just tell me why you asked me to come here today? What it is you think I can do for you?"

"We want our daughter back, Mr. Rose."

"I don't know what I can do to help you. You should be contacting the youth agencies, the shelters, not a newspaper reporter."

"They won't help us. Mr. Griffin has told us about your search for Jeanette and her friend Billy."

"He what?" Johnny faced Griffin, who was near the windows with Joellen.

"I've been asking a lot of questions in the same places you have. Your name came up, that's all," Griffin said.

Johnny stared at Griffin for a moment before turning to Rottman again. "Okay, let me ask you a couple of questions," Johnny said.

"Like what?"

"Like, did she have any friends besides the kids in that squat?"

"I wouldn't have the faintest idea about her friends," Rottman said.

"If she was in trouble, who would she contact? Any family friends or relatives?"

"Trouble, what kind of trouble?"

"Who would she contact, Mr. Rottman?"

"I don't know."

"Do you have any idea where she would go?"

"I don't know the answer to these questions, Mr. Rose. If I did I wouldn't need you. That's why I asked you to come here today. I want you to help me, ah, help us find our daughter."

"I'm not a private detective, Mr. Rottman. I think you'd be better off with someone else."

"But you know some of the kids. These kids won't talk with our investigators. Clay told me you met some of them when you were spending time with that cousin of yours. Maybe they'll trust you. And that woman from the shelter. Maybe she'll tell you something."

Rottman was staring at him, waiting, expectant. "No," Johnny said. "I can't help you."

"Five thousand dollars," Rottman said.

"What?"

"If you help us find her."

Johnny stared at Rottman for a long time. The sweat had dried on his neck and plastered his hair to the temples. But he still looked good, a man not used to worrying about details.

"I've got someplace I've got to be," Johnny said. "If you'll excuse me."

"If she contacts you, agree to meet her and call me. Or call if you find out where she is. One phone call. Five thousand dollars for one phone call. Think about it. You'd be helping Jeanette. Mr. Rose, our daughter needs help. Despite all she's done to us, we love her and we want to help her. If you help us find her, I'm ready to pay you five thousand dollars. Cash, if you want. There will be no records."

Johnny looked from Rottman to Griffin, and his gaze slid to Joellen, who turned away toward the backyard.

"If I see your daughter, I will ask her to call you. I will tell her you asked me to give her your love and tell her you want her to come home."

"Mr. Rose, that's not what we want," Rottman said, his tone petulant.

Johnny moved to the step. "I can show myself out," he said and walked out of the living room, through the house, and outside.

At the curb, Johnny hesitated before getting into the Z and looked at the tall hedge that grew along the sidewalk hiding the house from public view. He got in the car, started the engine, and had just slipped it into gear when Joellen Rottman bolted from behind the hedge.

Her eyes were filled with tears that sent black lines of mascara down her cheeks and ruined her carefully crafted makeup. She was breathing heavily and had obviously run to the street. She crossed the narrow grass area to the side of the Z, looked at Johnny, and waited. He leaned over and rolled the window down.

"I was afraid I would miss you," she said.

"Mrs. Rottman, I can't help you."

"I don't know what you can do, Mr. Rose. But if you see Jeanette, tell her I love her. Tell her she is all I have." Her eyes clouded up, and she began crying again. She sank to her knees in the grass next to the car and leaned against the door, her folded arms on the edge of the window.

"My husband's not an evil man. He loves her, too, in his own way. He just doesn't understand what . . . he just doesn't know." She seemed to be rambling, not talking to him as much as begging an unseen force for help.

"Mrs. Rottman, I have no idea where your daughter is. I may never see her."

"She's wanted by the police."

"What? Why?"

"Burglary. They came to our house about six months ago and questioned us. Ted's afraid they'll arrest her, and it'll get in the papers. But he thinks if we have lawyers and she turns herself in he can keep it quiet."

"What do you think, Mrs. Rottman?"

"I don't care about the papers. I just want my daughter." She looked over her shoulder toward the driveway and back to Johnny. "You asked if she had any other friends. There was a girl, a black girl named Bev. When Jeanette first ran away, she called me a few times. She told me about Bev. Maybe she can help you find Jeanette."

"Maybe, but I don't know. I just don't know," Johnny said, remembering Beverly, overdressed in the cheap clothes from My Home's closet.

Joellen Rottman rubbed her tears away. A gut-level anger seeped into her voice.

"What Ted told you isn't true. A friend of mine didn't call me. Jeanette called me and told me she was back in Holly-wood. I was thrilled. You have no idea how happy I was. I begged her to come home but she wouldn't. She stayed away but she called him. Called him at the hospital to throw it in his face."

"I don't think I understand. Throw what in his face?"

"Where she was. What she was doing."

"That she was in Hollywood?"

"Ted always wanted her to be a movie star. He had this fantasy life built for her. He never understood that she was just a child. God, she was just a child." She started crying again, but Johnny could see that the fury, which had been pushed deep inside her long ago, was emerging.

"Mrs. Rottman, I don't think I—"

"She called him, don't you see? Just called to humiliate him. She told him she was working for a movie star. Then she laughed at him. 'I'm cleaning her toilets and doing yard work for a big Hollywood star, Daddy. Are you proud of me now? I'm in Hollywood.' And then she hung up. That's when he called Clay. Then Clay told us about the fire and I thought I had lost her. But I made a vow to myself. I will protect my daughter, Mr. Rose. This will never happen again." She looked down at the grass for a moment, then stood up. Johnny could see the water stains on her stockings, her knees covered with mud from kneeling in the spongy grass. "I love Jeanette. If you see her, tell her to call me. Here." She searched through a pocket in her dress, pulled out a piece of paper, and handed it through the window to Johnny. "It's my cell phone. My husband doesn't even know I have it."

She stepped back from the car, but Johnny said her name before she moved away.

"Mrs. Rottman, did she say who the movie star was? Whose house she was working at?"

"No, and Ted didn't ask, I'm sure."

"It doesn't matter. I think I already know."

He slipped the Z into gear and sped away from the curb. Half a block away he glanced in the mirror and saw her standing at the corner of the hedge, and he had the feeling she was debating returning to her own house.

Twenty-one

*T*en minutes later Johnny was pounding on Carol Holland's door. He waited a moment and pushed the doorbell. There was no answer, and he banged again and pushed the bell harder, as if effort alone could make it ring louder. Still no one came. He stepped off the porch, walked back down the short walk to the driveway, turned, and looked again at the house.

"She left about a half hour ago."

Johnny turned and saw Henry using a push broom to move a small amount of dirt down his driveway toward the street. The old man took a couple more swipes at the dirt, stopped, and waited while Johnny crossed the street to him. He wore the same faded shirt and dark polyester slacks he'd had on when Johnny last saw him.

"Hi, Henry, how you doing?"

"I'm fine. You're that reporter, right?"

"Yes. Looks like I missed Miss Holland."

"Like I said, she left about half an hour ago."

Johnny looked back at her house, then smiled at Henry. "Tell me something, Henry. Do you ever see any teenagers up here, maybe doing yard work around her house? You know, in the last couple of months or so."

"Oh, sure. A while back she had some kids up here help-

234

ing her clear off that hillside. Even asked me if I had any stuff that needed doing, but I can pretty much take care of it all myself."

"How do these kids get up here? It's a long way to walk. Miss Holland go and get them, bring 'em up?"

"No, they came in that church van."

"What church van?"

"The church with the big neon sign."

"God's House?"

"Yeah, that's the one."

"You're sure."

"Sure, I'm sure. I know 'cause that minister was up here too. He'd talk to the kids, you know. He's the one asked me if I needed 'em to do anything around my place."

"You mean Reverend Roberts. The one from God's House?"

"Yeah, that's him. I read about him in some magazine. He won a gold medal in the Olympics. Did you know that?"

"Yes, I knew. Was he driving the van?"

"Nah, he always comes up in his own car."

"Thank you, Henry. I appreciate your time."

"Glad to help. She's a nice lady. You be sure to write a nice article about her."

"I'll try. Say, you don't have any idea where she was going, do you?"

Henry smiled and shook his head. "Nah. We chatted a little when she left. She always takes a minute or two to talk to me. Did you know she's going to be in *People* magazine? Oh, yeah, that's where she's going, to get her picture taken with that minister."

Johnny hurried across the street to his car and swung the door open, looking at the remnants of the side mirror. He started to get into the car but stopped suddenly, understanding what Henry had just said. He looked back and called, "Hey, Henry." He waited until the old man stopped sweeping and looked at him.

"You said the minister always comes up in his own car. Does he come up often, even when the kids aren't here?"

"Oh, sure. He comes up here a lot."

Johnny was speeding when he took the curves, sliding close to the edge of the street. Once he glanced in his rearview mirror and caught sight of a red Toyota Celica coming down the mountain after him. A moment later the car disappeared around a curve. It wasn't a police cruiser or a motorcycle cop, so Johnny paid it no heed. He shot through the light at Franklin, going through the intersection just before a car came from the east, its horn blaring. Moments later, he turned the Z up the narrow driveway of the Hank Jefferson Center. He parked in the back between a Mercedes and a Chevy Caprice. As he climbed from the car a young man in a blue blazer and gray slacks came from the house, waved, and called to him.

"You the writer?"

"I'm a reporter," Johnny said.

But before he could add more the young man stepped off the porch and walked toward him, smiling, his hand outstretched. "Hi, I'm Bill. Reverend Roberts asked me to keep an eye out for you in case you were a little early. We weren't expecting you for a few minutes yet. He said to have you wait in the study. It's just inside."

"I think maybe you have me mixed up," Johnny said. But the young man was paying little attention.

"Miss Holland's already here. She's in the center right now. She'll be over in a couple of minutes. The photographer's already here, too. He's in the center with Miss Holland."

Johnny looked at the boy, nodded, and walked into the house and down the hall to the study. He'd been there only a few minutes when he heard footsteps on the hardwood in the hall. Roberts was first through the door, looking behind him as he walked in.

"We can sit in here. It's probably not what you expected. Just because God's House is successful, people—" He turned into the room and saw Johnny. He hesitated, started to speak, stopped, then went on. "Oh! Johnny, ah, hi. I, ah, I wasn't expecting you."

Carol Holland was only a step behind and almost ran into Roberts when he stopped. She looked past him and saw Johnny. His sudden appearance in the small study jolted her. She stiffened, and he saw a flash of hatred and fear in her eyes, but the look was gone instantly and she recovered her composure.

"You must enjoy spending your employer's money, Mr. Rose. I'm sure the *Journal*'s lawyers are just as expensive as my husband's." She moved sideways to get past Roberts into the room. She stopped just inside the door and stared at Johnny.

"You hired Gem to work at your house, and Dallas, and probably my cousin too. What the hell's this all about? What are you hiding?"

"Johnny, this is not the time," Roberts said. His voice was gentle but firm and well practiced, the minister moving a loud drunk from the last pew to the door. "We're here for an interview with this writer from *People*." He gestured to the man standing in the hall. The reporter, short and thin with curly black hair, looked through the door from Johnny to Carol Holland and back again. "The photographer will be coming in a few minutes. He's just finishing up at the center. We can talk about this later," Roberts added, almost pleading for the scene to evaporate. But Carol Holland ignored him.

"I've never denied helping kids, Mr. Rose. I've hired a lot of street kids to do chores around my house. I told you that before," she said. Her voice was cold and hard, her eyes dark and narrow.

"Yeah, how many of them ended up dead?"

"That's slander."

"Tough."

"You'll hear from my lawyers."

"Yeah, what are they going to do, set my house on fire? Stuff me under a train?"

"You're sick."

A quiet settled on the small, crowded office. Johnny shifted his gaze to Roberts.

"Your van took 'em up there. You knew 'em, Dick. What are you doing? What the hell's this all about? I thought you cared about these kids."

"There a problem here?" Buddy appeared in the hall, staring at Johnny over the writer's shoulder.

"No, no, Buddy. Thank you." Roberts didn't even look at him. His eyes were on Johnny. "Johnny, I don't know who rides in the van. We take dozens of kids all kinds of places every day. I don't keep track. I see hundreds of kids every week. I don't know all their names. Look, this is not the time or the place."

"I'm going to call the police. This man is a menace," Buddy declared and walked away.

"No!" Roberts shouted after him. "Johnny's an old friend. We'll handle it here."

Johnny looked from Roberts to the writer in the doorway, whose eyes were darting from Johnny to the minister and back to Carol Holland. He was smiling, probably thinking he'd stumbled into a better story than he'd expected.

"Johnny, there's nothing for you here." Roberts's voice was low, beseeching. He raised his hands in a small gesture that begged his old friend to help. Johnny caught a smile from Carol Holland, the actress who's just had the wardrobe assistant fired for some imagined infraction.

Johnny moved past Roberts to the door, stopped, and looked back at the minister.

"What happened to you? You used to care about people, Dick."

"Johnny, I'll overlook that because we've been friends for a long time. But please, just go."

Johnny stepped past the *People* reporter into the hallway.

They were only inches apart. He looked at the other writer. "Ask her where she went to high school. She tells a good story." He started down the hall and out of the house.

"Hey," the reporter called. When Johnny turned, he saw the recognition in the man's face. "You're Johnny Rose. You're the guy the sniper tried to take out, right?"

Johnny spent a long moment struggling to think of some parting shot, something that would hit everyone like a brick in the face. But all he could do was say, "Yeah. That's me, the rifleman reporter."

The writer gestured back toward the study. "This little scene here have anything to do with that shooting?"

"I don't know what this is about," Johnny said and walked out of the building.

Buddy was waiting by the Z's back fender, his arms folded across his chest. He watched Johnny cross the lawn to the car, his eyes tracking Johnny's movements. As Johnny pulled the car door open, Buddy surprised him with a smile.

"You know, man, I thought you were smart. Reverend Roberts used to talk about his friend the newspaper reporter who always wanted the truth. But now I know who you are. You're like all them other losers I've known all my life. Just trying to destroy what they'll never be."

"No, you had it right the first time, Buddy. All I want is the truth. It just doesn't seem that anyone around here knows how to tell it."

Twenty-two

●────────────●

Kate came around her desk the moment Johnny appeared in the doorway of her office. She crossed the few feet to the door and embraced him.

"Oh, Johnny, are you okay? I've been trying to call you. I tried your house and office, but there was never an answer."

"Sorry, I wasn't answering my phone. But yeah, I'm fine, thanks."

"God, I'm so glad. I heard about it on the radio this morning, and when I couldn't reach you . . . I'm just glad you're here."

"I came straight from God's House. I needed to see you. I called last night but you weren't there."

"I was at the hospital with Billy. He's got major problems, way beyond the medical. I had to get him a lawyer." She shook her head and walked back to her desk. "It's never easy with these kids. Everything has to be the hard way."

"Is he going to be okay?"

"Okay? No. He'll live, but they couldn't save his leg. He'll need a prosthesis. And that's only the beginning. He had a warrant out, a ticket for jaywalking. He told the cops he was eighteen so they wouldn't pick him up as a

240

runaway. Now he's looking at criminal trespass charges as an adult, even though he's only seventeen."

"I'm sorry," Johnny said. He stayed near the door, not coming into the room.

"Thanks, but we'll get it straightened out."

"Good. Kate, have you heard anything from Gem?"

"No." She shook her head slowly.

"No idea where she is?"

"None."

"Billy threw her backpack on the train before he fell. So it's gone. She doesn't have anything."

"Yes." Kate nodded, accepting his statement as though Gem's plight were an everyday situation.

Anger and frustration filled him. He balled his fist and felt a throbbing in his arm.

"This is all wrong. Gem's mother told me she used to work up at Carol Holland's house. All three of them were there. I just saw her over at God's House."

"Gem's mom? At God's House?"

"No, no. I saw her parents this morning. God, what a pair. No wonder she's a mess. Gem was bragging about cleaning Carol Holland's toilet. And then Dick says he doesn't even know who she is. Gem or Sara either. Doesn't know any of the kids. He's lying too. I know it."

"Johnny!" Kate's voice startled him. "I'm not following you. Are you sure you're okay?"

"Yeah, I'm fine. I'm probably going to be fired, but what the hell. If you're not pissing 'em off, you're not doing your job, right?"

"Johnny! Come in, sit down! Talk to me! You're rambling, not making any sense. You're running on about God's House and Carol Holland and Gem's parents. I can't understand anything you're saying. Start at the beginning. Tell me about the shooting."

Johnny looked at Kate and suddenly felt like a fool, almost embarrassed. He crossed the room slowly and sat across the desk from her. "I'm sorry, I'm still running on adrenaline, I guess. And I'm mad as hell and I don't know who I should be mad at."

"Just tell me what happened."

He told her about Roberts's plea to leave Carol Holland alone, his visit to Hank Jefferson's house, and finally described the shooting and the phone call and the press conference.

"And after the press conference you went to Gem's parents' house?"

"Yes."

"How did that go?"

He shook his head from side to side. "No wonder she's messed up. God, what an awful place."

"Bad, huh?"

"Yeah. Get this. They offered me money to help 'em find her. It was weird. It was like they thought they could just buy her back."

"They offered you money?"

"Five thousand dollars if I find her and help them get her home. Like I'm a bounty hunter or something. Jesus, they're fucked-up people, especially the father. He's a piece of work. I've known major appliances with more warmth."

"She never talked about them."

"That's not surprising. They're rich. Live in Hancock Park. The father was trying to make her into another Shirley Temple before she ran away. They had a bunch of pictures lined up on their mantel, like she was a show animal. A prize possession. They must have had her in beauty pageants from the time she could walk. But you know the worst part?" He looked at Kate, but she didn't answer. "They didn't see it. These photos were like a damned scream, and they didn't hear it. Jesus, I'd have run away too. Any kid with an ounce of personality would die in that house." He leaned back in the chair and looked up at the ceiling for a moment.

"The mother chased me out to the street and begged me to help her. I think she's getting ready to split from the father. Begged me to find her." He grunted a half laugh. "It's almost funny. They think I can help them and I can't even help my-self. I don't even know what to do next, where to look."

"Johnny, if Gem's in Hollywood, we have to hope one of the kids sees her. I've already been asking. Telling them that it's really important that I talk to her. Most of the kids are looking."

"What if the men from the rail yard find her first?"

"We have to hope they won't."

"Yeah. One thing that may help. Gem's mom told me she used to hang out with a black girl named Bev. Is that the girl I met in the dayroom? Talked about going into the Job Corps?"

"Probably. She and Gem were friends. Remember, she took her pictures. I'll talk to her. She might help. It's hard to tell."

"God, I hope she will. We need a break. Look, I have to get going." At the door he stopped and looked at the floor for a moment. "You know, I misjudged her and I can't help but think that's one reason she's running. She was asking me for help and I missed it."

"What do you mean, you misjudged her?"

"I assumed she was some poor kid from the boonies. When I was taking her home and we got close to Hancock Park, I assumed she was lying about where she lived. Who knows, maybe if I'd believed her . . . "

"You had no way to know."

"No. But you'd think I'd know better. . . . Well, it doesn't matter now. Look, I've got to get back to the paper. I should be there to give my side of it if Carol Holland's lawyers decide to haul me into court."

Kate stood and came around the corner of the desk. She smiled, but neither one seemed to know the appropriate gesture, so they simply stood.

"Good luck," she said.

"Thanks." Still they stood.

"Hey, Johnny, you didn't tell me what happened at God's House."

"It's a long story."

"Why don't you come over tonight? Tell me then. I'll make us some dinner. Something quick and simple."

He smiled. For the first time in days, it seemed that something good was happening. "I'd love to."

"See you about seven?"

"I'll be there."

He stopped at the door and looked back. "Be sure to ask Bev if you see her, okay?"

"Of course."

"Thanks. See you about seven."

He had parked about a block away, and as he walked back to the car he could feel the heat radiate from the concrete and asphalt and the happiness he'd felt only minutes before begin to melt away.

September can be the cruelest month in LA. After a summer that often sees temperatures top ninety, Mother Nature nudges the thermostat a little higher and the air becomes slightly more sodden with fumes. Winter's rains and the chamber of commerce clear days are months away. LA's summers always reminded Johnny of the distance races he'd run. It was great in the beginning, but at some point it became a grind. The needle dipped close to E, and you ran on determination and habit to the end. Summer days were great at the beach. They were less wonderful in fresh ozone and recycled air-conditioning.

When he reached his car, he looked north and saw the God's House sign and thought of the comfort a church is supposed to bring. His thoughts quickly drifted to Maggie, and he wondered how she was holding up. Had the minister visited again? Would she find comfort in the church? He looked again at the sign, then got in the car and headed back to the *Journal*.

As he pulled into traffic, he saw a red Toyota Celica ease from the curb a block behind him. On the freeway he scanned the traffic around him but didn't see the car again. At the *Journal,* he picked a parking spot close to the building, stepped out, and saw a television crew—a reporter and cameraman—hustling across the lot toward him. The reporter wore a white shirt and tie with a blue sports coat over jeans and running shoes. The cameraman was actually a petite young woman with thick blonde hair.

"Oh, Mr. Rose, may we have a minute? Just a couple of questions, if you don't mind."

How the hell did they get into the lot? Had they stayed since the press conference? He thought of just walking away, but he'd seen too many people look stupid by fleeing. He stood his ground and faced them.

"How can I help you?" he asked. The camera's light clicked on. Johnny tried to ignore the glare and focus on the reporter.

"Can you tell us what happened last night?"

"Someone took a couple of shots at me."

"Do you know who or why?"

"No."

"Certainly you must have some idea? Are you working on a sensitive story?"

"I have no proof that the shooting was related to any story I'm working on. I'm in the dark on this as much as you are. I'm working with the police. I have every faith that they'll solve this crime." Johnny was amazed at his own words. He was sounding like the PR men he'd always hated—talking, sounding good, and saying nothing.

"Have you received any other threats?"

Johnny smiled and laughed. "Well, I'll tell you this. I've been a reporter for about twenty-five years and that's the first time anyone's tried to shoot me."

He turned and walked away, knowing he hadn't answered the question, that what he'd told the reporter was true but misleading. And he didn't care.

"Rose!" Kuscyk's voice caught him before he reached his cubicle. Johnny looked up and saw the metro editor striding toward him, his pace fast. He started speaking halfway to Johnny's cubicle.

"Goddamn it, Rose, I warned you. I told you to keep me in the loop. You walk out of the press conference and now this. Jesus! Next time . . . what the hell, there's not going to be a next time. I goddamn guarantee it."

Johnny watched him cover the last few feet to his desk and started to speak, but Kuscyk cut him off. The metro editor's face was red, flushed with anger.

"That stunt at Reverend Roberts's house this morning. You got shit for brains? What the hell were you doing? That's not the way we do business. We don't do ambush interviews. I never thought you'd do that. Come on, Knight wants to see us."

Johnny followed him silently down the hall. Kuscyk's fury filled the elevator. Johnny turned to the metro editor. "Stan, let's get something straight right away. I didn't ambush anybody. Carol Holland and Reverend Roberts are both lying to me. I went there to ask why. That's all."

"I don't give a shit why you went there. That's not the point. We had a deal, remember? You were going to keep me informed so I wouldn't get blindsided. Did you call me? Did I miss the call or something?"

"Stan, I didn't know I was going there until this morning. I didn't have a chance to call you."

"Bullshit. You walk out of the press conference leaving us looking like a couple of jackasses and disappear. What? You didn't have time for a call? Oh, yeah, I forgot you're too stubborn and old-fashioned to have a cell phone. Or maybe you just didn't have a quarter, is that it? Well, guess who did find time to call me? Some writer for *People* magazine. He wanted to know the connection between you and the shooting and Carol Holland. Jesus, what the fuck were you thinking?" Kuscyk was almost shaking. "Don't you get it, Rose? I went to bat for you. I told Knight we'd keep it under control. So now when we go in there, you're on your own. You'll be lucky to have a job when Knight gets done. Hell, I'll be lucky to have a job."

"Stan, listen to me. They're lying."

"Don't! Don't say a thing."

Knight's secretary, a tall, thin woman in her early forties who wore her dark hair short, smiled at Johnny and Kuscyk as they walked into the outer office.

"Oh, hello, Mr. Kuscyk, Mr. Rose. Please have a seat, Mr. Knight is on the phone at the moment."

"We'll stand," Kuscyk said. Neither man spoke. They didn't have to wait long. A few minutes later the phone on her desk rang. The secretary answered it, listened a moment, smiled sweetly again, and said, "You can go in now. Mr. Knight's off the phone."

The publisher wore a dark blue tie and a blue shirt with a white collar. He sat writing at his desk, a slab of cherrywood that reminded Johnny of a flight deck. He put down his pen as Kuscyk and Johnny walked in and looked at them for a moment, his eyes shifting from one to the other until they settled on Johnny.

"I don't even know where to start with you." His voice was tight with anger, and Johnny could see a vein pulsing in his temple, like a taut crane cable struggling to deadlift a one-ton steel girder.

"What do you think you're doing? You know, fifteen minutes ago I was ready to fire you for insubordination for walking out of that press conference. You left me and Stan standing there looking like a couple of jerks. The great Johnny Rose, the only lone-wolf reporter left in Los Angeles. Well, I'm sick of your go-it-alone attitude. But this time you've done it." He stood suddenly and leaned forward, his face reddening with the strain. "You've fucked everything up so badly I can't even fire you."

"What?"

Knight sat again abruptly and turned away. "I just got off the phone with Charles Carruthers. They're seeking a restraining order against the paper, and you personally, Johnny. They say you're harassing Carol Holland."

"I didn't—"

"Shut up! Just shut the fuck up and listen, Rose. I also got a call from display advertising. Plank's company has pulled all their ads for the next two months. We had them on a six-month schedule. They're reviewing the other four. Oh, and did I mention that Carruthers says they're considering a slander and harassment suit? Those bastards will never win but they can cause us a lot of grief, a ton of money, and generate a lot of bad publicity." He turned again and stared at Johnny. "What the hell were you doing trying to interview Carol Holland? Are you stupid or what?"

"I didn't try to interview her. She just happened to be at the same place I was."

"You accused her of being a liar in front of a reporter for *People* magazine." Knight threw his hands in the air like a man bedeviled by an unsolvable equation.

"That's not what happened. Can I explain?"

"No, you can't," Knight barked and turned suddenly to Kuscyk. "Where the hell were you? I thought you were on top of this."

"He didn't tell me he was going to see her."

"I didn't know I was going to see her," Johnny said. "I'm trying to tell you."

"Rose, you've said enough already," Kuscyk said.

Knight's head swiveled as he looked from Kuscyk to Johnny. His jaw worked as he ground his teeth.

"There's only one reason I don't fire you right now. I won't let some lawyers tell me how to run my business. So, I'm going to back you, Rose, but don't think for a minute I like it. And this is definitely a short-term deal. If I were you, I'd start looking, because you've got no future here."

Knight sucked in a deep breath. "We've got some major damage control ahead of us. The *Journal*'s reputation is on the line here. I'll talk to our lawyers, we'll work out a press release. Something about we support our reporters and the freedom of the press but we're checking Mr. Rose's conduct blah blah blah."

"You don't have to check my conduct. What I did was within professional bounds." Johnny took a quick step toward the publisher's desk but stopped, and Knight stared at him until he stepped back.

Knight turned to Kuscyk again, and his words came as a hiss. "I don't want him writing anything. Not a goddamned thing. Is that clear?"

"Yeah, sure, but—"

Knight jabbed the air with his index finger. "But what? What?" Neither Johnny nor Kuscyk spoke, and Knight picked up the pen and began writing again. They had been dismissed.

In the newsroom, Kuscyk said, "Shit, Rose, now I've got to figure out what to do with you."

"Yeah, well, you know where to find me."

"Don't be a smart-ass, Rose."

Johnny walked to his desk and dropped into the chair. He picked up a pencil from the desktop and hurled it against the side of the cubicle. He jumped to his feet, but realized he had nowhere to go. This time he sat more slowly. The pencil had rebounded to the middle of the desk, and Johnny picked it up again and threw it down hard into the wastebasket. He turned and slapped the side of his computer with his palm. The sound reverberated across the newsroom, but no one paid attention. Thirty minutes later Kuscyk walked up.

"Close it down, Rose. You're on vacation. If I put you on administrative leave, it sounds like you did something wrong. Vacation sounds like time to get over the shock of the sniper attack. So, go home. Don't come back until I call you."

"Come on, Stan, listen to me. This isn't about advertising or *People* magazine. This is about someone killing street kids."

The metro editor looked at him for a moment, and the fury in his eyes had faded. He shook his head slowly from side to side, like a disappointed parent. When he spoke, his voice was soft, almost gentle.

"You don't get it, do you? Go home. Just go. I'll call you. And don't come back into the office until I do. I'll try to handle Knight, but if he sees you here, it'll be even tougher."

The phone rang, and Johnny looked at Kuscyk for a moment, then reached for the phone. "Don't worry, Stan," he said as he answered. "One call and I'm gone."

"Okay."

"Johnny Rose," he said to the mouthpiece as Kuscyk walked away.

"It's Detective Bennett. I've been trying to find you all day. What's this about a phone threat you got last night?"

"That's right. Someone threatened me. Called right after you'd left." Johnny went on, telling him about the brief conversation.

"You recognize the voice?"

"No. Just some guy. I couldn't tell the age, but it wasn't a kid making a prank call."

"Who was the guy talking about? Who's the woman?"

"I think it's a street kid named Gem. I told you about her."

"Yeah, I'll check with Towers in Hollywood."

"Okay, thanks."

He hung up and looked at Kuscyk's desk. The metro editor was watching him. Johnny stood, raised his hands like a criminal surrendering, and walked out of the newsroom.

Twenty-three

●————————————————●

At home Johnny stopped at the door and looked toward the bushes. He could see the saucer but not the cat. "Hey, Archie," he called, but the animal did not appear, and Johnny went inside.

He changed into his running shorts and a ragged T-shirt. He stretched quickly, taking only a few moments to lean against the closed door, then bending to touch his toes. For a moment he wondered if he were being stupid, running outside, where he would be totally exposed.

"Fuck 'em, I'm not hiding," he said to himself as he jerked the door open and went out. Running north toward San Vicente Boulevard, he kept a slow pace at first. It was not as hot on LA's west side as it had been in Hollywood, but the temperatures were still in the seventies and the heat slowed him down. Ten minutes later he reached the wide median on San Vicente and turned west to follow the path worn in the grass down the long, gentle slope toward the ocean.

Once he heard a car slowing behind him and felt an edge of panic well up inside. He picked up his pace and glanced over his shoulder. But it was an old VW bug convertible driven by a teenage girl. Slowly his fear ebbed again and he thought of the scene in Roberts's office. Imaginary conversations arranged and rearranged themselves in his head, but regardless of the words or sentences he constructed, the scene always ended the same. Everyone was telling a tale, truth reflected in a carnival mirror. His pace picked up when he thought of Knight's orders and Kuscyk's refusal even to listen. They didn't understand, he told himself, and without thinking about his pace, he ran faster, pounding out his anger. By the time he'd reached the end of the boulevard the bitterness had faded.

He stopped and caught his breath at the end of the street. The Santa Monica Bay was spread before him, and the water looked cool, the waves inviting. He stared at the ocean and admitted to himself that confronting Roberts and Holland had been stupid. He should have just walked away, not stormed into the minister's office. He'd let his frustration take over, making his decisions on impulse instead of thought. After a few minutes he turned and started back up San Vicente, his pace steady and even.

When he got home, he stretched longer, paying special attention to his knees, calves, and hamstrings. He was drinking a glass of water when the phone rang. He leaned back against the counter and let it ring. At that moment there was no one in the world he wanted to talk to. But when it rolled into the answering machine and he heard the voice, he grabbed the phone.

"Hi, Johnny, it's Maggie."

"Hey, Maggie, hold on a second, let me turn off the machine." He punched the button and spoke again. "Sorry about that. I just got in from a run. Thanks for calling. How are you?"

"I'm doing better."

"Really? That's good."

"Yeah, really, Johnny. I've been thinking a lot about Sara, of course. But I've also been thinking about what you said. About Annie. I can't let her go under too. In fact, she went back to soccer practice today. She missed a lot of practices, but at this age I don't think it really makes much difference." She laughed suddenly, a bright, clear, and genuine laugh. "I still don't understand that game. It's good when the ball goes in the net. I know that much, but all this other stuff. I mean, what's offsides?"

"You're asking me?"

"No, not really. I mean, I wasn't expecting an answer. Anyway, that's not why I called. I just got a very strange phone call."

"From who?" Johnny could feel his muscles tighten, and he squeezed the telephone hard.

"Jeff's wife."

"Oh?" he said, suddenly curious. "What did she want?"

"She wanted to know if I've heard from him. She said she hasn't seen him in a couple of days and there was a message from his boss on her machine wanting to know where he's been. She said he'd been acting really weird ever since he saw you."

"Me?"

"That's what she said."

"What did you tell her?"

"The truth. I have absolutely no idea where he is. I haven't spoken to him since . . . " She was quiet for a moment. "Well, since I called him up and yelled at him. I guess I was out of line."

"Water under the bridge, Maggie."

"Yeah, I guess."

"Listen, you can't be looking at the past. You have to think of the future. You've got to take care of Annie and yourself now."

"I know that. It's just, sometimes it's hard to move on."

"I know, but you have to do it. You have to go forward."

"I'll try. So, have you heard from him?"

"He stopped by my apartment a couple of nights ago. He thinks I know who killed Sara. When I told him I didn't, he got pissed off and left."

"Do you?"

"Do I what?"

"Know who killed her?"

"No, Maggie, I don't. I'll call you when I know something for sure. I'm not giving up on this, Maggie. Believe me." She hadn't mentioned the shooting. Maybe the Atlanta papers hadn't picked it up, or she'd missed it.

"So you don't know where he is, either, do you?"

"I haven't got a clue. He stomped out of here and I haven't seen . . ." His voice trailed away. He remembered the red Toyota Celica he'd seen trailing him and knew without hesitation that it was Jeff.

"Johnny, you there?"

"Yeah, I was just thinking of Jeff. Don't spend your time worrying about him, okay? He'll be fine."

"Yeah, he always lands on his feet. Look, I gotta go. I've got to do the dinner dishes. If you see Jeff, tell him to call his wife."

"I will. Hey, Maggie . . ."

"Yes?"

"You sound better."

"Good. I am. I've got a long way to go, but I'll get there. That news about her being pregnant, that was really tough to take. For a while there I thought it was just one thing too many. But then . . . well, we'll get through this, we really will."

"I know you will. I'll call you again soon."

"You don't have to check up on me."

"I want to. Say hi to Annie. Tell her I love her."

"I will."

After hanging up, Johnny showered and dressed in shorts and a polo shirt. He paused again on his front step to watch for Archie, but the cat didn't appear. He was already smiling in anticipation of seeing Kate when he reached the car and backed into the alley. He slipped a tape into the deck, and by the time he reached the street he was humming along.

Kate banged open the door and ran to meet him when he was still coming up the driveway.

"Gem called," she said, catching her breath.

"Is she okay? Where is she?"

"She says she's okay. She wants to talk to you. She tried to get you at the paper but you were gone. I told her you would be here soon and to call."

"Good."

Kate shook her head. "She sounded scared. I've never heard her sound afraid before. Never. She was always tough."

"How soon will she call?" Johnny looked over Kate's shoulder toward the door, half-expecting to hear the phone ring.

"When she called, I told her I'd come get her right away. But she won't wait outside anywhere. She's going to find a squat and hide for the night."

"Ah, shit," Johnny said. "I can't be at the paper tomorrow. I've been suspended. They're not calling it that, but I can't go back. I'll be fired."

"She has your home number? You put it on the note you left for her, right?"

"Yeah, yeah, I did."

"Okay, come on. All we can do now is wait," she said and led him up the steps and into her house.

"I don't know if I can wait anymore. I just can't stand this," he said as he followed her through the screen door.

She turned to face him, reached out, and took his hands in hers. "Johnny, you care about these kids when no one else does. Someone's harming them, and you're the only one who understood it in the beginning. You're the only one who believed it. You can't give up."

"I'm not giving up, but I'm not getting anywhere. It's like trying to grab a handful of dust out of the air. I can see it. It's all right there but I can't get my fingers around it."

"I know. Believe me, I know." She shook her head, her eyes on the floor. She exhaled deeply, looked up, and tried to smile. "Hey, I invited you for dinner. We might as well eat."

"Yeah, okay."

"I promised simple and quick and that's what I've got.

Come on, we'll eat out back." She caught his look and answered quickly. "I have a cordless. We'll take it out with us."

"Okay," he said, and she led him through a dining-car kitchen to the back porch and pointed to a redwood table with two benches in the middle of the yard.

"Grab a seat, I'll be right out."

Johnny pulled out a bench and looked around the yard. A strip of dirt perhaps three feet wide paralleled the cement-block wall surrounding the yard. Tomato plants in round wire cages alternated with flowers along the wall. Long, leafy vines twisted from the black soil onto the grass and back toward the wall.

He heard the screen door bang, and Kate walked across the yard carrying a small tray.

"You're a gardener," Johnny said, waving toward the wall.

"It's a good change of pace." She set the tray down and looked at the garden that ringed the yard. "I can lose myself for hours out here."

"What do you like growing the best?"

"Flowers," she answered without hesitation.

She turned back to the table and handed Johnny a tall bottle of Corona and picked up one herself and took a long swallow. She set a plate of sliced tomatoes, cheese, and cucumbers, salt and pepper shakers, a small butter dish, and a basket of bread on the table.

"Beer's okay, right?"

"You have great instincts."

"In some things." A silence fell between them, and she gestured toward the wall. "I think these tomatoes are from that plant right there. Do you like tomato and cucumber sandwiches?"

"Well, I'll let you know."

They ate slowly, and their conversation quickly drifted into personal stories. Once again they talked of growing up in LA and how the city had changed. Once Kate retreated to the kitchen and brought out two more bottles of beer. Finally

Johnny helped her gather the dishes and carry them into the kitchen.

"What else can I do to help?" he asked.

"Nothing. It'll be faster if I do it myself."

She brushed past him several times as she moved through the narrow space, and each time he wanted to touch her, to run his fingertips along her arms and onto her neck and face. But he kept his hands pressed against the tile, afraid he would alienate her and knowing that he needed her help. Through it all he stole secret glances at the phone, wondering where Gem was. Would she call?

"Coffee?" she asked.

"Yeah, that'd be great."

"How do you like it?"

"With a little milk."

"Okay. Let's move to the living room. It's cool enough in here now."

Johnny sat on the couch, Kate on the futon seat across from him. He sipped his coffee. "So give me the details about your meeting with Dick today. I gather that didn't go too well," she said.

"No. Frankly, I think I made an ass of myself. But . . . there's something there. I know there is. How well do you know him?"

She gazed at Johnny, and a strange look of recognition played through her eyes. Then in one fluid movement she rose and walked from the living room into the bedroom beyond. Johnny watched her go and for a moment thought of following her, but waited, watching the doorway. She came back a moment later and handed Johnny a small framed picture. In the photo, Barbara Roberts, Dick's wife, hugged Kate around the shoulders, pulling her close to her as they both smiled directly into the camera.

"I told you a friend of mine got me the job at My Home." She stood next to the couch, inches from Johnny, looking down at him.

"Yes," he said, still staring at the picture.

"It was Barbara. I got to know her when I did an internship at God's House. We became like sisters. She's the one who told me about the job and made a few calls on my behalf. When she died, it almost killed me. I didn't think Dick was going to survive. I've known him for a long time, Johnny, and I've seen him go through some very hard times. I know him." She paused for a second and took the picture back from him and looked at it. "No, that's not quite true. I used to know him. I don't know him that well anymore. He's changed in the last couple of years. Becoming famous, it's . . . well, it's changed him. It's hard to describe exactly. I know he still cares about the kids and the poor and making the world better. But when I hear him talking it's like the passion is coming from memory."

"I know what you mean. Hungry isn't quite the right word but it's what comes to my mind. When I wrote about him, he was . . . well, hungry to save the world. He couldn't wait to get to it. It's a little like they say about an aging ball player. The instincts are still there but the reflexes are just a little slow."

"I guess," Kate said. She took the picture, walked into the bedroom, and came back a moment later without the picture. Standing in front of the couch, she looked down at Johnny.

"Dick and I have very different philosophies and a different way of working with the kids. He's changed a lot and I don't know him like I used to, but I can't believe Dick would hurt the kids."

Johnny laid his head back against the top of the pillow behind him. He closed his eyes and spoke into the darkness. "No, I don't really believe it either. At least I don't want to believe it. But I don't know what to think. I mean . . . Jesus, Kate, I was there too late with Sara. I can't be there too late for Gem."

She sank onto the couch next to him. He shifted to face her as she sat down only inches from him. "You won't be," she whispered.

Without thinking, he leaned toward her, and she moved to meet him. He kissed her gently at first, but quickly he slipped his hand behind her back and pulled her close, his mouth pressing hard against hers. She took his face in her hands, pressing his cheeks with her palms and sliding her fingers to the back of his head.

Johnny fell back awkwardly, diagonally across the couch, his legs almost completely off the sofa, and pulled her to him. She lay half on top of him, kissing him, and then she stopped and shifted until she was nearly on top of him again, straddling his leg. He held her tightly, his right hand on the back of her head, his left arm across her back.

He pulled her tank top up and gently ran his fingers along her bare spine. She murmured and squeezed his leg with hers. After a moment she slid off him, settling between the back of the couch and his side, resting her head against his chest. He put his arm across her shoulder and leaned his head back.

"You're a strange man, Johnny Rose," she said. "A very strange man."

He half-laughed. "I don't know if it's strange as much as it is stubborn and probably more than a little stupid."

"No. It's a blend of idealism and cynicism I've never seen before."

He stared at the ceiling and gently ran his fingertips along her bare arm, and she snuggled against him. "Sometimes I think I'm falling and that no one will be there to catch me and no one will care when I hit the ground."

"That's not true. I care." She rose up on an elbow and looked at him for a moment, studying his face before pushing herself up and standing next to the couch. She stepped over his legs and walked toward the bedroom door, pulling off her tank top as she went. Johnny sat up in time to see her reach behind her back and unsnap her bra and let it fall to the floor. He stood a little too fast and almost fell back onto the couch but caught himself and followed her into the bedroom.

* * *

They made love again in the morning. They had slept snuggled close, and at times in the night Johnny draped his arm across Kate's naked body and, half asleep, she would move closer to him. He had awakened with the first light that slipped past the shade, throwing a narrow beam across the foot of the bed.

Twice in the night, Johnny had gotten out of bed and walked quietly and carefully into the living room and checked his messages at work and home. But Gem had called neither place.

Now he watched Kate sleep next to him and eased onto his back and stared at the ceiling. He lay for perhaps half an hour, thinking first of Kate and of their lovemaking the night before, simultaneously gentle and intense. He would glance at her sleeping form, watching the barely perceptible rise and fall of her bare breasts, and try to pinpoint when he'd first known how much he cared for her and realized that he'd known from the beginning, from the first time they talked in her office, that she awakened something in him that had been so long buried that he'd lost all confidence in its very existence. But through it all he hadn't admitted it, hadn't allowed himself to peer deep enough into his own soul to acknowledge how much he cared until she had moved to the couch next to him and reassured him with a confidence he didn't share. A few simple words had made him realize how much he cared and wanted her affection and love.

She smiled at him when she opened her eyes, but a moment later something flickered through them, a quick note of fear, there, then gone in an instant.

"What? What is it?" Johnny asked

"Maybe this was a mistake," she said. But instead of moving away, she rolled to face him, pressing her cheek to his chest.

"No. This wasn't a mistake," Johnny said. "I care too much to think this was a mistake."

"It's not easy for me," she said, her voice barely above a whisper.

"Nor me."

"Will you leave?"

"You mean today, this morning?"

"No, Johnny, that's not what I mean."

They lay quietly for a moment, and Johnny gently ran his fingers through her hair to the base of her neck and leaned forward to kiss the top of her head. "I don't want to leave. I don't want to leave ever."

"I was married once," she said, a flat statement, adding no details, telling nothing more.

"I was too," he said. "It was hard. And I've had a relationship or two that have ended badly. But those are over, they're yesterday. We're here today, tomorrow."

She kissed his chest and reached between his legs and felt him stiffen, then rose on top of him and guided him into her and straddled him. When they were through, she stayed on top of him for a minute before slipping to his side. She said, "It's hard for me to trust adults. Especially men. It will take time."

"You build trust slowly, Kate. I know that. God, don't I know that. I don't think I've trusted anyone in . . . well, it's been a very long time."

She left the bed without replying and disappeared into the bathroom. A few moments later he heard the water running in the shower. He slipped on his jeans and went into the kitchen and shuffled through drawers and cupboards until he found the coffee and filters and started a pot dripping. He'd just picked the *LA Times* off the front porch when Kate called him from the bedroom.

"Your turn."

She stood in front of the closet in a terry-cloth robe, her wet hair spiked and disheveled. He walked up, bent slightly, and put his hands on her hips and kissed her on the side of the head just above her ear. She leaned back into him for a second and batted his hands away.

"I've got to get dressed," she said.

"Okay, okay," Johnny said and walked into the small bathroom with a tub/shower combination. Later, after he'd dressed, he found her at the table in the small kitchen reading the front page.

"I put a cup out for you." She waved toward the coffeemaker. A quart of milk sat next to it. "With milk, right?"

"Yes."

"You want some toast?" she asked.

"No, I'm fine, thanks. I don't usually eat much breakfast." He slipped into a chair across from her.

"Ah, Kate."

She lowered the paper and shook her head no. "Don't say anything," she said. "I'm going to work in a few minutes. I'll be home tonight. I hope you'll come back. I want to see you again, but I'm not going to count on it. Okay? You do what you want. There are no strings here." Her tone was detached, businesslike. He could tell she was already distancing herself from him.

"What time do you get home?"

"I'm usually here by six."

"I'll be over after that."

"If you don't come, you won't owe me an explanation."

"Kate," he started to protest, but she held up her hand.

"No, don't say anything. We'll take this as it comes. Like I said last night, I've learned not to put too much faith in what adults tell me. That goes double for men who just got laid." She laughed lightly, but Johnny's response was serious.

"I'll be here."

"I hope so. Anyway, when I get to the center, I'll look for Bev again and I'll tell all the kids to let me know if they see Gem. Now that we know she's in Hollywood, I've got more hope."

"Yeah."

He finished the coffee and stood. "I'd better go too. I've got to get home. Who knows, maybe she'll call me this morning. Or maybe Kuscyk's even ready to let me out of the penalty box. But I'll be back. Whether you believe it or not, I will be back."

"I hope so," she said.

Johnny moved next to her, reached down and took her hand, and pulled her to her feet. She came into his arms, and he held her tight against him. "I'll probably think about you all day."

She craned her neck to look up at him and smiled. "I hope so."

Twenty-four

———————•———————

*B*ut Johnny thought of her only until he listened to the message on his voice-mail at work.

"Rose, get in here. Something's come up."

He pulled the door to Kate's house closed and ran to the Z. Fifteen minutes later he was at the *Journal*. He hurried down the corridor from the elevator and across the newsroom to the metro editor's desk.

"What is it, Stan? What?"

Kuscyk looked at him and smiled. "I don't know what the hell you did, Rose. I don't know if the lady felt sorry for you because of the shooting or what."

"What lady? What the hell are you talking about?"

"Carol Holland."

"Carol Holland? What about her?"

"Plank's not pulling his ads and the lawyers decided not to seek a restraining order. I also got a call from that *People* reporter who said he was going to credit you and the *Journal* in his piece. Called it the best thing he's ever come up with. What the hell did you do?"

"I don't know." Johnny shook his head and looked past Kuscyk into the newsroom without focusing on anything. He felt an odd, unfathomable blend of despair and elation. It wasn't about Gem. She hadn't been hurt or killed. But she hadn't called either. This was all about Carol Holland.

264

"You didn't go talk to her?" Kuscyk pressed.

"No. I spent the night . . . No I didn't talk to her."

"Well, they want to talk to you."

"Who?"

"Reverend Roberts and Carol Holland."

"Why?"

"How the hell should I know? They want to meet you in his study in about an hour. I told Knight you'd be there."

"Roberts's study? At his house?"

"Yeah. Find out what the hell's going on. And this time, keep me informed. You got that?"

"Stan, Gem called last night. She's going to call again. I need to be here to take the call."

Kuscyk stared at him, his face expressionless. "This is the end of the line, Rose. Either you're on board or not. Go see them, find out what this is all about."

"But, Stan . . . "

Kuscyk held up his hand. "Look, I'll have Lawrence sit at your desk. He'll personally answer every call. You know, if you had a cell phone—"

"Jesus, Stan, don't start with me. I hate those things. You can't ever get away from people. Not even in your car in the middle of the freeway at rush hour. Maybe I don't want people calling me all the time."

"No one ever calls you anyway, Rose." Kuscyk waved his hand as though clearing the air. "Do you at least have a beeper?"

"No."

"Jesus, Rose. Here." Kuscyk pulled a beeper off his belt and handed it to Johnny. "I'll have Lawrence beep you if she calls. Now go and find out what the hell's going on here."

"Okay, sure. But you'll beep me if Gem calls, right?"

"Yes. Don't worry, Johnny. We'll cover it."

Carol Holland's Mercedes was the only car in the lot behind the Jefferson Youth Center. Johnny parked next to it, climbed out, and crossed the small crabgrass lawn to the porch of Roberts's house. The door was open, and he knocked lightly on the screen door. A few moments later Buddy appeared and looked at him through the mesh. Even in the dim light inside the house, Johnny could see Buddy's lifeless expression, his eyes dull and focused on a space just beyond the end of his nose. He didn't appear to be looking at Johnny but obviously saw him.

"You just wouldn't leave 'em alone, would you?" he said. "I told you, hell, I almost begged you, to leave 'em alone, but you wouldn't listen."

"What are you talking about?"

Buddy shoved the screen door. It swung open, missing Johnny by less than an inch. Buddy walked into the living room and sat on the couch, staring straight ahead.

"They're waiting for you in Reverend Roberts's study." He didn't look at Johnny.

The door to the study was closed, and he knocked lightly.

"Come in." It was Roberts's voice.

The minister was behind the desk, and Carol Holland sat in a chair at his left, near the end of the desk facing the door. Johnny stopped just inside the room and looked at her. She wore dark slacks, a white blouse, and an unadorned, short-waisted black jacket. She had on lipstick but no other makeup and no jewelry. She looked older, the lines in the corners of her eyes deeper, and a sense of worry hovered at the corners of her mouth. She smiled weakly at him.

"Johnny, please come in," Roberts said.

He hesitated a moment, but when the minister said "please" again and motioned to another chair in front of the desk, Johnny moved to it and sat down.

"You know, sometimes you face very difficult decisions that force you to choose between core beliefs. Suddenly you're faced with ethical dilemmas you never expected, never believed could happen. What do you do when you have to choose between telling the truth and protecting the innocent?"

Johnny looked from the minister to the actress and back to Roberts.

"What's this all about, Dick?" Johnny's eyes wandered to the telephone on Roberts's desk and back to the minister.

Roberts swiveled in the chair and took a picture of the youth choir off the wall and put it on the desk. "You know that our choir members were always street kids. The ones living on rooftops and behind Dumpsters. They were kids nobody wanted. You know that, don't you?"

"Yes, of course."

"Here." He handed Johnny the photo. "Study the choir carefully, especially the middle row."

Johnny looked at the faces slowly, studying each one, moving left to right. He took his time, and once he recognized her, he looked again to make sure before handing the picture back to Roberts.

Johnny looked at Carol Holland.

"That's you?"

She didn't answer his question directly. Instead she simply started speaking, and as she spoke, her sentences picked up speed and intensity and, Johnny thought, a sense of relief. At first she spoke to the floor, but after a moment, she looked up, her eyes directly on him, her hands folded neatly in her lap.

"I was raised in Trenton, New Jersey. I grew up in an incredibly abusive household. You can't imagine it. My parents never beat me, not physically. But psychologically and emotionally they were terribly cruel. They practiced on each other with amazing regularity. They had a sick, perverse relationship that was based solely on giving and getting pain. I would go to sleep at night praying that the next day they wouldn't scream at each other, wouldn't hit each other, that they wouldn't demean me, wouldn't tell me that I was a worthless mistake that ruined their lives. Just one day, that's all I wanted. One normal day. Just one day when I'd come home from school and they'd be glad to see me. But that wasn't their way." She paused for a second and dropped her eyes to her hands, then looked at him again and went on.

"I decided to run away on Christmas Day the year I was fourteen. We had been to my mother's sister's house and we had taken all our presents there to open. I had saved all the money I'd made baby-sitting and bought my dad a tie and tiepin." She laughed a dry, mirthless chuckle. "I thought if I got him the right present maybe he . . . it doesn't really matter. Dad and Mom fought all the way over, and once we got there they both started drinking before dinner and it just got worse. They said horrible, mean things to each other and ruined the day for everyone with their sickness. They kept at it in the car on the way home. I was in the backseat with all the presents. My dad was driving. They were yelling at each other the whole time until we were almost home. We were on a two-lane highway and had started to cross this bridge. The weather had been unusually warm and a lot of snow had melted so the creek was high and running fast and suddenly Dad pulled the car to the side and leaped out. He came around and jerked open the back door and screamed at both of us. 'I'll show you, I'll show you how much I give a shit about either one of you.' And he took all his presents. The ones my mom had given him, the tie and tiepin I'd given him, everything everyone had given him, took them and threw them all in the water." She paused and cleared her throat before going on.

"You know, Mr. Rose, I can still hear the splashes and see the boxes and the ribbons and the red and green tissue paper being carried along that surface. And suddenly it was all gone. It was one of the cruelest, most selfish things I've ever witnessed in my life.

"It was perfect. He insulted us, made us feel guilty, and got to be a martyr all in one gesture. I started dreaming about running away that night. But I didn't know where I would go or what I would do. I was smart enough to know I couldn't run away in the winter. But the next summer, the day after school was out, you know, it's funny but it seemed important that I finish school. Anyway, I packed a single suitcase and stole all the money my father had in his wallet and my mother had in her purse and I ran away.

"I decided to go to Hollywood where I could be discovered. A week after I got here, someone stole my suitcase and all my money. I ended up sleeping in a doorway, hungry and scared to death. That's where Dick found me. He told me about the love of Jesus and made me believe that I was worth loving. He got me into a shelter and I started singing in the God's House choir and realized that I had a talent. I got a GED here and . . ." She paused for a moment, collecting her thoughts. "I was lucky, Mr. Rose. I never had to do survival sex, I didn't have to sell myself to eat, like some of these kids do. I didn't have to steal or beg, but I might have if Dick hadn't found me."

Roberts picked up the story there. "Barbara told me about her talent. Once I heard her sing, I knew God had given her a great gift. I had a friend in regional theater in Georgia," Roberts said. "After she got her GED, the church paid for her to go there. She was a natural and it was just the beginning. It turned out she was an even better actress than a singer. She was back in Hollywood just a few years later."

"So, Mr. Rose, no, I didn't really go to Hollywood High," Carol Holland said. "I lied to you. This is a part of my life that I never wanted to tell anyone. But it's also why I want to help these kids. I should have told you the truth when you first started asking questions, but I've been telling this lie for so long. It was just so easy. I had no idea you'd check. There's also the movie. It's going to be out in a few weeks. It could make a huge difference in my career. I thought that if this came out, it would ruin it."

"But you're telling me this now."

She looked at him with expressionless, almost dead eyes. "You weren't going to stop. I could tell. Nothing I did seemed to matter to you." She blew her breath out and shrugged. "Then yesterday Dick had to answer all those questions from the *People* reporter. He didn't lie, not directly but, well . . . I guess I knew all along that someday it all had to come out. It was bad enough that I was telling lies, but then other people had started shading the truth just to protect me. Last night I came to see Dick. To ask his advice. We prayed for a long time about this."

"Does your husband know?" Johnny asked.

"About my living on the streets? Yes, I told Mel before we were married."

"And you called me over here to give me an exclusive. Is that it?"

"No, Johnny," Roberts said. "We wanted to apologize for any trouble we've caused you. Carol has told her lawyers not to seek a restraining order, and Mel's agreed not to pull his advertising from the *Journal*."

"And in exchange, I've got to do what? Sit on the story?"

"No, Mr. Rose," Carol Holland said. "This morning I called the writer for *People* magazine and told him the whole story. Now, I've arranged to tell the whole world. I want the truth out. I'm tired of living this lie. I'll be on *Access Hollywood* tonight. We're taping this afternoon. I'm going to tell the whole thing. I'm not going to hold anything back. If you want to write a story, that's your business."

"Did you know my cousin Sara or her boyfriend, Dallas? Or the girl named Gem?"

"I don't know. I asked Dick to send some kids up to clean the pool house and clear the brush off the hills behind my house. They could have been there. I don't know. I didn't really talk to any of them. I didn't know their names or who they were."

"Johnny, I don't even know myself who we took up to Carol's house. We had kids up there three or four times. When we get a request like this we just ask around, see which kids are available. I honestly don't know if I ever even met your cousin. I might have, I don't know. I'm sorry about her death. You have to believe me. I'm sorry about the boy who died near Carol's house. But I don't know anything about him or the fire in that house."

The room was quiet. The sound of a prop airplane gaining altitude in the distance drifted though the window. Johnny looked at Roberts for a moment and turned to Carol Holland. He stood and stepped behind the chair and rested his hands on its back.

"And all this happening today is just coincidence, right? It has nothing to do with someone trying to shoot me? Is that what you want me to believe?"

"Johnny, you have to believe me. We don't know anything about that. Carol came to me last night and we prayed and decided that we had to call you today. It had nothing to do with the shooting. You have my word."

Johnny stepped to the door. He looked at Roberts and shifted his gaze to the actress.

"Thank you for telling me all this. I'll pass your story on to the Hollywood beat reporter. She may want to interview you. This is not a story I'm going to write."

"Please accept my personal apology, Mr. Rose," Carol Holland said. She stood. "I'm very sorry for all the trouble my lying caused you. If you want, I'll call your publisher personally and apologize to the paper."

Johnny stared at her and wondered. Had he just seen a woman pouring out her heart or a very talented actress? Her offer to call Knight troubled him. Carol Holland was a woman who had to be in control, but she was offering a mea culpa way beyond what was necessary.

"Thank you for telling me, but you don't have to call Mr. Knight," he said.

He left the study and walked down the hall and out the door. He didn't look back until he was in the Z. But once in the car, he sat for several minutes looking at the front of the minister's small house, thinking how the two of them had just explained everything. Everything they said made sense. But as he sat there, he remembered a tough lesson he'd learned as a cross-country runner in high school. You've got to save something for the end. It doesn't matter who's ahead in the first turn around the track or at the top of the first hill.

You can keep them on your shoulder and match them stride for stride through all the tough miles of hills and flats, but in the end, it usually comes down to who has the juice over the last hundred yards.

Twenty-five

•━━━━━•

Kuscyk was smiling. He watched Johnny walk into the newsroom and check with Lawrence, then waved the reporter to his desk. When Johnny was a few feet away, the metro editor leaned back in his chair and laced his fingers behind his head.

"Well, what did the lady have to say?"

Johnny took the beeper off his belt and put it on Kuscyk's desk.

"She used to be a street kid. Ran away when she was fourteen. She was afraid I'd find out. That's all there was to it."

"That's it?"

"So she says."

"And now she's decided to tell all?" Over Kuscyk's shoulder, Johnny could see a story, half edited, on the screen, the cursor blinking. The pace was picking up in the newsroom. The editor at the desk next to him was talking to someone, asking for something "on background. I won't quote you." Kuscyk seemed oblivious.

"Yeah, she's going on *Access Hollywood* tonight. She's taping the show this afternoon."

"Well, what the hell, this ought to get her some publicity. Going to Betty Ford doesn't generate the headlines it once did. Being a street kid, now that's new and sexy. Could even make her new movie a big hit."

273

"Yeah, that had occurred to me," Johnny said.

"You know, Rose, you don't seem very pleased. You're back at work, Knight's not pissed off anymore. I'd think you'd be happy."

"I'm waiting on the call, Stan. Waiting to hear from Gem. Besides, there are too many unanswered questions."

"Like the fire?" The phone behind Kuscyk began ringing. Johnny glanced at it, but Kuscyk ignored it, and after a few moments it quit.

"Yeah."

"What's Holland say about the fire?"

"Says she doesn't know anything about it."

"And the dead kid on the hillside near her house?"

"Coincidence."

"You know, Rose, the first paper I worked at I had a city editor, a runty little guy who always wore a bow tie. He asked me a question one time, and I started to answer by saying 'I assume.'" Kuscyk chuckled lightly, remembering. "I can still hear him. 'Stan, when you assume, you make an ass out of you and me.'"

The phone rang again, and Kuscyk reached behind him and grabbed it. "I'll call you back," he said, hung up, and looked back at Johnny.

"It's an old line, Stan."

"Yeah, but the point is, I've been trying to think of something clever like that to say about the word 'coincidence,' but I haven't come up with anything. You get my drift, though, don't you? I don't believe in coincidence."

"I get it, Stan." They were quiet for a moment, and then the editor leaned forward. "Look, Johnny, you don't have to stay on this. Sometimes shit happens and we never understand it, never get to write a story, bring it to an end. Maybe you're never going to hear from Gem. This might be a good time to call it a draw. No one's going to blame you if you do."

Johnny didn't hesitate. "No," he said, his voice low. "Sara's dead, and Gem's still out there in the wind someplace and someone wants to hurt her, maybe even kill her. This isn't just about finding out who killed Sara. It was in the beginning, but it's not anymore. Now it's about saving a kid and it's got to be me, Stan, or it's nobody. She'll call me. At least, I hope she will."

"I hope you're right, but listen to me—and I'm getting really tired of saying this. Don't do anything stupid."

"Well, I'm tired of hearing it."

Kuscyk laughed. "I'll bet you are. So what are you going to do now?"

Johnny smiled. "Wait for a phone call, then make dinner for a friend and wait some more."

Kuscyk started to speak, but Johnny was already walking toward his desk. He grabbed his phone and dialed.

Kate answered on the third ring.

"Hi, Kate, it's Johnny."

"Hi, have you heard anything from Gem?"

"No," Johnny said.

"I'm not surprised. She may be afraid to come out until dark."

"I hope that's it."

"I'm sure it is. Listen, I'm glad you called. I think we may be in luck. Bev's here. She's downstairs now."

"Should I come over?"

"No. I've already talked to her. She remembers you. Thought you were nice."

"Does she know where Gem is?"

"She says she doesn't."

"Do you believe her?"

"Well, yes, but . . ."

"But what?"

"I think she knows where to look. She told me she'll check a couple of places tonight. I gave her my phone number."

"Give her mine too."

"Johnny, you know our policy, we don't—"

"Please."

He waited, listening to the silence for a moment before Kate said, "Yes, of course I will."

"You know, maybe I should come over and look around anyway."

"Gem's hiding. You won't find her. You don't know where to look. You don't even know where the squats are, where they hide. I don't know half of them myself. If she's in Hollywood, Bev will find her. Right now Bev's our best chance. Besides, you need to be home if Gem calls."

"I don't know, I hate sitting around."

"There's no choice. You could spend weeks looking and never find her. You could ask dozens of kids on the streets and not get anywhere. Most of them wouldn't help you, wouldn't trust you. Bev trusts you. She says you treated her like a real person."

"She is a real person."

"Yes, I know, but some people don't."

"Okay, listen, Kate, about tonight."

"Wait, don't say anything. If you can't make it, I understand. No strings, remember?"

"No, that's not it. I just want you to come to my place. I'll make dinner for you, okay? Simple and easy. What do you say? Besides, Gem has my home number. She might call."

She laughed. "That'd be great. I'll see you soon."

"Be sure to give Bev my number."

"I will."

"Hey, guess what? I'm back on the job."

"Really?"

"Yeah, I'll tell you all about it tonight. I'd like to get your take on the whole thing."

"Mine?"

"I'll explain tonight." He gave her his address and directions and hung up.

Johnny sent Kuscyk a simple e-mail. "Leaving early. In tomorrow." He shut down the machine and was a few feet from his cubicle when his phone rang. He lunged back, grabbing it before it rang a second time.

"Johnny Rose."

"Mr. Rose, it's Detective Towers from Hollywood."

"Oh, hi."

"You okay?"

"Yeah, I was just expecting someone else, that's all."

"Well, Mr. Rose, I talked to Detective Bennett today. He filled me in on a few things. It got me thinking and I wanted to ask you a quick follow-up question."

"Sure."

"You doing anything on street gangs? Maybe an investigative piece, anything like that?"

"Gangs? No. Where did that come from?"

"It was the shooting. I've only been in Hollywood a couple of years, so I checked with a guy who's been here a long time and sure enough, I was right. There used to be a gang here called the Hollywood Jackals. I'd heard of 'em even before I came to Hollywood. Some very bad people. About eight years ago the Jackals were having problems with some guys dealing on their corners. Now other gangs send someone up close and use a handgun or maybe they drive by with a semiautomatic. But the Jackals used a sniper. One shot and the guy was dead. Never knew what hit him. They did two guys that way, and the fear, never knowing when or where, pretty much drove their competition out. Kept their own casualties down too."

"The Hollywood Jackals?" Johnny saw himself in Hank Jefferson's living room listening to the music man's story about Buddy. He'd belonged to a gang called the Hollywood Jackals, Jefferson had said.

"The outreach director at God's House, a guy named Buddy, he's an ex-con. He used to be in the Jackals. He thinks I'm trying to do in the Reverend Roberts. Maybe there's a connection there."

"I'll check him out."

"Thanks. It's probably just a . . ." He couldn't bring himself to call it a coincidence. "Well, who knows?"

"I'll check it." Towers's voice was serious. "Listen, Rose,

I'm beginning to think you're right about all this being connected. When you first came in here and talked to me, I didn't put much store in it. But after talking with Bennett and hearing about the sniper attack, well, it all just tells me something's happening. I'm going to have a little talk with Buddy about all of this." Towers paused for a second. "Listen, write down my beeper number, okay? You need something, you call me. And be careful."

Johnny jotted down the number, hung up, and looked at the phone for a few minutes, feeling the excitement rise, the sense he got when a story was coming together.

He listened for the phone while he walked to the elevator, but it didn't ring again, and as he walked out of the *Journal*, he started thinking of dinner.

He shopped quickly at a small market near his house, buying angel hair pasta, asparagus, shrimp, a small package of pecans, a garlic bulb, a small bottle of olive oil, two bottles of white wine, and a couple of cans of cat food. At home he again circled the block, parked two streets away, and entered through the back door. He quickly checked his messages, showered, and dressed, putting on shorts and a faded T-shirt. He took a moment to straighten up his bedroom, changing the sheets, making the bed, and throwing his dirty laundry in the closet. He gathered the old newspapers in the living room and threw them out. He fluffed the pillows on the couch and ran a wet rag on the top of the coffee table. After putting on an Iguanas CD, Johnny went into the kitchen, stuck a bottle of the wine in the freezer, and began cooking. He chopped the asparagus into pieces, tailed the shrimp, and put a pot of water on to boil.

The sun was almost gone, but the evening had not yet begun to cool when Johnny pulled the top off a can of cat food, grabbed a quart of milk from the refrigerator, and walked out the front door.

This time the cat was waiting. It sauntered into the open grass and sat a respectable distance away while Johnny picked up the saucer and carried it a few feet closer to his door. He spooned the food out and poured a little milk on it.

"Okay, Archie, chow time," Johnny said and backed up a few steps. The cat didn't hesitate. It walked nonchalantly across the grass and began eating, not bothering to keep its usual watchful eye on Johnny. But when Kate came up the path a few moments later, the cat hissed at her and walked slowly away from the empty saucer and disappeared into the bushes.

She wore a yellow sundress that hung to midcalf and white sandals, and she held a bottle of wine in her right hand. She stopped next to Johnny and looked at the bushes.

"Your cat?"

"We're working that out."

"Really, what's its name?"

"Archie."

"As in Bunker?"

"No, as in Moore. Ageless Archie Moore. One of the great fighters of all time. Guy won the light heavyweight championship at age thirty-nine. Had more knockouts than anyone in the history of boxing. This cat reminds me of him, kind of old and beat up, but still fighting."

She looked at him for a moment, a knowing grin on her face. "Kind of reminds me of someone I know too." She smiled sweetly when he scowled at her.

"Come on in, I was just starting dinner."

The moment she stepped into his apartment, he pulled her close and kissed her. She put her left arm around his neck and held his embrace, the bottle of wine still in her hand. Finally, she pulled away.

"That was nice," she said.

"Yes, it was."

She held up the bottle. "Here, I didn't know what you were cooking, so I brought chardonnay."

"I'm sautéing a little asparagus with shrimp and garlic. I'll toss it with a little angel hair pasta and some chopped pecans."

"I'm impressed."

"Wait till you've tried it. It's been a long time since I did much cooking."

He put the wine she'd brought into the refrigerator, pulled the bottle from the freezer, and poured two glasses.

"Can I help you?"

"Nah, it's a small kitchen. Just sit and we can talk."

Kate sat at the table and watched as he cooked the asparagus and tossed the shrimp into the pan.

"Where'd you learn to cook?" she asked.

"Right here. My ex-wife didn't like to cook much. She was more the restaurant type. But I got tired of eating out all the time, so I got a few cookbooks and started teaching myself. Whatever was easy."

"Well, it smells wonderful."

He took his glass from the counter and sipped and turned to look at her.

"You know, I haven't cooked for anyone in a long time. It's kind of nice."

"I'm glad you asked me."

He put his glass down and turned back to the stove. The phone rang and Johnny's heart accelerated. He grabbed it.

"Hello."

"Hey, Johnny, it's Terry Fox from KJTV. Sorry I missed you earlier. That was quite a performance at the press conference. Wish I'd been there but I saw the film. You should have seen the look on Knight's face." The man chuckled.

Johnny looked at Kate and shook his head no and turned away. "Hi, Terry, what can I do for you?"

"I'd still love to get you into the studio, talk about that shooting. Cops know anything more about it?" The man's voice was smooth, relaxed, but with an undercurrent of urgency.

"Terry, this isn't a good time to talk. I'm in the middle of cooking dinner and besides there's nothing new. I said everything I had to say at the press conference."

"Oh, come on, Johnny, I know you better than that. It'll

make a great piece. Everyone wants to be on TV. Get your fifteen minutes, you know what I mean?"

"Good-bye, Terry." Johnny hung up and looked at Kate. The words "fucking reporters" were on the tip of his tongue, but he caught himself, and a sheepish grin spread across his face. "Damned TV types," he said.

Turning back to the stove, he lifted the lid to see if the water was boiling when the phone rang again. "Damn," he said and grabbed it off the stand.

"Hello," he barked. A second later he heard Bev's voice. His muscles tensed instantly and he held his breath.

"Mr. Rose, I know where Gem is."

"Where?" He breathed again.

"She's hiding in this crack house."

"Ah, shit, where is it?"

"It's an abandoned apartment building a couple of blocks north of Sunset. I figured it was maybe one of the places I should check. She's in one of the apartments that them junkies ain't taken over yet."

"Did you see her?" He turned to Kate and mouthed the word Bev, and pointed to the phone.

"No, I didn't see her myself. This crackhead old boyfriend of mine named Roy, he saw her."

"Is he sure it's her?"

"Yeah, that's how I know. I saw him talking to this guy then this guy gives him some money and leaves. So after this dude left, I went up and asked Roy what was that all about and he said the man had asked about Gem and offered to pay him, if he could tell him where she was. So now that man knows where to look too."

"Ah, shit."

"I think maybe you better hurry, Mr. Rose. He gonna be telling somebody to be looking in that house real soon I'll bet."

"Where is the place?"

"I don't know the address, but here's how you get there."

Johnny copied the directions, put the phone down, and turned to Kate. "It's Bev, she knows where Gem's hiding."

"Where is she? Is she okay?"

"In an abandoned apartment building near the freeway. It's a crack house north of Sunset."

"I know it. Get a flashlight, we're going to need it."

"I've got one in the car."

"Where's your car?"

"Out back."

"I'll meet you there. I gotta get shoes."

"What?"

"I can't go in there in sandals. You could step on a needle in the dark. I've got shoes in my car. I'll be back in a minute."

"I'll pick you up out front."

Three minutes later, Johnny rounded the corner from the alley and pulled to a stop in the middle of the street. Kate jerked open the door and slipped in.

"This time of the day the freeway's the fastest way," she said.

He rolled through the stop sign at the end of his block, glancing in his rearview mirror for police. There were no cops, but in the dim streetlight Johnny caught a glimpse of a red car accelerating behind him. It looked like a Celica, but he couldn't be sure. He watched for the car, but if it was lingering among the traffic behind him, it was well hidden and he quickly forgot about it. He was only interested in getting to Hollywood as fast as possible.

Johnny pressed the Z past eighty-five as he moved in and out of lanes, pushing the car hard, his foot on the accelerator just above the floorboard, his hands gripping the wheel. Kate stared straight ahead, never flinching as he swerved from one lane to another. She guided him through Hollywood's streets until they skidded to a stop in front of a dark two-story rectangular stucco-and-frame building. Johnny could just make out the outlines of the windows and the two stairwells facing the street. The windows were boarded up with graffiti-covered plywood, and the stairwells were pitch black, like the entrances to caves. At one time, the builder had stretched a chain-link fence around the property, but the crackheads had peeled it back from the poles at the corner and it sagged in the middle.

"A developer was going to tear that old place down and put up some condos. I don't know if he ran out of money or what, but it's been empty for months. The junkies use the bottom floor. The two on the end there. Some of the kids squat in the places upstairs."

"They dealing out of here? Should we worry about guards?"

"I don't think so. They just go there to get high."

"Okay, Beverly said it was the top place on the end." Johnny gestured through the window.

"Let's go," Kate said. She was out of the car before Johnny got his door open.

Johnny pulled back the fence as Kate stepped through, and he followed a second later. They walked diagonally across the dead grass to the narrow cement walkway that at one time had led from the sidewalk to the stairwell. As they drew close, Johnny could see the outline of something on the stairs. At first it was indistinguishable, but he quickly realized it was a person slumped on his side. He nudged Kate and gestured to the figure, and she nodded.

Suddenly the door to a bottom apartment banged opened. They stopped and stared. Johnny gripped the flashlight, ready to wield it as a weapon. His eyes darted from the door to the figure on the stairwell and back. The door hung open for a second, and a dim, flickering light leaked out of the apartment, illuminating the small landing and the steps to the second floor. He caught a whiff of marijuana and cigarette smoke and shifted his weight, standing on the balls of his feet. A second later a man, tall and thin, his face pale, his eyes unfocused, stumbled through the door and stood on the landing.

He saw them and froze. Johnny met his eyes and realized

he couldn't guess the man's age within twenty years. Defiance and shame seemed to blend in his face. Then he shoved the door closed, stepped off the porch, and walked toward the fence without a word.

"Give me the flashlight," Kate said.

She flicked it on and pointed it to the figure on the stairs. In the light Johnny saw a young man in blue jeans and T-shirt, passed out, his breathing shallow, his head in the crook of his arm. Kate paused a second, playing the beam quickly up and down the stairway littered with the scraps of old newspapers and broken glass.

"Come on," she said and rushed to the stairs and up them, the beam of light bouncing off the walls ahead of her. She stopped at the top, and Johnny was at her side a second later. A gaping hole where the door and frame had once been led into the upstairs apartment, and they stepped cautiously through the opening into what had been the living room. The smell of vomit, moldy carpet, and incense struck them like a vicious slap.

"God," Johnny whispered. It was worse than the bridge squat.

But if Kate noticed the filth or was repelled by it, she gave no outward sign. She played the light across the living room. A sleeping bag was spread on the floor near the far wall, and just beyond, two blankets had been rolled into a pile. But they saw no one in the room, so they moved farther into the apartment, Kate alternately casting the beam across the room and down to the floor.

They went quickly into the kitchen. The beam cut a swath across the room, revealing the warped and peeling doors of the empty cabinets. A drainpipe rose from the floor where the sink had been. Cockroaches scurried away from the light.

"The bedrooms," Johnny said, his voice tight. The first one was empty, the carpet strewn with newspapers, the sliding closet door hanging off its track, a hole punched in the thin wood. A moment later they were in the hallway going toward the back bedroom.

They heard a low moan from down the hall, and Kate rushed forward into the dark, playing the light ahead of her as she went. Gem was on the floor, her back against the wall next to a space heater. Her T-shirt was slashed and soaked with blood, her hands pressed to the sides of her face. Blood trickled between her fingers down her throat. She moaned and looked up at them, and seemed to pass out.

"Gem!" Johnny yelled and knelt beside her. He grabbed her face, his hands on the sides of her head. "Gem! Come back here, don't go. No!"

Her eyes opened, glassy and unfocused. "Please don't hurt me," she whimpered. "No more, please."

"She's in shock," Kate whispered and flicked the light off and knelt next to her. "Gem, it's okay. I'm Kate from My Home." Kate looked back at Johnny. "She's been cut up. We've got to call an ambulance."

"He wanted the pictures," she said. "But I don't have them. I don't know where Dallas put them."

"It's going to be all right, Jeanette," Johnny said.

"We've got to call the paramedics," Kate said.

"There's no phone here. She'll never make it."

"Queen of Angels isn't two miles from here."

"We'll be there in four minutes," Johnny said. He swooped Gem into his arms, surprised by how light she was. Her skin was cool and clammy.

"Stay with us, Gem. Stay here," Johnny said to the girl as they hurried back down the hall. They were through the living room a moment later. Johnny took the steps as quickly as he could without falling and ran across the dried grass to the fence, clutching Gem to his chest as her arms dangled and flopped at her side. Kate pulled back the fence, and Gem moaned when Johnny ducked through.

"You'll have to hold her in your lap," Johnny said. Kate got in and slid the passenger seat back as far as it would go, and Johnny gently put the girl atop her, then ran to the driver's seat. A moment later the Z's tires spit gravel and left the smell of burning rubber in the air as Johnny dropped the clutch and sped from the curb.

He pushed the Z past the redline in first and shifted into second, and the car surged forward. They shot through the red light at Vine, barely missing a late-model Camry. Johnny could hear the engine whine as he pushed the limit in third gear. The car shuddered when Johnny jerked it around the corner onto Vermont and a few seconds later downshifted and hit the brakes and whipped it into the emergency entrance of Queen of Angels.

The car was still rocking on its springs when Johnny leaped from the driver's side and ran to the passenger door. He lifted Gem from Kate's lap. Her head lolled against his shoulder as he walked. Blood still ran from her face. It dripped across his shoulder and smeared on his neck, leaving a trail of drops on the cement.

The doors opened automatically, and they rushed into the emergency room. Straight ahead a wall of thick glass rose from a low counter. At this hour the chairs facing the counter usually filled with patients checking in were empty. Only one person, a woman wearing flowered surgical scrubs, sat behind the glass.

"We need a doctor. She's been stabbed," Johnny yelled. The woman leaped to her feet.

"Around here, through the doors, down the hall," she yelled and gestured past the end of the counter to the area behind her. She met them in the hallway. "Down here," she said and hurried ahead of them, her shoes squeaking on the linoleum.

"Jeanette, who did this to you? Who hurt you?" Johnny said.

"I told him I didn't know where the pictures were," she mumbled. "He didn't believe me." She was slipping in and out of consciousness.

"What pictures?" Johnny asked.

"The pictures Dallas took." She closed her eyes again.

"Pictures of what?" Johnny asked, but she didn't respond.

"Put her here," the nurse barked. "Put her on the exam table," the nurse said and pushed aside a curtain. He moved close and laid Gem gently on the bed. "What happened?" the nurse demanded.

"Someone attacked her. We don't know who," Kate said.

"Is she your daughter?"

"No, but we know her parents."

"The doctor will be right here. We'll need some information, and I'm going to have to report this to the police."

"Yes, of course," Johnny said. "Don't worry, I'm sure she has insurance. Her father's a doctor."

Gem opened her eyes and looked at Johnny for a moment. "Dallas told me he hid the pictures."

"Where?"

"Where he took them. He said they'd never look there. But I don't know where." Her head seemed to fall sideways, and her eyes closed. But a moment later she stirred again and looked at Kate. "I want my mom. Can you call her?" Her voice was weak and pleading.

"Yes, of course," Kate said.

"You'll have to wait outside," the nurse said. She grabbed the curtain and began to pull it closed around the bed.

"We'll be in the waiting room," Kate said as they left.

They sat numbly, silently, side by side in the formed metal chairs next to the tall windows that looked onto the small lot just beyond the doors. They said nothing for several minutes, each in their own world. Finally, Kate reached over and touched Johnny's neck.

"You look as bad as she did. You'd better clean up."

He focused on Kate for the first time since they'd run from his apartment. He saw the red smeared down her front and where she had cradled Gem as they sped to the hospital.

"You've got blood all over you too."

"That's okay. She's alive, Johnny. She's going to pull through. I just know it. You were there in time. Sara would be pleased."

"I know it's just . . . I still don't understand." A wave of exhaustion swept through him.

"What did Gem say? I couldn't hear it," Kate said. "Did she tell you who did this?

"No. All she said was that Dallas hid pictures someplace. That's what they're after. Pictures."

"Pictures of what?"

"I don't know." He slumped in his seat, stretching his legs in front of him, and thought again of Gem's words, and suddenly he knew. "I know where they are," he whispered.

"What?"

"Call Gem's mom, tell her what happened. Ask her to come to the hospital, okay?" He stood suddenly and began digging through his pockets. A moment later he pulled out two pieces of paper.

"I don't know how to reach her. I don't even know Gem's last name."

"It's Rottman. Jeanette Rottman. Here." He handed her the papers. "It's Gem's . . . This is Jeanette's mom's cell phone. She gave it to me and asked me to call her if I saw her daughter. Day or night, anytime. Call her, okay? I've got to go. I've got to get there before they figure out what she told them."

"Get where? What are you going to do?"

"I'm going to get the pictures."

"What pictures?"

"I don't know what they are, but I think I know where they are."

"What? How do you know?"

"She said Dallas hid them where he took them."

"I don't understand."

"You remember the pictures of Sara on your bulletin board?"

"Of course."

"You said he only took one roll. He liked the darkroom work better."

"I still—"

"They're at Carol Holland's. I'm going up there. I've got to find them. That second number is Detective Towers's beeper. Call him and tell him to meet me at Carol Holland's house, okay? I don't have time to wait for him."

"Johnny, this isn't a good idea."

"Look, it won't take 'em long to figure out where the pictures are. They may already have them. I've got to try to get there first. Call Towers, then call Gem's mom. The cops will be here soon. Give them a statement and tell them I'll be back."

He hurried toward the door but stopped a few feet shy of it and turned back.

"I still owe you dinner. Don't forget, okay?"

Twenty-six

Johnny stopped half a block from Carol Holland's house, leaned forward across the steering wheel, and looked down the street to the end of the cul-de-sac. He first scanned the neighbors' houses, but they were all dark, as though the street had been abandoned at nightfall. He then looked up the empty street for any sign of Towers. The street was empty, and Johnny picked up the flashlight from the passenger's seat. Blood was smeared across it, but he made no attempt to wipe it away.

He got out and approached the house, his pace picking up as he drew near. He broke into a run and sprinted across the grass to the far corner of the house near the edge of the hill. He eased the latch on the wooden gate and slipped through to the backyard. A moment later he had scrambled up the steps in the darkness to the balcony. The night was warm, and the smell of jasmine hung sweet in the air, like too much cheap perfume. He picked his way slowly along the balcony and was almost to the steps when a muffled thump, the sound of a car door slamming, came from the street. Johnny whirled and looked back at the gate. Was it Towers? Johnny waited, beads of sweat gathering on his forehead and running from his armpits down his side. The smell of jasmine seemed to intensify, almost overpowering. Should he go out and look? And if it wasn't the detective, then what?

His stomach was knotted and his breathing quickened. He strained to hear every sound and stared at the gate, its outline just visible in the darkness. But he heard only his heartbeat in his ears and the laugh track of a television show, the noise drifting up the canyon from the darkness below.

After a moment he turned and stared across the canyon to pick out the hillside where Dallas's body had been found. But he could see nothing in the dark. He forced himself to exhale, to breathe slowly as he listened. The sound of the television stopped suddenly, and now the only noise he heard was the distant buzz of the city stretched below him, an urban white noise you don't even know you hear until it's gone.

He sucked in a deep breath and exhaled slowly to calm himself again, then ran the last few feet across the balcony to the steps. As he ran, he glanced back at the floor-to-ceiling glass windows. The vertical blinds were open, but the interior was completely black—not a night-light, nor a pinpoint of red from a smoke alarm, nor a stray beam reflected from a source deeper in the house broke the darkness. Johnny realized suddenly how vividly he stood out, a shadow moving against the ambient light of the city. He might as well be wearing neon. If someone were inside, they could watch him and he would never see them.

His feet beat a quick staccato on the wooden steps as he switchbacked to the terrace below. At the edge of the pool, he stopped and looked at the brick fence cutouts filled with wrought iron. It was where the picture of Dallas had been taken. But what were the other pictures of and where had he hidden them? Johnny scanned the deck and the fence, letting his gaze move over the dark water in the pool, jumping quickly from one object to another.

He glanced back up the hillside at the dark house. Where was Towers? Had Kate even reached him? "Concentrate, damn it, concentrate," he whispered to himself, and he looked again at the pool area. His eyes swept over the potted plants, the deck chairs, and the short, round glass-topped tables to the pool house and stopped. He knew the moment he saw it.

The lounge chairs were pushed well back from the coping, and Johnny ran along the edge of the pool to the house's louvered door. He pushed it open and stepped into the pitch-black interior. The sound of his own breathing seemed to fill the small building like a roar. From somewhere below he heard a car working its way up a canyon, struggling to gain enough speed to get out of second gear. But he also heard another sound, metal scraping metal, like a sliding door opening. He looked at the door, then stepped slowly outside to the pool deck and searched the stairs and main house but saw nothing. Sound traveled in the night air in the hills, and he told himself the noise could have come from anywhere in the canyon. It had seemed close, and he again looked up at the house a moment longer, staring into the darkness on the balcony, but saw nothing.

"Shit," he whispered, and he stepped back into the pool house.

He flicked on the flashlight and swept the beam around the room. Straight ahead he saw the slatted door of a changing room. He moved the beam across a short rattan couch and matching end chairs arranged to face a bar at the end of the room. The light reflected back from a mirror decorated with a beer company slogan on the wall behind the bar. Three short-backed stools faced the bar.

Unsure where to start, Johnny moved to the changing room. It was the size of a hall closet. He dropped to his knees and checked under a short built-in bench but found nothing. He moved on to the couch and chairs, pulling the cushions onto the floor and turning them over. Sweat was pouring off him now, and his throat was dry.

Behind the bar, a stack of thick, fluffy beach towels shared the shelves with six-packs of soft drinks still in their plastic ring holders. Johnny grabbed a towel and wiped his forehead and hands. He moved the cans and shined the light underneath the shelves. He searched the refrigerator, then stood and looked across the bar at the rest of the pool house. Then he slowly turned and looked at the mirror on the wall behind him and he knew.

As he stared at the glass and beer slogans, Johnny felt a sudden and deep sense of sorrow. In the end, they were just kids, not very sophisticated or particularly clever. Just kids trying to find an edge.

The mirror was heavy, and Johnny had to struggle when he lifted it off its hook and set it gently down and leaned it against the wall. He reached behind it, felt the large rectangular envelope taped to the back, and peeled it off. Unfastening it, he dumped its contents, six black-and-white pictures and a strip of negatives, onto the bar.

Johnny put the beam on them and stared. The photos were grainy, poorly lit, but printed crisply and clearly. But what Johnny saw made him wince. Carol Holland was almost naked on the middle barstool, leaning back, her mouth open as though panting, her legs wide and the bottoms of her feet resting on the hips of a tall man facing her. A bikini top was pushed up off her breasts and the bottom of her suit hung from her left foot. The man's buttocks were tight with the strain of penetrating her. It wasn't sex, it was pornography.

And then he saw the rest and his stomach muscles tightened as though someone had sucker-punched him in a crowded elevator, and he looked away, not wanting to see it. After a moment, though, he shined the light on the photo and bent forward and looked carefully at the picture again. In the mirror behind the bar, he saw Richard Roberts's face. A far-off, fierce look filled his eyes, as though he were suspended on a razor's edge between fury and pleasure.

"Oh, Jesus," Johnny whispered. He leaned against the bar for a moment and looked across the pool house to the dressing room. Dallas must have hidden there to take the pictures. Had he known the minister and the actress were having an affair? Or had he just happened to be there working on the hillside and seized the opportunity? In the end, Johnny knew, it didn't matter. The pictures had gotten Dallas and

Sara killed and Gem hunted and hurt. He shook his head slightly. Dallas had been right. It was the perfect hiding place, the last place anyone would look.

Johnny slipped the photos and negatives back into the envelope and turned off the flashlight. The sound of a radio low and muted, the Stones singing "Satisfaction," drifted into the pool house. But a split second later it was gone. Johnny froze and looked toward the door. It hung open, waiting for him. There was no other exit. Still, he hesitated, staring at the door. The music was just another night noise drifting through the canyon, he told himself. Walk out and go home, it's that simple. You have it all now. It's all clear. Just go home. Walk outside, up the stairs, into the car and gone. Hell, Towers is probably pulling up out front right now.

Johnny stuck the flashlight into his rear pocket and left the pool house. He knew instantly that something was wrong, something had changed, but he wasn't sure what it was. He paused, looked, but saw no one and hurried on, moving to the pool coping to skirt a lounge chair that sat almost on the edge of the pool. Suddenly he understood the change. The pool was lighted, the bottom visible, the water cool and inviting. It had been dark before. The realization came too late. He heard a noise and tried to turn. But it took only a slight shove and he was in the water. He swallowed a mouthful as he sank below the surface and rose spitting and gasping for breath. His clothes and shoes weighed him down. The envelope floated only inches from him. He treaded water awkwardly and grabbed it. Suddenly the Stones were wailing from the edge of the pool, the volume turned high. Johnny slipped back under the water and could see someone standing at the edge of the pool.

His head broke the surface, and he wiped the water from his eyes, his toes just touching the bottom. Carol Holland was on the coping, holding a huge radio. She looked at Johnny, and anger pinched her face.

"I didn't know where that little bastard hid them. Then I

saw you out front and I knew they were here and that you'd find them for me. Now, give me the pictures and I won't drop this in the pool."

She held the radio in her left hand and raised the cord in her right. "I'll drop it in, if I have to. I'll fry you up just like I did that kid."

"You don't want to do this, Ms. Holland."

"Oh, I don't know. I don't think I'll mind too much." In the half-light reflected from the pool he could see her fingers tense, the knuckles white from gripping the radio. She wore shorts, and her legs looked skinny and white. She was barefoot and moved across the wet pavement to the pool's edge. Johnny looked at her and knew she would do it. There was no question. The anger he'd seen a moment ago was gone, replaced by desperation and naked fear at what she was about to do. Johnny looked at the radio and understood how Dallas had died.

"I'll tell the police I heard a noise and came down here just as you fell in. I'll have to try to save you, but it'll be too late. They'll sort it out. Remember, you were the one harassing me. Maybe you're up here trying to dig up a little midnight dirt on me. Now give me the pictures."

"You killed those kids for these pictures? Jesus, what kind of person are you?"

"The little bastard said he'd sell them to an Internet porn site. He tried to blackmail me to get money for him and that slut he'd knocked up. If those get out, I'll be through. Mel wouldn't . . . oh, it doesn't matter, just give me the pictures."

"You started the fire, you killed Sara over pictures?"

"No. Buddy did. Don't you see? We had to burn the pictures. The slut just got caught in it, that's all."

"And Dallas?" Johnny was inching toward the steps. He had to keep her talking, distracted. If he could just get to the steps maybe he could get out before she threw the radio. Maybe.

"Well, he was in the Jacuzzi. Me and him. Thought I could seduce him, get him to give me the pictures. I fucked his brains out and he still wouldn't tell me where they were. So I dumped the radio in on him. Now stop moving! Give me the pictures or I swear I'll drop this in on you." She raised the radio and held it over the water.

Johnny held his hands high, a man under arrest. "Wait, wait. Okay, just move back a step, you're making me real nervous here." He stared at the actress and she stepped back. Johnny moved slowly toward the steps again, not trying to hide his movement. "Okay, I'm getting out of the pool, I'm just going to walk to the steps and climb out. Then you can have the pictures, okay? Just move back a step, okay? I don't want to die here."

"No! Give me the pictures first." Her words were full of panic and Johnny stopped.

"Right. Okay. I'm throwing them to you." Johnny looked at her as he cocked his arm. The Stones were gone and Roy Orbison was singing "Pretty Woman." They stared at each other, frozen for a moment.

"Just tell me one thing. Does Dick know about this? Does he know what you're doing, that you're killing these kids?"

Carol Holland tilted her head back and laughed. "No. He's blind when he wants to be and if he doesn't see it, it doesn't exist. This was just me and Buddy."

"Buddy and the Jackals."

"Buddy'll do anything to protect Dick. Anything. 'I got Dick's back.'" She mimicked his voice. "And he knew the right people. All I had to do was point him and he got his friends to do the rest. I'm tired of this. You had your chance. She stepped to the edge of the pool and raised the radio above his head.

"Hey, don't do that, Carol. I'm giving you the pictures. Here." He flicked the envelope onto the side of the pool. It hit with a splat.

But in that same instant, a noise came from near the end of the pool, a lounger scraping on the cement. They both turned. In the light from the pool Johnny saw a man standing with a gun held steadily in two hands pointing directly at Carol Holland.

"Jeff, what the hell . . . ?"

"Is she the one that killed Sara? Is she, Johnny? I'll fucking blow her away right now. I don't give a shit. Is she the one?"

"Whoa, Jeff, you don't want to do this. Hold on, man, be cool here. Put the gun down. It's going to be okay, Jeff. She's not going to hurt me. Now just put the gun down."

"I've been following you for days, waiting for this. I almost lost you when you went to the hospital. But I found you again. I knew you'd take me to Sara's killer. I just thought it would be some guy. I couldn't hear it all coming down the stairs. Got some of it, though. She's the one, isn't she? Tell me!"

"Who the hell are you?" Carol Holland asked. She'd turned to face Jeff, forgetting about Johnny. "Look, mister, I don't know who you are, but you have this all wrong. Do what he says, just put down the gun."

"The lady's right, Jeff. Let's all be really calm right now, okay?" Johnny said.

Later Johnny would see it all again and think of the difference a few inches would have made. If Carol Holland hadn't been so off balance, if she'd had a better angle or reacted more quickly, it might have ended differently. But at that moment, Johnny thought only of getting out of the pool. He moved through the water to the steps and slowly climbed, praying Carol wouldn't suddenly wheel around and see him.

"Jeff, this isn't what you want to do. You've got a lot of people who depend on you, you've got a wife and kids. Don't do the wrong thing here. What about Annie? You gotta think about her." Johnny spoke as he climbed the steps. Carol Holland and Jeff stood staring at each other, less than ten feet apart.

Then Johnny was safe, out of the pool, on the cement. He moved slowly, cautiously, toward the long extension cord that led from the wall to the radio in Carol Holland's hands. If he could just get the cord, he could yank it from the wall. Maybe he could defuse it all. Keep everyone alive.

"Jeff, I know everything that happened now. I'll tell you about it. We'll call the cops. They'll handle this. Just be calm, okay?"

But Jeff was on the edge, a look of sleep-deprived insanity filling his eyes.

"What the fuck you doing, Johnny?" Jeff screamed and took two quick steps forward. Carol Holland spun to look back but lost her footing on the wet coping and fell. As she went into the pool, she desperately heaved the radio toward the side. It landed on the coping, bounced and fell against the pool ladder, and balanced precariously above the water. Amazingly it still played. Roy Orbison was gone and some disc jockey was screaming about the weather, a lame late-night attempt at humor.

Carol Holland broke the surface. She looked at Jeff, the fear gone, her eyes filled with arrogance and contempt. "You dumb fuck," she muttered.

In two quick strokes she was at the ladder, grabbed it, and began to climb out. It was over in an instant. As she pulled herself from the water, the radio fell, lodging on the top step in less than half a foot of water and only inches from her foot. Holding onto the metal, she made a perfect conduit. The electricity shot through her. She jerked and fell backward.

There was a hiss and crackle, the circuit breakers snapped, the lights disappeared, and Carol Holland was dead. A second later she was floating facedown.

"Oh, my God," Jeff said. He stared at the body for a moment, and then his legs seemed to weaken and he slumped to the lounger. "Is she dead, Johnny? Is she?"

"Yeah, Jeff. She's dead."

"Oh, God, what did I do?"

"Give me the gun." Johnny held out his hand, and Jeff handed him the pistol.

"There's a phone in the pool house. I've got to call the police."

"Yeah," Jeff said and lowered his head between his knees.

Johnny made the call, then walked out of the pool house, stood next to the brick wall, and looked down on Los Angeles. Amid the spread of lights he could make out the back of the God's House neon sign, but he didn't dwell on it. He shifted his eyes away, feeling the cool air of the late evening.

He didn't look at Carol Holland in the pool or Jeff sitting only a few yards away. After a while he heard the sirens, far off and faint at first but growing louder as they gained altitude. For a moment he thought he saw the flashing lights of the cruisers and paramedics coming up the canyon, but they disappeared behind a curve, and Johnny tried to pretend it had all been an illusion. He heard Towers's voice then.

"Hey, Rose, that you? What the hell's going on here?"

Johnny turned and saw Towers crossing the deck toward the steps.

"Yeah, down here. I'll explain," Johnny called. But as he watched the cop descend toward the pool, he wondered what he would say. How could he explain that the chance intersection of the rich and famous, the powerful and renowned, with a few children who lived on the farthest ragged edges of society had led to such a tragedy. He looked away from Towers, turning his gaze to the lights of the City of Angels and knew the story was as old as heaven itself but that knowledge offered little comfort because the pain was as real as the sounds of the sirens that grew louder with each second.

Twenty-seven

•────────────────────•

Johnny's shoes were still wet, his feet cold, and the backs of his legs felt clammy where his slacks clung to them. The air-conditioning in the small interview room didn't help. Johnny rubbed his hands together, ran them across his face, and looked at the acoustic-tile walls for a moment. He started to stand up, but Detective Towers pushed the door open and stepped in carrying two cups of coffee.

"I didn't know how you took it. Hope black's okay." He held out the cup, and Johnny took it and sat down again.

"Black's great."

Towers pulled the other chair from the table. "I just sat in on the interview with the minister. He's pretty shook up. Says he didn't know anything about the pictures or about the kids being killed. You believe him?"

"Roberts is here?"

"We sent a squad car for him. He was more than happy to come down, try to straighten out Buddy's problems. I don't think he expected us to start asking him questions." Towers paused. "So, like I asked. You believe him?"

Johnny sipped the coffee and looked at the detective and nodded his head, a barely perceptible dip.

"She said he didn't know. You wonder, though, how he could not. But some people don't see what they don't want to see. He just didn't want to put it together, I guess. What about Buddy?"

Towers nodded, and a look of weary knowledge filled his eyes. He sipped his coffee. "Ah, that took some doing. The guy's smart, been through the system. He denied everything at first. Didn't know what we were talking about. Said Carol Holland never told him about any pictures, never asked him to start a fire or hurt anyone. Said we couldn't prove anything about the girl or the sniper attack on you. All we've got is the word of a dead woman against his. He's right, of course. The fact is, we don't have much right now. I mean, we can put something together, but it would take some time. Maybe the girl he cut up can identify him, maybe she can't. She's been through a lot, I don't know how good her memory will be. Anyway, it might be pretty hard to make a case against him. But then I remembered what you said about the guy. How he'd done it all to protect the minister. So I told him how with your testimony and Jeff's statement backing you up, we could probably make it stick. No guarantee, of course, and he might get off. But either way we'd have to go to trial and I'd make sure the prosecutor showed the pictures. If they didn't want to use 'em in the trial I'd personally leak 'em to the press, make sure the tabloids got 'em." Towers swallowed and lowered his eyes to the table. "Then I told him my personal favorite was where the minister had the look of the devil in his eyes. Buddy almost came across the table at me."

"And?"

"He says he wants to talk to his lawyer about a plea. He'll plead out as long as there's no trial. He's still protecting Roberts."

"Faith can be a strange thing."

"Yeah, he probably figures he can save the souls of his fellow prisoners."

"You don't seem very happy about all this."

"No, you got that wrong. I'm happy. I'm glad Buddy's

going to be off the streets. I really am. Mr. Rose, I take great pride in my job, take pride in putting scum like him away. But I don't take great joy in it. Those are two different things."

"I understand. Let me ask you one more thing, though."

"What?"

"Why didn't Buddy go straight to the pool house himself? He had to know where the pictures were. Gem told him. He had to know where they were."

Towers smiled. "I guess that's where we got a little lucky. He didn't have a chance. I hauled him in to question him about the sniper attack. He stopped at the halfway house to change, take off his bloody clothes. That's when I got there."

"What's going to happen to Jeff?"

"I don't know yet. We're not done talking to him. In the end, it's going to be up to the DA. Personally, I think that'd be a pretty hard case to make too. Probably even tougher to win. He can claim he was trying to save your life, that Carol Holland's fall was an accident. It was an accident, wasn't it?"

Johnny thought for a second, seeing the actress slip and fall and the look of total panic in her eyes as she tried to throw the radio. "Yes. Yes, it was," he said. He finished the coffee. "Is that it? You need me for anything more?"

"No. You can head out. Keep in touch, though."

Johnny stood and moved from behind the table to the door. Towers had to scoot sideways to give him enough room to open it. Johnny paused, his hand on the knob, and looked at the detective. "You know where to reach me."

"Yes, I do, and, ah, well, I'm sorry this had to end like it did. Maybe if we'd listened more carefully, done a little more, it would have been different."

"No. You did all you could. I really don't know what more you could have done."

"You going to write a story about this?"

Johnny thought about it for a moment, then shook his head. "No. It won't be me. I'm too close to it. I've got to give it all to my editor, though. He'll assign someone. When a Hollywood star gets electrocuted in her own swimming pool, it's news. The rest of it . . . Hell, I don't know. There's only my word to connect her death and Buddy's arrest. I can tell them what the connection is, but if Buddy denies it . . . I don't know. That's the editor's call. Whoever gets the assignment might be able to do it but only if he's got good police sources."

"Don't look at me. I don't see the point in dragging anyone through the mud, especially dead people. I say just let it go."

"Thanks again," Johnny said and pulled the door open.

"Hey, Rose."

"Yeah?"

"I'm sorry about your cousin. I really am."

"Thanks."

The sun was just coming up, and some of the deepest canyons were still in shadow when Johnny walked out of the substation. He crossed the street to his car and glanced back just as the Reverend Richard Roberts came out the door. Roberts walked down the steps alone, his shoulders hunched forward, his head down. He wore a pair of old, blue sweatpants and a T-shirt with the God's House logo on the front. He was unshaven and his hair uncombed, his T-shirt only half tucked in. He moved slowly, like an old man dreaming of long-ago victories.

Roberts looked up and saw Johnny and from reflex smiled and started to wave. But he lowered his hand, and for a second Johnny thought he would turn away, but the minister surprised him. He walked across the street and stopped a few feet away.

"I am terribly, terribly sorry, Johnny. I can only pray for your forgiveness and the forgiveness of the Lord."

"You told the police you didn't know." It was a statement, a question, and a dismissal.

"I didn't know. I really didn't. They showed me the pictures." He lowered his eyes, unable to look at Johnny, and for a second Johnny thought he would cry, and when he spoke, his voice was shaky but clear. "We began our relationship about a year after Barbara died. I was just so lonely, I needed . . . I just needed . . . Her husband was always away and when he was there he didn't, he wasn't very interested . . . but we couldn't at my house. There were always people around, no privacy. So I started visiting her. The boy must have seen us when he was working up there. I don't know. Maybe he didn't take the van home or maybe he came back." Roberts stopped and raised his head to look at Johnny. "I guess it doesn't really matter, does it?"

"No, it doesn't."

"Please tell the girl's mother how sorry I am."

"Yes."

Roberts looked at him for a second longer, but there was nothing for either man to say, and the minister turned and walked away, heading north toward Hollywood Boulevard. Johnny watched him walk up the street for almost a block and looked into the distance at the huge God's House neon sign. In the daylight, it looked colorless and dull. He got in his car and drove away.

Kate was asleep in the waiting room chair. Her head lolled to one side, and her breathing was shallow. The bloodstains on her clothes had turned a dark rust color, and she'd missed a few smudges high on her forehead when she washed her face. Johnny eased into the chair next to her and stroked the side of her face with the back of his index finger. She opened her eyes slowly at first, then sat up suddenly.

"Johnny, where have you been? Is everything all right?"

He smiled at her for a second and looked around the waiting room before turning back to her. He didn't know how to answer the question.

"Carol Holland is dead."

"God! What happened?"

"She was electrocuted."

"What? How?"

Johnny put his arm around her shoulders, pulled her

close, and kissed her gently on the cheek. "I found the pictures," he said. He leaned back in the chair and described what had happened in the hours since he last saw her. They sat quietly for several minutes when he finished until Kate said, "Dick and Carol Holland? It just sounds so, I don't know, just so . . ."

"Sleazy." Johnny finished her sentence for her.

"Yes, that's the word I guess, and he claims he didn't know about the killings?"

"So he says. I've got no reason not to believe him. When you start seeing the world through your ego, you can get tunnel vision pretty quickly."

"And Buddy was trying to protect him. I'd never have put that together."

Johnny sat straight in the chair and ran his hands over his head, flattening his hair and pushing it back from his forehead.

"How's Gem?" he asked.

Kate smiled. "She's going to be all right. The guy sliced her up pretty good, cut her face and shoulder, and cut her stomach. The doctor said she could have died if we hadn't found her and brought her in. She'll have scars, including one on her face, but it could have been a lot worse. Her mom's with her now."

"Good."

"She's an interesting lady."

"Mrs. Rottman?"

"Yeah. She came out here and we talked a little bit. She thinks you saved Gem's life."

Johnny shook his head and was quiet for a moment. "What about her father? Did he come?"

"No, no, he didn't. You know, it's funny. I asked Mrs. Rottman if she'd like me to call him and she did the funniest thing. She rubbed the side of her face with her finger, like she was tracing Gem's cut on her own cheek, and said, 'No, he won't care now. Besides, he's done enough already. Now he can pay for it all. He'll do it too. I'll make him do it.' You know, Johnny, unless I misread the situation, Mr. Rottman is just about to have his privates handed to him."

"I'd say good, but I don't know if I really care." They were quiet for a minute, and Johnny stood and looked down at Kate.

"Can we see Gem?"

"No, not now. Visiting hours are this afternoon. We can come back then, okay?"

"Sure."

They stood, and Kate slipped her arm around Johnny's waist and pulled him close. "You know, Mrs. Rottman's right. You saved her."

"I wish I could have saved Sara too."

"We lose kids, Johnny. We save those we can."

He made them coffee at his apartment, but Kate stood up after one cup. "I've got to go. I've got to go home, take a shower, and get to the center. Some of the kids may have heard about Gem, I want to make sure they know she's going to be okay. Also, I want to check up on Billy and let him know that Gem's okay." She moved along the edge of the table until she was close enough to touch him.

"Okay, but I still want to make you dinner." He glanced at the half-cooked meal that sat on the stove.

"I'd love that. Why don't I come over about seven? But frankly, I may be too tired to eat." She smiled and held out her hand. Johnny took it, and she bent down and kissed him gently.

After she left, Johnny peeled off his rumpled clothes and took a long shower, standing in the stream of hot water until his skin was red and the steam ran off the bathroom mirror and puddled on the countertop. He dressed in cutoff jeans and an old, baggy T-shirt and went downstairs and called Kuscyk.

He told the metro editor the story and added, "So I'm not coming in today. I gotta get some rest."

He could hear Kuscyk grunt. "So the lady was hiding more than a stint on the streets."

"Yes, she was."

"Yeah, I'll bet if those pictures were posted on the Web, old Mel Plank would have cut her off in a heartbeat. No more movies for the wife. Listen, I'll get a couple of people on this now. You have any suggestions on how we can corroborate this?"

"I'd call Roberts. Better yet, send someone over there."

"He'll never talk, Johnny."

"Maybe not, but you've got to give him a chance to tell his side anyway. But, Stan, my guess is he'll want to talk. They say confession is good for the soul. Tell whoever goes over there to get it on tape, just in case he forgets later what he really said."

"Okay, get some rest. We'll try not to call for a couple of hours anyway."

But Johnny didn't go to bed. Instead, he poured himself another cup of coffee and sat at the table for a moment, then got up and walked to the front door and opened it wide to let in the light and the fresh air. When he opened the door, Archie walked out from under the bush and stood in the middle of the grass. The cat stared at Johnny, waiting.

This time, Johnny moved the saucer almost to the edge of the porch. Archie was wary but eventually came and ate. When the animal was done, it sat on its haunches and cleaned its face and looked at Johnny standing above him as though they'd reached a simple understanding. Two old fighters always ready to go another round.

Johnny left the door open when he returned to the table and picked up the phone and dialed. He got Maggie at work.

"Hi. I was just thinking about you. I'm glad you called." Her voice was solid. She sounded healthy, alert.

"Yeah, me too. I've got some news." He went on then, telling her of his search for Gem and his confrontation with Carol Holland.

"All this because of dirty pictures? You can't be serious."

"I'm afraid I am, Maggie." The line was silent for a moment, and Maggie said, "But, it just doesn't make any sense."

"No. None. Carol Holland said no one was supposed to get hurt. But I think that was a lie. I don't think she cared how many people were hurt or killed."

"I just can't believe it. And Jeff actually saved your life? I can't believe that son of a bitch did anything right."

"I don't think I'd be here if it weren't for him."

"You know, sometimes I think this world is so strange, I'll never understand it. Then I hear something like this and I think I don't want to understand."

"Yeah," he said. But he added nothing more, and a long silence filled the line before Maggie said, "Johnny, I don't know if I ever said thank you."

"Sure you did."

"It's easy to talk about how much we miss Sara now. How we wish she was here. But when she was alive, when she was living on the streets, you were the one who made sure she knew she was loved and wanted."

"Maggie, I—"

"No, Johnny, let me finish. You helped her when she was alive and tried to save her when she was dying. Thank you."

"I loved her too, Maggie."

"I know, Johnny. So, how's the other girl, what's her name?"

"Jeanette."

"How is she?"

"She's going to be okay."

"You should be proud of yourself."

"Thanks."

"Well, I gotta get back to work. But listen, Johnny, remember what you told me, okay?"

"What?"

"We're going forward. Both of us. I came back to work. We're starting again. It's a beginning."

"I'll remember."

He said good-bye, put the phone back in its holder, and turned the coffeemaker off, leaving the almost-full pot to cool. For a moment he stood near the kitchen table and listened to the sounds of the birds outside and the noise of a neighbor vacuuming a carpet. He crossed the living room, closed the door, and climbed the stairs to his bedroom, where he shed his clothes. Despite his exhaustion, he lay awake for a moment, thinking of what Maggie had said. She was right. It was a beginning. His thoughts drifted to Gem and what was ahead for her and her mom. Finally, though, he fell asleep thinking of Kate and the evening ahead. He slept without dreams or demons to disturb his smile.

New York Times Bestselling Author
Stuart Woods

THE RUN	0-06-101343-9/$7.99 US/$10.99 Can
WHITE CARGO	0-06-101423-0/$7.99 US/$10.99 Can
ORCHID BEACH	0-06-101341-2/$7.50 US/$9.50 Can
UNDER THE LAKE	
	0-06-101417-6/$7.50 US/$9.99 Can
RUN BEFORE THE WIND	
	0-380-70507-9/$6.99 US/$8.99 Can
CHIEFS	0-380-70347-5/$7.99 US/$10.99 Can
DEEP LIE	0-06-104449-0/$6.99 US/$8.50 Can
CHOKE	0-06-109422-6/$7.99 US/$10.99 Can
IMPERFECT STRANGERS	
	0-06-109404-8/$6.99 US/$8.99 Can
HEAT	0-06-109358-0/$6.99 US/$8.99 Can
DEAD EYES	0-06-109157-X/$7.50 US/$8.99 Can
L.A. TIMES	0-06-109156-1/$6.99 US/$8.50 Can
SANTA FE RULES	
	0-06-109089-1/$6.99 US/$8.50 Can
PALINDROME	0-06-109936-8/$7.99 US/$10.99 Can